'What can I do

The question of his name hung in the warm air around them, testing and challenging him. Charlotte stood tall as his astonished gaze travelled down her body, taking in her dishevelled appearance. Her skin tingled as those eyes all but caressed every part of her, making her breath catch as if he'd actually touched her.

'*You* are Sebastian's sister?'

Accusation and disbelief laced through every word, but it was lost on her as the grief she'd thought she'd finally begun to get over hit her once more when he said her brother's name.

The urge to defend herself rose up, but she had no idea from what. 'Yes,' she said curtly, hearing the irritation in her own voice. 'And you are…?'

She asked the question although she knew the answer—and it was not one she wanted to hear. She curled her fingers into her palms, knowing that the one man she'd never wanted to meet—the man she held responsible first for taking Seb away from her and then for his death—now stood impudently in her garden. Looking for her.

Rachael Thomas has always loved reading romance and is thrilled to be a Modern™ Romance author. She lives and works on a farm in Wales—a far cry from the glamour of a Modern story—but that makes slipping into her characters' world all the more appealing. When she's not writing or working on the farm she enjoys photography and visiting historic castles and grand houses.

Visit her at www.rachaelthomas.co.uk

Books by Rachael Thomas

Mills & Boon® Modern™ Romance

Claimed by the Sheikh
A Deal Before the Altar

**Visit the author profile page at
millsandboon.co.uk for more titles**

CRAVING HER ENEMY'S TOUCH

BY
RACHAEL THOMAS

Published in Great Britain 2015
by Mills & Boon, an imprint of Harlequin (UK) Limited,
Eton House, 18-24 Paradise Road, Richmond, Surrey, TW9 1SR

© 2015 Rachael Thomas

ISBN: 978-0-263-25063-3

Harlequin (UK) Limited's policy is to use papers that are natural,
renewable and recyclable products and made from wood grown in
sustainable forests. The logging and manufacturing processes conform
to the legal environmental regulations of the country of origin.

Printed and bound in Spain
by CPI, Barcelona

CRAVING HER ENEMY'S TOUCH

For Ruth and Sarah Jane and our enjoyable
writing retreat weekends in our little Welsh cottage.

CHAPTER ONE

THE PURR OF a sports car broke the quietness of the afternoon, taking Charlie's mind hurtling back to the past. To events she'd been hiding from for the last year.

She had grown up in the glamour of the racing world, but her brother's death had sent her retreating to the country and the sanctuary of her cottage garden. It was a place that was safe, but instinct warned her that this safety was now under threat.

Unable to help herself, she listened to the unmistakable sound of the V8 engine as it slowed in the lane beyond her garden, appreciative of its throaty restraint. All thoughts of planting bulbs for next spring disappeared as memories were unleashed. Images of happier times filled her mind, colliding with those of the moment her world had fallen apart.

Kneeling on the grass in the corner of her garden, she couldn't see the car on the other side of the hedge, but she knew it was powerful and expensive—and that it had stopped in the lane outside her cottage.

The engine fell silent and only birdsong disturbed the peace of the English countryside. She closed her eyes against the dread which rushed over her. She didn't need visits from the past, however well meaning. This unexpected visitor had to be her father's doing; he'd been pushing her to move on for weeks now.

The heavy clunk of the car door shutting was followed by purposeful footsteps on the road. A few seconds later they crunched on the gravel of her pathway and she knew that whoever it was would see her at any second.

'*Scusi.*' The deep male voice startled her more than the Italian he spoke and she jumped up as though she were a child with her hand caught in the sweet jar.

The six foot plus of dark Italian male which stood in her garden robbed her of the ability to think, let alone speak, and all she could do was look at him. Dressed in casual but very much designer jeans which hugged his thighs to perfection, he appeared totally out of place and yet vaguely familiar. Over a dark shirt he wore a leather jacket and was everything she'd expect an Italian man to be. Self-assured and confident, oozing undeniable sex appeal.

His dark collar-length hair was thick and gleamed in the sunshine, his tanned face showed a light growth of stubble, which only enhanced his handsome features. But it was the intense blackness of his eyes as they pierced into her which made breathing almost impossible.

'I am looking for Charlotte Warrington.' His accent was heavy and incredibly sexy, as was the way he said her name, caressing it until it sounded like a melody. She fought hard against the urge to allow it to wrap itself around her. She had to. She was out of practice in dealing with such men.

Slowly pulling off her gardening gloves, she became acutely aware she was wearing her oldest jeans and T-shirt and that her hair was scraped back in something which almost resembled a ponytail. Could she get away with not admitting who she was? But the arrogance in those dark eyes as they watched her made her want to shock him.

He was undoubtedly her brother's business partner, the man who had whisked him deeper into the world of performance cars, so far that he'd almost forgotten his family's existence. Indignation surfaced rapidly.

'What can I do for you, Mr…?' The question of his name hung in the warm air around them, testing and challenging him. She stood tall as his astonished gaze travelled down her body, taking in her dishevelled appearance. Her skin tingled as those eyes all but caressed every part of her, making her breath catch as if he'd actually touched her.

'You are Sebastian's sister?' Accusation and disbelief laced through every word, but it was lost on her as the grief she'd thought she'd finally begun to get over hit her once more as he said her brother's name.

The urge to defend herself rose up, but she had no idea where it came from. 'Yes,' she said curtly, hearing the irritation in her own voice. 'And you are?'

She asked the question although she knew the answer and it was not one she wanted to hear. She curled her fingers into her palms, knowing that the one man she'd never wanted to meet, the man she held responsible, first for taking Seb away from her, then for his death, stood impudently in her garden. Looking for her.

If that wasn't bad enough, there had been a spark of attraction in that first second she'd seen him. Already she hated herself for it. How could she feel anything other than contempt for the man who'd deprived her of her brother?

'Roselli,' he said and stepped off the path and onto her newly cut lawn, confirming her worst suspicions.

He smiled at her as he walked closer, but it didn't reach his eyes. 'Alessandro Roselli.'

She glared at him and he stopped a few paces away from her. Had he felt the heat of her anger? She certainly hoped so. He deserved every bit of it and so much more.

'I have nothing to say to you, Mr Roselli.' She stood firm, looked him in the eye and tried not to be affected by the way his met and held hers, shamelessly, without any trace of guilt. 'Now, please leave.'

She walked across the lawn, past him and towards her cottage, sure that he would go, that her cold dismissal would be enough. As she neared him the breeze carried his scent. Pure, unadulterated male. Her head became light, her breath hard to catch. In disgust at the way he distracted her thoughts, she marched off.

'No.' That one word, deep and accented, froze her to the spot as if a winter frost had descended, coating everything in white crystals.

A tremor of fear slipped down her spine. Not just fear of the man standing so close to her, but fear of all he represented. Slowly she turned her face to look directly at him. 'We have nothing to say. I made that clear in my response to your letter after Sebastian's death.'

Sebastian's death.

It was hard to say those words aloud. Hard to admit her brother was gone, that she'd never see him again. But, worse, the man responsible had the nerve to ignore her early grief-laden requests and then invade the cottage, her one place of sanctuary.

'You may not, but I do.' He stepped closer to her, too close. She held his gaze, noticing the bronze sparks in his eyes and the firm set of his mouth. This was a man who did exactly what he wanted, without regard for anyone else. Even without knowing his reputation she'd be left in no doubt of that as he all but towered over her.

'I don't want to hear what you've got to say.' She didn't even want to talk to him. He had as good as killed her brother. She didn't want to look at him, to acknowledge him, but something, some undeniable primal instinct, made her and she fought hard to keep the heady mix of anger and grief under control. An emotional meltdown was not something she wanted to display, especially in front of the man she'd steadfastly refused to meet.

'I'm going to say it anyway.' His voice lowered, resembling a growl, and she wondered which of them was fighting the hardest to hold onto their composure.

She lifted a brow in haughty question at him and watched his lips press firmly together as he clenched his jaw. Good, she was getting to him. With that satisfaction racing through her, she walked away, desperate for the safety of her cottage. She didn't want to hear anything he had to say.

'I am here because Sebastian asked me to come.' His words, staccato and deeply accented, made another step impossible.

'How dare you?' She whirled round to face him, all thought of restraint abandoned. 'You are here because of your guilt.'

'My guilt?' He stepped towards her, quickly closing that final bit of space between them, his eyes glittering and hard.

Her heart thumped frantically in her chest and her knees weakened, but she couldn't let him know that. 'It's your fault. You are the one responsible for Sebastian's death.'

Her words hung accusingly between them, and the sun

slipped behind a cloud as if sensing trouble. She watched his handsome face turn to stone and even thought she saw the veil of guilt shadow it, but it was brief, swiftly followed by cold anger, making his eyes sharper than flint.

He was so close, so tall, and she wished she was wearing the heels she used to favour before her life had been shaken up into total turmoil. She kept her gaze focused on him, determined to match his aggressive stance.

'If, as you say, it was my fault I would not have waited a year to come here.' His voice was cool and level, his eyes, changing to gleaming bronze, fixed her accusingly to the spot.

He took one final step towards her, so close now he could have kissed her. That thought shocked her and she resisted the need to step back away from him, as far as she could. She hadn't done anything wrong. He was the guilty one. He was the one who'd intruded on her life.

'It was your car that crashed, Mr Roselli.' She forced each word out, his proximity making it almost impossible.

'Your brother *and* I designed that car. We built it together.' His voice, deep and accented, hinted at pain. Or was she just imagining it, reflecting her grief onto him?

'But it was Sebastian who test drove it.' She fought the memories he was dragging up. Demons she'd thought she'd finally shut the door on.

He didn't say anything and she held her ground, looking up into his eyes as they searched her face. Her heart pounded wildly and deep down she knew it wasn't just the memories of Sebastian. It was as much to do with this man. Instinctively she knew his potent maleness had disturbed the slumbering woman hidden within her—and she hated him for that.

'It couldn't have done your company's reputation any good when an up-and-coming racing driver was killed at the wheel of your prototype.' She injected a jaunty edge to her words, issuing a challenge. At the same time she wished she could run and hide—from the memories he stirred as much as from the way her body reacted to each glance from his devilishly dark eyes.

He didn't move. He didn't flinch at all. He was in complete control as his eyes glittered, sharp sparks like diamonds spiking her soul.

'It wasn't good for anyone.' His voice was icy cold and, despite the warmth of the September sun, she shivered, but still he remained, watching as if he could read every thought that raced through her mind.

She drew in a ragged tear-laden breath and swallowed hard. She couldn't cry, not now. Not again. She was done with crying. It was time to move on, time to forge a new path through life. She couldn't go back to what she'd been doing before. Her time in front of the cameras, representing Seb's team, was over. The memories would be too much, yet this man seemed hell-bent on bringing the past into the present.

'I think you should leave, Mr Roselli.' She stepped away from him, out of his shadow and into the sun as it crept out from behind the clouds. 'Neither is it doing me any good.'

With eyes narrowed by suspicion, he watched her as she took another step back and away from him. 'I am here because Sebastian asked me to come.'

She shook her head, the emotional meltdown she'd wanted to keep at bay threatening to erupt. 'I still want you to leave.'

She didn't care if he remained standing in her precious garden; she just wanted to escape him, escape the aura of a man obviously used to getting all he wanted, no matter what the cost to anyone else.

Alessandro closed his eyes and sighed as Charlie fled across the garden, heading for the open door of the cottage. Hysteria had not been on his agenda. He didn't need this now. For a moment he thought about turning and walking away, getting in his car and driving as fast and as far away as he could. He'd kept part of his promise to Sebastian, after all. But had he even achieved that?

'Maledizione!' he cursed aloud and strode after her, his legs brushing against the lavender which tumbled from the borders, raising the scent. Just being in the garden, with its proud display of flowers, made him remember the time he'd looked after his sister while she'd recovered from a car accident. It was a memory that wouldn't help at all right now.

As he neared the open back door he heard Charlie's frustrated growl. He didn't knock, didn't pause. He just walked straight in. He wasn't going to be dismissed so easily.

This woman had stubbornly refused her brother's requests to go to Italy and see the car they'd been working on and it had angered him. Then, after the accident, he'd offered his support, but he'd never expected her rejection or her cold and furious denial of his existence.

With her arms locked rigidly tight, she leant on the kitchen table, her head lowered in despair. She spun round to face him. 'How dare you?' Hot angry words hurtled across the small space to him, but he stood tall, despite the low beams of the old cottage, and took her anger.

'I dare because I promised Sebastian that I would.' He moved nearer to the small table, nearer to her, until only a pulled-out chair, left as if recently vacated, separated them.

'I'm sure Seb would not have made anyone promise to come and hassle me like this.' He watched as her full lips clamped shut on further words and he felt the strangest desire to kiss those lips, to taste her rage and frustration, to draw it from her and replace it with hot desire.

'Hassle?' He frowned at her and saw her green eyes widen, liking the swirling brown within their depths, reminding him of autumn.

'Yes, hassle. Hound. Harass. Call it what you like, but he wouldn't have wanted that.' Her words were short and sharp. Irritation made her breathing shallow and fast. Her breasts rose and fell rapidly beneath her T-shirt, snagging his attention as lustful hormones raced to places he just didn't need them going right now.

'He made me promise to bring you to Italy and involve you in the launch.' His words were sharper than he'd intended, but then he'd never expected to meet a woman who unleashed such a cocktail of fury and fire within him. She was not at all the sweet and happy girl Sebastian had told him about; she was sexy and passionately angry.

'He what?' She pushed the chair under the old pine table and moved closer to him.

Not a good idea, not when his body was reacting so wildly to her sexy curves. He wanted to drag the damn chair back out, keep the barrier between them. Maybe then he'd be able to think about the reason he'd come here instead of this long neglected need for a woman's body.

'The car is due to be launched. I want you there.' The words rushed out and he had the strangest sensation that she was depleting his control, weaving some kind of spell around him.

'You want me there?' Her voice raised an octave and he blinked hard, then realised how it had sounded to her. A little pang of conscience surged forwards but he pushed it back. Clearly she held him responsible for that night and he couldn't sully her memories with the truth. Not after the promise he'd made.

'Sebastian wanted you there.' What was the matter with him? This woman wasn't at all what he'd expected. She didn't look glamorous and the idea that she had, until recently, been living a luxury lifestyle didn't seem remotely possible.

Why did this ordinary and plain version of Charlotte Warrington, tousled and unkempt from the garden, arouse him so instantly? He couldn't process thought coherently, his body flooding with lust, demanding satisfaction.

She shook her head. 'No, he wouldn't have asked that. But then he wouldn't have been killed if it wasn't for you and your stupid car.'

'You know he lived for cars, for the thrill of speed. It was what he did, what he was good at.' Sandro pushed back the image of the accident, shelving the terror of all that had unfolded minutes after the crash, which had proved, within hours, to be fatal. He could relate to her pain, sympathise with her grief, but he couldn't and wouldn't allow her to apportion the blame to him.

He'd kept the truth from the world and the gossip-hungry media, out of respect for the young driver who'd quickly become his friend. Now it was time to carry out Seb's final request. He'd wanted his sister at the launch, wanted her stamp of approval on the car, and that was what Seb would have—whatever it took.

'It is also how he died.' Sadness deflated her voice and he saw her shoulders drop. Was she going to cry? Panic sluiced over him.

As she composed herself, his gaze scanned the small country kitchen, typically English and not at all the sort of thing he'd imagined her living in. Herbs hung drying from a beam and various fresh versions adorned the windowsill. Nestled among them, in a small frame, was a photo of Sebastian and Charlie.

He reached for it and saw her gaze dart from him to the photo, but she said nothing as he picked it up and looked at the picture. Instead of being drawn to his friend, he looked at the image of the woman who now stood close to him. A woman he knew through the media but had never met. The same woman who was now having a strange effect on him—or was that just his conscience?

From the photo her eyes shone with happiness, her deliciously full lips spread into a smile. She was leaning against a sports car, her brother, his arms wrapped protectively around her, pulled her close, equally happy.

'Rome. Two years ago,' she said, her voice almost a whisper, and he sensed her move closer to him, felt the heat radiating from her body. 'Before he became embroiled in your project and forgot about us.'

He took a deep breath in, inhaling her scent, something light and floral, like jasmine, mixed with an earthy scent from her time just spent in the garden. Carefully he replaced the photo on the windowsill, ignoring the barb of accusation in her last words. That was not a discussion for now. 'You are alike.'

'Were.'

That one word ratcheted up his guilt, the same guilt he'd told himself again and again he shouldn't carry and, finally, he'd thought he'd convinced himself. He should have known that coming here, facing this woman wouldn't be easy. That it would only increase the self-apportioned guilt instead of lessen it. The fact that he still kept Seb's darkest secret from everyone didn't help.

He looked down at her as she stood at his side and when she looked up, her mossy green eyes so sad, so vulnerable, his chest tightened, almost crushing him with a need to chase away that sadness, to put that happy smile back on her sexy lips once again.

'It's what he wanted, Charlotte,' he said softly, unable to break the eye contact.

'Charlie. Nobody calls me Charlotte. Except my mother,' she whispered. The kind of sexy whisper he was used to hearing from a woman after passionate sex. Inside his body, heady desire erupted as he imagined her lying in his bed, whispering with contentment.

'Charlie,' he repeated as wild need pumped through his veins. He really should stop his mind wandering to the subject of sex. He was in danger of complicating this mission beyond all proportions. She was the one woman he shouldn't want, couldn't desire. 'Seb did want you there.'

'I can't.' Her voice, still a throaty whisper, tugged at his male desires as they rampaged ever wilder.

'You can,' he said and, without thinking, he reached out and stroked the back of his fingers down her face. Her skin was soft and warm. Her breath hitched audibly and her eyes darkened in a message as old as time itself.

Slowly she shook her head in denial, moving her cheek against his fingers, and he clenched his jaw against the sensation, reminding himself he didn't mix business with pleasure and this had always been about business—and concealing his friend's downfall.

He thought again of the recent conversation with her father, of the assurances he'd made to him, binding him deeper into the promise Seb had extracted from him as his life had ebbed away.

'Your father thinks you should.'

It was as if an explosion had happened. As if a firework had gone off between them. She jumped back from him, the chair scratching the tiled floor noisily, her eyes flashing accusation at him.

'My father?' Her voice, laden with shock, crashed into his thoughts, bringing his mind well and truly back into focus. 'You've spoken to my father?'

Charlie was numb with shock. How dare he speak to her father? And why had her father not mentioned it? Why hadn't he warned her Alessandro Roselli, owner of one of Italy's biggest car manufacturers, was looking for her, wanting her to do something he knew she couldn't face yet? She'd only seen her father yesterday. He should have told her.

'What exactly have you spoken about with my father?' She kept her words firm, her fingers curled around the back of the chair as if the pine would anchor her, keep her thoughts focused and in control. Just moments ago she'd wondered what his kiss would be like, had revelled in the soft caress of his fingers like a star-struck teenager. What had she been thinking? 'You had no right.'

'I contacted him to ask if I could visit, to invite you to be at the launch. Your father knows it is what Seb wanted.' He folded his arms across his broad chest and leant against a kitchen unit, his eyes never breaking contact with hers.

For the second time that morning her shoulders sagged in defeat. She pressed her fingertips to her temples and closed her eyes briefly. Hopefully, when she opened them he wouldn't be watching so intently, so knowingly.

But it didn't make any difference. Those bronze-flecked eyes, which strangely felt so familiar, now bored into her. Right into the very heart of her, as if probing for every secret she'd ever hidden.

She dropped her hands and gripped onto the back of the chair again. 'You had no right to speak to my father. He doesn't need to be reminded of what we've lost and I'm more than capable of deciding for myself if I want to see you or not or if I want to be involved in the launch.'

'And do you?' He raised his brows and a smile twitched at the corners of his lips. The same lips she'd just imagined kissing her.

Did she what? Focus, Charlie. Her mind scrabbled to regain rational thought. She didn't know what she wanted except not to allow this man, this prime specimen of raw maleness, to know how unsure and undecided she was.

'I certainly didn't want to see you.' She raised her chin and injected calm control into her voice. 'If you recall, I asked you to leave. I don't want any part of the motor racing world any more.'

'Is that why you've hidden yourself away in the depths of the English countryside?'

The curiosity in his voice was barely disguised and the question came rapidly on the heels of the confusion he'd caused just by being here. She found it difficult to think about such things, but this man's presence was making it harder still.

'I withdrew from the frenzy of the media out of respect for my brother. I'm not hiding,' she said, aware of the curt tone of her voice. 'I couldn't continue to be on camera, promoting the team, not after Seb died.'

'Do you think he'd want you to stay that way?'

As he leant against the kitchen unit, unable to help herself, her gaze flickered to his hips and strong thighs. A sizzle of sexual awareness shimmied over her. Why did she have to find this man, of all men, so undeniably attractive?

'Meaning?'

'The cottage is very nice, but a woman like you shouldn't be ensconced here for ever.'

She looked back into his face, taking in the slant of his nose and the sensual curve of his lips. He looked directly into her eyes, almost knocking the breath from her body with the intensity.

Was he right? Would Seb want her to be involved? Then his last words finally registered in her mind. 'What do you mean—a woman like me?'

He walked around the table, appearing confined within the small kitchen. A room she'd never thought of as so compact, not until Alessandro Roselli had walked into it. He stopped at the opposite side of the table and she was thankful to have something more substantial between them.

'You live life in the fast lane—or did.' His accent had turned into a sexy drawl and his eyes raked over her. Again she was conscious of her casual and slightly grubby clothes.

'Well, now I don't and I have no intention of going back to it. Nothing you—or my father—can say will change my mind.'

'"Look after my little Charlie. She'd like you."' He

spoke firmly and she knew exactly who he was quoting. Only Seb called her 'little Charlie'.

He pulled out another chair and sat down. He was taking root, making it very clear he wasn't leaving any time soon, but his words unsettled her. She could almost hear Seb saying them.

'I don't believe you.' She folded her arms across her chest, trying to deflect his scrutiny, but she remembered the phone calls from Seb. He'd always tried to get her to date again, insisting that not all men were as heartless as her former fiancé. 'He would never say that.'

Absently, he reached out and pulled last night's local paper towards him. He looked as if he belonged in her home, in her kitchen. He looked comfortable.

'It is true, *cara.*'

'Charlotte to you.' Her previous thoughts linked in too easily with his term of endearment and it unnerved her. She wished she'd never invited him to use 'Charlie'.

'Charlotte…' he said, so slowly, so sexily he caressed each syllable. Heat speared through her body. She stood rigid, trying to ignore the heavy pulse of desire scorching through her. What the heck was the matter with her?

Maybe she'd been out of the *fast lane*, as he'd called it, for too long. Should she believe him, that Seb had wanted her involved? Not that she'd ever admit it to him, but those words could well have been spoken by her brother.

'What exactly did my father say?' She had to divert his attention. She couldn't stand here any longer whilst his gaze ravished her. It was too unnerving.

He looked up at her, the paper forgotten, and the heat level within her rose higher still. She swallowed hard. Her brother had been right. She did like him, but purely on a primal level. It was just lust, nothing more. Something she would get over and she could do without that particular complication at the moment.

'He said,' he taunted her, his brows lifting a little too suggestively, 'that it was time you got back in the driving seat.'

His words hung heavy in the air. Words which were true. Hadn't her father said exactly that to her only a few weeks ago?

'I wasn't aware there was more to you than the glamorous façade you've always displayed on camera—that you'd been taught to drive high-powered cars.' He watched her intently and she had the distinct impression he was trying to irritate her, push her into accepting that her brother had wanted her to be involved.

She thought of her job promoting Seb's team, following them to every racetrack in the world and being interviewed by the press. It was a jet set lifestyle, one she'd enjoyed and had been good at. She'd got there by working her way up from the very bottom and had learnt all there was to know about cars and driving. Despite the glamorous image she portrayed to the world whilst on camera, she'd always felt safer, less exposed when she was doing what she really loved. Working on the cars and driving them—something her mother had been set against.

Was it time to stop hiding away and be part of that life again? She pondered the question, aware of his gaze on her, watching and taking in every move.

'You'd be surprised,' she flirted, shocking herself by doing so. What was she doing? She never flirted. It only ever caused trouble. She knew that better than most and had seen it many times in her line of work. Light-hearted flirting always led to more. Her mother had fallen victim to it, leaving her and Seb as teenagers whilst she pursued her latest love interest.

He raised a brow, his eyes sparking with sexy mischief, doing untold things to her pulse rate. It had to stop. She couldn't stand here any longer beneath his scrutiny. She'd melt.

'I hope I get to find out.' His voice was almost a drawl, making her stomach clench.

'Coffee?' Diversion tactics were certainly required and coffee was the first thing to come to her mind.

'Sì, grazie.' The effect she was having made him slip automatically into Italian. Coffee was the last thing he wanted. Even a good cup of espresso wouldn't distract him from the fire in his body.

She looked at him, her tongue sliding unconsciously over her lips, and he almost groaned with the effort of staying seated at the table when all he could do was watch her. Desiring a woman dressed in elegant evening wear was normal, but the way he wanted this casual and rumpled version of Charlie was totally new and unexpected. It was also extremely inconvenient.

He watched as she moved around the kitchen, taking in her curves as she turned her back to him to prepare the coffee. He liked the way her jeans clung to her thighs, accentuating the shape of her bottom. Her scruffy T-shirt couldn't quite hide the indent of her waist, just as it hadn't hidden the swell of her breasts from his hungry eyes moments ago.

She turned and passed over a mug of instant coffee, then sat at the table. Inwardly he grimaced. Not what he was used to, but if it meant he had time to convince her to at least be present at the launch then he would have to put up with it.

He took a sip, watching as she blew gently on hers, almost mesmerised by her lips. He had to rein in his libido. She was an attractive woman and in any other circumstances he would have wanted more—much more, at least long enough for the fire of lust to burn lower. But he had to remember she was Sebastian's sister and, out of respect for his friend's memory, she was off limits. He shouldn't have allowed his attraction to show, shouldn't have lit the fuse of attraction.

'Back to business,' he said tersely and put down his mug.

'I wasn't aware it was business,' she said lightly. A little too lightly, giving away that she was battling with emotions, that she was stalling him. 'I thought this was all about salving your conscience, freeing you of guilt.'

He did feel guilt over Seb's death—who wouldn't in the circumstances?—but it wasn't what drove him, what had made him come here. He'd come because of the promise he'd made. 'It is business, Charlotte. I want you to be at the launch of the car. Seb always wanted you there. He knew how good you were with the media.'

'He never said anything to me about being at the launch.' She put her mug down, pushing it away slightly, as if she too had no intention of drinking it.

He was about to say how much Seb had missed her. How he'd looked forward to her going to Italy. Anything to persuade her, when her next words jolted him with the raw pain entwined in them.

'But I suppose he didn't know he was going to die.'

He nodded, fighting his conscience and sensing she

was coming to the right decision by herself. He just needed to give her a little more time. 'Sadly, that is true.'

'When is the launch?'

Her eyes, slightly misted with held-back tears, met his. Despite his earlier thoughts, he did feel guilt. Guilt for her sadness, and worse. He felt compelled to make it right, to bring happiness back to her life. After all, she wouldn't be hiding away from the world, the racing world in particular, if she wasn't unhappy.

'Friday.'

'But that's only two days away! Thanks for the advance warning.' Her tone was sharp and he saw a spark of determination in her eyes that he recognised and related to.

'*Bene*, you will be there?'

'Yes, I will,' she said as she pushed back her chair and stood up. Dismissing him, he realised. 'But on my terms.'

CHAPTER TWO

'What terms?' Alessandro asked suspiciously, looking up at her from where he'd remained sitting at the table.

Charlie watched his jaw clench and his eyes narrow slightly. He hadn't expected that. It annoyed her that he'd thought he could just turn up at the last moment and ask her to go to the launch of the car, as if she was merely an afterthought. Until now she hadn't wanted anything to do with the car, but she'd started to realise that by being involved she might be able to find answers to the questions she still had about the accident.

She mulled the idea over, trying to ignore his scrutiny. If—and that was a big if at the moment—she did go, she'd want much more than just being a last-minute guest. One invited only because Alessandro's conscience had been nudged. She'd want to know all there was to know about the car.

She regretted deeply that she hadn't seen Seb in the months before the accident. If she had gone to Italy to see the car as it had turned from dream into reality, would she have been able to prevent the fateful night of the accident?

The launch could be the exact catalyst she needed to regain control of her life. It was time to put the past to rest, but she could only do that if she had answers. This could be the only opportunity she'd get to find out what had really happened to her brother. He had been, after all, a professional driver, trained to the highest standard, and for Charlie his accident was shrouded in questions.

'Before we discuss my terms, I need to know what happened that night.' She folded her arms in a subconscious gesture of self-protection and leant against the kitchen cupboards, watching intently for his reaction.

She'd expected guilt to cloud his face, to darken the handsome features, but his steady gaze met hers and a flicker of doubt entered her mind. She'd always held him responsible, blamed him, but right now that notion was as unstable as a newborn foal.

'What do you want to know?' His calm voice conflicted with her pounding heart. The questions she'd wanted answers to since the night of the accident clamoured in her mind. The answers now tantalisingly close after having eluded her for so long.

'Why was he even in the car? It wasn't fit to be driven—at least that's what I heard.' She straightened her shoulders and took a deep breath, desperately trying to appear in control. She was far from that, and deep down she knew it wasn't just because she had to face the man she blamed. It was the man himself.

Alessandro Roselli's powerful aura of domination and control filled the kitchen, but she couldn't allow herself to be intimidated. She met it head-on, with determination and courage. She would find out the truth, one way or another. She was convinced it hadn't yet been revealed and she wanted to put that right.

He sat back in his seat, studying her, and she had the distinct impression he was stalling her in an attempt to divert her attention. It was almost working. She'd never been under such a hot spotlight before. *Think of Seb*, she reminded herself, not wanting to waste this opportunity.

'Do you always believe gossip?' He folded his arms, looking more relaxed than he had a right to. Far too self-assured.

She frowned, irritation at his attitude growing. 'No, of course I don't.'

'So if I tell you there was nothing wrong with the car, would you believe me?' He unfolded his arms and turned in his seat, stretching his long legs out, one arm leaning casually on the table. But he was far from casual. His body might be relaxed but, looking into those dark eyes, she knew he was all alertness. Like a hunting cat, lulling its quarry into a false sense of security. But not this mouse. No, she was on her guard.

Forcefully, she shook her head. 'The only thing that will convince me of that is to see the report of the accident.'

He stood up slowly, his height almost intimidating, walked towards the window and looked out across her garden and the countryside beyond. 'Would that really help? Every last detail is in it.'

'Yes,' she said and moved towards him, drawn by an inexplicable need to see his face, see the emotion in it. 'I want every last detail.'

'Why do you think your father hasn't shown you the report?' His broad shoulders became a barrier, as if he was hiding something, concealing something he didn't want her to know, like his guilt. 'What are you hoping to find?'

'The truth.' Anger surged through her again as she imagined him talking to her father, conspiring to hide all the details. She still couldn't understand why her father wouldn't tell her everything. She'd always suspected he was covering something up. Did he have loyalties to this man which exceeded those to his daughter—or even his son's memory?

He turned to face her, his expression hard, making the angles of his face more pronounced. 'Sometimes not knowing the truth is best.'

'What?' She pressed her fingertips to her temples, hardly able to believe what he was saying. Her father and this man were keeping things from her. He might as well have told her exactly that. 'What are you talking about?'

Alessandro heard the exasperation in her voice and gritted his teeth against the urge to tell her what she wanted to know. A truth that would tarnish all the happiness she'd ever shared with her brother and a truth her father had expressly asked him to conceal from her. That had been the one and only condition her father had made when he'd contacted him. He intended to honour that—and the promise he'd made to Seb.

She stood before him, not able to look at him as she pressed long fingers against her temples, her head shaking in denial. The rise and fall of her shoulders as her breath came hard and fast gave away the struggle she was having. Instinctively, he took hold of her arms and she looked back up at him, the beauty of her green eyes almost swaying him from his purpose. 'Your brother was in a high speed accident. You do know that, don't you?'

'I know,' she whispered, thankfully a little more calmly, and looked up into his face, her eyes searching his, looking for answers he couldn't give. 'But I need to know what happened and why.'

'It is better to remember him well and happy, believe

me, Charlotte. It is for the best.' Her ragged sigh deflated all the anger from her body and he felt the resignation slip through her, defusing the fight which had raged moments ago.

'I know, but so many questions need answering.' She closed her eyes and he watched the thick dark lashes splay out over her pale skin. The urge to kiss her rushed at him, almost knocking the breath from his body.

When he'd arrived he'd never expected to find a woman he desired so fiercely. Only once before had such a need raged in him and he'd acted impulsively on it, marrying quickly, only to discover his wife had had ulterior motives all along. Under no circumstances would he put himself in such a position again.

The attraction which had sprung between him and Charlie the second their eyes had met complicated things, made his promise even harder to keep. He let her go and stepped back away from her, away from the temptation, curling his fingers into tight fists. The whole situation was testing far more than his ability to keep his promise.

She looked up at him, her chin lifting in determination. 'I will find out, Mr Roselli. Your and my father's insistence to keep things from me only makes it more important to do so.'

'Some things are best left alone. For Seb's sake, accept what you know and do as your father wants.' He moved away from her, back to the chair he'd sat in earlier—anything to put distance between them—but still the heady need which rushed through him persisted.

'For Seb's sake?' Her question jolted him and he realised how close he'd come to pointing her in the direction of the cause of the accident.

'Seb asked for you to be at the launch. It was one of the

last things he said to me.' There was no way he was going to tell her Seb's actual last words and he guarded himself against letting the truth inadvertently slip. He held her partly accountable for Seb's problems. She'd never been to see him in Italy, had never shown any interest, but that wasn't something he was prepared to discuss now. All he wanted was for her to agree to be at the launch.

'He really said that?' Her voice was so soft it was hardly audible, but it did untold things to the pulse of desire he was fighting hard to suppress.

'He wanted you there.' He watched the indecision slide over her face and waited. She was coming to the right decision slowly. All he had to do was wait.

Charlie couldn't shake the feeling of unease. Yes, she knew Seb's accident would have caused horrible injuries, but she couldn't rid herself of the notion there was something else. Something her father wanted to keep from her as much as Alessandro did. Did that mean he was to blame?

She changed tactics and adopted an attitude of acceptance, realising it was possibly the only way to find out. Slowly, she walked back to the table and stood looking down at him where he calmly sat, watching her.

'If I come to the launch I want to know all about the car first. I want to see everything you and Seb worked on. I want to live it, to breathe it.' A hint of the passion she'd always felt for her job and the world of racing started to fizz in her veins after being unmoved for many months, infusing her with excitement that she hadn't felt for a long time.

'There isn't much time for that.' He sat back in the

chair and looked up at her, observing every move she made until she wondered if he could read all her thoughts.

'If I'm going to be at the launch I want to be able to talk about the car, to bring it to life for everyone else. I need to know all there is to know.'

It was more than that, she admitted to herself. It was much more than just promoting the car. It was seeing what Seb had seen, feeling the excitement he'd felt as he'd driven it for the first time. Her thoughts halted as if they'd slammed into a brick wall.

Was she ready to know all the facts? She looked at the man she'd blamed for her brother's death. As far as she was concerned, he'd allowed Seb to drive a faulty car, despite the fact that her father had told her all the reports stated driver error. She'd blamed Alessandro and now he was here, offering her the opportunity to find out the truth for herself. Would he really do that if he had something to hide?

'I want to see all the files and every drawing Seb made.' She kept her voice firm, trying to hide the waver of confidence growing within her.

Alessandro got up and made his way around the table, coming closer to her, his face stern with contemplation. 'I can't allow it. There isn't enough time.'

Not allow it. Who did he think he was?

'If you knew anything about me, Mr Roselli, you'd know that I need to be involved—if I'm to do my job right, that is. You do want me to promote this car, put my seal of approval on it, do you not?'

She held his gaze, looked directly into his eyes. She would not be intimidated by him. He might be used to getting his way in business, but so was she. He pressed his lips together in thought, the movement drawing her attention briefly, but quickly she regained her focus, refusing to allow the pull of attraction to him to cloud her mind. Confirming her suspicions of his blame for the accident would surely curb any misguided attraction she was experiencing.

'It's more than that, isn't it, Charlotte?' The firmness of his tone dissipated as he said each word until he caressed her name, sending a hot fizzing sensation racing over her. It was worse than when he'd called her Charlie.

It was soft yet insanely hot, but she couldn't pay heed to that now. 'I need to know something about the car if I am to promote and endorse it. You understand that, surely.'

He took a deep breath in and she watched his broad chest expand, waiting expectantly, holding her own breath.

'I do but, given the circumstances, is it really wise?' He looked up at her and she tasted defeat as his dark eyes hardened in determination. But defeat wasn't on her agenda. She'd do this her way or not at all. How could he expect anything less when he'd been the one who'd let Seb get in the car, allowed him to drive it that night?

This was the only option. Her only chance to find out what had truly happened. At least then she might be able to move on from it. 'Don't worry—I won't dissolve into a heap of female hysteria again.'

'Maybe you should,' he said and stepped closer to her—too close—but she wouldn't move away. He must never know of the heat he fired within her, just from one look. Thankfully, he'd stopped his flirting of moments ago and had become more professional and she had to ensure it would stay that way.

'No, it is past time for that. I intend to do what my father advised last week.'

'And that is?'

'To get back in the driving seat.' She wouldn't tell him just yet that was quite literally what she intended to do.

He raised his hand to his chin, his thumb and finger rasping over the hint of dark stubble, the sound tying her stomach in knots. She couldn't listen to her body now, to the way it reacted just to being close to him, not that she really understood what it was asking of her. Heightened desire and intense awareness of a man was something she'd never experienced before.

Her previous relationships had been short-lived and unsuccessful. Back then, the breakdown of her parents' marriage had still been too fresh in her mind. Those relationships had also been a long time ago. The mess her parents had made of their marriage had ensured that life-long commitment wasn't something she considered possible. There was no way she was going to expose herself to more hurt and humiliation.

'I'm not convinced it is for the best, but if you are sure then so be it.' He spoke slowly, his accent heavy, as he continued to watch her closely.

'I am,' she said quickly before he had a chance to change his mind. Before she too changed her mind.

'Then we have a deal.' He reached out his hand, the same one that had been thoughtfully touching his face, and she took it quickly, anxious to seal the deal.

'We have a deal.' Her words came out in a rush as a jolt shot up her arm, setting off sparks all over her body as if she'd become a firework. Her breathing almost stopped as his eyes locked with hers, his fingers clasped tightly around her hand, the warmth of his scorching hers.

'Bene,' he said firmly, so firmly it was obvious he didn't feel any of the drama from touching her and she'd do well to remember that the next time he smiled at her as if she was the most beautiful woman in the world. He was flirting, just like all the men she'd known, including her father. And it was flirting which had destroyed her parents' marriage, driving her mother into another man's arms, tearing the family apart.

She closed the door on those thoughts. Now was not the time to become embroiled in them, not when she had the perfect opportunity to find out the truth of Seb's last hours.

Alessandro held onto her hand and looked into her eyes. Did she feel it too? Was the same sizzle of passion creating havoc in her body? She regarded him with a steady gaze, her full lips pressed into a firm line. Evidently not. Her beautiful face was a mask of stone; not a trace of emotion there.

He should be pleased, grateful that the deal they'd just made wasn't going to be overcomplicated by sex. His friendship with Seb and the promise he'd made when he was in hospital, hooked up to all sorts of machines, dictated this arrangement should be business only. At least with her cool demeanour it would be exactly that.

'If it becomes too painful, too much, you must tell me.' She frowned at him and pulled her hand free of his, ceasing the torment just that innocent touch had created within him.

'It won't.' Those two words were so full of strength he didn't doubt it for one moment.

'You are very sure of that, considering you told me to

leave only a short while ago.' Was he trying to reassure himself or her?

'You caught me off guard.' She reached past him and gathered up their discarded coffee mugs and as she turned to wash them he couldn't help but take another look at her curves, admire the womanly softness of them.

Enough.

Business. That was all it was—business. He also sensed that this was a woman who wouldn't accept a no-strings-attached affair. He had, after all, become adept at avoiding such women since extricating himself from a marriage which should never have happened.

He shrugged his shoulders, trying to shake off the pulse of passion. 'Then we shall travel to Milan today.'

'We?' Her eyes flew wide with shock.

'I have much to do ahead of the launch and if you seriously want to learn more about the car it would be a good idea, no?' He wondered at the wisdom of travelling with her when he found it hard to focus on much other than her glorious body.

'I'm not packed or anything. I'll travel out later. You'd better get back to your family.'

'That will not be necessary.' His voice was firm, perhaps a little too firm if the surprise on her face was anything to go by. 'There isn't anyone awaiting my arrival.' Those days were over and if he had any sense it would stay that way.

He didn't miss her raised brows, or the look of suppressed curiosity which crept into her eyes, and wanted to deflect any questions. 'There are also plans for the weekend, with customers going to the test track to drive the demonstration car. Seb had been really excited about that, told me you'd be in your element there.'

'But still,' she said, her soft voice torturing his un-expected need for her, 'I can make my own way there.'

Was she deliberately being difficult, provoking him to the point of frustration? 'I have a plane waiting. We can be there before nightfall.'

She looked at him, doubt clouding her eyes, and a vice-like grip clutched at his chest. Seb had always spo-ken very protectively of his sister—and now he knew why. She was woman enough to bring out the protective streak in any man. For years he'd avoided any such sen-timents, having had them destroyed by divorce. He was far from the right man to protect her and he wished he'd never made Seb any promises.

He couldn't do this, couldn't risk it. She was sweet temptation even though he knew she was off limits. He couldn't do anything against Seb's memory. This was Seb's sister, the woman his friend had always wanted to protect. If he allowed this carnal need to take over, he would be failing in his promise to Seb. He wouldn't be protecting her at all.

'So what are you going to do while I pack?' Charlie asked tersely, annoyed that she hadn't even left her home yet and he was already making decisions for her. She tried for flippancy. 'Drink more coffee?'

'No,' he said, sounding very Italian, even with just that one word. 'I will wait here.'

He was infuriating and she recalled what Seb had said about him once when they'd talked on the phone about his new venture. *A man who knows what he wants and allows nothing to get in his way.*

Alessandro did want her at the launch. That much was clear. But why? Was she disrupting his plans by dictating her own terms? She certainly hoped so. It was probably about time he learnt he couldn't have it all.

'Very well. I will be as quick as I can.' She made to move past him and he stepped back away from her, giving her room. So much room that anyone would think he didn't want her near him, but the heavy hint of desire in his eyes gave an entirely different message.

'I'm not going anywhere, *cara*.' The silky softness of his voice stirred the throb of desire which still lingered inside her body. She clutched the door frame of the kitchen as if it was the only thing that would keep her upright.

'I wouldn't expect anything less from a man like you.' Before he even had time to respond, she fled, dashing up the stairs to her room, enjoying the rush of anticipation that ran through her. She paused briefly. She'd always been excited by the prospect of jetting off when she'd worked for Seb's team, but never had such a handsome man been part of the reason.

He's not, she scolded herself and quickly changed, before applying light make-up. Then, with practised speed and efficiency, she packed a small bag, just enough for a few days in Italy. She'd shop for anything else she needed once there.

His expression of shock made her smile as she returned to the kitchen. He hadn't expected that. At least it proved he didn't know as much about her as he claimed.

'Have you your passport?' His accent was heavy as he moved towards her to take her bag.

His fingers grazed hers as she gave him the bag and heat scorched her skin. She looked up at him and a flush crept over her face. In his eyes she thought she saw desire, the same desire she was sure must be shining from hers. Would he see it? Recognise it?

She hoped not. From the first second her eyes had met his, the pull of attraction had been strong. With each passing minute it had strengthened, but she could not and would not act on it. To do so would be disloyal to Seb. Whatever had happened the night of the accident, this was Seb's business partner.

She hesitated. Could she do this? Should she be considering going anywhere with this man? The desire he lit within her contrasted starkly with the anger she felt at her brother's death. As far as she was concerned, he was the reason her brother had crashed.

She'd do well to remember that.

This was going to be harder than he'd imagined. Sandro took the case from Charlie, taking in her change of clothes. Heels, tight jeans of soft beige with a white blouse and dark brown jacket. Chic. Elegant. Not at all like the dishevelled gardener he'd met on arrival. She was now very much the woman he'd seen on television promoting Seb's team. The woman he'd admired more and more as Seb had enthused about her.

Don't go there. He pushed thoughts of her to the back of his mind, focusing instead on maintaining a business-like manner. One that would keep her where she needed to be in his mind.

He watched as she opened a drawer and pulled out her passport.

'I should really let my neighbour know I'm going away.'

He frowned, unsure where that comment was going. 'Why is this?'

'She'll keep an eye on the place, water the garden.' Absently she picked up her phone and began tapping quickly onto the screen. 'At least for a few days.'

Garden, he pondered. That didn't fit with the glamorous image she'd built up as she'd promoted the team. Had this cottage, this garden been her escape from the media frenzy that had followed? He knew well about the need to escape. It had been something he'd had to do twice in his life now.

'You gave up your career to become a gardener?'

She turned to face him, putting her phone in her handbag at the same time. 'Why is that so shocking?'

'Seb never mentioned you were a gardener.'

'It is something I've always enjoyed, but I didn't feel the need to change my life before Seb's accident.' She looked up at him, her expression serious and focused. 'Seb's death changed all that. That's why I want to know all he did that day. I have to understand why it happened.'

Each word echoed with her accusation, leaving him in no doubt she blamed him. The only other person who knew the truth was her father—and he'd insisted that she must never know all the details of Seb's accident.

Thoughts of Seb grounded him and the urge to tell her everything, just to clear his name of blame in her eyes, was overwhelming. But he wasn't doing this for himself; he was doing it for Seb. He would do well to remember that when he next thought of succumbing to the temptation of Charlie. She was out of his reach. Put there by his sense of honour and his promise to Seb and subsequently her father. Out of his reach was where she had to stay.

CHAPTER THREE

As DARKNESS BEGAN to descend the car pulled to a halt outside Alessandro's offices and Charlie got her first view of the place she'd heard so much about from her brother. His calls had always been full of excitement and pride as he'd enthused about the Roselli factory, workshops and test track.

Sadness crept over her too. This was where Seb had spent his final weeks and she could have been part of that if she'd accepted his offer to come out and visit instead of being so tied up in her career. The same career she'd dropped after Seb's death.

She got out of the car and stood looking up at the buildings, wishing she had come to see what he was doing. 'I should have come when he asked me to,' she said softly and was startled when Alessandro responded.

'Seb always hoped you'd come here one day.' His voice was gentle and not at all judgemental as he placed his hand in the small of her back. She drew in a ragged breath, her emotions all over the place. Memories of Seb mixed with the undeniable attraction she felt for Alessandro. Guilt added to the mix and washed over her. How could she even be thinking such thoughts? Quickly she blocked them out.

'I wish I had.' Her voice was a croaky whisper of raw emotion. She stood next to him in the warm evening air, her emotions exposed and vulnerable, as if she stood before him totally naked. She was certain that not only was he able to see every bit of her skin, but into her heart and soul.

He stopped outside a glass door and keyed in his pass code, his other hand sliding away from her back, the heat of his touch cooling, giving her space to think. Judging by the shiver which had run up her spine, she needed that space. Badly.

'Why didn't you?' he asked, pushing open the door, stepping inside and holding the door open for her, but she didn't miss the lightly veiled accusation in his voice.

'It was busy. You know how the end of the racing season gets.' She saw his jaw tighten, saw the sceptical look on his face and shame heated her cheeks. She'd also been worried about Seb's blatant attempts at matchmaking. He'd often teased her on the phone about finding the perfect man for her.

She could have come. She'd wanted to come, but she had been a tiny bit threatened by this new life Seb had found. They'd always been so close and when he'd met Alessandro all that had changed overnight. She was pleased he'd found something he was so passionate about; she'd just never expected it to take him so far away from her, physically or emotionally.

He shrugged nonchalantly but she knew what he was thinking. She could almost hear his words, heavy and accented, telling her she was selfish, and she retaliated as if he'd actually spoken. 'I didn't know time was against me.'

He let the door go and she stood in the semi-darkness of the large reception. His face was a mask of hardened

fury as the accusation in her words hit him. Did he feel
any guilt? Did he have regrets? Did he want to go back
and change things?

He stepped forward, coming closer, and she wished
there was more light, something to lessen the presence
of a man who excited and angered her so intensely. She
veered wildly between those two emotions as he looked
directly at her.

'Whatever guilt you carry, Charlotte, I do not need it
added to what I feel.' His voice had deepened, become
growly, anger lingering dangerously beneath the surface
like a serpent waiting to strike. He loomed over her in
the dim light, every bit the predator, but she wasn't going
to be his next victim.

'Just by saying that you are admitting guilt.' She
rounded on him. The hours spent on the plane and in
his car, when she'd thought everything through silently,
had allowed her temper to brew and now it flared to life.

For a moment his gaze held hers, his eyes hard and
glittering. Tension stretched almost to breaking point
between them as silence settled after her angry words.
In her head she could hear her heartbeat, the fast thump
of blood rushing around her body. It should have been
ignited by her anger, but the flutter in her stomach as he
stepped closer made it something else entirely.

It was raw attraction. Something she didn't want to
feel. Not now and not for this man.

He stepped even closer, his height towering over her
in the darkness, and she looked up into his eyes, wanting
to appear fearless but afraid he'd see just what an effect
he could have on her. Could he hear her heart pounding?
Had he noticed her breath, ragged and unsteady?

'Dangerous words, *cara*.' Each word was low and soft

like a cat purring, but she sensed the coil of tension in him, the cool detachment from the emotions that careered inside her. He was more like a tiger preparing to strike.

'I came here to see what Seb had been working on,' she said, trying hard to beat down the flutter of emotions, and walked away from him towards the stairs. 'So, can we just do that? Then I'd like to check into a nearby hotel.'

She didn't wait for his answer, didn't look at his face, but every nerve in her body told her he was watching her—intently. She was about to go up the stairs when light flooded the reception area and she blinked against it and turned to face him. The sleek clean lines of the interior of the building were exactly as she would have imagined and, unable to help herself, she looked around her, trying hard to ignore the man who stood in the centre of the marble floor and the superiority which radiated from him.

'This way,' he said and passed her as she waited at the foot of the stairs, his scent of musk and male trailing in his wake. 'We'll take the lift.'

She bit her bottom lip, anxiety rushing at her. Was she really ready to see what Seb had been working on? She wasn't, but this was what she had to do, what she needed to do before she could put the last year behind her.

She became aware that Alessandro was watching her, waiting for her to enter the lift. 'We don't have to do this tonight.'

Was that genuine concern in his voice? Her gaze locked with his and everything around them spun. Everything blurred as the dark depths of his eyes met and held hers. Time seemed to be suspended, as if everything was standing still. She lowered her lashes. Now was not

the time to get fanciful. She'd never been that way in-
clined, had never hankered after notions of instant attraction. So why now? And why this man?

'I want to.' The words rushed from her as she stepped
quickly into the lift. 'I just hadn't anticipated it. Today
started just like any other, then you arrived...' Her voice
trailed off and she looked down at her hands, feigning
interest in her unpainted nails.

'I should have contacted you first but I didn't think
you'd see me.' His tone was calm and so matter-of-fact
she glanced up at him. He appeared totally unaffected
by the whole situation.

'I wouldn't have.' She flashed him a smile and, from
the expression on his face, he hadn't missed the sarcasm.
'I wouldn't have seen you and I would never have come
here.'

The lift doors opened onto a vast office but she paid
little attention to the hard masculine lines and marched
out of the lift, drawn inexplicably to the wall of windows,
offering an unrivalled view of Milan's twinkling skyline.

She should feel too irritated by his assured presence
to notice even one thing about his office, but that was so
far from the truth it was scary. She should be thinking
of Seb, should be focusing on what he'd done here, not
the man he'd worked with.

'*Grazie.*' The deep tone of his voice unsettled her and,
as she stopped to look out over the city, she saw his reflection behind her, saw him move closer.

'What for?' Her gaze met his reflected in the glass
and a coil of tension pressed down inside her. She knew
at any minute it could snap.

'Your honesty. Saying you wouldn't want to see me.'
His reflection shrugged nonchalantly, his gaze so intense

it obliterated the view. All she could see was him. Then her heart plummeted in disappointment. None of this really mattered to him. It was all about the Roselli image and launching a new car.

'I have no reason to conceal my dislike of you, Mr Roselli.'

Liar! a voice called in her head. She didn't dislike him. She should. The fizz of attraction was at war with the blame she still laid at his door, despite his earlier assurances that the accident had been nothing more than a tragedy.

'Dislike. Is that not a bit strong?' He moved unbearably close, his eyes holding hers in the reflection in the window.

She had to stop this now, whatever *this* was. Something she couldn't control was happening between them and she didn't like it. Or did she?

'Oh, I dislike you intensely, Alessandro.' She turned, her words a hurried whisper. Who was she trying to convince? 'And right at this moment I have no idea what I'm doing here.'

His eyes turned blacker than the night sky, their swirling depths mesmerising. She couldn't break eye contact. The power he'd had as he'd looked at her reflection had been intense, but this all-consuming fire which had leapt to life in her was too much.

'You are here, *cara*, because you couldn't help yourself.' His voice was deep and gentle, caressing every heightened nerve in her body into submission. 'Because this is what you need to do—for Seb.'

At the mention of her brother's name the spell slipped away like morning mist as the sun came up. She could see everything sharply and in focus again. She was here for Seb—a fact she had to keep in the forefront of her mind—or lose it to the seductive charms of the worst man she could possibly fall for.

'Exactly.' Her eyes maintained contact with his and she saw the moment they turned to glittering blackness. 'So I'd like to see where he worked, what he did.'

Alessandro couldn't move, mesmerised by the intensity of what had just passed between them. For the last few weeks he'd been irritated at the thought of contacting Seb's sister, had put the moment off for as long as possible. But, whatever he had been expecting when they'd finally met, it wasn't the raw desire that coursed wildly through him.

If she'd been any other woman he'd have acted upon that need; he would have kissed her and explored the passion that lingered expectantly, just waiting for the touch-paper to be lit so it could explode into life.

'*Si, così,*' he instructed her to follow, unable to gather his thoughts quickly enough to use English, a situation he'd never known before.

'Thank you.' Those two words were so soft, so seductive he almost couldn't move. He fought the urge to press his lips to hers. Thankfully, she stepped back, enough to remind him what he should and definitely shouldn't be doing.

With intent, he made his way across the vast expanse of his office, resisting the urge to look in the windows and see her reflection following. He didn't need to. His body told him she was; even if he hadn't heard her footsteps on the marble behind him he would have known she was there.

'This is where Seb worked.' He went through a door

at the end of his office into the room Seb had claimed as his own, the emptiness of it almost too harsh. On the far wall was the first drawing that Seb had done of the car. But still the office looked stark.

Something akin to guilt touched him. He should have brought Charlie here sooner and not left it until the last days before the launch. He should have done this a long time ago, but he'd been anxious to conceal the truth— for Seb's sake as much as his sister's.

As Charlie walked past him he caught a hint of her perfume; instantly he was transported back to her garden and the sweet smells of an English summer. Her deep ragged breath, inhaled quickly, drew his attention back to the present.

'Is this what he did?' She stood next to the desk, her fingertips tracing the outline of the car drawing. He noticed her hand shook slightly and, when she looked back at him, hesitation weaved with panic sprang from her eyes. He had the strange sensation his heart was being crushed.

'*Sì.*' His voice was so raw he couldn't say anything else, painfully aware he was intruding on her moment of grief.

'What else?' She looked at him and he saw the gleam of tears collect in her eyes and the pressure on his chest intensified.

Thankful for the diversion, he walked over to the desk and opened the laptop, turned it on and looked across the desk at her. Her pretty face was pale, her eyes wide, reminding him of a startled doe. 'There are lots of photos on here, as well as all he created in the design programme.'

She hesitated for a moment and he wondered if it was

all too much. She stood and watched him as he opened the photos up on the screen and turned the laptop to face her. He felt her scrutiny and questions press down on him.

Slowly she reached out, one fingertip touching the screen. He watched her eyes, the green becoming much more intense as she looked at the photo of Seb sitting in the driving seat of the test car, and he inwardly cursed. Couldn't he have selected a more appropriate photo for her to see first?

'When was this taken?' Her voice was fragile as she continued to look at the screen. She swallowed hard, trying to keep the tears at bay, and for the first time ever he wished a woman would cry. She needed to let out her grief.

He hated the answer he was going to have to give. 'The day before the accident.' It took huge effort to keep his voice calm, to keep it steady, but even to his ears each word he'd just said sounded cold. He'd studied the photo since then, shocked to see a hint of trouble in Seb's eyes. Would she notice too?

She looked up at him and tears filled her eyes, making them shine like gemstones. Before he'd thought about the consequences, he moved around the desk and took her in his arms. Without hesitation, she sought the comfort he offered and pressed her face in her hands, her forehead on his chest as sobs racked her body.

'*Dio mio.* This is too much for you.' He wanted to clench his fists in anger but instead spread them over her back as the sobs continued, smoothing them over her and pulling her closer against him.

'No, it's not.' The strangled words came out in a rush, muffled by her hands and his body.

'It is, *cara*, it is,' he soothed, just as he'd done for his sister many times as they'd grown up, but this wasn't his sister. This was a woman he desired with every nerve in his body.

'I should, I should.' Sobs prevented her words from coming out and, without thinking, he lowered his head, pressing his lips into her hair. She stilled in his arms momentarily and he closed his eyes against the memories of when he'd thought his life was complete. He pushed back the knowledge that he'd failed to be the man his wife had wanted, lifted his chin and took in a deep breath.

It seemed like for ever that he held Charlie as she cried, each sob transferring her pain to him, increasing his guilt for not having been there the night Seb had decided to take the car out again. He would have seen the drink- and drugs-induced euphoria and could have stopped him. The discovery still shocked him now. How had they worked so closely together for all those months without him noticing Seb had such a problem?

He lowered his head, once more pressing his lips against her hair, his aim to soothe both of them. But, as he held her tighter, uttering words of comfort in Italian, he knew he had to stop, had to let her go. It shocked him to admit he wanted to be more than just a shoulder to cry on.

Thankfully the tears subsided and a huge sob shuddered through her. She looked up at him and they were so close they could have been lovers. Without any effort at all he would be able to press his lips to hers, but her tear-stained cheeks reminded him they were not lovers and exactly why they were here.

'I should have done this a long time ago.' Finally she spoke a little more calmly, her words slightly wobbly after crying.

'This is the first time you have cried?' Incredulity made him pull back slightly as he watched her expression change, become softer, less pained.

She smiled up at him, nodding. 'Thank you.' Her voice was barely above a whisper and she blinked as tears escaped her eyes. She rubbed one cheek roughly with her fingers but, before she could reach the other cheek and before he could think about what he was doing, he gently wiped the tears away.

Everything changed in that second. They became cocooned in a bubble of sizzling tension. Unable to stop himself, he held her face in his hands, her skin warm and damp from crying. Her green eyes locked with his, sadness and grief swirling with something quite different and completely inappropriate.

'Prego.' His natural response sprang to his lips but his voice was husky and deep. He couldn't take his gaze from hers, couldn't break that tenuous contact which held them together.

She closed her eyes and leant her cheek against his hand. Instinct took over and he caressed her face then pushed his fingers into her hair, the silky softness of it almost irresistible. He wanted to kiss her, to lower his head and taste the fullness of her lips.

He moved towards her and she opened her eyes. For what seemed like an eternity she looked up at him, her breathing fast and shallow. His heartbeat sounded so loud in his ears as he watched the green of her eyes change until they swirled with browns, like trees as autumn approached.

He wanted her. That was all he could think of at that moment. Nothing else was important. Nothing else mattered.

She moved nearer, her eyes closing, spreading her long damp lashes on her cheeks, and then her lips met his. It was a gentle kiss, full of hesitancy at first, but, as he pulled her close, one hand buried in her long hair, it deepened, became something much more. He shouldn't be doing this, not now, not ever.

Charlie's head spun and she knew she shouldn't be kissing him like this, knew it would only mean complications, but the need to feel his lips against hers was overwhelming. Her senses were on overdrive, every nerve in her body responding to him. Heat exploded deep inside her and she pressed herself against him. His arm tightened around her back, pulling her closer, and his fingers scrunched in her hair, holding her head at just the right angle as his tongue moved between her lips, entwining with hers.

Her arms slipped up around his neck, pulling him closer, deepening the kiss until she could hardly stand, her knees were so weak. Never had a kiss felt like this, so electrifying, so right.

With a force and suddenness that nearly knocked her backwards he released his hold on her and pushed his hands against her shoulders, forcing her back and away from him. She was so shocked she didn't know what to say, even if her laboured breathing had allowed her to speak. After a few seconds he let go of her, stepping backwards, a wary look in his eyes and a furious rush of Italian sprang from his lips.

Her grasp on the language was slight and she had no idea what he'd said, but his body language left her in no doubt. He had not enjoyed or wanted that kiss. So why had he encouraged her? Was this some kind of game?

'That shouldn't have happened.' She forced herself to stand as tall as possible, even though her knees were so weak they might crumple beneath her and a fire of heady need still raged inside her.

'Damn right it shouldn't have.' He flung his hand up in agitation, turned and marched across the office to the doorway. 'That can never happen between us, ever.'

Hurt scolded her but she kept her eyes firmly fixed on him, refusing to be intimidated. He didn't want her kisses—so what? 'I didn't think…' she stammered the words out '…I didn't know what I was doing.'

His eyes narrowed but he remained at the far side of the office. 'Apparently not. It's time we left here.'

'No—' she panicked, her embarrassment at his obvious dislike of her evaporating '—I haven't seen nearly enough.'

'Enough for tonight.' His voice was deep and hard, the complete opposite to the husky tones that had soothed her just moments before. 'You will stay with me tonight.'

'You?' The question shot from her lips before she could think.

'You are upset, acting irrationally. I cannot leave you in a hotel alone, not tonight.'

The firm words brooked no argument and if she was honest she had little fight left in her. The last twelve hours had been nothing short of shock after shock. From the moment he'd arrived in her garden she'd been on a roller coaster ride of emotions.

'Just call me a taxi to take me to a hotel in the city.' With bravado she was far from feeling, she walked towards him but he didn't move aside for her to leave the office. Instead, he looked at her, his brown eyes cold and remote.

'Seb was right.' The firmness of his voice caught her attention and she looked up at him, her gaze locking with his.

Angered at the mention of her brother, she glared at him. 'And what is that supposed to mean?'

A hint of a smile lingered at the edges of his mouth then he pressed them into a tight line of exasperation. 'I know more about you than you might think, Charlotte Warrington.'

'You've got a nerve,' she said as her own expression mirrored his.

'*Sì.*' He shrugged casually and turned away from her, leaving her wide-eyed with shock.

If she was sensible she'd just walk out of here, get a taxi to the airport and go home. But right now she wasn't sensible and she wanted this chance to get answers to questions that would otherwise niggle at her for the rest of her life.

The only problem was these answers were tied up with the man she blamed for Seb's death, the very same man she'd just thrown herself at, kissing him with a passion she'd never known before.

'I'm not going anywhere with you, especially after what just happened.'

He turned round so swiftly she almost walked straight into him, leaving her perilously close to him again. 'Do I need to remind you, *cara*, you kissed me?'

Her cheeks burned as the sexy depth of his voice practically caressed her body, reigniting the heat that had flared between them earlier. 'That,' she hissed at him, 'was a big mistake. One that won't be happening again.'

'*Va bene!*' His gaze searched her face, resting briefly

on her lips. 'In that case, there is no danger in you staying at my apartment tonight.'

'Danger? You make me sound like some sort of predatory female.' She was becoming more and more infuriated by him. Maybe a hotel would be the best option, but as that thought settled in her mind she knew she didn't want to be alone right now. Not after all she'd been through in the short space of time since he'd forged into her life, but her only choice of company was Alessandro Roselli.

He just quirked his brows at her, the humiliating spark in his eyes clear. She held his gaze, refusing to back down.

'Why do you want to do this? Why is it so important I'm at the launch?' She gestured around the room, glancing back at the drawing on the wall.

'As I explained, I made a promise to your brother. One I intend to keep.' He walked through to the large office they'd entered earlier and across to the lift. 'This way, *cara.*'

Charlie couldn't shake off the feeling that he'd won. What he'd won she didn't quite know, but he had. One night in his apartment wouldn't be that hard, would it? First thing, she'd arrange a hotel in Milan and as soon as the launch was over she could go back to her cottage and get on with her life. The quiet life she'd led since Seb's accident; the one that kept her safe.

Alessandro shut the door of his apartment and watched Charlie as she walked into the open-plan living area. She hadn't said a word since they'd left his office but, despite that, the tension between them had increased. So much that he now questioned his sanity in bringing her here.

'The guest suite is ready for you,' he said sternly, eager to create some boundaries because if there was one woman who needed to be behind them it was this one.

'Thank you,' she said so softly it was almost a whisper.

He watched her as she walked around the apartment, judging the artwork he'd collected over recent years, taking in just about every detail with a hint of suspicion on her face. There was nothing modern about the apartment, from the grand façade of the old building to the ornate interior. It was a complete contrast to the office they'd just left—exactly what he'd wanted it to be. It was a showcase for the real Alessandro.

She wandered over to the balcony doors and looked down onto the busy streets of Milan. He used that time to rein in the hot lust which pumped around his body after the journey back from his office. Since the moment her lips had touched his something had changed and he feared it might be irreversible.

'Would you like anything to eat or drink?' The polite question gave him just that bit more time to regain control and bring normality to the evening.

She turned and looked back at him. 'No, thank you. I'm tired. It's been an unexpectedly busy day and I need to be fresh tomorrow.'

'Fresh?' The word sprang from him, a frown furrowing his brow, but she kept her gaze on him.

'Yes, there is a lot to do before the launch, lots I need to know.' She looked completely focused but the gritty determination in her voice rang alarm bells in his head.

'You're right,' he said and turned from her, picking up her small overnight bag before heading towards the guest suite. A good night's sleep would be beneficial to him too, but somehow he doubted he'd get it. His body still craved hers, still yearned for her touch, her kiss.

He crunched his hand tightly around the handle of the bag. He'd made a promise to Seb and he would keep that promise, no matter what. The thought of his friend, who had also been a partner in the business venture, reminded him that Seb had been the last person to stay in the guest suite.

He pushed aside the guilt. Seb had been staying with him. He should have seen the signs, spotted the problem. He couldn't change that now, but he could keep the painful truth from Seb's beloved sister.

He paused outside the door and turned to look at her. 'Your brother stayed here too. Did you know that?'

'No.' A startled whisper formed the word and she looked at him, confusion marring the beauty of her face. 'I don't understand. He was looking for somewhere to rent.'

'That is true.' He opened the door to the suite and walked in and she followed him, looking around her. There wasn't any evidence that anyone had ever stayed here. 'It was a sensible option. We were both working on the same project.'

'Did he find somewhere to move to, or was this the last place he stayed?'

The very question he'd dreaded had just been delivered with clear words. 'This was the last place.'

'But his things?'

'I sent them on to your father.'

She looked around the room, from the large bed to the dark wardrobe and drawers, as if she didn't quite believe him. 'I see.'

Silence floated down around them, a silence so heavy

he wanted to break it, to say something. But what else could he say? Everything so far had caused hurt and pain. 'There is another room. Much smaller, but if you would prefer it…'

She shook her head, the light above them catching the darkness of her hair, making the brown tones glow and come alive. 'I'd like to stay here, please.'

Now he really did question his sanity. Not only had he kissed her, responded to the invitation her lips had made, but now he'd put her in the very same room Seb had last stayed in. The promise he'd made to his friend to look after Charlie, to involve her in the project was becoming more difficult to keep by the minute. As was concealing the truth.

CHAPTER FOUR

'DID YOU SLEEP WELL?' Alessandro's polite enquiry pulled Charlie from her thoughts as they sat having breakfast together in the tranquillity of his apartment. The jeans and shirt he wore hugged his body to perfection and she fought hard to keep her mind where it should be—on her brother and the car she was here to help promote. Thinking about the handsome Italian she'd kissed last night wasn't going to help her at all and she forced herself to be as rational and in control as he appeared.

'Yes, thanks,' she replied, taking a sip of freshly squeezed orange juice. Sleeping in the room Seb had used should have helped her, but it hadn't. It had had the opposite effect. She'd wept silent tears for her brother, finally finding release from the grief she'd kept locked away, but little comfort. It hadn't banished the idea that Alessandro was to blame for the accident or that he was hiding something from her.

He looked at her, his keen gaze lingering on her face just a little too long. She was aware the dark circles beneath her eyes would tell him she hadn't slept well at all. Thankfully, he had the good grace to let it go.

'There are a few things I need to do this afternoon in

preparation for the launch, but we can either go to the office or to the test track this morning.'

Test track. Those words careered into her, dragging her back to a time when she'd always been at the test track, her father and brother at her side. It was where she'd learnt to drive, really drive, much to her mother's disgust.

'I'd like to see the car,' she said thoughtfully. 'It feels as if I haven't been at a track for a long time.' She'd missed the thrill and excitement of the place. Her garden, whilst a safe sanctuary she'd been happy in, suddenly seemed tame.

'*Sì,*' he said as he sat forward, placing his now empty cup back on the table. 'Seb told me it was a big part of your childhood too.'

She looked into her juice, not able to meet the intensity in his eyes. They made her feel vulnerable and she didn't do vulnerable. 'I spent a lot of my time there. I loved it.'

'What did your mother think of that?' His question nudged at issues which had erupted often when she was a teenager.

'She didn't have any objection to Seb being there.' Charlie hesitated and looked up into his handsome face and instantly wished she hadn't.

He appeared relaxed as he sat back in his seat again, but something wasn't quite right. He reminded her of a big cat, lulling its quarry into a false sense of security. Any moment he would pounce, strike out and get exactly what he wanted with unnerving accuracy.

'I sense a *but.*' He spoke softly, then waited, the silence hanging expectantly between them.

Before she could think, his question had thrown open things she'd do better to keep to herself—because it was a very big *but*. How much had Seb told him? Did he know of her mother's disapproval of her involvement in the racing world? Did he know she'd hated the lifestyle, hated the way her husband had flirted with all the women. Her mother had resented being second best so much she'd left the family home, deserting her teenage children.

'My mother didn't like me being there. She didn't think I should be driving those cars and certainly not working on them. She thought I should behave more like a lady instead of a tomboy and it became a constant battleground as I grew up.' She wasn't bitter any more. In fact she could now see why her mother had been so against the racing world, why she'd wanted her daughter as far away from it as possible. But she wasn't about to go into all that now, especially not with Alessandro.

He smiled, a gorgeous smile that made his eyes sparkle, full of mischief. 'Now I understand. Your insistence on being called Charlie was to remain a tomboy.'

'Something like that.' She finished her juice, wondering how she had become the topic of conversation.

'But you are a beautiful woman, Charlotte, why hide it?' The intensity in his eyes scared her, made her heart pound, and she bit down on her lower lip, suddenly very much out of her depth.

'I was a rebellious teenager,' she explained, giving in to the need to offer some sort of explanation. Heat infused her cheeks and she looked out over Milan to hide her embarrassment. It was time to change the subject; she'd said more than enough to him. This wasn't about her—it was about Seb. 'Can we go now? I'd like to see the car.'

'Of course,' he said as he stood up, preparing to leave. 'If you are sure this is what you want to do.'

She'd never been more certain about anything, which

was strange, given that just twenty-four hours ago she'd thought she never wanted to see this man. His timing had been impeccable, arriving so soon after the conversation she'd had with her father about getting her life back again.

'Before we go,' she asked, unable to keep the hint of suspicion from her voice, 'what did my father say to you when you told him about the launch?'

He looked directly at her, his stance bold and intimidating. 'It appears he wants only your happiness.'

'I need to contact him, tell him I will be at the launch.'

'He knows.' She looked at him. There was not a hint of conceit on his handsome face, but she sensed he was keeping something from her. She decided to let it go—for now. At the moment, seeing the car which had become Seb's world was at the top of her list and talking like this wouldn't help at all. She tried to deflect his interest with light-hearted words.

'And will he be there too?'

'He hopes to be.'

'That sounds like Dad.'

'This way,' he said as he picked up his keys and slipped on a leather jacket. The understated style only emphasised the latent strength of his body and she had to pull her gaze away, force herself to think of other things. This was not the time or the place to become attracted to a man—especially not this man.

Alessandro wasn't able to negotiate the morning traffic of Milan with his usual ease. He could hardly concentrate on driving. His main focus was instead on the woman beside him. She didn't say anything, merely looked around her, taking in the vibrancy of the city he loved.

'Have you always lived in Milan?' Her voice was soft

and should have soothed his restless mind, but it didn't. The slight husky tone to it only intensified the way his body seemed on high alert just being next to her.

'For most of my adult life, yes.' He knew it was only small talk, but discussing his family with outsiders wasn't what he usually did. But Seb had become like a brother to him, even in such a short time, so didn't that make Charlie anything but an outsider?

'Seb mentioned your family lives in Tuscany and produce wines.' Her voice was light in an attempt to make conversation, but such questions made him uneasy. When a woman asked about family, there was usually intent behind it. But what motivation could Charlie possibly have?

He shrugged and turned onto the open road, leaving the city behind as they headed for the test track. The sun shone with the promise of another hot day. 'That is true, but my love was for cars, not wine. So I moved to Milan, finished my education and began working for my uncle, turning the company around and making it the success it is today. The rest, I believe you would say, is history.'

'And this car? Was that also part of your love for cars?' She almost caressed the words, setting his pulse racing at an alarming rate.

He glanced across at her, watching as she looked around the interior with genuine interest, proving all that Seb had told him about her was true. She wasn't much older than his sister but, at twenty-four, had made her way to the top of her career, promoting first her father's racing team, then Seb's. She was a successful woman in her own right, and that success had been born out of her passion for cars and racing, which was why Seb had wanted her at the launch of the car.

She ran the tips of her fingers across the dashboard in

front of her, leaving him in no doubt of her love of cars—
and that she was a woman of passion. She'd shown him
that much last night with her kiss. He pressed down on
the accelerator in a bid to focus his attention on anything
else but her, and the car responding willingly. Thinking
of last night's kiss wouldn't help to quell the lingering
desire she'd awakened.

'Impressive,' she said quickly, laughter filling her
voice.

Inwardly he groaned. She thought he was putting the
car through its paces for her, when all he'd been doing
was giving his mind something other than her to focus
on. Again he glanced at her, shocked to see a smile on
her lips, and instantly he wished he wasn't driving, that
he didn't have to concentrate on the car so that he could
enjoy her smile—the first real smile he'd seen on those
sweet lips.

'It is not far now.' *Grazie a Dio!* He didn't think he
could take much more of this enforced proximity, the way
her light perfume weaved its scent throughout the car.
His body was excruciatingly aware of each tiny movement she made.

The streamlined car willingly ate up the miles as they
drove in a silence laced with tension—not angry tension but that of restrained desire. Her kiss last night had
more than hinted at her attraction for him. He couldn't
deny that he was tempted by her but it was something
he wouldn't act on. To do so would be to dishonour his
friend's memory and the promise he'd made.

A sigh of relief left him as they turned off the road and
down a smaller road which led to the Roselli test track.
Never before had a drive here been so long and so tense.
Thankfully, he parked the car behind the large building

which housed the prototypes for all his cars currently being tested.

Charlie got out of the car, her full attention now on the building before her, and he knew she was anxious. The tight set of her shoulders betrayed her nerves. 'You don't have to do this. We can just go back to the office.'

She turned to look at him, her hand reaching up to keep her hair from her face as the wind toyed with it. Instantly he remembered how he'd pushed his hands through it just hours ago, how he'd clutched it hard to enable him to kiss her deeper, and the way she'd responded.

Maledizione! Did he have to keep going back to something that should never have happened?

'Mr Roselli, I want to do this and I will, no matter how many times you try to dissuade me.' The fire of her spirit sounded in every word and, as she looked at him, her pretty face set in fierce determination, he fought the urge to smile.

'I think we can dispense with formalities now, don't you, Charlie?' He saw her green eyes glitter as he used her preferred name.

'As you wish, Alessandro.' The sweetness of her voice didn't mask her irritation.

'Sandro,' he said as he locked the car and came round to her. 'I'd much prefer it if you'd call me Sandro.'

Her gaze locked with his, challenging him with unsaid words. They held the same fire and courage Seb's always had, although the green of hers was more like emerald. Hard and glittering.

'As you wish, Sandro.' She shrugged casually and turned to look up at the building. 'Now, can I see the car?'

'It is only the test car. The actual car will be revealed at the launch.'

She glanced briefly at him before returning her attention to the modern building, its streamlined design which curved around them. 'Even better. I'd like to know what changes have been made since Seb drove it.'

There it was again. Accusation.

'It is an exact copy of the prototype Seb drove. There weren't any improvements to be made.'

She turned and looked at him, her brows raised in surprise. 'None at all?'

He watched her intently for a moment as she did anything other than look at him. 'No. This way.' He moved purposefully towards the door, keyed in his code and stood back for her to enter, hoping she wouldn't pursue the conversation further. He didn't want to lie to her, but at the same time he didn't think she would be able to handle the truth.

His team of mechanics were working on another project and glanced up as they entered. He noticed she ignored their speculative gazes and instead walked towards the grey test car parked in the centre of the white workshop floor, ready for them.

He followed but held back as she approached the vehicle, wanting to give her time with something that had been as much a part of Seb's life as it was his.

She paced slowly along the car, her long jeans-clad legs doing untold things to him, and he gritted his teeth against the sizzle of attraction. This was one woman he couldn't have but, as she slid her hand over the front wing of the car, following the sleek angles of the bodywork, he couldn't help but wish he was the car.

'Can I?' She gestured towards the door and he nodded, not able to string even a few words together in any language after those thoughts.

As she slid into the driving seat he moved towards the car and leant on the open door. He looked down at her, trying hard not to notice how the seat curved around her thighs. Instead, he kept his eyes on her face, watching as she openly devoured everything with hungry eyes. Slowly she wrapped her fingers around the steering wheel, clutching it tight until the leather creaked. She looked as if she belonged behind the wheel of a car and as if this particular car had been made for her.

'It's amazing.' Those words were so light and husky. He gritted his teeth hard, trying to subdue the lust which now throbbed in his veins, demanding satisfaction.

With a sudden movement which caught her attention, he pushed his body off the car door. 'We'll take it out now,' he said as he gave the signal to his team to raise the doors. Sunlight poured in as they silently opened.

'I'd like to drive.' Her words were firm as he walked back to the car, reminding him of the stubborn little girl he'd grown up with. His sister had nearly always got her way with such a tone, especially with him.

'Maybe it would be better if I drove first.' He didn't want her thinking too much about her brother whilst behind the wheel. It was obvious she blamed him for Seb's accident and grief could manifest itself in various forms. 'You can sit back and enjoy the ride, just as Seb would have wanted you to.'

'You didn't know Seb that well if you think that.' She raised her delicate brows suggestively at him and smiled. He knew he was beaten. 'Seb would want me to drive so he could sit there and listen. He'd want to feel the car and be at one with it.'

He leant on the car, one hand on the roof, one hand on the open door, and lowered his head, bringing him very close to her. The enticing scent of her perfume met him and he resisted the urge to inhale it. Her passionate little speech just now had already done enough.

'*Va bene*, you may drive, but carefully and I will, of course, be with you.'

She smiled up at him, a genuine heartfelt smile that made her eyes light up. Right there and then he decided he wanted her to smile more and assigned himself the mission of making that happen.

'I am able to drive.' Her lips formed a sexy little pout as she put on a show of pretend petulance and it was all he could do not to lean down and kiss her. The first woman who'd stirred his dormant body since he'd extricated himself from the mistake of his marriage and she was out of bounds. So far off limits she might as well be on the moon.

'I don't doubt that you can, but having dealt with one female who drove too fast I'm reluctant to do it again.'

'Oh.' The word was full of disappointment and he couldn't hide his smile.

'My sister. A while ago now. She took a corner too fast, despite my warnings, and ended up a bit the worse for wear.' He made light of it when really he wished he could go back and change things, make her listen. Just as he now wished he could with Seb.

'Well, you don't need to worry about me,' she said and started the engine, the throaty growl forcing her to raise her voice slightly. 'Sebastian Warrington was my brother, after all.'

She was wrong, so wrong. He did have to worry. His promise to Seb meant that not only would he involve her in the launch but he'd look after her, be a brother figure to her, and he couldn't do that when hot lust shot around his body like off-course fireworks.

He walked around the front of the car, watching her through the windscreen. Her face was full of concentration as she studied the array of information on the driver's screen. As if she sensed his scrutiny, she looked up and smiled, this time a more hesitant smile. Should he be letting her do this? He knew only too well what could happen if someone drove beyond their capabilities.

Her gaze followed him as he moved to the other side of the car and opened the passenger door. 'Ready?' He kept the word light as he slipped down into the seat and shut the door. It was a lightness he didn't feel, not when they were suddenly very close, much more so than in his car.

She nodded her head and looked forward, focusing on the task, but he couldn't concentrate. The engine growled in anticipation and the car moved slowly out into the morning sunshine. He breathed a sigh of relief that she wasn't as hot-headed as her brother had been the first time he'd taken it out.

Carefully she manoeuvred out onto the track and with a steady speed began the first circuit. He looked over at her, taking the opportunity to study her as she focused on driving. Her thick hair was scrunched up in a haphazard sort of style, looking as if she'd just left her lover's bed. Her lips were pressed together in concentration, the same gesture Seb had used when he really focused on driving, but on Charlie it was cute, sexy even.

The engine grew louder as she pushed the speed up, bringing his mind back from the dangerous territory it had just wandered to.

'Relax.' The laughter in her voice didn't match the

intense concentration on her face and, probably for the first time ever, he didn't know what to say. With shock, he realised she was making him nervous. He sensed she was holding back, that, just like her brother, she wanted to take the car to its upper limits, but was she capable? Could she really drive a car like this to its full potential?

'You're not nervous, are you?' The teasing question finally focused his mind. 'I have been taught to do this properly.'

'No,' he lied as he tried to sit back and relax. With each passing second it was obvious she could drive and if she'd had the same tutor as Seb, what more guarantee did he need? 'I make a bad co-pilot. I like to be in control at all times.'

She glanced quickly at him, the green of her eyes flashing with amusement. 'Are we just talking about driving?'

He couldn't help the laugh that rumbled from him. 'I was only referring to driving, but now you come to mention it…'

'Let's see what she's made of then.' The laughter in her voice gave way to a serious tone full of purpose.

Before he could utter one word of protest, the car lurched forward like an angry stallion, pressing him back in the seat. The trees around the track blurred as the engine roared. His heart pounded and he had images of arriving at the scene of his sister Francesca's accident and comforting her while he waited for help to arrive.

'Slow down!' he demanded, hating the sense of being totally unable to avert a crisis.

'Don't spoil it now. I know what I'm doing.' Her raised voice did little to assuage the doubt he had in himself to trust her driving ability.

'Charlotte!' He snapped her name loudly, keeping his eyes firmly fixed on the corner they were hurtling towards.

Charlie could barely hear Alessandro. Her heart was thudding with the excitement of being behind the wheel of a powerful car again. It had been too long and she had no intention of stopping now. This was exactly what she needed to chase the demons away.

She pressed harder on the accelerator, elated to find the powerful engine still had more to give. As the countryside blurred to a sway of green she knew this was the right thing to do. Seb had driven this car, felt its power and had been at one with it. Driving it now brought her closer to him; it was as if he was here with her.

'Slow down, Charlotte. Now.' Alessandro's curt tone was full of authority but she couldn't stop now, couldn't deny herself this moment.

'This is amazing,' she enthused, pushing the car to its limits around a corner. Tyres squealed but held the track like nothing she'd known before.

'Do you ever do as you are told?' The rich timbre of his voice was edged with steely control. She sensed him sitting there, rigid with anger at her disobedience. The thought made her laugh.

'Didn't Seb tell you that I'm exasperating?' Another corner took her concentration and beside her he cursed fluidly in Italian. Was she really worrying him or was it just that she wouldn't do what he wanted? There wasn't any doubt in her mind that he was the type of man who liked to be in total control of every situation.

'That, *cara*, is something we didn't discuss. Slow

down.' His voice was firm, full of discipline, making her smile and itch to push the car harder.

'Do you always spoil everyone's fun?' She slowed the car enough to be able to talk with him, but the engine protested, tempting her with its power once more.

'Only when my life is on the line.' The acerbic tone of his voice didn't go unnoticed as he raised it to be heard over the engine. They headed down a long straight and she had to resist the urge to push the car harder.

'Your life is not on the line, Sandro—don't be so dramatic. I've been trained to the highest level to drive cars just as powerful as this.' She drove into the next bend, restraining herself from showing him just how capable she was of handling the car.

'By whom?' Those two words were curt and heavily accented and she wondered again if he genuinely was afraid.

'My father. He taught Seb and me everything he'd learnt, so relax and enjoy your car, feel it, be at one with it.'

She pushed the car into another bend, her body infused with adrenaline, something she'd missed when she'd taken up the more genteel pursuit of gardening. It just hadn't given her the same buzz.

A long straight stretch spread out before her again as she came out of another bend and, forgetting everything, including the hurt and pain of losing Seb, she pushed the car to its limits one last time.

It felt so good. Nothing like it on earth had ever come close. It was exhilarating. The car ate up the tarmac as they sped along the straight stretch.

'*Dio mio*, stop!' The harsh command penetrated the bubble of excitement she'd slipped into and she let her foot off the accelerator, the car slowing.

'We're halfway around the track; I can't just stop!' she protested, but moderated the speed to a more sensible level.

'Stop. Right now.'

'Right now?' Anger sizzled inside her. Anger because she had to do as he told her. Anger because she'd lost control in front of him but, most of all, anger at him. If things had been different, it might have been Seb at her side.

'Now, Charlotte.' His hard tone brooked no argument.

'Okay, have it your way.' As the words snapped from her she pressed hard on the brake pedal.

Tyres squealed in protest as the front of the car lowered dramatically to the tarmac, but it was nothing compared to the anger which still hurtled around her. This was all his fault.

'Are you insane?' The car jolted to a stop and those words rushed at her.

She couldn't look at him yet. Her heart thumped so wildly in her chest she was sure he could hear its wild beat. She was mad, yes, she'd lost control. In her bid to forget the real reason she was here she'd been reckless, but it was still his fault.

'Yes—' she turned her head sharply to look at him, her breathing coming hard and fast '—I was mad to come here with you.'

Before she could think in any kind of rational way, she threw open the door, unclipped the seat belt and bolted—from him and the car. She ran from everything she'd tried to hide from these last twelve months.

'Charlotte!' She heard the deep tone of his voice, now edged with exasperation, but she didn't turn, didn't stop. She marched off the tarmac and onto the grass without any idea of which way to go. All she wanted was to get away from him, away from the car and away from all the pain which now surged through her.

Pain he'd induced.

As she began to break into a run he reached her, grabbed her arm and pulled her so quickly to a stop that she was turned and jolted against the hardness of his chest. For an instant all the breath seemed to leave her body and she couldn't speak. All she could do was stand looking into his eyes, glittering with anger as he held her captive with his firm grip. Her breathing was now so rapid she was panting as if she'd just run a hundred-metre sprint.

'Let me go.' Her furious demand only made his hand tighten on her arm.

'Not until you calm down.' He said the words slowly, but she didn't miss the glinting edge of steel within them.

'It shouldn't have been you.' A cocktail of emotions rushed to find expression. 'I should have been here with Seb. Not you.'

'I should never have brought you here, not after what your father told me.' Each word was delivered in a cool and calm tone, but there was still that underlying steel.

'My father?' She gasped in shock, trying unsuccessfully to release her arm from his grip. 'What has he said?'

'That you've been hiding from this since the funeral.' He released her arm but remained excruciatingly close. It was all becoming too much. Memories of Seb entwined with whatever it was between her and this man. She couldn't deal with either of them at the moment.

'I have not been hiding from anything—except the cruelty of the media.' She looked up into his face, so close she could smell his aftershave, but fury kept her expression hard.

He blinked, his head drawing back from her just a fraction. 'The media?'

She pulled free from him, turned and stalked away, tossing her next words over her shoulder. 'Yes, the media. You know the ones. They like to dig all the dirt on you and your family when you're down.'

'Charlotte, don't walk away from me.' His tone was harsh but she carried on walking—or was she running yet again?

'Just leave me, Alessandro. Take the car back and leave me.' She stopped and turned to look at him; his strides were so long that he was almost directly behind her and again she found herself against a wall of pure maleness.

'No, *cara*.' He spoke more softly, looking down at her.

Infuriated, a well of exasperation opened deep within her. 'Worried what everyone will think when you go back alone?' She couldn't prevent the tart edge creeping into her words.

'I don't give a damn about anyone else. The only thing that matters right now is you.'

She looked up into his eyes; the angry glitter was gone from them now. She resisted the urge to close hers, to give in to the invitation of his words and let him care for her, soothe her. But that hadn't been what he'd meant.

'Why? Because of your promise to Seb?' she retorted, fighting back once more.

His brow furrowed and he shook his head in denial. Guilt niggled at her. She was deliberately provoking him. *It's his fault Seb isn't here*, she reminded herself sharply.

'Not completely.' He stepped closer, so close she could just reach up and kiss him if she wanted to. Just as she'd done last night.

Mesmerised by his nearness, the heady scent of his aftershave doing strange things to her senses, she remained exactly where she was. Their eyes locked and she was sure he was thinking the same thing, feeling the same hot sizzle arcing between them.

Slowly, maintaining eye contact, she raised her chin up and saw his eyes darken to the blackness of a starless sky. She paused, an unspoken question emanating from her. His answer was to claim her lips with his.

CHAPTER FIVE

CHARLIE CLOSED HER eyes as every limb in her body weakened beneath the power of his hungry kiss. Just when she thought she wouldn't be able to stand any longer his arms wrapped around her, pulling her so tight against him that she was in no doubt he wanted her.

What was she doing? Kissing this man—and, worse again, wanting so much more?

Although she knew she shouldn't, she couldn't help herself and, just as she had done the previous night, she wound her arms about his neck, sliding her fingers into the curls he had tried to disguise.

Adrenaline from the drive still pumped around her, fuelling this new heady passion to heights she'd never before experienced. Every part of her was on fire, burning with desire for the man she supposedly hated above all others.

'This is...' she began as his lips left hers, scorching a trail down her throat until she couldn't utter another word.

'Amazing, no?' His husky voice sent a thrill of shivers through her.

No, not amazing. It's wrong. It shouldn't be happening.

Inside her head the words formed, but that was where they stayed as he claimed her lips once more, so deeply and passionately she gasped in pleasure against him. She couldn't think any more. The only thing that mattered was satisfying the hot need which blazed inside her.

'And this…' He almost groaned the words out as he lowered his head to kiss down her throat. She arched her back, leaning against the strength of his arm, knowing exactly what he wanted.

A sigh of total contentment slipped from her and she let her head drop back as his kisses moved down her throat until he reached the soft swell of her breasts, visible at the opening of her blouse.

Then passion exploded as he kissed her nipple, dampening the silk of her blouse. Her bra offered little defence against the persuasion of his seduction and she buried her fingers into the thickness of his hair, a soft sigh escaping her lips as she surrendered to the pleasure of his mastery.

'This is good too, no?' His accent became heavier with each word as desire engulfed them, wrapping them up together. He nipped at the hard peak of her nipple, sending a spark of urgent need straight to the very core of her.

'It's so good, but so wrong.' Her voice was a throaty whisper as she pushed her fingers deeper into the curls, pressing him against her, even though she knew it was reckless. Each breath she took intensified the sensation until she couldn't do anything but close her eyes to the pure pleasure of the moment. Wrong or right, she gave herself up to it.

'Oh, *cara*, it's wrong, so, so wrong, but so right.' He moved his attention to her other breast and she almost sank to the grass beneath her feet as his tongue worked its magic, her breathing ragged and fast.

'We shouldn't.' Barely a whisper now, her voice sounded hoarse as each breath rushed from her.

It was so good she thought she could hear horns—car horns blasting around them, their fast rhythm matching the pulse of desire inside her. The sound became louder and suddenly he straightened, pulling her upright with a jolt.

'*Maledizione.* I should have known we'd be seen.'

The sound of horns was very clear now and she realised it wasn't just horns, but emergency sirens. She jumped back from him as if scalded by his very touch, wanting to put as much distance between them as possible while she fought to regain control over her body, extinguish the heady need he'd ignited. Thankfully, he seemed to want the same and walked abruptly away.

What had she been thinking? Nothing. Absolutely nothing. That was the problem. She hadn't been thinking at all. She'd allowed her seesawing emotions to get the better of her and when she next spoke to her father she'd find out just what he and Alessandro had discussed. Had her father tried to continue the matchmaking Seb had started?

Alessandro took in deep breaths, trying to cool the heat in his body as he strode back to the track. The approaching ambulance was almost upon them as he reached the car. He didn't look back at her, but knew she'd started to follow him. Every nerve in his body responded to each step those lovely long legs took.

After a few quick words with the ambulance crew he sent them back to the workshop, by which time Charlie was at his side. What would have happened if they hadn't been interrupted? The thought of what he could at this minute be doing sent his pulse sky-high.

'Get in.' The command was gruff, but that was the

only way to deal with this. Denial wasn't usually his style, but right now it suited perfectly. He got into the driving seat and waited, his gaze firmly fixed ahead as she got in beside him.

'Sorry.' That one word from her was so soft, so quiet he wondered if he'd imagined it.

What was she sorry for? Driving like a maniac or setting light to the fire between them? Either way, he didn't want her apology. He just wanted to get as far away from her as possible so that he could reassemble the barrier he always kept around him.

He didn't ever want to be so emotionally exposed with a woman, but Charlie had slipped under his radar, almost destroying the defence he'd erected after his marriage. It had taken just one kiss.

'I can't believe you'd drive like that. What would Seb say?' He clutched at the first thing that came to mind to use as a weapon against the hum of desire threatening to rise once more, just from being close to her. He could still smell her scent, still taste her and his body craved more, wanting absolute satisfaction.

'Seb would be pleased. He taught me to drive like that but, judging by your reaction, I guess he didn't tell you that I am a test driver for the team. I can drive as fast and as safely as any racing driver.'

'That may be so, but he wouldn't have wanted you to risk your life.' Angrily, he rebuffed her explanation.

A heavy silence filled the car and he wished the words unsaid. When she didn't say anything else he started the car and gently moved off, keeping the speed to a sensible level.

'Did I scare you?' The question flew out and he

gripped the steering wheel, the muscles of his forearms flexing.

She had scared him, but he wasn't about to admit that to anyone. As the speed had increased all he'd been able to think of was Seb, lying in the hospital bed in pain, and the way he'd forced him into a promise he now had serious doubts he could keep. How could he look after Charlie as if she were his sister when all he could think of was taking her to his bed?

'Yes, damn it, you scared me. You knew I had to deal with my sister after she'd had an accident.' He wasn't about to confide in her the real cause of his fear. That would mean looking deeper at what had just happened between them. Accepting that there even was something there, some undeniable attraction that was so powerful it took over, given the slightest opportunity.

'I don't see how me driving on a test track has any connection with your sister having a bump on the road.' He could hear the irritation in every word and was relieved to see the workshop coming into view.

'That *bump*, as you put it, caused her to defer her last year at university and all because she couldn't slow down, as I'd asked her to do.' His mind began to tie in knots, talking on one subject, trying to rationalise another and fighting the need to pull over and finish what he'd started back there.

He'd never been this off-kilter before. Shock and the unrelenting need to regain control had unbalanced his emotions, but he couldn't let her know that.

'What happened?' Curiosity filled her voice and it was all he could do not to look at her. The heat of her gaze burned into him.

He drove back into the workshop, switching the engine off. Silence settled around them and he looked about the workshop, thankful the mechanics had had the presence of mind to make themselves scarce. He'd have some smart talking to do with them later; of that he was sure.

He threw his hands up in frustration. 'She drove too fast. That's it. Just as you did out there.'

He didn't need this conversation right now. It wasn't what they should be discussing, even though it went part way towards his reasons for demanding she stop.

He could feel her watching him and turned to look at her, instilling as much control as he possibly could into his voice. 'She took a bend too fast, hit the wall and ended up in hospital. All because she couldn't slow down.'

'But I'm a skilled driver; I test drive for Seb's team.' Her expression served only to exasperate him further. Couldn't she see the similarities between her and Seb? He was a skilled driver too and now he was dead.

'Skill isn't everything, *cara*. Seb was incredibly skilled.' Her eyes widened and he had the strangest sensation that he'd walked into a trap. One of his own making.

'Seb went out in a car that should never have been on the test track. Is that what you are saying?' The accusation was hurled at him, but he knew it was the driver that shouldn't have been out on the track that night. If he hadn't been meeting with potential customers, maybe he would have seen the state Seb was in. Stopped him from taking the car out to the test track.

'Nobody knew he was here, Charlotte. He took it upon himself to take the car out.' He desperately tried to instil patience into each word. She was hurting and this was the moment he'd been dreading, the moment she'd accuse him of negligence and he wouldn't be able to deny it. Not if he kept the horrible truth from her.

'I thought he was staying with you. Surely you knew he'd gone to the test track?' Her eyes narrowed and he knew for certain she blamed him.

'He was staying with me, but he also did his own thing. I thought he was on a date that night.'

'And you just happened to be at the track within minutes of the accident.'

'Am I on trial here?'

'By me, yes.'

'*Va bene.* For the record, I was on my way back from a meeting and called in to collect paperwork. I wanted to go over the problem we had with the first prototype. The second had just come out of the workshop so I wanted to talk to Seb about it.'

Her face watched his expectantly and he wondered if she'd already heard this from her father, or read about it in the press. It had been a tough few months after the accident and he'd had to deal with the guilt he felt, even though no blame had been apportioned to him or his company.

'But Seb was out in the car?' she asked, pre-empting him.

'I'd seen Seb's car outside when I parked, but thought he'd gone out with one of the mechanics. When I noticed the test car gone, I knew he was out in it and jumped into the pickup. That's how I was able to be there just minutes after it happened.'

He could still hear the sickening thud and scrunch of metal, then the protest of the engine before the ominous silence. He'd known instantly it wasn't going to be good and was on his phone, calling for the emergency services as he'd pulled up alongside the twisted wreck.

'Thank you,' she whispered, her gaze lowering so that

her thick long lashes brushed against her cheeks and he had to fight hard not to reach out to hold her or offer her comfort. He just didn't trust himself, he wanted her so fiercely.

'Come, that is enough for today. I'll take you back to the apartment.'

A little sigh escaped her as she got out of the car and, without a backward glance at it, walked towards the door. Quickly he caught up with her and as soon as they were outside the workshop he put his arm around her shoulders in an attempt to console her.

'Don't.' She pulled away from him and stood by the passenger door of his car, looking anywhere else but at him and very much like she was hurting.

Damn it. He should never have responded to her kiss last night and certainly shouldn't have done what he had today. Now he couldn't offer her comfort, couldn't keep his promise to Seb and look after her—like a brother. How could he go back from that intensely heated moment they'd shared at the trackside?

The drive back to the apartment had seemed to last for ever, but Charlie kept up the act of hurt and betrayal. It was hard, but more preferable to the role of wanton seductress that she'd just played out with him at the trackside. She was completely shocked by her behaviour. She'd never thrown herself with such abandon at a man and couldn't understand what had possessed her to do that today—other than hot lust. All she wanted now was to lie on her bed and be alone, to calm her body and her heart.

'I have work at the office this afternoon.' His words were firm but she knew he was looking for a way out, trying to avoid a discussion about what had happened between them. Well, that suited her just fine. She didn't want to acknowledge it either, much less discuss it.

'I may go shopping,' she said, trying to sound light and carefree. 'I need something to wear at the launch tomorrow evening.'

'I will send a car for you in a few hours. Rest first.' He stood tall and proud in the middle of his living room, the opulence of it still not quite fitting with the picture of the man Seb had painted in her mind.

Rest. She wasn't sure she could, but she was glad that at least she'd be alone. His gesture of comfort had been hard to shrug off earlier. She wanted nothing more than to be held by him, to be safe in his arms, but she didn't trust herself. Whatever it was between them, she could only ignore it if she physically kept her distance.

'Alessandro?'

'Yes.' He looked at her, his dark eyes no longer full of the passion she'd seen in them at the test track. Now they were cold, full of dismissal.

'Your sister? Is she all right now?'

'Yes, thankfully, she made a quick recovery and even graduated with full honours.'

She nodded, unable to say anything, the pain of losing Seb more raw than it had ever been. She wished she could allow Alessandro to hold her. She'd never felt so alone. 'But Seb didn't.'

Without another thought, she went to him, needing his strong embrace and the warmth of his body. He didn't say a word as he took her in his arms, infusing her with his strength, but it felt different. Every muscle in his body was tense.

She pulled away. She shouldn't have done that, not after this morning.

'I won't be back tonight,' he said curtly, picking up his car keys.

She blinked in shock. Was she driving him out of his own home? 'Because of me?' Her voice was hardly a whisper and she bit her bottom lip with her teeth.

'Not you—me.' The sternness in his voice didn't go unnoticed. 'I think it's for the best. Boundaries have been crossed, but it won't happen again.'

She stepped back further from him. 'Good, but you don't have to stay away on my account.'

'I do, Charlie, I do need to—for Seb and the promise I made him to look after you.'

'You are looking after me.' She really should let him go, simply because she didn't trust herself not to want him. His offer to leave her alone became more tempting by the second as her heart hammered harder while he stood before her.

'My staff will see to your every need and a car will be available to take you wherever you need to go. I will see you at the launch.'

'Not before?' Stunned, she couldn't believe it. The launch was the next evening. Was he going to keep as far from her as possible for the next twenty-four hours? Did the boundaries they'd crossed mean that much?

Alessandro stood and looked at her, wanting nothing more than to take her back into his arms, hold her and inhale her sweet scent. But he couldn't. It would be disastrous if he did. He'd already proved she was the one woman who made him lose his mind and he knew if he stayed there would be no stopping him.

'No, it will be better if I don't.' He kept his voice level and stood rigidly straight, but didn't miss the look of disappointment slide across her face.

'But this is your home.' Her delicate brows furrowed in confusion and concern.

'Tonight it is yours. I will go elsewhere.' He had to. He already knew beyond doubt that he had very little self-control where she was concerned. He didn't want to be involved with any woman, but especially this one.

'To a friend?' She dropped her gaze and he knew exactly what she thought. That he was going to warm the bed of another woman. Well, so much the better if it stamped out the electricity that raged between them and the heady lust he felt for her. One thing was for certain; it couldn't go on, not if he wanted to honour his promise to Seb and keep his sanity.

'Something like that, *sì*.' He moved towards the door, needing to go before he relented and told her he was intending to spend the night in his office, something he did on occasion. His office was all geared up for such nights, but this would be the first time he'd been driven there by a woman.

It certainly wouldn't be as hard as staying here with Charlie when all he wanted was to make her completely his. But she could never be that to him, not now.

'*Buonanotte, cara.* Sleep well.'

CHAPTER SIX

IT WAS ALMOST twenty-four hours since Alessandro had left her at his apartment. Charlie had enjoyed the indulgence of being alone to begin with. She'd spent the first hours in her room, the same room Seb had stayed in, looking for anything left behind that connected with him. Any clues as to what he'd been doing in the days before the accident, but that had proved futile. She realised it was foolish to think there would be any evidence left in the room a year after he'd last been here. So she'd turned her attention to the rest of the apartment to learn about the man who owned it.

Old and new blended tastefully with the ornate interior of the grand building and she still couldn't help but be shocked that he didn't live in a new and modern apartment with the same masculine lines as his office. She wondered which was the real man—the one who worked in the modern minimalist office or the contented man who surrounded himself with fine art.

Now, she stood looking out over Milan as she waited for the car to take her to the launch party, unable to comprehend how much she was looking forward to seeing Alessandro again. A brief call from him, which had sent a sizzle of anticipation down her spine, had informed her he would send his car at six. As an ornate clock struck the hour she began to have second thoughts about the long red dress she'd bought that morning.

Second thoughts were too late. The car pulled up and her breath hitched as Alessandro got out. From her vantage point at the window above him she could see that he now wore a tuxedo and looked more sexy and stunning than any man had a right to. She drank him in. He looked like every woman's dream, the strength of his body still evident despite the high-class tailoring.

She watched as he shut the car door, grateful she had time to get her wayward thoughts reined in. She saw the black fabric stretch across his broad shoulders as he leant down and spoke to the driver. Unable to tear her eyes away, she stood watching, enjoying her unobserved vantage point.

As if he sensed her presence, he looked up at her. Despite the three floors that separated them, his gaze met hers, sending her pulse rate into freefall. If he could do this from that distance, what was it going to be like when she was actually with him?

She didn't have to wait long to find out as the key turned in the lock of the front door and he walked into the apartment, overpowering the splendour of the living room completely.

He stood and looked at her very slowly, his gaze moving down from her head to her toes, peeping out of the red sandals that gave her a few inches more height. Defiantly she looked at him, desperate not to let him know that inside she was melting from the heat of his gaze.

'*Sei bellissimo.*' He moved towards her, each step making her heart pound harder. His Italian was more sexy than his accented English. Her heart soared. He thought she was beautiful.

Shyness swept over her and she lowered her gaze. The vibrant red dress she had bought in a moment of defiance was having more of an effect than she'd imagined possible. She'd been drawn to the red sequins which sparkled on the bodice, and the jaunty single shoulder which had slashed red across her pale skin. But now she wondered and looked down at the silk of the floor-length dress. 'It is not too much, is it?'

'Too much,' he said in a husky tone as he stepped closer and lifted her chin with his fingers, forcing her to look into his handsome face. 'You look beautiful.'

'Thank you.' She shyly accepted his compliment and stepped back, away from temptation. All she could think of was kissing him again, feeling his arms pressing her against his hard body. But she couldn't; she had to remain aloof, keep him at a distance. He'd already proved what he was capable of doing to her. 'I'm glad you approve.'

He didn't say anything. He didn't have to; the intensity in his dark eyes told her he more than approved. His gaze was so hot she could hardly breathe and she caught her bottom lip between her teeth.

'We had better go.' A ripple of awareness cascaded through her as his deep, sensual voice left her in no doubt that he wanted to kiss her, that he too was fighting an attraction so strong the outcome now seemed inevitable.

'Yes.' Aware how husky her voice had become, she moved quickly towards the door, the silk of her dress moulding to her legs as she moved. He followed her, his shoes beating a purposeful rhythm on the marble floor.

Whatever it was that had simmered between them that

first afternoon in her garden had ignited spectacularly, threatening to engulf them at any second. She drew in a deep breath as she realised she wanted the increasing desire to burn freely between them. After several years of pushing men away, using her off-camera tomboy image to discourage male attention, this was what she now wanted. Was it just lust or was she ready to risk her heart again?

He shut the door of his apartment with a resounding bang which echoed in the coolness of the marble hallway, startling her and knocking all those tempting thoughts out of her mind. She turned to face him. 'Is something wrong?'

Purposefully, he walked towards her, stopping so close she could smell the heady scent of his aftershave, feel his breath on her face. She looked up at him and swallowed hard against the urge to kiss him.

'This is wrong.' The deep tones of his voice were heavy with accent and raw with unquenched desire. The sheer potency of his sexual magnetism made any kind of reply impossible. All she could do was look into his increasingly black eyes.

He lowered his head and brushed his lips over hers, the kiss so light her lips tingled. She sighed in pleasure, swaying towards him. She wanted him and whatever she said, however much she denied it, her body would call to his. Could something so potent be so wrong? Did she have to give her heart to taste the desire between them?

'So, so wrong, *mia cara*.' His lips left hers fractionally as he spoke, his voice husky with the same passion which flowed around her body. Her stomach churned nervously as her body heated in response to his desire-laden words.

'How can it be wrong?' She drew in a deep breath, trying to calm the erratic beating of her heart. She looked deep into his eyes, searching the bronze-flecked brown as they became inky black.

'It's wrong because I promised Sebastian I would look after you.' He stepped back away from her, breaking the powerful spell and leaving her so weak she thought she might crumple on the floor. 'I did not promise to seduce his sister and right now that is all I can think of doing.'

Her breathing was becoming ever harder to control, the sequin-encrusted bodice of the dress tightening with each attempt to breathe normally. He'd admitted he wanted her and her body hummed with a need she'd never known before, one that demanded satisfaction.

'We will be late.' She said the first thing that came to her mind to avoid confronting what sparked between them.

He laughed, a sound so sexy and throaty she blushed. Why had she said that?

'Is that an invitation, *cara*?' He pulled the cuff of his jacket back with long tanned fingers and looked at his watch. 'When I make love to a woman I take my time, give pleasure and enjoy it. You're right, if I take you back in there now we will be late. Very late.'

The smile on his lips, the invitation in his eyes were all too much, shocking her and giving her a much-needed reminder why she was even here with him. 'That can't happen, Alessandro. I'm not here to be your latest conquest.' Desperately, she tried to hide her desire, her confusion behind the words.

'Are you sure about that, *cara*?' He folded his arms across his broad chest and leant back against the wall, looking so handsome and sure of himself.

'You're impossible,' she fumed and turned towards the stairs, rushing down them so quickly her dress billowed out behind her and her heels tapped out an angry rhythm. His gentle laughter followed her, teasing and so sexy. She let out an exasperated groan.

Once at the bottom of the stairs, she pulled open the door of the building, drawing the warm early evening air deep into her lungs, wanting to banish the lustful throb that still hummed inside her. Seconds later, he was at her side, his hand in the small of her back, guiding her towards the door of the car as the driver opened it and stood back.

Swiftly, she got in, thankful of the roomy interior. At least she didn't have to sit close to him. But that roomy interior vanished as soon as he got in and, despite the expanse of leather seats between them, he felt too close. Her pulse, still unbalanced from that fleeting kiss, raced, making her light-headed.

She looked out of the window as the car pulled away, leaving the historic centre of Milan and the impressive Duomo behind. She feigned an interest in the passing streets she was far from feeling after their *encounter* outside his apartment. She couldn't trust herself to look at him, didn't want to see the hot desire in his eyes. Not now, on the night of the launch—a moment that was for her brother.

Relief surged through Alessandro as they reached the exclusive hotel where the launch party was being held. At least with other people around him he could distract himself. From the second he'd seen her, the red silk of her dress clinging to her narrow waist, enhanced further by all the red sequins, he'd been lost. Her one bare shoulder distracted him so completely that all thoughts of keeping her at a distance after the test track kiss had vanished.

He wanted her. More than he'd ever wanted any woman.

The driver opened his door and he got out amidst flashes from the waiting press and made his way around to Charlie's door. He held her hand as she stepped out, fighting the sizzle that shot through him from that contact. He didn't miss her hesitation as the photographers went crazy, flashes lighting up the ever darkening sky, their calls resounding around them.

'I hadn't expected so many,' he said sternly as she came to stand at his side. He should have warned her. Escaping the intrusion of the press had been her reason for retreating from the racing world and now she was in the thick of it again. 'Sorry, I didn't think to tell you they'd be here.'

'I expected it.' She smiled up at him, then faced the cameras as photographers shouted at them. 'Just not so many.'

He put his arm around her, pulling her close, feeling only a slight resistance as she continued to pose for the media. Seb had told him she was the best, knew just how to work the press to the team's advantage and, despite his doubts, he saw immediately this was true. But she was smiling and posing under duress and a tinge of guilt slipped over him.

The tension in her body increased and he turned her away from the press, heading into the hotel. All around, people chatted, sipping the champagne being circulated, but as they entered a hush fell on the room. Beside him, Charlie drew in a deep breath, straightened and as he looked across at her he saw a smile light up her face.

'I had not anticipated such a turnout.' He spoke softly, for her ears only. 'It seems you have many people wishing to meet you.'

'My presence here is a way of absolving you of any wrongdoing…in the eyes of the media and public, that is.' She whispered the words with her smile still in place and he suddenly saw how she must be feeling, how this whole evening must be for her.

'That was not my intention.' He placed his hand against her back, felt the heat and tried to ignore it.

'No, I don't think it was.' She looked up at him and, despite the smile on her lips, he knew that inside she was hurting. He could see it in her eyes and wanted to protect her from it.

She turned her attention to those around them, her smile easing the tension in the room, and a hum of conversation gradually started again. He took two flutes of champagne, handed her one and moved into the room, aware that every man there was looking at her with admiration.

A stab of jealousy spiked him, but instantly he dismissed it. She wasn't his and never could be. His urge to protect her and keep her at his side was thwarted as they were engaged in conversation before being separated.

Even though she was on the other side of the room, deep in conversation with several Italian racing drivers, he was aware of her. Each time she laughed, the gentle sound rippled through the air and he had to defuse the heady pulse of passion or he'd be in danger of dragging her away and doing just what his body demanded.

He made his welcome speech, repeating it in English for her benefit, but he couldn't look at her because if he did he wouldn't be able to stay here in front of everyone and remain calm. His prepared lines became jumbled and he improvised. Something he'd never had to do before.

'Now, to the moment everyone is waiting for,' he said as the doors of the hotel courtyard were folded back to reveal the shape of his car beneath a black cloth. Appreciative sounds came from those around him but, instead of giving the signal to pull off the cloth, he turned back to the audience.

Charlie looked up at him as he stood on the presentation stage, questions in her eyes, but he continued with his original plan.

'I'd like to introduce, for those who don't know her, Charlotte Warrington, sister of the late and very much missed Sebastian Warrington, who played a big part in developing this car.'

He turned, ignoring the need to look at her again, and gave the signal to reveal the car. Delighted sounds and applause came from everyone as the brilliant red of the car sparkled beneath the lights.

Finally he looked towards Charlie. She was slowly making her way towards the car, the red of her dress a perfect match for its gleaming paintwork, but the expression on her face sent alarm bells ringing. The smile she'd hidden behind from the moment she'd arrived in front of the cameras was gone. In its place was an expression of sadness that stilled the applause.

He stepped down and briskly made his way over to her, the audience parting ahead of him. He didn't know what to say, didn't know how to offer her support, and he cursed the fact that she'd only seen the plain grey test car until now.

'Charlotte?'

Slowly she turned to look at him. 'It's beautiful, Sandro.' The fact that she'd shortened his name didn't go unnoticed. All her barriers were down; she was exposed, vulnerable, and it was because of his carelessness.

'You were meant to see it yesterday afternoon.' She looked up at him, her eyes greener than he'd ever seen them. He didn't need to add that their test track kiss had thrown all his plans into disarray. Her expression and hint of a blush told him she knew why.

'Seb would be proud.' Her soft voice was firm and she turned to those around her, the smile she'd been using all night firmly back in place. The shutters had rolled back.

Charlie looked at Alessandro, blinking back the tears that momentarily threatened. 'Thank you.' Her voice was almost a whisper and, despite the throng of people around them, eager to get a good look at the car, it seemed as if it was only them there.

He moved closer, his eyes holding hers, and her heartbeat sped to an alarming rate. His height and broad shoulders made her feel small and defenceless but the intensity in his eyes cancelled that and she basked in his bold desire for her.

'Seb would also be proud of you.' His gentle words focused her attention back on the task at hand, giving her a chance to quell the almost primal need racing through her, need that only he could satisfy. 'You outshine the car.'

She laughed gently. 'That's not what I intended.' She hadn't. If she'd known the car was red she would have chosen a different colour dress, but red had been Seb's favourite. 'I should have known Seb would have wanted the car to be red.'

He didn't say anything and worry flitted through her.

His mouth was set in a firm line and she used the offer of more champagne to dilute the tension between them. He followed her lead and took a flute, clinking it against hers as he raised it to her. 'To Seb.'

The tribute, spoken sternly, poured cooling water over the fire which was still raging inside her since the kiss a few hours ago outside his apartment. How did he manage to awaken her so completely yet still leave her yearning for more?

'To Seb.' She took a sip, her gaze remaining locked with his. Those flecks of bronze became more diluted as his eyes darkened again. Whatever was between them wasn't going away; it was intensifying. Each glance, each touch and definitely each kiss increased the sizzle of attraction.

She couldn't deny it any longer.

She didn't want to deny it.

She wanted to be with him, wanted to feel his lips on hers and keep kissing him. She craved his touch and caresses, needed to feel his body against hers. But men like Alessandro Roselli, who had looks and wealth on their side, never wanted more than a brief affair. She'd learnt that the hard way, rebounding from a broken relationship with her childhood boyfriend into the arms of an up-and-coming racing driver, only to find he was using her to further his career.

Despite that, she still wanted to explore what was between them, but only if he didn't want any kind of commitment from her. She didn't want her heart exposed to pain. But would one night be enough to quench the thirst of desire?

'It's been a successful evening, *grazie*.' His words dragged her attention back, his gaze a soft caress and his words so tender and warm, making her yearn to hear it as he kissed her again and again.

'It's not over yet.' She couldn't believe she'd said the words aloud, offering something she'd only just realised she wanted. Judging by the look of surprise on his face, neither could he. But it was what she wanted, she realised as she watched his expression change, riveted to the spot by her bluntness. She wanted to forget all reason and abandon herself to the pleasure of his kisses, his caresses.

He raised his glass fractionally, not breaking eye contact, and her stomach twisted into knots of excitement and apprehension. 'Then I will drink to its continued success.' His rich voice was vibrant and warmth surged through her faster than lightning.

Shyness took over, banishing the boldness that had made her promise something she wanted but knew she shouldn't. She lowered her gaze and looked into her champagne as if the bubbles could give her the answers. 'Sorry, I shouldn't…'

Her words of apology, withdrawing her bold statement, were cut off by a familiar voice and she whirled around to see her father. He shook Alessandro's hand warmly and she marvelled at the ease with which they greeted one another.

'My flight was late.' Her father smiled at her, seemingly unaware of the tension between her and Alessandro. 'But I see you have done yourself—and Seb—proud.'

'I didn't know you were coming.' She sent up a silent prayer of thanks. Her father's arrival had stopped her from throwing herself at Alessandro and making a fool of herself into the bargain.

'I'm not staying. I will be leaving for Rome in a few hours, but I had to come and see you emerge like a butterfly back into the real world, and what a very beautiful butterfly you are.' He looked at her, his smile gentle, and she knew he really was proud and very pleased she'd stepped back into the limelight.

'So, the car—has it gone down well?' Her father turned to Alessandro and within minutes they were immersed in conversation. One she would normally relish hearing, but she needed to put space between her and Alessandro, cool things down. Maybe now it was time to mingle with potential buyers, do what she'd come here for.

Alessandro watched as Charlie talked animatedly with other people about the car, about its performance, and he recalled how well she'd driven it. She was more than qualified to sing its praises but it wasn't the drive, however fast, he was remembering. It was the kiss. Holding her in his arms and feeling her body against his.

Just a few guests lingered now, along with the racing drivers she'd been talking to earlier. Had she given them the same hints she'd given him? The way they hung on her every word certainly suggested as much.

An unknown need to be territorial made him stand as close to her as possible, but just doing so infused him once more with sizzling need. 'Thank you, gentlemen,' he said firmly, ignoring the way she shot him a startled glance. 'Any more questions you may have can be directed to my office.'

The remaining guests left, animated discussion of speed and performance trailing in their wake, but Alessandro watched Charlie as she leant back against the wing of the car, her red dress so perfect a match she almost became one with the slumbering beast.

Heat scorched through him as he remembered her earlier words and he undid his tie, letting it hang down, and pulled loose his top buttons. He'd never been so suffocated by desire before, had never experienced this continuous aching need.

He wanted her with a ferocious need, his promise to Seb becoming lost in the mists of heady desire. He should turn and walk away. To have kissed her at the test track had been so wrong. It had unlocked a thirst that needed quenching. Did she feel the same?

He looked at her and her eyes met his, darkening by the second. She smiled, a shy seductive smile that made his pulse leap. Instantly, he closed the distance between them, taking her in his arms and claiming her lips. She tasted better than ever; the anticipation of the last few hours had been worth the wait.

He caressed her cheek as he deepened the kiss, her response setting fire to his senses so instantly there was only one way to put out the flames now. Her skin was so soft and as his fingers caressed her bare throat he felt the wild pump of her pulse.

She wrapped her arms around his neck, her breasts pressing against his chest, and he moved her back against the car, pressing into her as heady lust robbed him of all thought.

'Sandro,' she murmured against his lips, pushing him almost too far.

It was all he could do to stop himself ripping the red dress from her, wanting to reveal her glorious body to his hungry gaze. Somewhere on the periphery sense prevailed.

This couldn't happen here and if he didn't stop kissing her there was a very real probability that it would. He pulled back from her, seeing her thick dark lashes flutter open to reveal eyes swirling with passion. 'My car is outside.'

Would she remember her covert promise to him that the night was still young? Her kiss certainly suggested as much, but did she want him enough to put all their differences aside for one night?

Shyly she looked up at him, a small sexy smile lifting her lips. Then, without further words, he took her hand and led her away from the car, through the brightly lit room where the hotel staff had started to clear up.

Movement caught his eye and he glanced over to see a photographer at a table, packing away his camera. Alessandro scrunched his eyes in suspicion, then, as her hand touched his arm, bringing her so close again, he dismissed the idea. He had far more important things to worry about than a rogue photographer.

He looked down into her upturned face as they stepped out into the warmth of the night, her smile reaching her eyes. 'It has been a very successful night,' she said as the car stopped outside the door.

'One I hope will continue in the same way.'

Demurely she looked down as he opened the car door. Once inside the car, he pulled her close against him, her head resting on his shoulder as if they'd known each other for ever. He didn't want to kiss her now. He didn't trust himself to be able to stop if things got heated. No, this was going to be played out in the comfort of his bedroom, where nothing and nobody could disturb them.

CHAPTER SEVEN

CHARLIE LIFTED THE front of her dress with one hand, the other still firmly in Alessandro's as they made their way up the marble staircase to his apartment. It was late and she should be tired. Last night she'd hardly slept and this evening she'd enjoyed the champagne just a little too much, but every sense in her body was on high alert.

Alessandro turned the key in the door and then looked at her, a seductive gentleness in his eyes. 'I want to kiss you again.' His voice was hardly above a whisper and his eyes searched her face.

He was so strikingly handsome, his tie hanging loosely and his white shirt open at the top button—exactly the romantic image that turned a girl's head. She smiled up at him, suddenly so sure that this was what she wanted. He wasn't the kind of man to want commitment and, for once in her life, neither did she. She wasn't looking or thinking beyond this moment.

'I shouldn't, but I do.' He moved closer, his height almost as overpowering as the tension that fizzed between them.

'Why shouldn't you?' Her voice was husky and she looked up at him, unsure what he meant.

'I promised Seb to look after you, not seduce you.'

The resolute growl in his voice made her heart race faster than any car she'd driven.

'Seb wouldn't be cross.' She couldn't keep the light teasing note from her voice. He was fighting this attraction as much as she was, which made her want him even more. She wanted his kisses, his touch and to be totally his—tonight, at least

She wanted him more than she had wanted any other man and it scared her, but at least with Alessandro there wasn't any danger of anything more than a brief affair. The idea of getting involved in another relationship didn't appeal. She'd been hurt once before and that was enough. 'I want you to kiss me again, Sandro.'

'But if I do—' he lowered his voice and his eyes softened as he looked down at her '—I'm not going to be able to stop. Not this time.'

She walked away from him and into the apartment, feeling empowered by his desire for her. Slowly she turned as he shut the apartment door, its click ominous, warning her she'd passed the point of no return. But she didn't care. She didn't want to stop. Not now. This passion, which had ebbed and flowed between them since the moment they'd met, needed to reach its conclusion. There wasn't any other option now.

He might be the man she still saw as responsible for Seb's accident, even though her father didn't, but he was also the man who'd ignited a fire of hot need within her. From the second she'd seen him standing in her garden she'd fallen for him. This attraction was something she couldn't turn her back on. Not yet. It was a totally new experience for her.

'I don't want you to stop, Sandro.' The husky whisper that came from her sounded so unreal and she watched as he stepped towards her, his tie hanging loose, his shirt unbuttoned and the hint of golden skin of his chest creating an evocative image. One which seared into her mind and would, she knew, remain there for ever.

He took her hand once more and, with a seductive look which whispered a thousand words, he drew her towards him, pulling her close. '*Mia cara*, I have wanted you since the moment I first saw you.'

A tremor of panic slipped over her, his words too serious. Did he want more than just this moment, this night which held the promise of so much pleasure? It wasn't what she wanted. She couldn't give him more. She pushed her hands against his chest, the firmness of it making her breath catch, but she refused to let it sway her from what she had to say, what she had to make clear.

'I don't do for ever, Sandro.' She'd been sure all along he just wanted a fling, a brief affair. The image of her and Alessandro, together and happy in the future, didn't fill her mind. It was more than just risking her heart. It was about letting go of pain and grief and she wasn't ready to do that yet. But one night meant only putting it aside and not engaging her heart. 'It's all I can give you.'

'So serious, *cara*,' he said and pressed a light kiss to her forehead. 'Isn't my divorce proof that I'm not able to commit to a relationship? Tonight belongs to us, *cara*.'

Before he could say anything else she looked up, bringing his lips tantalisingly close to hers, the shock of discovering he was divorced dulled by the passion which sizzled inside her. It proved he didn't do forever either and all she wanted now was to lose herself in the moment, forget the world existed. 'Kiss me, Sandro.'

In answer he kissed her so gently she thought she might actually cry. His previous kisses had been hard and demanding, but this was so tender, so loving. He held her as if she were a delicate flower he was afraid he might crush. She swayed towards him, desire making her light-headed as he continued the kiss.

Just when she thought she couldn't stand the torment any longer he stopped kissing her and, with blatant intent, led her through to his bedroom. As with the rest of the apartment, old blended stylishly with new and the corner of the room comprised of windows offering unrivalled views of the Duomo, lit up and sparkling like a thousand jewels against the night sky. But all that was lost on her. All she could see was him.

'*Un momento.*' He released her hand and closed the cream curtains before flicking on the bedside lamps, creating a room for romance. Then he walked back towards her, slipping off his jacket as he did so and tossing it carelessly onto the armchair that filled another corner of the room.

'Wait,' she said and walked towards him, smiling coyly, her gaze meeting his from beneath her lowered lashes. With unashamed enticement she reached up, flattened her hands against his chest, revelling in the strength and his ragged intake of breath. Slowly she pulled one end of his tie until it fell from his neck. Holding it up, she dangled it in front of him like a trophy, her brows raised suggestively.

'Tease.' He reached out, took hold of her waist and pulled her against him, his hold keeping her there, leaving her in no doubt he wanted her.

Still believing she was in charge, she undid first one button of his shirt and, meeting no resistance, continued with each button until she was forced to gently pull the shirt from his trousers. As she unfastened the final buttons she slid her hands inside and over his chest. Hair covered his muscles, but couldn't hide them from her exploring hands. The heat of his body emboldened her further.

She looked at his face, his eyes so dark and heavy with desire that shivers of delight rushed over her. Very slowly she pushed open the shirt and kissed his chest, little kisses as light as a feather all over him, his musky scent invading her senses. She heard him groan with pleasure, his hold on her waist tightening, and she smiled.

She pulled back from him and pushed the shirt from his shoulders. 'This has to go.' Her voice was husky and she almost didn't recognise it, but then she'd never done anything so bold before.

One-night stands had never been for her, not after the devastation caused to her parents' marriage, when her mother had succumbed to temptation. But this was different. Deep down, she acknowledged that if it had happened at a different time, in a different place it could have been so much more than one night.

She pushed that thought aside, refusing to allow it to defuse the sexual tension which filled the room.

He lifted his arms behind her as he unfastened the cuffs of his shirt, pressing her unbearably close. Before he released her, his lips pressed hard to hers, his breathing deep as his tongue slid into her mouth, teasing and tasting. She kissed him back, demanding more. For a moment his kiss matched hers, then abruptly he pulled back. 'The shirt?'

She smiled, feeling more brazen by the second. 'Yes, the shirt,' she whispered. 'It has to go.' She slid her hands up his chest, making him groan and close his eyes as she lingered there before pushing the white material from his shoulders. He moved first one arm from her, then the other and the shirt fell to the floor.

Again he pulled her close, but this time his fingers caught the zip at the back of her dress, slowly pulling it lower and lower; all the while his eyes held hers. Shyness swept over her and she resisted the urge to look away as his hand slid over her shoulder, pushing the one sleeve away and revealing her skin to his kisses.

The dress slipped down her body and slithered into a heap of silk and sequins at her feet. She stood against him, conscious of the fact that she now only wore the red underwear she'd bought to go with the dress and the strappy sandals she'd fallen in love with instantly.

Before she had time to think, he'd swept her off her feet and carried her to the bed. She lay where he'd placed her and looked up at him. He kicked off his shoes and was reaching for the fastener on his trousers when she knelt up on the bed and pushed his hands away. 'My turn.'

Who was this bold woman, this seductress? And why did it have to be this man who'd revealed her? This was a side of her she'd never known existed. Never before had passion taken over, making her want things with scant regard for the consequences.

A string of Italian that she was unable to understand flew from his lips as she opened his trousers, letting them slip down, leaving him in only a snug pair of black hipsters. As she looked up at him he caught her face between his hands and bent to kiss her. The spark was well and truly lit. Electricity shot between them. There would be no stopping now.

Before she had a chance to catch her breath he tumbled her onto the bed, his body pressing her into the softness of the covers. His kiss became urgent and demanding and she surrendered willingly to his domination.

His hands cupped her breast and inside her something exploded as she arched herself up to him, wanting his touch and so much more. Kisses trailed down her throat and she sighed in pleasure as her fingers slipped into the silky thickness of his hair. His tongue teased her nipple through the red lace of her strapless bra and her fingers tightened in his hair.

As if reading her urgent need, his hand slipped under her arched back, his fingers expertly flicking open her bra, releasing her breasts to his erotic kisses. Possessively he took a nipple in his mouth, swirling his tongue around it, making her cry out with pleasure. Moments later he moved his attention to the other nipple as his hand slid down her side and over her thigh, pulling her closer to the hardness of his erection.

'So beautiful,' he said huskily in between kisses and he moved back up her throat; the warmth of his body scorched hers until she felt as if flames licked around her.

She moved her hands down his back, savouring the latent strength beneath her fingertips. Lower she moved until she slipped her fingers in the back of his hipsters but, before she could make any attempt to remove them, he moved quickly onto his back, taking her with him until she sat astride him.

'That was…' she blushed beneath his open admiration, once again empowered by his need '…very masterful.'

His hands held her hips, keeping her exactly where he wanted her, and a hot stab of desire rushed over her. Following his need, she moved against him. With eyes as black as ebony he held her gaze until, drawn by something inexplicable, she lowered her body over him, bringing her lips against his.

'I am,' he said hotly between fast passionate kisses. 'Now, all night you will be mine.'

Charlie liked the sound of that; she wanted all night with him, wanted to enjoy this wonderful feeling again and again. 'Make me yours,' she whispered against his lips. 'Now.'

With the same suddenness of moments ago, she was once more lying on the bed, Sandro at her side. His fingers hooked into the lace of her panties and slowly pulled them lower, his eyes holding hers all the while.

She quivered as his fingers moved back to touch her, closed her eyes as a wave of pleasure rushed over her like the tide washing over the sand, taking her higher, almost to the point of no return. He took her lips in a hard and bruising kiss, his tongue as demanding as his touch, and her breath came hard and fast. It was too much and not enough both at the same time, leaving her wanting more.

Just when she'd almost slipped over the edge he pulled away from her. She opened her eyes, looking up at him and blinking against the pounding and unsatisfied passion of her body. He reached across her and roughly pulled open the drawer of the cabinet beside the bed.

Of course. Protection. How had she not thought of that? His eyes met hers, a knowing light in their depths, as if he knew she'd almost lost control. She watched as he dispensed with his underwear and rolled on the condom. Anticipation zinged through her and a pulse of heady need throbbed heavily between her legs.

He moved over her and she opened to him, wanting him deep inside her, but he paused. Propped up on his hands, his muscles straining with the effort, he looked down at her, his breathing deep and fast.

'Sandro?' She couldn't keep the question from her voice. Was he having doubts? What had she done?

Then his mouth claimed hers in a hungry and possessive kiss as he pushed into her, taking himself in deeply. She gasped against his lips, his kiss smothering the sound as he moved inside her, sending firecrackers of explosion all around her.

She moved with him, taking him deeper still. He dropped down against her, his warm skin pressing against her body as he kissed her neck, his hands grasping her hair tightly. A flurry of hoarse Italian erupted from him as he thrust harder, sending her over the edge and beyond. Further than she'd ever been before.

She dug her nails into his back, moving with him as the ecstasy crashed into her. His grip on her hair tightened as he gasped out his release and kissed her hard. Then, as the heady lust ebbed slowly away, their bodies tangled, she wrapped her arms around him, keeping him against her, and softly kissed the dampness of his face.

She'd just experienced something she'd never before known and wanted to hold onto the moment just a little longer.

Alessandro could hardly think, the beat of his pulse was so loud. He couldn't move; every muscle in his body had been weakened by the power of hers. She kissed his face and he closed his eyes against the tenderness of that kiss. It was too intimate, too loving and he didn't deserve it.

He didn't deserve any of this and had almost stopped, but his name on her lips, husky and seductive, had made that impossible. Quickly he pushed aside the guilt. She'd wanted this as much as he had, leading the seduction like a temptress.

In a bid to hide the turbulent emotions racing through him, he propped himself up over her and looked down into her flushed face. 'You make love as wildly as you drive.'

She trailed her fingertips over his chest and looked up at him, coyness and temptation filling those emerald-green eyes. 'Are you going to insist I stop again?'

He should do—this wasn't what he'd imagined when he'd promised Seb he'd look out for his little sister, but then he hadn't expected to be so attracted to her and certainly he'd never have guessed at the passion hidden within her.

Gently he kissed her, tenderness that he hadn't felt for such a long time filling him. She responded, her kiss telling him that the fire of passion still burned within her, as it did inside him. He needed to cool things down, needed to calm the riot of emotions which raged within him. Emotions that were so intense and completely unwelcome.

'*Sì.* For now.' He pushed his protesting body away from hers, trying to ignore the wounded look on her beautiful face. Before he had a chance to question his motives, he left the bed and made his way to the bathroom.

Moments later, his face stinging from the cold water he'd splashed over it, he returned to the bedroom, but the bed was empty, the rumpled covers the only hint of the passion that had just played out there.

A rustle caught his attention and he looked towards the door where, clutching the red silk dress against her nakedness, Charlie stood. She was running away again. Was this what she always did? He should let her walk away—every rational sense inside him shouted the advice—but the hot-blooded man she'd resurrected wasn't about to let her slip away from him now.

He strode over to her, heedless of his nakedness and empowered by the shock and need that filled her eyes. She still desired him, just as he desired her. This passion wasn't spent yet.

'Come back to bed, Charlotte.' His voice was deep and raw, leaving him with the distinct impression that his emotions were as naked as he was.

'But…'

He silenced the hoarse whisper by tilting her chin up and kissing her lips, still swollen from his earlier kisses. She sighed and kissed him, dropping the dress carelessly to the floor. He pulled back but still held her chin and looked deep into her eyes, saw the green darken to resemble the heart of the forest, hidden from the sun.

'*Tornare a letto, cara.*' He brushed his lips on hers as a frown of confusion slipped over her face. Desire rushed through him and all he could think about was making love to her again and again. This might not be for ever, but it was certainly for now and, as far as he was concerned, *now* would last all night. 'Come back to bed, *cara.*'

Charlie all but melted at his feet, almost as crumpled as the sea of red silk on the floor between them. The raw and potent desire in his eyes couldn't be ignored. Neither could the kiss that promised so much more. She couldn't deny she wanted him. She knew she shouldn't and briefly wondered if this was how it had been for her mother. Had her mother been drawn inexorably towards the flame of desire, a flame that had then extinguished all the love she'd had for her husband, Charlie's father?

'Don't look so worried, *cara*.' His soft words broke her thoughts. Now was not the time to worry about the past. Unlike her mother, she wasn't married or committed in any way. She was free to enjoy this for what it was, a short and passionate affair.

But what of Seb? What would he have said? Hurriedly, she pushed that thought to the back of her mind, remembering what she and Sandro had enjoyed earlier. Seb had always wanted her to be happy and right now her whole body was alive with happiness.

She smiled at Sandro as he took her hand and led her back to the bed, the passion that had raged between them earlier beginning to heat again. Desperate to drown her misgivings, she wrapped her arms about his neck, pressing herself against his nakedness, and kissed him as if her life depended on it.

Suddenly he tumbled her back on the bed, his body over hers as his hot kisses stoked the fire of passion ever higher and she was lost once more.

CHAPTER EIGHT

'BUONGIORNO.' THE SOFT Italian greeting stirred her senses and Charlie opened her eyes. Sunlight poured in around the closed curtains, but all she could focus on was the man beside her. Every limb in her body was replete with Alessandro's lovemaking and she stretched, smiling up at him, enjoying the way his eyes clouded with passion. 'Breakfast awaits.'

'Breakfast? How long have I slept?' She sat up, pulling the soft sheet modestly against her. He stood by the bed, dressed in jeans which hugged his strong thighs and a black T-shirt which highlighted the contours of his chest to perfection.

His gentle laugh knotted her insides and she dragged her gaze from him, to look at the clock which ticked beside the bed. 'Long enough, *cara*, but then we didn't sleep much last night.'

She turned quickly to look at him, heat infusing her cheeks as his words confirmed her memory was correct. Was it all over now—the one night of passion she'd willingly entered into? Was this now time to go back to her room, to return to the professional relationship they'd had initially? There was still more promotion scheduled for the car over the weekend and into the following week.

How was she going to get through the weekend after what they'd shared last night?

'Thank you.' She was confused by the way she felt and the need to distance herself from him. Wanting to return to the businesslike dealings they'd had with one another until last night. 'I'll get dressed, then we can discuss what's next on the promotion agenda.'

'Oh, no, *cara*. There is only one thing on the agenda right now.' A teasing smile lingered on his lips and the suggestive tone of his voice made her stomach flutter wildly. He still wanted her.

Her heart thumped as he strode back to stand beside the bed. Her mouth was as dry as a desert and she tried to moisten her lips but, from the smouldering look in his eyes, that was a mistake. 'There is?' The strangled whisper only just managed to squeeze out.

He leant on the bed, so close that her lips parted without her consent, waiting for his kiss. When it came it was soft and teasing and loaded with promise. She closed her eyes, slipping under his masterful spell far too easily. 'I'm taking you somewhere we can be alone, somewhere we can explore what is between us.'

She pulled sharply back from him. 'But the launch… the promotion? You're supposed to be hosting a promotional afternoon at the test track.' She'd already expressed a wish to be there and was torn between the idea of spending time alone with him and being with the car her brother had designed.

'Someone else can handle that.' He moved towards her again, stretching his body across the bed, making her want to reach out and touch him, feel his strength. 'We have far more important things to do.'

'But…' She raised her hand, pressing it against his

shoulder, stopping him coming any closer. The sheet she'd pulled against her slipped down, exposing her breasts, but she held her ground, keeping a firm expression on her face.

His eyes looked down at her, his appreciative gaze sending heat to the centre of her again, and her breath hitched audibly as if he'd caressed her. '*Per Dio*, but you are so hard to resist.' His accent became heavy and she released his shoulder and clutched the sheet quickly against her once more, shyness rushing over her now that daylight flooded the room.

'It was only meant to be one night, Sandro.' Her voice was barely above a whisper and she felt emotionally exposed and vulnerable.

'You need to stop running, Charlie, and face what scares you.' His body, tall and overpowering, dominated the room but his expression was gentle. Did he understand her fears? Empathise with her?

She looked up at him, willing the carefree attitude she'd had last night to infuse her again. With alarming clarity she realised she was using not just Seb's accident but her disastrous love life as a shield. Retreating behind it and potentially denying herself more pleasure than she could imagine.

'I want to be at the test track.' She injected a firmness she was far from feeling into her voice and, from the look on his face, he knew she was already running.

'It is not necessary, not after last night.' He stood back up, his height dominating the room. 'We will spend the weekend at my villa. I intend to explore what you started last night, enjoy it. Do you not feel the same, *cara*?'

Should she lie? Tell him she didn't want to be with him any more when the heat of her body and the pounding of her heartbeat told her she did? She slipped from the bed, dragging the sheet she clutched with her. 'What about the car?'

'The car will still be there on Monday.' His voice was deep and the darkness of his eyes told her he wasn't thinking about the car at all.

He was right. The car would still be there after the weekend, but the passion which still burned fiercely between them wouldn't be. She didn't want it to be anything more than a brief affair. This way, it would burn itself out, enabling her to concentrate on what she'd come to Italy for. The truth about Seb's accident.

'Just the weekend.' She smiled at him, enjoying the power she seemed to have over him. 'But no more.'

'Bene.' He moved to the door of the bedroom, filling it with his oh-so-sexy body, and she could hardly think. 'We leave in an hour.'

Alessandro revved the car along the open road, the bustle of Milan far behind them, but tension still filled him. He'd seen the panic in her eyes as she'd sat in the bed, but he'd also seen the desire. Whatever was holding her back hadn't been quite strong enough and he sensed it was more than just her brother. That was only a smokescreen.

His body longed for the moment he could make her his again, but he questioned if he was right to do so. If he was a betting man he'd stake everything on the fact that Seb had never intended this to happen when he'd made Alessandro promise what now turned out to be impossible. How could he possibly look after Charlie when all he wanted to do was make love to her again and again?

Inwardly he cursed. The idea behind bringing her to

his villa was to be somewhere the ghost of her brother's memory couldn't reach. Whatever had happened last night wasn't about Seb—or the car. It was about them and the hot lust which zipped between them from just one look. After last night the temperature of that lust had risen instead of cooling, as he'd thought it would have done.

'*Benvenuti* Villa Dell Angelo.' Pushing his doubts and thoughts of Seb aside, he pulled off the road and into the driveway of his villa, perched on the hillside. Beyond it, Lake Garda glittered like a thousand jewels in the midday sun. This was his new place of sanctuary and Charlie was the first woman he'd ever brought here.

'It's beautiful.' Her soft gasp of pleasure did untold things to his body and he tried to keep his mind on the here and now instead of roaming back to last night or fast forwarding to the pleasures that would await him as darkness fell once more.

'*Sì, grazie.*' He stopped the car, turned off the engine and looked across at her. 'But not as beautiful as you.'

She blushed and dropped her gaze, amazing him that a woman who had been so bold in the bedroom just hours ago could be so shy from his compliment. That boldness did, however, salve his conscience and ease the guilt he felt at breaking his promise. Whilst it was true he had needed little invitation last night, she had instigated it, even warning him she didn't do for ever. She'd wanted last night as much as he had, despite the innocent blushes which now coloured her cheeks.

He got out of the car before he gave in to the temptation to kiss her again. 'I have arranged for lunch on the terrace, then we will drive down to the local town of Desenzano for the afternoon, maybe take a ferry across the lake.' If he didn't take her out he knew they would spend the whole afternoon in bed and, whilst the sex was amazing, he wanted to know her better. That thought shocked him and he frowned as he watched her taking in the view. She was beginning to get to him, tear down his wall of protection.

'Sounds lovely.' Her heels tapped out a gentle beat as she walked towards the terrace, the warm wind pressing her white sundress against her body, making him draw in a sharp breath as he fought for control. He'd never been this affected by a woman before, not even the woman he'd married, foolishly believing he loved her.

'I'm glad you approve,' he said with a smile as he watched her walk and pushed the memories from the past to the back of his mind where they belonged.

Charlie couldn't help but stop as they rounded the corner of the ornate villa. A large infinity pool stretched away, blending with the views of the lake far below, becoming one with it. Under the shade of trees, a table was laid out for lunch, looking so luxurious she felt as if she'd stepped into another world. This was on another level to the glamour her career had showed her so far. It was pure indulgence.

'If we take a ferry maybe we should do a little exploring before returning to dine in Desenzano.' He gestured her to sit and then took his seat opposite her. Beyond him the view seduced her almost as much as the man himself and she tried hard to keep her mind focused on the here and now, instead of allowing it to drift towards thoughts of what their time together would bring.

'And then?' What was the matter with her? Why did she need to act the seductress still? *Because that's what you were last night and that's what he's expecting.* The reprimand shot swiftly through her mind. She had been brazen, but they'd both agreed this was just an affair, a short dalliance. Right now she might be someone she'd never been before, but that didn't mean she couldn't enjoy it. Once it was over and the launch complete she would return to her life in England and try to move on.

He raised his brows, leant back in his chair and smiled—a slow lazy smile that was so sexy she almost couldn't breathe—but his next words made that breath catch in her throat. 'Then we spend the night making love.'

His bluntness shocked her, but she smiled teasingly back at him, enjoying the freedom to be different from normal. It was as if he'd unlocked a new and completely unexpected version of herself, one that lived a carefree and happy existence. 'Promises, promises.'

'All night, *cara*, you will be mine, that I do promise, but first we eat.' He watched her with a steadfast gaze that dissolved the few remaining doubts which lingered in her mind. He wanted her, she wanted him. Was it so wrong to put aside everything else and enjoy the mutual attraction until it fizzled out?

It *was* wrong. It went against everything she believed in. She didn't do affairs and certainly didn't want a relationship with anyone and definitely not with Alessandro, but the connection between them was impossible to ignore. For the first time in her life she was throwing caution to the wind, almost seeing it being snatched away to float above the blue waters of the lake.

She picked up her glass of wine and lifted it to him. 'To tonight,' she toasted, enjoying the smile that tugged at his lips and the hum of anticipation that warmed her body.

'Salute!' He raised his glass to her and she watched his eyes become as black as midnight, the desire-laden and smouldering look on his face making her heart constrict and her body heat.

The ferry from Desenzano to Sirmione offered a cool breeze which was a welcome relief from the heat of the afternoon. Charlie, feeling like a child, wanted to sit at the front of the paddle steamer to gain a prime view of the lake and surrounding countryside and Alessandro seemed happy to indulge her. He made her feel special and cherished with his attention.

Passengers chatted and laughed all around them but still she felt as if she were in a bubble, just the two of them, wrapped up in the attraction which sizzled stronger than ever between them. He put his arm around her as they sat, pulling her close, and the moment took on a magical quality, as if they were in love and not just lovers.

In love.

The words rang in her mind. It couldn't be possible to be in love so soon. She was just being seduced by the sunshine, the luxury of this life she'd stepped into, but most of all by the man himself. Love didn't just happen. It grew and flourished within a happy relationship and this wasn't a relationship. It was an affair.

'I suppose this is a regular trip for you.' She tried to quell the unease of her emotions and distract her thoughts. She was probably just one of many. A man like Alessandro would never be short of female company.

'I bought the villa a year ago but have been too busy with the car to use it.' He looked ahead of them, the wind playing in his hair, his eyes hidden by dark glasses, then suddenly he turned to look at her. She saw herself reflected in his sunglasses and hated that she couldn't see the expression in his eyes.

'Did Seb ever come here?' The light question made his mouth set in a firm line and she wondered what she'd said wrong.

'No. It's why I brought you here. I wanted it to be just the two of us. No memories. There will be enough of those when we return to Milan.' His voice was hard and the clipped edge to it warned her off further questions.

He had at least confirmed one thing. This was still nothing more than a weekend affair. Once they were back in Milan it would be over and just a few days after she would leave for England and the life she needed to get back together. A brief affair was all she'd wanted, so why did it hurt to know she could so easily be dispensed with?

'I'm glad you brought me here. It has been a hard year and right now I feel I have a reprieve from thinking about Seb and the accident,' she said honestly. Certain aspects of her time in Italy had been painful. 'It's time to put the past behind me.'

The sound of the ferry's motor as it manoeuvred towards the shore halted further conversation, something she was grateful for. She didn't want to admit to him he'd been right, that being at the launch was not just what Seb had wanted but what she'd wanted.

She looked ahead of her as the ferry docked with a bump. The medieval castle dominating the town of Sirmione as it rose up from the blue waters of the lake unleashed a childlike need to explore. She pushed aside all other thoughts, determined to enjoy the day and Alessandro's company. 'I can't believe you've never been here or done this,' she said as she stood up, trying to lighten the mood.

'No, but now I will share the experience with you.' The smile on his lips almost melted her heart; it was far hotter than the sun. As the holiday-makers scurried off the ferry he pulled her into his arms and kissed her. The passion in that kiss must have been obvious to anyone who saw them, but she didn't care. All she wanted was to lose herself in his desire, to enjoy the short time they would have together before reality intervened.

'Sandro,' she murmured against his lips as her eyes fluttered open.

'We need to go now.' His voice was gravelly. He lifted his sunglasses onto his head and looked into her eyes, leaving her in no doubt as to why they had to go.

He took her hand and led her off the ferry. A knowing smile from a crew member was cast their way, making her blush again. Could everyone tell how much they wanted one another?

'The castle is the place to see,' he said as they walked alongside the walled moat of the impressive building. Swans moved gracefully over the rippling water and she wished she could be as free as them. Free to let go and love, to pair for life. But she couldn't, and certainly not with Sandro. She'd set the boundaries and he'd set the time limit. They would be lovers—for the weekend only.

Swept along with the tourists, they walked over the long bridge towards the impressive arched entrance and into the courtyard of the castle, its thick and high walls offering respite from the sun. He pulled her close, his arm around her waist, and she shivered, but not from being in the shade.

She feigned an interest in the history which oozed from the walls, desperate not to look at him or show just how much she wanted him. With his arm around her,

they walked slowly over the cobbled courtyard and towards the steps up to the wall. As they reached the top,
applause and cheers caught her attention and she turned
to look back down into the courtyard, where a radiant
bride posed with her new husband for photographs.

'Wouldn't it be fantastic to be married here?' She said
the words aloud, without thinking how they would sound
to him.

'If you find the right partner, yes.' His brittle words
snagged her attention but she didn't look at him; instead
she kept her attention on the happy scene playing out
below them—a scene she'd always secretly hankered
after. That was until her mother had destroyed all faith
in fairy tales and happy ever afters.

'Sorry.' She was. A moment ago they'd been happy—
smiling, laughing and kissing like lovers without a care
in the world—and now she'd said the wrong thing.

'You have nothing to be sorry about, *cara*. Mine was a
marriage that should never have happened. We were too
young and wanted such different things.' She glanced at
him to see that he too was watching the happy couple,
his face set in hard lines of repressed anger.

'Love can deceive all of us,' she said and leant against
the railings, preferring to look at him instead of the bride
and groom.

'It wasn't love.' He snapped the words out and looked
down at her. 'It was deception.'

'Deception?'

'We had known each other since childhood,' he began,
keeping his attention focused on the events unfolding
in the castle courtyard. 'It stood the test of time when I
moved to Milan. Marriage seemed the normal progres-
sion and very much expected by our families.'

'So what went wrong?' She asked the question quietly, sensing his simmering anger.

'It wasn't me she really wanted, but the lifestyle she thought I could give her. What she hadn't accounted for in her scheming was that I would be putting every last cent back into my uncle's business. She soon tired of my frugal ways and found a man who could give her what she wanted.'

Charlie touched his arm, compelled to reach out, and he turned quickly to look at her, his eyes hard and glacial. She understood his feelings of betrayal. They almost mirrored hers.

For a moment he was silent, looking at her with unguarded curiosity. She held his gaze, trapped by the intensity of it.

'Seb told me you were once engaged.' Her heart plummeted but she smiled up at him, keeping her expression emotionless.

'Yes and, like you, we were too young. I was also far too naïve.' The sudden need to talk about something she'd hidden away surprised her. Was it his honesty that had triggered it? Whatever was happening between them, she was conscious of the earlier buoyant mood deflating as vulnerabilities were exposed. 'Let's not talk about it now; let's just enjoy our time together.'

'That is why you don't do for ever? Your heart has been broken?' He ignored her attempt to change the subject and lifted her chin with his fingers, brushing a kiss on her lips, sending her already distracted body into overdrive.

'I'd much prefer a wildly passionate affair,' she lied and moved closer to him, pressing her lips against his. A broken heart was only part of it and for the first time she realised what was really holding her back. What if she had the same capability to leave as her mother had?

'My sentiments exactly.' He deepened the kiss and she was vaguely aware of people passing them on the walkway and the wedding celebrations below moving away.

'Come on, let's explore.' Finally she pulled away from him, a teasing note in her voice. A little bit of distance between them was needed. Her heart was pounding and imagining all sorts of happy-ever-after scenarios with him.

'We shall go back a much faster way,' he said as they emerged from the castle, his voice full of laughter but the intent in his words clear. 'I've arranged for a private trip back; that way I can kiss you without feeling the world is watching.'

Excitement fizzed inside her at the thought of being alone with him but, as they stepped into the small speed-boat waiting within the moat of the castle, the reality was very different. It was compact, forcing them close to-gether, but it also meant they were very near to the driver.

Heat from Sandro seeped into her as she sat next to him. The boat made its way under the small castle bridges which reminded her of Venice, out of the medieval port and onto the lake. Soon they were speeding across the water and quickly she knotted her hair into a ponytail as they rushed back towards the small town of Desenzano. Alessandro pulled her tight against him and she closed her eyes, relishing the rush of air past her as the boat sped along and the feel of his strength. This was like a dream, so romantic and loving it would be easy to get carried away.

'I have a table booked at the best lakeside restaurant,'

Alessandro said as the powerboat slowed and pulled alongside the quay. Flags flapped erratically in the wind and she grabbed her hair again with one hand to stop it from blowing all over her face as he took the other and helped her from the boat.

Time was passing too quickly. It hardly seemed possible they'd been together all day, but already the sun was slipping lower in the sky. Once dinner was over they would go back to his villa, a thought which sent shivers of anticipation zipping rapidly through her.

All through dinner Alessandro had fought the urge to take her back to his villa. The tension had mounted rapidly, almost to boiling point. She felt it too, of that he was sure, and, as she'd sipped her coffee, her eyes became as dark as moss, suggestion in their depths as to what the night would bring.

They were kindred spirits, both healing from failed relationships, both wanting only the here and now. But, as they made their way back to his car, he imagined what it would be like to be with Charlie every day, to spend weekend after weekend like this.

Such thoughts had to be stamped out. She didn't do for ever, she'd made that perfectly clear, and the promise he'd made Seb to look after her as if she were his sister loomed over him, mocking him as his desire for the one woman he couldn't have raged ever stronger.

Now he powered the car along the road, the setting sun casting an orange glow all around them. He'd enjoyed his day with her but he knew he would enjoy the night much more. Here in his villa he was free to let go and love her. No promises hung over him, taunting him with guilt at what he was doing. Hurt from the past couldn't reach him any more and for just one more night she was his.

He sensed her watching him and glanced over at her. Did she guess at his eagerness to get her home?

'We have all night, Sandro.' She smiled lightly but the passion in her eyes told a very different story, as did the sexy purr when she said his name.

Would it be enough? he asked himself as he turned into the driveway of the villa, the last glimmer of the sun slipping beneath the horizon before them. Sunrise would mean their last day. They could only be lovers for the weekend. A weekend that was drawing rapidly to a close.

'Ma per amare una donna...' He tried hard to bring English to the fore as images of them together made his pulse race. Finally he managed to. 'But to love a woman like you I need more than one night.'

She reached up and touched his face, her fingertips snagging over his light growth of stubble. 'We only have tonight, Sandro. This can never be anything more. We don't belong together.'

Reminded of her earlier warning, he caught her hand and kissed her palm. 'Tonight only, but it will be one you will remember for ever.'

CHAPTER NINE

IF THAT FIRST morning waking in Alessandro's bed had been amazing, this morning was delicious. Charlie luxuriated against the warmth of his body like a kitten, content and sleepy. She lingered on the edge of sleep a moment longer, her back against his chest and his arms possessively keeping her close.

It was bliss and she didn't want to wake and face the day. Their last day together, and after their night of hot passionate sex she wasn't sure she wanted to begin the day. Birdsong drifted in through the open balcony doors and finally she opened her eyes to see the soft linen curtains stirring gently in the breeze.

It was like a dream, her body still singing from the hours of lovemaking, and now she felt safe. Loved. It was something she could get used to, but she mustn't. Thoughts of love drifted perilously close to the surface and she pushed them aside, aware something had changed. Deep down she wanted to be loved, but her disastrous engagement made that almost impossible. *This is just a weekend affair*, she reminded herself sternly as his arms pulled her tighter against him.

'Would you care to join me for a morning swim?' His lips brushed against the back of her neck and a flutter of butterflies took flight in her stomach. She closed her eyes against the heady sensation, ignoring her doubts of moments ago. It was still the weekend and still time to enjoy this affair.

'I don't have anything to wear.' She wished she did. The pool had looked inviting in the morning sun yesterday, but the thought of Sandro in it too made it infinitely better.

'Not a problem.' He kissed her ear and whispered to her, 'We are totally alone; nobody can see us.'

She turned in his arms, her pulse rate leaping wildly at the thought of swimming naked with him. 'Are you sure? No staff.'

'No staff. Nobody except you and me.' His words were heavy with accent and much more, making her body sing with desire she thought had long since been quenched.

He pulled her against him but she pushed at his chest with her hands, delighting in the chance to tease him again. 'I thought you wanted to swim.'

'I've changed my mind.'

In one swift move she leapt from the bed, the shock on his face making her laugh. Suggestively, she raised her brows. 'Well, I'm going for a swim.' Not wanting to pass up on the opportunity of such a luxurious pool, she rushed through the open balcony doors and down the stone steps that led to the pool. She glanced around briefly, checking they were as alone as he'd said, acutely aware she was still totally naked.

Without waiting to see if he followed, she dived into the cool blue water, glided forward then broke the surface. The sense of freedom was immense and she struggled to comprehend how just a bikini could hinder the feel of water against the skin. Only a short time ago she had been asleep but now her whole body was alive, invigorated by the cool water and the prospect of Alessandro joining her.

It was already warm. She swam to the end of the pool and, with her arms over the edge, looked out over Lake Garda as it stretched out below her. The sun's morning rays cast a golden glow over the tree-covered hills and mountains and already she could see the ferries, like tiny white shapes on the water, as they started their daily cruises.

Behind her she heard a small splash and moments later felt the water ripple against her neck as Alessandro dived in. She smiled but continued to survey the view, waiting with anticipation for him to join her. Her body trembled and her heart rate soared as she heard his strong strokes through the water. Then he was beside her, his arms on the edge, looking at the view too.

Embarrassment filled her. Swimming naked was not something she had ever done before and yet here she was, naked in Alessandro's pool. With breathing becoming difficult and her heart thumping hard, she needed to divert her attention, cool things down. She didn't even dare look at him.

'Stunning, isn't it?' She really couldn't believe she was here, enjoying a weekend of total luxury with the sexiest man she'd ever met.

'Semplicemente bellissimo.' Whenever he spoke Italian she got shivers of excitement down her spine, but this time she was certain he wasn't referring to the view and she turned to face him.

Shyness rushed over her at her nakedness and the hungry look in his eyes. She tried to mask it with bravado. 'Race you.' Without waiting to see if he'd taken up her challenge, she pushed away from the side of the pool, propelling herself through the water before beginning to swim back towards the villa.

Just as moments ago, she sensed him coming closer. Splashes of water landed around her as his strong arms carried him past her and to the end of the pool. His hand on the edge, his bronzed shoulders glistening in the morning sun, he waited for her to draw closer.

'I should have known you'd win.' She breathed out the words after the exertion of a brisk swim. Of course he'd win. She doubted he ever lost—at anything.

'You shouldn't challenge me, *cara*.' His voice was mocking and, without thinking, she splashed water at him, laughing in a way she hadn't laughed for a long time. 'And you shouldn't splash me either.'

Before she could do anything more, he hauled himself out of the water and effortlessly sprang to his feet to stand on the side of the pool looking down at her. She couldn't help but look at him and as her eyes travelled downwards shock set it.

'You cheat!' The words rushed from her as she took in the trunks clinging to him, water dripping from them. 'You tricked me. You let me believe we would both be naked.'

She hung on to the side of the pool, embarrassment colouring her cheeks. The smile on his face was too much. 'I never mentioned that I would be naked. Now, are you coming out or not?'

'Not.' She pouted up at him then swam slowly away, knowing he would be looking at her body.

She looked over at him as she swam, saw him grab a towel from a lounger and ruffle his hair dry, then stretch out on the lounger, watching every move she made. Her pulse rate went into overdrive.

'Do you make a habit of this, Miss Warrington?' His teasing question irritated her, yet made her smile too. He was playing games with her, toying with her like a cat did a mouse.

'Swimming naked or passionate weekend affairs?' She tossed the question at him as she reached the end of the pool, this time turning her back on the view of Lake Garda. There was a much more interesting view to take in now.

'Both.'

'I've never swum naked before.' She pushed away from the side, this time on her back, revelling in the chance to tease him just a bit, making her feel that little bit more in control. She had never had an affair, no matter how long, but she wasn't going to tell him that. She was tiring as she reached the end of the pool again but didn't want to come out of the water, not whilst he watched her so intently.

'I've never had a naked woman in my pool before.' His look was playful and the smile that moved his lips incredibly sexy.

She looked over at him, liking the way the sun gleamed in his damp hair. His long legs were as tanned as the rest of him and she feasted on the image he created, adding it to the one from their first night together, storing it away. This would be a scene never to be repeated.

'Well, that does surprise me. A man like you.' She kept her voice light and flirty, trying to echo his mood, but her heart was racing as heady need spread through her.

'A man like me?' He leant forward on the lounger, placing one foot on the floor. 'Just what is a man like me?'

She wished the words unsaid but continued with her carefree tone as she slowly swam to the side of the pool, holding the edge in front of him and trying to hide her nakedness. 'Don't try to deny you don't have women dropping at your feet.'

'Only those who are looking for something I can't give.' The brusque words, in complete contrast to his sexy and carefree stance, made her smile.

'Oh, and what's that?' she said, laughing teasingly at him.

'Marriage and security.' The air stilled around them and his mouth hardened just enough to warn her she'd strayed into dangerous territory. He sat back in the lounger again, as if to get as far away from the conversation as possible. Yesterday he'd talked of the end of his marriage to his childhood sweetheart. Was that the reason he'd never settled down again? She could certainly relate to that.

'And you don't want that?' She rested her arms on the side of the pool and looked at him, seeing an array of emotions flash across his face.

'No.'

The word was so final a chill slipped over her despite the warm sun on her back. She moved in the water, rippling sounds filling the heavy silence, but she couldn't look away, couldn't break the eye contact.

'I totally understand.' She did, but wished she'd kept that to herself as his eyes narrowed suspiciously.

'You do?'

'Oh, you know, once bitten, twice shy, as we say in England.' She turned her back and swam away from him, not wanting this discussion she had inadvertently started.

They should be enjoying their last hours together, not mulling over the past.

'You shouldn't hide from it, Charlie.' She stopped swimming as he said the very same words her father often said. Treading water, she turned to face him and swam back to the side of the pool, wishing she was wearing something so she could get out—of the pool and the conversation.

'Hide from what, Sandro?'

'Love.'

She blinked in shock, not quite able to believe a man who freely admitted to not wanting commitment would even use that word. 'I'm not hiding from it. I just haven't found it yet.'

'And when you do?'

She couldn't understand where the questions were coming from. She'd made it clear she didn't do for ever, so why channel the conversation this way? 'My mother left us as teenagers, Sandro. She left my father, turning her back on us. I haven't believed in happy ever after since.'

'And the man you were engaged to? Did you love him and dream of living happily ever after?' His scrutiny was intense and she hated the feeling of being trapped in the pool, forced to answer his questions.

'Maybe I wasn't ready to love after that.' That statement stunned her and she blinked against the admission, realising the truth of it.

'And if you were to fall in love?' His dark eyes fixed hers and she clutched harder to the side of the pool.

'If I was sure I'd found a man to love, one who would love me, then I might just think about for ever.'

'So you'd get married?' His voice rose in question and disbelief.

'Marriage isn't the only way to have love, Sandro.' He furrowed his brows speculatively at her and she turned the heat on him, deflecting it from herself. 'What about you—would you marry again?'

Alessandro looked down at Charlie, her wet hair slicked back from her face, highlighting the beauty of her eyes. She was stunning, but she was also talking of things he'd begun to question as he'd held her sleeping body against him this morning.

He'd been adamant he was done with love, done with marriage, but such thoughts had begun to filter from the back of his mind. Images of him and Charlie, sharing love and happiness, lingered on the edge, hazy images that hadn't yet become sharp and focused. Images that shouldn't even be there.

Just as he had done as she'd curled against him and slept, he wondered what it would be like to wake every morning, take her in his arms and kiss her awake. In just a few days she'd weaved a spell so potent he didn't want to let her go. Because she still blamed him for Seb's accident, he couldn't ask for more—not until he cleared himself of blame in her eyes. And he couldn't do that without telling her everything. And that would break his promise to Seb.

'Your silence says it all.' Charlie's voice hurtled him back to the present.

'With the right woman,' he said truthfully. He had thought the right woman didn't exist for him. His first marriage had been testament to that. Now the woman he wished could be *the right woman* had made it perfectly clear she didn't want anything more than this weekend.

'I hope you meet her then.'

He watched as she pushed away from the side of the pool, once again swimming on her back, exposing her pert breasts to him. The water sparkled under the sun but it couldn't detract from the beauty of her naked body as she swam. He was beginning to think he had.

'Are you ever going to come out of that pool?' Desperate to change the subject, he stood and picked up a towel. 'You'll be a mermaid before long.'

She laughed and swam to the steps at the far end of the pool, her slim figure clearly visible in the water, unleashing coils of lust within him. Lust. That was all this was—all it could be. He had to keep that at the forefront of his mind when dreams he'd long since hidden away threatened to reappear.

'I'm not mermaid material.' Slowly, as if aware of his eyes on her, aware of the hot lust she evoked within him, she climbed up the steps. Water rushed off her skin as she stood at the edge of the pool, pulling her hands down her hair, scrunching it into a ponytail to wring the water from it.

He couldn't move, couldn't take his eyes off her. Rivulets of water rushed over her breasts, down her stomach, and he fought hard against the urge to carry her back to his bed. She was so beautiful as she stood like a nymph with the morning sun glistening on her wet skin. It was like watching a film play out in slow motion as she walked towards him. Her angelic beauty stunned him into silence.

Unaware of what he was doing, he walked towards her and wrapped the towel around her, pulling her close against his now dry skin, relishing the wetness of hers. His gaze met hers, her green eyes heavy with unguarded passion that made his heart thud.

She reached up and brushed her lips over his and he closed his eyes as an intensity pressed down on his heart. Would he ever get enough of her? He knew the answer to that as her arms reached around his back, locking them together. No, he never would. She deepened the kiss, sending heat and need rushing through him again.

'We should take this inside,' he ground out as she pulled back and looked up at him. Her smile told him she knew exactly what she did to him and fully intended to continue the teasing she'd started as soon as she'd woken this morning.

'Yes,' she whispered. 'One last time.'

'One last time.' He repeated her words and kissed her, drinking her in, wanting more than one last time, but she hadn't set the boundaries for their weekend—he had and now he couldn't take this any further. He was already guilty enough of abusing the trust Seb had placed in him. As soon as they returned to Milan he had to put their relationship back where it belonged. On a professional level.

She pulled back from him and clutched the towel around her shoulders, although it didn't hide her luscious body completely from his view. With a coquettish little smile she took his hand and led him back up the stone steps and into the bedroom.

The sun now poured into the room, its rays falling onto the bed he'd hastily left after he'd heard her splash into the pool. The cream covers strewn aside, evidence of the hot hours they'd spent there last night.

She dropped the towel as she walked towards him, the makeshift ponytail hanging over one breast sending a rivulet of water down her sexy body. He took in a deep breath, savouring every last detail about her. Her impatience was clear as she closed the distance between them.

Before he knew what had happened she was in his arms, her body pressed hard against his, the torment of her nakedness too much. With an urgency he'd never experienced he lifted her from the wooden floor, her legs wrapping around him, only his trunks between them.

He carried her towards the bed, the heat of her against his arousal almost too much. Gently he lowered her onto the bed, watching as she slithered up towards the pillows. He crawled up the bed after her, his heart pounding in his chest so hard she must hear it. He wanted her so very much and intended to make the most of these last moments as lovers.

With frantic moves he tugged his trunks down, kicking them away as his gaze held hers, then took one slender ankle in his grasp and pulled her slowly back towards him. Her eyes flew wide but her heavy breaths, which made her breasts rise and fall provocatively, drove him on.

He moved over her, wanting to be deep inside her, to make her his one last time. He should be taking it slow but he couldn't hold back any longer.

'Sandro, stop.' She pushed against his chest, the urgency in her voice breaking the mind-numbing lust which robbed him of all coherent thought. 'We need protection.'

'*Maledizione.*' He shook with the effort of regaining control and looked at her face. With her eyes so wide and so green, all he could do was lower his head and kiss her. 'Forgive me.'

He didn't recognise the hoarse voice that had said those words. Never had he lost control quite so spectac-

ularly and somewhere deep inside he was thankful that
at least one of them had retained some sense.

He reached across to the bedside table and grabbed
the box of condoms, tipping the last one out. Her words
of moments ago floated back to him. *One last time.* He
pushed the thought roughly aside as he rolled the protection on.

'Sorry,' she said shyly. 'But we don't want any consequences from this weekend.'

He looked at her, realisation hitting him. There were already consequences from this weekend, though not in the
form of pregnancy. The consequences for him were that
he'd unwittingly given his heart away, fallen for a woman
he shouldn't even have had an affair with, let alone love.

'You're right, *mia cara.* There cannot be any consequences.'

She kissed him gently, her lips so light and teasing,
sending him almost over the edge. 'None at all.' Her
words whispered against his lips and he pushed all other
thoughts from his mind until he couldn't hold back any
longer.

'No,' he ground out as she pulled him towards her,
wrapping her legs about him, taking him deep inside
her. For the last time he made her his, the passion all-
consuming.

His release was swift and she clung to him as he buried his head in her damp hair. '*Il* mio *amore,*' he murmured softly in Italian as he kissed her neck, not knowing
what he was saying, his thoughts translating to words involuntarily as passion took over.

Was it his way of saying goodbye? He didn't know, but
was grateful the words of love he'd voiced in his language
hadn't appeared to have been understood, or even heard.

* * *

Charlie smoothed down the white dress she'd arrived in yesterday and glanced around the room one last time, not sure if she was checking for forgotten items or committing it to memory. Both, she told herself, because there wouldn't be any coming back. It was over. In just two more days she'd be back in England, back to her life. The moments of passion they'd shared would be locked away for good.

She walked around the room, her sandals tapping slowly on the wooden floor. She could still hear the soft words of Italian Sandro had spoken as they'd made love that one last time. She hadn't understood much of it, but one phrase now replayed over and over in her head.

Il mio *amore.*

My love.

She shook her head in denial. It must have been in the heat of the moment, something he said to every woman he made love to and nothing more. She clung to this idea, knowing she didn't want it to be anything more. Especially not from Alessandro.

They might have put aside their differences for a weekend of passion, enabling them to explore the explosive attraction that had been present from the very beginning, but as soon as they returned to Milan those differences would return. They would engulf them and mock her for her weakness at giving in to lust, because lust was all it was, all it ever could be.

As she thought of returning to Milan, she knew that, deep down, she could never forgive him for failing to ensure that the prototype that Seb had crashed that night was fit to drive. Their differences encroached like a menacing shadow. What had she done? Not only had she slept with the man responsible for Seb's death, but had enjoyed a whirlwind affair. One that had jumbled her emotions and tied her in knots.

Quickly she grabbed her bag and left the room, not daring to look again at the bed which had been the focal point of so much pleasure, so much passion. She should be ashamed of herself. And, deep down, she was, but at least she'd got it out of her system, cleansed away the irrational desire she'd felt for him the instant her eyes had met his. There wouldn't be any *what ifs* when she returned home. But there would be recriminations.

Her heels clipped down the marble stairs, echoing around the vast hallway, and she paused as she saw Alessandro stood by the door, keys in hand, looking as desperate to get back to normal as she was.

Despite her bravado and knowing this was how it should be, her heart sank. If things had been different, if she didn't hold him responsible for Seb's accident, would they have been leaving as lovers too? She swallowed down the thought, straightened her shoulders and met his gaze head-on.

'It is time to go, no?' Her step faltered briefly at his heavily accented question, or was it a statement? Whatever it was, it was right. It was time to go, time to leave their passion within the luxury of this villa.

'It is,' she said and continued down the stairs, her chin held high. 'Time to get back to reality.'

CHAPTER TEN

CHARLIE HAD NEVER been so tense. The drive back to Milan had been almost silent, with the exception of a few attempts at polite conversation which had withered like flowers in parched earth.

She followed Alessandro into the apartment, trying not to notice the masculine scent of his aftershave, which trailed tantalisingly in his wake. She might have decided to distance herself from him but her body was having a hard time accepting it.

'I will book into a hotel, if you can recommend one close by.' She forced the words out, knowing it would be for the best. What they'd shared over the weekend had no place in the present and certainly not the future. She'd made it very clear to him she wasn't looking for more than a passing distraction and he'd made it easy, setting the time limit and taking her away.

But now they were back in Milan. Back with their problems. All she wanted was to get through the next two days and leave—but not until she'd found what she'd come to Italy for. Answers.

He turned to face her, his expression set in a hard mask, his eyes unreadable. 'That will not be necessary. The room you occupied on the first night is ready for you.'

Her room was ready for her. Didn't that tell her enough? He'd obviously instructed his housekeeper to put the few things she'd left behind back in the room Seb had once used, effectively removing her presence as a lover from his apartment. It was what she wanted, what she needed, so why did it hurt so much?

'Under the circumstances, it would be best if I stayed in a hotel.' She forced herself to believe her words. After all, she had little hope of him doing so if she didn't.

'No.' The word snapped from him as he tossed his car keys onto the marble worktop of the kitchen in an irritated fashion. 'The circumstances, as you so nicely put it, are that we are back after a weekend away. Our weekend of fun is over. It was not a for ever arrangement and nothing more than an affair.'

'All the more reason I stay in a hotel, don't you think?'

He looked at her sternly and the hard businessman he was showed through. 'You said it wasn't for ever, so why do you need to leave? The weekend affair we agreed on is over, now it is back to business.'

'Very well,' she relented, but knew she had to go back to England sooner than originally planned. Once their meeting at the test track was over tomorrow she would be on the next plane home. She'd walk out right now, if only she had the answers she needed.

Resigned to staying in his apartment one more night, she walked over to the windows, looking out at the Duomo. When she'd first arrived its magnificence had captured her imagination, now she just looked blankly at it. So much had changed in just two days, but each mile they'd driven on their way back to Milan had wiped out their weekend, kiss by kiss. They were back where they had started, but the simmer of sexual tension was now tinged with regret. At least for her it was; for Alessandro it had been replaced by indifference.

With a small sigh she turned and absently looked at the newspaper neatly placed on the ornate desk which occupied the corner of the living area. Already a photograph of her and Alessandro arriving at the launch party had a front-page position. The few words written beneath were incomprehensible and she turned the page. Maybe more of the launch would be on another page.

She froze.

The image which leapt to life from the page scorched her with hot memories. She and Alessandro were there, in the paper. Not the happy smiles of their arrival, but the passionate kiss against the car. The kiss that had happened after everyone had left.

She looked down at the picture, which sparked with passion, showing lovers locked in their own world, oblivious to everything, even the intrusion of the photographer. When and how had this been taken? Then her body chilled. Had Alessandro known of this? She recalled his intent as he'd taken her in his arms, the way he'd rendered all thought impossible as his lips had claimed hers.

He hadn't kissed her because he'd wanted to, because he'd been unable to resist, but to set up the perfect photo opportunity. One that would show to the world he wasn't in any way to blame for Seb's accident, that she and her family had more than given their stamp of approval to a car which had taken the life of a young driver.

'Did you know about this?' She closed the paper, unable to look at the sizzling photograph a moment longer. He approached the table, a frown on his face, and she looked up at him, hostility masking her shock.

'*Sì*. It is what I requested.' His calm words did little to soothe her jangled nerves. So he had set her up, used her like a pawn in his game. Not only did her presence at the launch suggest she didn't blame him or the Roselli company, it showed an intimate moment she had no wish for the world to see.

She blinked in surprise. 'What you requested?'

'Come, Charlotte—' his accent lavished her full name as he looked down at her, having glanced briefly at the paper '—a front-page photograph of us together is exactly the sort of advertisement I'd hoped for. You brought glamour and style to the occasion and, of course, your family's blessing.'

'What about this?' Furiously she dashed back the front page and watched as he looked down at the photo of their passionately hot kiss. 'Did you request this?'

He scanned the words beneath the photo, words she didn't understand. His silence was almost too much as he placed one palm on the desk, leaning down to read. The suspense of what it all meant was wrapping up with her initial anger until she thought she might explode. 'Did you?'

'No.' He shook his head, continuing to study the piece. 'Not this.'

'What does it say?' Anger overtook the suspense, filling her mind and her body. He'd set her up. He'd used her. Had that been his intention even as he'd entered her home and tried to convince her to go to Milan? She swallowed down the sour taste of deceit, determined not to let her feelings out. She had to remain calm.

He turned to look at her, his eyes locking with hers, but the brown of his were devoid of any emotion and her stomach lurched sickeningly. What had she done—to herself and to Seb? She'd sullied Seb's memory and her reputation into the bargain, falling into the worst trap imaginable.

Alessandro looked into the confusion of her eyes and tried to push back all the guilt he'd so far managed to keep at bay. She was angry, there wasn't any denying that, but she also looked scared and he didn't blame her.

'It says your passion shows your approval of the car which claimed the life of your brother.' He didn't translate word for word what had been written beneath that blisteringly hot photograph. He didn't think her anger would allow him enough time, so quickly he'd summed it up, leaving her to draw her own conclusions.

'What's next, Sandro? A photo of me, naked in your pool?' The accusation in her voice cut hard and deep. Did she really think he was that callous?

What could he say? This photograph alone went against everything he'd said to her that day in her cottage. He'd persuaded her to come to the launch in Milan, telling her Seb had wanted it. Now, thanks to a rogue photographer, something he would swiftly sort out, she thought he'd set her up.

'That will not be possible. You would not have been seen by anyone.' He pushed the image of her swimming naked aside. Now was not the time for such heated recollections.

'Damn you, Alessandro. You tricked me into swimming with nothing on, even had the nerve to come out in your trunks. What will the next headline say?' Her eyes were sharp, her expression strained as she pressed her lips tightly together, expectantly waiting for his answer.

He clenched his fists against the urge to hold her, pull her towards him and calm her. Instinctively he knew that would be the worst possible thing to do. She was pushing him further away, something he was certain she would have done even without the help of the newspaper report.

He glowered at her, his pulse racing erratically. 'I did not trick you at all. Your swim this morning will remain between us.'

'I don't believe you.' The words fired from her like bullets and she stepped closer to him, chin lifted and standing so tall with indignation he would hardly have had to lower his head to kiss her lips. The temptation was great, but he resisted.

'Have I lied to you, *cara*?'

Of course he'd lied to her. From the night of the accident and the moment he'd discovered the truth, the real reason Seb had crashed, he'd been lying to her. But they were lies to protect her and Seb, to keep the Warrington name out of the papers. They were lies he had to continue with. He'd made a promise, first to Seb, then to her father and he would keep both of those promises. He was a man of honour, whatever the cost.

'If you can set up publicity like this—' she flicked the paper, not taking her eyes from him '—then you are capable of anything, any lie, just to get what you want.'

He shook his head slowly, admiring the fire of anger emanating from her, not wanting to dampen the passion. But her passion was something he could no longer have; there were too many secrets, too many lies between them.

She made a sound that was like a growl and put her hands to her face, fingers splayed over her eyes. Then she dropped her hands, letting them fall with a slap against her as exasperation got the better of her. 'I was stupid ever to have believed you—or trusted you.'

He shook his head and reached for her, desperate to offer some comfort at least. She flinched, stepping back out of his reach.

Her eyes, angry and glittering, searched his face, finally narrowing in suspicion. 'You've done nothing but lie to me, Sandro; since the moment you arrived at my cottage it's been nothing but lies.'

'*Dio mio!* How can you say that?' Exasperation coursed through him and he pushed his fingers through his hair, unable to comprehend the circles she was spinning around him. Circles that made the temptation to tell the truth almost too much.

'Because of this.' She snatched the paper from the desk, shaking it in front of him. 'You used me. This has nothing at all to do with Seb. You're just trying to ease your conscience, ease your guilt over the accident.'

'My conscience is clear, Charlie.' It was—he was doing this for Seb.

'Charlotte.' Her voice cracked like a whip as she corrected his use of her name, glaring up at him. 'And once again you are lying. I don't believe Seb really asked for me to be at the launch. It was you who wanted me there all along; you were just preying on my emotions.'

'Seb did ask for you to be there; that much is true.' Her anger lacerated him but he stood firm against it, holding the truth inside.

'That much? So you are lying about something?' Her voice lowered in suspicion and she looked at him through narrowing eyes.

He had to think fast, keep ahead of her suspicions. 'I

have not lied, but certain things need to remain out of the limelight.'

'Like this?' She stabbed at the photo of them kissing and inwardly he breathed a sigh of relief. He'd almost blown it, almost revealed there were things he was holding back on. Her anger fizzed around him, preventing her from thinking in any rational kind of way.

Charlie couldn't take any more and tossed the offending newspaper back onto the desk, glaring angrily at the man she'd been stupid enough to fall in love with.

Fall in love?

Panic rushed through her faster than any car she'd ever driven. She couldn't love him. Not Alessandro Roselli. Not the man she blamed for Seb's accident and the man who had cruelly tricked her and used her emotional weakness for his own ends.

'You can't run and hide from this, Charlotte.' Alessandro's words filtered through the hazy fog of anger and shock that obscured just about everything. Hadn't he used that phrase earlier? Then he'd been referring to love. Now it was truth. She sensed he was keeping something from her—and she was sure it wasn't love, despite his murmured words of endearment just hours ago.

'I don't run.' She stood in the doorway of the room she'd used the first night at his apartment, swallowing down the bitter taste of reality, refusing to admit any such thing to him.

'Then what are you doing now, *cara*?' His words were softer, coaxing and cajoling. She was running, she was hiding; they both knew it, but she'd never admit it to him. Especially as it was love she was running from. She had no choice. This man didn't love her and never would.

He'd agreed to the weekend affair for exactly the same reasons as she had. He didn't do love.

'I'm not the only one running or hiding, Alessandro.' She spoke calmly even though her heart was thudding painfully in her chest and her knees were suddenly weak.

His eyes narrowed in suspicion. 'What is it you want to say, Charlotte?'

She ignored the way he used her name, the way his accent caressed it, keeping herself focused on what she really wanted. 'You are hiding the truth of Seb's accident.'

'I've told you all there is to tell,' he said, his eyes searching her face.

'We both know that's not exactly true.' She lifted her chin in a show of defiance, looked him in the eye and continued. 'You told me what you want me to know.'

'It wasn't the car, Charlotte.'

'So it was the driver. It was Seb.' She wasn't about to let this go now. Whatever the truth was, she had to know.

'It was. I'm sorry.' He reached out to her but she flinched.

'Don't.' The word was spat out as she battled with the idea that the accident had possibly been Seb's fault and that Alessandro, for whatever reason, wasn't going to tell her.

'You should talk to your father,' he said quietly, seemingly indifferent to her anger.

'I intend to. Right now.' She turned and moved into her room, purposefully keeping the door open. She wanted him to see her ring her father, watch whilst she asked for the full facts.

Angrily grabbing her phone from her bag, she dialled the number. It rang out before going to answerphone. But she wasn't beaten yet. 'If you will excuse me,' she said tartly as she began to shut the door, 'I have packing to do.'

With that she turned her back on him, resolutely shutting the door behind her. She dropped to sit on the bed, all the fight deflating from her. Outside, a nearby bell tower chimed the hour and she fought against threatening tears.

It was time to go home. Time to go back to her life and pick up the pieces that had been discarded the day she'd heard that her beloved brother had died. Just as her father had been trying to persuade her to do for many months. But she was sure he wouldn't have wanted her to fall in love with Alessandro Roselli and that was just what she'd done.

She thought of her mother, but she dismissed the idea of confiding in her. She was always too willing to blame the racing world for bringing her family down and tearing it apart. It would only give more weight to her argument against the whole lifestyle.

Resigned to the pain that Alessandro's betrayal had brought, she pulled out her tablet and searched for London-bound flights, booking on one the next evening. At least that would give her time to go back to the test track in the morning. She had one last thing to do before she went.

Then it would be goodbye and this time she meant it to be for ever.

Alessandro had watched her walk away, desperate to call her name, to make her turn and look at him. But it wouldn't do any good. They should never have become lovers and they could never be together. The hours they'd shared at his villa must be forgotten and he hoped they hadn't been tailed by any more photographers. It was bad enough her father might see the one of them kissing, but what if he saw her, cares cast aside, enjoying time with him? Not that they'd be shots of her at his pool—security was good at the villa—but they'd spent a lot of time out and about, doing tourist things.

She had paused in the doorway and turned to look at him, her green eyes large and full of sadness, and as they met his he'd felt the disappointment crash over him like a stormy sea.

'Goodnight, Alessandro.' Her voice had lost the anger and hard edge of earlier but he remained where he was, rooted to the marble floor, unable to decide what course of action was best.

'*Buonanotte*, Charlotte.' He couldn't stand and watch her any more, not if he wanted to keep his distance, so he turned and marched off to his study, a place he could lose himself in work. Behind him, he heard the bedroom door click softly shut but it sounded loud and piercing in his head, like a gunshot.

He didn't sit at his desk, didn't open his laptop and work. He couldn't. His mind was going over every single detail of the last few days. From the moment he'd seen her working in her garden to the hot passionate nights they'd shared.

What was the matter with him? He couldn't want her, couldn't have her, but he did. He wanted to wake up with her each and every day. He paced the room, stopping to look out across the rooftops of Milan as the sun slipped lower in the sky, casting its orange glow onto the old buildings.

When he'd promised Seb he'd look after her as if she was his own sister he had never imagined it would be so difficult. What would he do if the situation was reversed, if it was his sister involved with a man who would break her heart?

He clenched his hands into tight fists, the thought of anyone hurting or taking advantage of his sister filling him with rage like an aggressive and territorial lion. Yet that was what he'd done. He'd gone back on his promise to Seb, just by kissing Charlie and by taking her away to explore the passion that had sparked to life the instant they'd met—he hadn't looked after her, as he'd promised her father he would.

The only thing he had been able to do right was keep the truth from her and even the success of that seemed in doubt as she probed into every drawing and detail Seb had made, and asked the manufacturing team pointed questions about whether certain design developments had been made before or after the accident.

He closed his eyes and memories of the day Seb had told him the truth descended. He could still hear Seb, his voice weak as he lay in the hospital bed, begging him to keep the drink and drug problem from his sister.

Please, Sandro, don't tell her. It will break her heart. Whatever else you do, don't tell her.

Seb's words came back to him, as clear as if he was at his side again. Alessandro rubbed his hands together, the light pressure of Seb's grasp once again on his hands, and in his mind he could see Seb's face, so like Charlie's, begging him to keep his secret.

Had he known then he wasn't going to make it?

With a furious curse, Alessandro strode back out of his office. He couldn't let Charlie sit there alone, worrying about everything. Outside her door, he paused. Was he doing the right thing? He was normally so decisive, so sure of what needed to be done, but where this woman was concerned he was the opposite.

He knocked on the door and almost instantly it was opened. 'You can't stay in there all night.' He attempted light-hearted chatter, something she'd proved to be very good at over the weekend. The frosty glare she sent him told him that he hadn't yet mastered that art.

'We could go out for dinner.' He didn't like her silence, as cold as her eyes, and he had the feeling he was in ever-deepening quicksand.

She raised a haughty brow at him. 'So you can set me up again, get yet another photo of us together?'

'Charlotte…' He stepped closer but she moved back, using the door as a shield.

'No, Sandro. I'm not prepared to take the risk. We should never have spent the weekend together.' She moved further behind the door. Hiding from him, from what they'd shared.

She was right and he moved away, not missing the relief on her face. 'I knew nothing about that photograph and I'm sorry it has upset you.'

'Please, I don't want to talk about it now.' Her green eyes looked moist and guilt tugged at him. He wasn't doing a very good job of looking after her at all.

He nodded his acceptance of her reason, knowing he was only making the whole situation worse. 'I will find whoever it was who took the photo and personally deal with him.'

'It won't take away the fact that you used me and Seb to promote the car, to clear its reputation and your name.'

'I have no need to clear my name, Charlotte.'

'You do to me.' Those words stung him as they hit

home and finally his business sense returned. He needed to step back, assess the situation and plan his next move.

'Very well, I will.' He walked away, not stopping to see how his words had been received. If she wanted proof he'd find it, but how could he do so without giving away Seb's secret—or his true feelings for her?

CHAPTER ELEVEN

CHARLIE HAD SECRETLY hoped Alessandro would have gone to wherever it was he went that first night, but as she'd emerged from her room earlier that morning he'd been preparing coffee, looking so handsome she'd actually stopped to take in every detail, from his expensive charcoal suit to the shiny black shoes.

Now, enclosed in his car, painfully aware of every move he made as he drove, she wished she'd taken the early morning flight to London. Instead, she'd been lured by the opportunity to be at the test track again, hoping she would find out what Alessandro was keeping from her about Seb's accident. Because something was, of that she was certain.

'I have a meeting at lunchtime.' His accented voice jolted her from her thoughts as they drove. She wanted to look at him, savour his handsome profile, but couldn't allow herself to. She'd imprinted more than enough images into her mind during their weekend. It was time to stop, to let go of something that could never be and should never have happened.

'I need to be at the airport this evening, so I will arrange a taxi.' Her words, though flowing and easy, didn't feel it. She was sure it sounded as if she was stumbling over each one and she ran her fingers through her hair nervously.

He turned to look at her just at the moment she gave in to temptation to look at him and for a split second their gazes met, then he focused back on the road as they turned into the test track.

'You said you weren't running.' His voice was deep and stern, but she fixed her attention on the workshops as he pulled up and parked. The engine fell silent and her heartbeat thumped so loudly she was sure he would hear it.

'I'm not running.' The angry words flew from her before she had time to think. 'I'm going back to my life, to the things I did before Seb's accident. It's what he would have wanted. The only good thing that has come out of this visit.'

She got out of the car, anxious to put some distance between herself and Alessandro. It didn't matter how much her body craved his, she had to remember what he'd done, how he'd manipulated her to get what he wanted in an attempt to assuage his guilt and clear his name.

She all but marched off towards the workshops, hearing the driver's door shut behind her then feeling his presence closing the distance as he caught up with her. Her pulse leapt as she reached the door but, before she could do anything, he pressed his palm against it, preventing her from opening it, stopping her from escaping him.

'That is all? There must be something else you want to accuse me of?' His voice deepened and she raised her eyes to meet his, determined not to let him know how much he affected her.

'"Something else" being the fact that you virtually sold me to the press for your own gain?' She hurled the words at him, indignation spiking her into action. 'Or is it the fact that you seduced me? You let me believe I was doing all this for Seb, when it wasn't. It was for you.'

His brows lifted suggestively, his expression of smug satisfaction almost too much to tolerate. 'As I recall, *cara*, it was you who seduced me.'

She clenched her hands into tight fists, digging her nails into her palms. Pain made her gasp, emotional and physical pain. It was just what she needed to remind her of what was at stake. Not only her brother's good name and her reputation, but her heart.

'Don't flatter yourself. What I did, I did for Seb.' She flung the first words that came to mind at him, then bit down on any more. She didn't want to let him know how much she was hurting, how hard she had fallen for him. He must never know. It would give him the trump card.

'Not because you wanted to, because you couldn't resist the fire that leapt to life between us the moment we met?' He loomed over her, trapping her and forcing her to confront this.

'Okay. So I couldn't resist the *fire*, as you put it. But that fire is well and truly out now.' She pushed his hand aside and opened the door, thankful to see mechanics and drivers busy at work. He'd never pursue her now, not so publicly.

Behind her, she heard him talking rapidly in Italian, heard his footsteps as he marched across the spotless floor of the workshop. She had no idea what he was saying, but it seemed that everyone was ready to do as he asked, waiting for their instruction.

At a loss as to just what she should do now they were here again and with so many curious glances her way, she went over to a car she hadn't seen here last time. Obviously it was a new prototype for yet another road sports car. The black paintwork shone beneath the bright lights of the workshop and the elegant curves of the wing of the car caught her eye. It was very different from the flashy red one her brother had played a part in. That had been exactly what she would have expected from Seb.

This had more style, as if designed for speed and comfort. The grille at the front was far more sedate, more classical and looked much less aggressive than Seb's. It was still low and sporty, its power subtly evident, but with a sophistication that made her immediately think of Alessandro. Was this car all his work?

As he spoke to his team, Alessandro watched Charlie walking towards the car. He saw her head tilt to one side in contemplation as she stood by the front wing, looking along the line of the car. He could almost hear her mind working, assessing the car's capabilities.

With a few final instructions, he left his team and walked over to where Charlie was now looking inside the latest prototype. This was his design; everything he'd ever wanted in a car was going into it.

'This looks like it has the potential to be a car in a league of its own.' Her voice oozed enthusiasm that no amount of animosity between them could disguise. 'Who designed it?'

He wasn't about to tell her it was his work, not so soon after the launch of Seb's car. He'd never intended for her to see it, worried she'd think he'd moved onto a new project before Seb's car had even been launched. 'A team effort.'

'A good one,' she said, running her fingers along it, just as she had done with the first car. 'A really good one. Black suits it.'

He couldn't listen to her praise for his work, even if she didn't know it as such. This was the woman he'd done nothing but try to protect, the woman who heated his blood, making him want her more than any other. Now she hated him and was about to walk out of his life. But he couldn't stop her.

'I have arranged for Giovanni to take you back to the apartment to collect your belongings and then on to the airport.' He had to keep the conversation on neutral territory. If she continued to talk about the car, he knew his passion for it would show, just as his passion for her could so easily come out.

'Yes, of course, thank you.' Her curt tone reminded him of her earlier anger and he knew he was doing the right thing. If he stayed any longer he would tell her anything to disperse that anger which hovered around them and relight the passion they'd shared at the weekend.

The best thing he could do was go. Walk away and never look back.

'*Arrivederci*, Charlotte.'

Before he lost control of his emotions he stalked from the workshop, his footsteps echoing loudly across the floor. He could feel her eyes on him, feel the intensity of her gaze, and he reminded himself of her warning that first night they'd spent together.

I don't do for ever.

Audaciously, he'd echoed her warning, using his first marriage to back up the claim, but had he really meant it? At that moment he had, but now, as he strode out of her life for ever, he knew that it was no longer true. He wanted for ever and he was turning his back on the one woman he wanted. Truly wanted.

As the sunlight dazzled him and the door shut behind

him he knew it was over. Whatever it was between them, it was gone. All that was left was his one-sided desire for a woman who thought he'd set her up and who held him responsible for her brother's accident.

This really was goodbye.

He got into his car and reversed hastily backwards, tyres squealing in protest, then he sped off, wanting only to get as far away from her as possible. The sooner she returned to England, the better.

Embarrassment washed over Charlie as she suddenly became aware of someone standing at her side. She was still looking at the closed door, could still hear the screech of tyres that suggested Alessandro couldn't get away fast enough.

'*Scuzi,*' the man at her side said; thankfully, he seemed unaware of her emotional turmoil. 'We will leave for Milan in one hour, but you may wait in Signor Roselli's office.'

She smiled at his heavily accented English, as appealing as Sandro's, but it didn't have the same effect on her. It didn't melt her from the inside, making her want to close her eyes as he spoke. 'Thank you; I will be ready.'

She turned and walked to the office, nerves cascading over her. This was the one place she hadn't been able to look for evidence of Alessandro's guilt. Was this where she could find out the secret he was keeping?

She opened the door and immediately felt Alessandro's presence. How could he affect her so, even when he wasn't anywhere near her? She took a gulp of air into her lungs, focusing on what she'd come to Italy for in the first place. Proof of who was to blame for her brother's death.

She sat in the chair at his desk, unable to shake the

feeling of unease, and glanced out at the workshop to see the team working on other cars. Her presence at Alessandro's desk didn't seem to worry them and she relaxed a bit.

At first she flicked through some design drawings, spread out and pushed to one side, then turned her attention to the files on the shelf above the desk. One stood out, as if calling for her attention, and she reached for it, feeling more and more like a spy.

The first few sections held nothing but engine reports but, as she flicked through the file, one unmarked section at the back caught her attention. She opened the page and looked at the photo of the car, a grey prototype the same as she'd driven, its specification listed below. With trembling fingers she turned the page.

Accident Report.

The words rushed at her and her stomach lurched sickeningly. She blinked, as if doing so would erase the truth that was set out in black and white before her.

'Oh, Seb,' she whispered and closed her eyes, but the words were imprinted there already. 'Why didn't you tell me?'

The question bounced around the office and she glanced at the team beyond the window, sure they would have heard it. Satisfied they hadn't, she looked back at the page, the words still a shock.

'Driver error.' She whispered the words, then paused before continuing. 'The driver was found to have significant levels of alcohol and drugs in his system.'

She leant her elbows on the desk and pressed her hands against her face. Could this be true? Could she believe it? She read the rest of the report, each point stating the car was in good working order.

With a heavy heart she closed the file and pushed it away from her, not wanting to read another word of it and wishing Alessandro was here to explain why he was using her brother as a scapegoat.

Alessandro had already shown how calculating he could be with the photo of the launch. Had this accident report been fabricated too?

The man she'd spoken to earlier knocked on the office door, dragging her from her thoughts. 'Now we shall leave.' He'd discarded his overalls and was every inch the Italian in his jeans and leather jacket, but he was far from the Italian she really wanted. The one she hated and loved.

Did that mean it wasn't hate? Or did it mean it wasn't love? Two powerfully strong emotions and they were tearing her apart. So what did she want it to be? Hate would mean staying in the past, never moving on, and she couldn't do that any longer. Love would mean forgiveness.

She stood and smiled, pushing her jumbled thoughts about all she'd just read to the back of her mind. 'Yes, I have a plane to catch.'

'Sì, sì,' he said as he walked towards the same door Sandro had left from an hour earlier. Where was he now? In his meeting, not giving her a second thought? Or was he relieved she would now be about to leave Italy and his life?

She pondered those questions as the car left the test track and within a few minutes they were on the busy roads and heading back to Milan. Charlie sat in silence, watching the countryside flash past, so caught up in her emotions she didn't even give the car they were in any thought. Her mind was with the man she loved. A man she should never have fallen in love with.

'Goodbye is hard, no?' The driver spoke, dragging her from her despondent thoughts.

'Yes,' she said before she'd realised it, adding quickly, 'but only because it is also saying goodbye to my brother.'

She hadn't expected this personal conversation and was glad to see they had reached Milan. Very soon she would be on her own, which was what she craved more than anything right now.

Thankfully, the traffic congestion took the driver's attention away from the conversation and she smiled at his exasperated sighs as they negotiated the streets towards Alessandro's apartment.

'I will get a taxi from here,' she said as she got out of the car outside the old building that she still couldn't believe was home to such a modern and powerful man.

'No, my instruction was to bring you here,' he said as he pressed the required numbers into the keypad, obviously used to letting himself in. Was this Sandro's right-hand man? Could he tell her the truth about the accident report? 'Then we go to the airport.'

She sensed he wanted to deliver her to the airport as soon as possible. Maybe that would be for the best. Alessandro had obviously asked that she be escorted all the way, to ensure she had actually left. 'Thank you. I will only be a few minutes.'

The driver handed her a key and she rushed up the stairs, into the apartment, trying not to think of all that had happened there in such a short time. Not wanting to linger, she grabbed her already packed case and left. As she shut the door, she closed her eyes briefly, pushing memories of being with Sandro to the back of her mind. But it wasn't easy. Even though she knew she shouldn't, she loved him. How did you switch that off? Finally, she went back down to where the driver was waiting.

Moments later they were once again in the traffic, heading towards the airport. She kept her eyes firmly fixed ahead of her as she thought of all that had happened. Would Seb have approved of her and Sandro—would he have been happy they were together?

'Did you know my brother?' She asked the question casually. This would be the last chance she got to talk to anyone from the test track and she wasn't going to waste this opening, no matter how small.

'*Sì*, he was a good driver, a very good driver, but things got too much for him. We tried to help.' His attention was kept on the busy road, his words had been said in such a distracted way, he obviously hadn't thought about them.

So it *was* true. She tried hard to keep her voice normal when all she wanted to do was scream and shout, but she couldn't. It was obvious this man thought she knew all about it.

'I didn't realise you'd helped him too,' she said as calmly as possible, luring him into divulging more of the truth. Each word he said confirmed all she'd seen in the report.

'Alessandro helped most, but I was also there that night and it became my secret too.'

What kind of sister had she been, not to have noticed Seb's problems? Guilt spiked cruelly at her. Not a hint of what she'd read had reached the press. Part of her clung desperately to the hope that this was because it was all part of an elaborate fabrication by Alessandro. She didn't want to believe it of Seb; it was too painful.

'Sorry, I didn't mean to upset you,' he said and she

opened her eyes to see him looking at her whilst they'd stopped at a red light.

'I do still find it upsetting, sorry.' She dabbed the corner of her eye with her fingertips, glad when the lights changed and they moved off, taking his gaze from her. Did he know he'd walked into her trap?

'The airport,' Giovanni said as the terminal buildings came into view and the relief in his voice would have been comical if she hadn't been so strung out by his conversation.

He pulled into a space and got out, but she wasn't done yet. Whatever he knew, she had to find out. Good or bad, she just had to hear it. Could it be any worse than all she had just read?

'Please—' she put her hand on his arm, using all her feminine charm, bombarding him with questions. 'You said you were there too. How bad were Seb's problems? Did they really cause the accident?'

He looked at his watch. 'You will be late for your flight.'

'Please.'

He sighed and then put his hand over hers as it clutched at his arm. 'He'd been drinking heavily that day—and the drugs…' He shrugged, his face apologetic. 'They made him wild, irrational. We couldn't stop him.'

'We?' she whispered, scared to let go of his arm in case she fell to the floor with shock.

'*Sì*, Signor Roselli and myself. Of course, we said nothing after the accident that would blacken your brother's name.' He took her hand and held it between both of his and looked at her, genuine concern in his face. 'I thought you knew.'

'I did,' she bluffed, not wanting to tell him she'd only

just discovered what now appeared to be the truth. 'It hurts to hear it again. I'm sorry.'

'Now you must go; you will be late for your plane.' The relief on his face only cemented the bad images of her brother, under the influence of drink and drugs, driving the car. How had she not known he had problems? How had he managed to hide it so well from her?

'Yes, my plane.' She forced the words out slowly. They sounded hollow to her ears, but she picked up her small case and walked away from this man and the truth that had shattered everything she'd held dear.

Once inside the building she ran to the Ladies, her insides churning alarmingly. She splashed cold water over her face, not caring about her make-up, just wanting to stave off the nausea. She looked at her reflection in the mirror, as if for reassurance.

Could it be true?

She didn't want it to be, but certain things were slotting into place, suddenly becoming much clearer. Seb had dropped out of the final races of last year's season, claiming injury, but had dismissed it as they'd spoken on the phone, telling her to stop mothering him. Had he had a problem even then?

'No, it can't be true... Sandro would have said something.' She spoke aloud to her shocked reflection.

Then it hit her like a brick being hurled through the air. Alessandro Roselli had been covering for her brother, not to keep Seb's good name but to save his own damn reputation. To do that he'd dragged hers through the mire too. That photograph of them kissing backed it all up.

She pressed her palms to her face and took in a deep breath. There was only one person other than Alessandro who could confirm this.

Her father. He'd flown out to Italy as soon as news of the accident had reached them. Seb had died just hours after he'd arrived, but her father would know if drugs and alcohol had been the cause.

She frowned at herself in the mirror. Why hadn't he told her? Why had he kept it a secret and then still supported Alessandro? There was only one answer. It wasn't true and he knew nothing of the cover-up story that was being used. The report must be a cover-up. It had even been left in easy view, just waiting for her to find it.

Frantically she searched in her bag for her phone and with shaking fingers pressed call on her father's number.

'Hello, Charlie.' Her father sounded cautious and not his usual self.

'Is it true, Dad?' She didn't waste any time on pleasantries.

On the other end of the phone her father sighed, then horrifyingly she knew it was. She clutched the washbasin with her free hand, watching the colour drain from the shocked face with hollowed eyes which looked back at her from the mirror.

'Oh, Dad, why didn't you tell me?' She shook her head in disbelief, feeling ever more disconnected from the woman staring back at her in the mirror.

'You didn't need to know. Where are you, Charlie?' She could hear the restrained panic in her father's voice and her heart clenched.

'On my way home. We'll talk soon. I have to check in or I'll miss the flight.'

'Charlie?'

'Yes, Dad.'

'See you soon.'

Her heart constricted as if a snake were torturing her,

squashing every last beat from her, and she couldn't say anything else. Instead she cut the connection before she cried, before she lost complete control. That was something she had to save until later. Much later. Right now she had a plane to catch.

CHAPTER TWELVE

ALESSANDRO STALKED AROUND the check-in desks, scanning the throng of passengers, but with each passing minute his impatience increased. Where was she? He still didn't want to accept what had drawn him to the airport instead of his meeting, but when the call from Giovanni had come through he'd been glad he was only minutes away. He couldn't let her leave without talking to her, checking she was all right.

The queue for the London flight was diminishing fast and his agitation increased. Giovanni had told him she'd acted as if she'd known everything. But how? He stalked over to the desk again, the operator who'd denied him passenger information earlier giving him a suspicious look.

Maledizione! Where was she? It was as if she'd just vanished. That or she'd got through security so quickly because she hated him. He didn't blame her. He hated himself right now. He should have found a way to tell her, found a way around the promise he'd made to Seb and her father. Hadn't he done just that so he could have a weekend affair with her? So why hadn't he been able to do the same with the truth of the accident?

Angrily he stabbed his fingers through his hair and

marched away from the check-in desk. Even his charm had deserted him as he'd tried to find out if Charlie had checked in or even what flight she had booked. Now what? Book on the next flight to England?

Suddenly his attention was caught as he saw a woman hurriedly leaving the terminal building and quickly he raced after her. His heart beat like a drum with the hope that it was Charlie, that she'd changed her mind, but once outside in the evening sunlight he couldn't see her. Taxis pulled away in rapid succession. He had no idea if she was in one—or if it had been her.

More deflated than he'd ever been in his adult life, he stood as everyone bustled past him, hurrying to or from the airport, all seemingly happy. The roar of jet engines as they soared into the sky sounded like a death knell. Each time he heard one, his heart died a bit more. She could be on board.

But what if she wasn't?

What if the woman he'd seen, the one he'd wanted to be Charlie, was her? Where would she go?

Realisation hit him. There was only one place she'd go to be alone with memories of her brother. One place she'd be sure he or his staff wouldn't be. But should he go there and disturb her?

The answer was simple. He had to. He had to find her and tell her everything, explain why he'd kept the secret. She already hated him. He didn't have anything to lose. He'd rather she hurled accusations at him than disappear with a revelation like that on her mind. Purposefully, he strode back to the car park and set about the tedious task of negotiating Milan's traffic.

The drive to the hotel proved almost impossible as a minor bump had closed the most direct route, forcing him down narrow side streets and testing his patience to the full. All the while he imagined her there, with the car that had been at the launch, alone and hurting. Hurt he'd caused.

With a big sigh of relief he pulled up at the hotel, jumped from the car, tossed the keys at the doorman for parking and went through the revolving doors. Slowly he made his way towards the room that had become a temporary showroom for the sleek red beast that had consumed Seb so utterly. Benign and innocuously it sat there, its secrets hidden within its beauty. The silence of the room hit him. Quickly he looked around, but couldn't see her.

Then a small movement caught his attention at the far end of the room. She was there, sitting at a table with her back to him. Relief rushed through him at top speed. Cautiously he moved towards her.

Charlie sat, totally lost in thought, the feeling of betrayal stinging more than a swarm of bees could. The two men she loved had betrayed her. She looked down at the cup of coffee, now very cold, as if it could answer her problems, tell her what to do.

Why had she come here? Why hadn't she just got on the plane and left? Because she needed answers and she couldn't go anywhere until she got them. The only problem was that Alessandro held those answers—and he'd just driven away from her at top speed.

With a sigh she looked at the sleek red car. The secrets locked within it had only just started to slip from its powerful clutches.

'Why, Seb?' She whispered the question aloud but silence came back at her, a painful echo.

Suddenly a sizzling sensation hurtled down her spine

and she knew she wasn't alone. There was only one person who had that effect on her. The man she hated and loved with equal passion. Alessandro Roselli.

'Haven't you done enough damage already?' The venomous tone of her words surprised her as much as him, but she kept her back to him, looking resolutely at the car.

'I did what I had to.' He came to stand beside her but still she didn't look at him.

'Of course you did.' The crispness of each word was colder than a frosty morning. 'You did exactly what you needed to do to keep your name from being dragged through the dirt.'

'You've got it all wrong, Charlie.'

'Charlotte,' she snapped and looked up at him, confused by the anger and the raw betrayal which filled her. 'And I haven't got it wrong at all.'

'It isn't what you think.' He moved to stand in front of her, obscuring her view of the car, her link to her brother.

She stood up and moved past him, towards the car, anything other than stay beneath his intense gaze. 'So you deny you brought me here under the pretence it was what Seb wanted, seduced me so that you could get the ultimate photograph for the press and then keep the truth of Seb's problems from me.'

'I never meant to hurt you, Charlie.'

'Charlotte!' She whirled round and stood to face him, catching her breath at the hard look in his eyes. Where had the loving man she'd spent the weekend with gone—or was that also part of his game plan?

'I can see you aren't prepared to listen to anything I have to say.' He sat down in the chair she'd just vacated but couldn't disguise the tension and irritation in his body.

'Too right I'm not. Everything else you've said has been lies.' Memories of the last time they'd made love, the tender words of Italian he'd whispered to her, slipped into her mind and she realised they too must have been lies.

She turned from him and closed her eyes against the pain. She'd opened her heart to him, given herself and her love, only to find he'd used her as a scapegoat. Behind her, his silence confirmed everything she thought and, despite the pain, she had to hear it all. Maybe then she'd stop loving him.

Purposefully, she returned to the table, pulled out another chair and sat down. She was going to get to the bottom of this if it was the last thing she did. Part of her didn't want to hear it, didn't want to accept that her brother had become embroiled in such a world. But she had to know—everything.

'I saw the report, Sandro.' He didn't say anything but his firm gaze held hers.

'Giovanni told me, or rather confirmed, about the drink…' her breath hitched in her throat and she could hardly form the words as she sat at the table with him '…and drugs. Why didn't you?'

He leant forward in the chair, his elbows resting on his knees and his hands clasped together. His expression was one of concern as he looked up at her and his eyes met hers. 'It was what your father wanted.'

She shook her head. 'Don't use my father. He would never keep such a thing from me.' Even as she said the words she recalled the brief call she'd made to him at the airport. The silence as she'd challenged him. He hadn't admitted anything, but his silence had been deafening.

'Have you spoken to him?'

'At the airport, yes.' She looked into his eyes and the

fight began to slip from her, receding like the tide going out. 'I don't understand why he'd do that.'

'He didn't want you to know. He wanted to keep your memories of Seb untainted.' The gentleness of his voice was almost too much and she shook her head rapidly, wanting to deny everything she was hearing. Her father might have wanted to protect her, but what about Sandro? What were his motives?

'And what about you? Why did you lie to me?' Fierceness exploded from deep within her, a need to shield herself from the fallout of his deceit.

'What do you think would have happened if the press had found out?' His firm question almost knocked the breath from her as she realised the implications of what he said. Shock sank in, washing away the strength she'd just found, and he reached out and took her hand.

Her gaze darted to his tanned hand covering hers, the dusting of dark hair which disappeared under the cuff of his shirt. She could feel the heat from his touch infusing her, awakening all she wished to suppress.

She pulled her hand from under his at the same time as jumping up from her chair, making it scrape noisily on the marble floor. 'What would the press do?' She gulped the words out, hardly daring to form an answer to that question.

'What would they do with a story like that, Charlie?' He sat back in his chair, all cool, calm sophistication, but the glittering hardness of his eyes told her he knew exactly what they would do.

'That's easy,' she retaliated harshly. 'They'd ruin your reputation.'

He stood up, his body full of restraint and composure, but ice had filled his eyes, chilling her to the core.

'Whatever you may think, Charlotte, I have done nothing wrong.'

'You lied—to me and the world.'

'Damn you, don't you see?' He strode towards her, his face full of anger, the angles sharp. 'I wasn't protecting myself. I was protecting Seb—and you.'

In exasperation he flung his hands up and marched towards the gleaming car and, before she could say anything more, he turned to look at her across the room, but it might as well have been across a continent.

The first bubbles of anger rose up like a shaken bottle of champagne and her breathing deepened, but still she couldn't find her voice. How could he stand there and use Seb again, after all that had happened?

Just like she'd seen happen on the podium, the champagne burst out, showering her with fizzy drops of anger. 'How dare you hide behind my brother's reputation after engineering that photo of us kissing? Right here.' She pointed at the car as she crossed the floor to him, her footsteps hard and forceful. 'That photo alone was enough to clear your name. That kiss absolved you of any blame and now it's splurged all over the papers and probably the Internet too.'

He looked taken aback by her outburst but he didn't move. He stood tall and strong as she moved closer and closer, stoking the fiery anger higher and higher.

'I didn't force you to kiss me.' His cool words poured cold water over the flames and for a moment she just looked at him. She couldn't answer that, couldn't offer any defence, because he was right. He hadn't forced her. She had wanted that kiss so badly.

'You manipulated the situation.'

'By "the situation" I assume you mean the heated pas-

sion that raged between us from the moment we met?'
Suddenly the frozen depths of his eyes heated, so intense
they almost scorched her skin.

'That was just a convenient smokescreen.' Despite
the bravado, her voice trembled—and she hated herself for it.

She should never have given in to the heady desire
that had filled her body and starved her heart. Somewhere deep down she was sure she'd known that, but at
the time she'd known she would regret not tasting the desire which had been between them from the beginning.
She hadn't wanted to spend the rest of her life wondering *what if?* Now she was going to have to live with the
fact that not only had she been used so callously, she'd
fallen in love with the man who'd lied and cheated his
way into her heart.

Alessandro saw the emotions play out across her face
like a movie. Shock, denial, hatred. They were all there.
Even passion and longing, but not once did he see anything which resembled what he felt for her.

'So you don't deny it existed.' It was like walking a
tightrope. At any moment he could lose his balance and
fall. He held his nerve, calling on every bit of control he
had. 'You don't deny you wanted me when we kissed
right here.'

She looked at him, her eyes saying things he hoped
were true but her lips stony silent. He moved forward but
she stayed rooted to the spot.

'Don't run from the passion which exists between us,
cara.'

'I don't need to run from that. I can handle the passion.' Finally words tumbled from her with a force so

fierce he drew in a sharp breath. 'But it wasn't passion, Sandro. It was lust.'

He remained still and silent, sensing there was more, but right now she was visibly shaking with emotions so powerful. He watched her beautiful face as she closed her eyes against them, her long lashes spreading across the paleness of her skin. His heart twisted and it was all he could do not to reach for her and hold her against him.

'Lust I can deal with.' She spoke again, her voice firm and resolute. 'What I want to run from is your deceit.'

'My deceit?' He knew what she was referring to and regret piled on top of the guilt because he hadn't had the strength to find a way to tell her everything. This guilt was intensified because he'd pushed aside the promises he'd made to spend the weekend with her, to indulge the lust, as she called it.

'You lied to me, kept the truth from me, then used the spark of lust which was there, even at my cottage, to lure me to the launch night. To this very spot, and engineer the photograph that would prove to the world my family had forgiven you.'

Slowly he shook his head. How was he ever going to prove he had nothing to do with the photo, that it was just a lucky shot for the photographer? 'I know how it must look,' he began, but she cut his words off.

'What would Seb say if he knew what you have done, how you tricked me so cruelly? What would he say about us?'

A glimmer of hope trickled through him at her mention of 'us' and he gave voice to the conclusion he'd reached just a few hours ago. 'Maybe it was what he wanted all along.'

'How can you know that? Much less say it.' She turned

from him and for a moment he thought she was going to
walk away. He knew he couldn't go after her again. As
she stood, lost in thought, he moved towards her cautiously.

'Seb made me promise to look after you,' he said softly
and saw her shoulders rise and fall with each breath she
took. 'Not just that night after the accident, but several
times before. He played on my loyalty to my sister.'

'That doesn't mean anything.' She turned her head
slightly and he saw her profile as she looked distractedly
at the floor. Pain and hurt lingered on her face.

Her voice trembled and finally she turned to look at
him and, like the moment he'd unveiled the car, he saw
her with all her vulnerabilities exposed, all her barriers
down. 'You should still have told me about the drink and
the drugs. I had a right to know. I don't care about anything else, not even that stupid photo, but that was the
one thing you shouldn't have kept from me. Not even
because of a promise.'

He fought really hard against the urge to hold her, to
soothe all the pain, but right now he didn't dare. If she
ran again it would be for ever; he knew that much.

'Seb was beside himself, desperate that you should
never know, and I made the promise to keep him calm.
By the time your father arrived I was firmly fixed into
it. I'm sorry, Charlotte. I had no choice at all.'

As he spoke he thought of why he was here, what had
made him race to the airport in the first place. All he'd
been able to think about was taking her in his arms and
holding her, comforting her as he had that night in his
office. He should have told her the truth then but she'd
been too fragile, so he'd kept the secret.

How did you tell the woman who had just kissed you

with such passion news like that? Selfishly, he'd kept silent, enjoying the spark that had been lit between them. Now he knew that spark wasn't just lust, not for him at least. It was love.

He loved her. He didn't just desire her—he loved her, so much it hurt.

He needed Charlie, or Charlotte, as he thought of her, when passion blazed in her eyes. She was Charlie behind the wheel of a car and Charlotte in his arms, and he loved her—completely and unconditionally.

Charlie thought of what Alessandro had just said, the situation he'd been forced into. He had kept that promise to Seb. He hadn't been the one who had told her the truth, so did that make the whole situation any more honourable?

She closed her eyes against the pain of finally knowing the truth and the knowledge that it was time to move on, time to leave her garden of sanctuary and live life as Seb would have wanted her to do. As the realisation dawned, Alessandro put his arms around her and pulled her close. This was where she wanted to be, in the arms of the man she loved, but that still didn't mean he loved her. He'd agreed to her terms of 'not for ever' as they'd stood in his apartment on that first night, had even taken her away to his villa to enable him to distance the affair from everything else.

'Why are you here, Sandro?' She looked up at him, hardly daring to hope. But he *was* here, holding her so tenderly—didn't that mean something?

'I couldn't let you go, not without explaining.' His face was full of concern, but she searched for more, desperate to find even a trace of something else.

'So, *cara*. Why are *you* here?' The term of endearment, said in the most gently seductive tone, gave her just enough hope. 'You know the truth yet you are still in my arms.'

She looked up at him, wondering if he'd see the reason shining from her eyes. He'd been protecting her from the truth all along. She didn't hate him. She loved him. He had honoured Seb's promise at great cost to himself and that just made her love him even more, but could she say those words aloud?

'I couldn't go, not yet.' She lowered her lashes, not wanting to see what was in his eyes, not daring to hope. 'I needed the truth.'

Was it her imagination or had his arms loosened slightly around her? She swallowed hard and took a deep breath.

'And now that you have it?' He let go of her, walked towards the car, pressing his palm against the fiery red paintwork. 'Now that you know the truth, will you return to your life, move on?'

It was as if he was letting her go, allowing her to walk away and find her destiny. Did he not know *he* was her destiny? That if he didn't want her she didn't have a life to return to? She couldn't stop her limbs from trembling and couldn't find the words to tell him what he needed to know.

'Sandro, I...' Her shaky voice deserted her; she began to feel suffocated, as if she couldn't get enough breath into her lungs.

He looked over at her, his brow furrowed into a frown, but it was his eyes that finally showed her what she needed to see. His gaze darted to her as her words died as she saw it. In the dark depths she saw the same hopelessness which filled her heart and she knew she had to say those words. With a jolt she also realised why he wouldn't say them first.

I don't do for ever.

Her words on that first night they'd made love drifted through her mind like a haunting spirit. 'Sandro, I have to say this. I can't go without telling you.'

Slowly she walked towards him, her heart pounding so hard in her chest she almost couldn't think. He looked away from her and jabbed his fingers through his hair, turning his body away, deflecting anything she might try to say. Had she misread the hope in his eyes?

'Just go, Charlotte. If that's what you want to do, there is nothing more to say.' She saw his jaw tense as he gritted his teeth, felt the raw pain and knew she hadn't misread anything.

'I love you, Sandro.' The silence that suddenly shrouded them was so heavy she almost couldn't stand and for a moment he didn't move, frozen in time.

When he did, it was such a small movement, disbelief all over his face as he stepped towards her. In slow motion he reached for her hands, taking them in his and drawing her towards him. She was desperate for him to speak, to say something, but he just looked at her, his hands firmly wrapped around hers.

'*Ti amo, ti amo...*' His seductive accent caressed each word and his lips, which had moments ago been pressed into a hard line, smiled. Wonder and happiness sparked from his eyes and she fell into his embrace, feeling as if she had come home. She'd found where she needed to be to move on in life.

Right here in the arms of the man she loved.

* * * * *

'I'm tougher than you think, Boss.'

Luke smiled. 'You haven't called me that in a long time. I think I like it.'

The wrestling stopped. The air in the taxi turned a little thick. Amy stopped moving and stilled her hand where it rested, on his thigh. High on his thigh. His hands stilled too.

'You like it when I call you Boss?' Amy's eyes skirted to Luke's lips. They were slightly parted. She wanted to kiss him. She wanted to touch him. She wanted to do bad, bad things to him.

'I like you having your hand there.' Luke's voice was deep and he shifted his leg a little, underneath where her hand sat.

There was no mistaking what he wanted and how he felt. And it sent a thrilling ripple through her to think that she could finally have what she'd wanted all those years ago. Time alone with Luke. Luke wanting her. It was everything she'd wanted as an eighteen-year-old and she could finally take it—if she wanted.

Jennifer Rae was raised on a farm in Australia by salt-of-the-earth farming parents. All she ever wanted to do was write, but she didn't have the confidence to share her stories with the world until, working as a journalist, she interviewed a couple of romance-writers. Finally the characters who had been milling around Jennifer's head since her long years on the farm made sense, and she realised romance was the genre for her and sat down to release her characters.

Books by Jennifer Rae

Who's Calling the Shots?
Sex, Lies & Her Impossible Boss
Confessions of a Bad Bridesmaid

**Visit the author profile page at
millsandboon.co.uk for more titles**

THE HOTEL MAGNATE'S DEMAND

BY
JENNIFER RAE

Published in Great Britain 2015
by Mills & Boon, an imprint of Harlequin (UK) Limited,
Eton House, 18-24 Paradise Road, Richmond, Surrey, TW9 1SR

© 2015 Jennifer Rae

ISBN: 978-0-263-25063-3

Printed and bound in Spain
by CPI, Barcelona

THE HOTEL
MAGNATE'S
DEMAND

This book is for the boys in my life.

For the boys who loved me when I wasn't very lovable,
the boys who cheered me up when I was feeling down,
and the boys who took care of me when I needed it.

I'm grateful for you all.

But mostly this book is dedicated to the two boys
who mean more to me than any other boy
ever has or ever will.

To Archie and Max

The two boys I love the most.

CHAPTER ONE

THREE MILLION DOLLARS. The sweet, stupid lunatics at Amy McCarthy's work were seriously trusting her with *three million dollars*? No matter how many times it happened Amy was still amazed that she'd managed to convince people she knew what she was on about. Didn't they know that she was a five-year-old dressed in a twenty-six-year-old's clothing? If they had, perhaps they wouldn't have opened that bottle of champagne tonight and toasted her success.

Perhaps they wouldn't have told her how proud they were of her for landing the biggest account in the company's history. Perhaps they would have done what they should have and handed the account to Maree, or Thomas, or another of one of the senior PR consultants. The grown-ups. The sensible, reliable, practical grown-ups who knew what the hell they were doing. Not her. Who considered it a win when she managed to find matching socks to wear to the gym.

The grin on Amy's face was almost manic as she pushed open the heavy door to Saints, the hip bar and restaurant in Surry Hills where she was meeting the others. Seriously. She totally had no idea what she was supposed to do with these new clients. They were the biggest luxury hotel chain in the entire Asia Pacific region.

She knew nothing about hotels! She was all talk. She knew that. She'd been able to sweet-talk people into anything since she was little. She'd even considered using her sales ability as her talent when she'd entered the Miss Northern Suburbs competition in high school. But she'd gone with magic instead. Which was probably why she'd lost. Either that or the fact that she'd been the dumpiest, plumpest, most unfashionable girl in the competition.

Amy remembered the long flowing bohemian dress she'd chosen for the 'formal wear' part of the competition. She'd loved it. It had made her feel pretty and feminine and free. But the judges had called her a hippy, and apparently hippies didn't win beauty contests. So she'd lost. But her mother had hugged her and told her she was cleverer than those silly judges and her father had insisted she was the most beautiful girl there.

Her parents were two more sweet, silly people in her life. Thinking she was so much brighter and cleverer and better than she actually was.

Perhaps that was why, Amy thought, she had a tendency to make bad decisions. Too many people telling her she could do anything. Maybe she needed to surround herself with some more realistic people.

Grounded, sensible people, who didn't hope for the impossible but had their feet firmly set on the ground.

People like Willa. Amy spotted her best friend as soon as she alighted from the small flight of stairs that led to the dark bar that had become her local in recent months. Willa's bright smile caught on the light and Amy smiled. Funny, clever, crazy Willa.

Amy couldn't wait to tell her friend about her latest mad scheme. Of course Amy would exaggerate and make it seem even more outrageous than it actually was. She knew that would make Willa laugh and she loved to make Willa laugh. Because that made Amy laugh and there was nothing Amy liked to do more than laugh. And go out. And work. And stay as busy as possible. Staying busy meant staying high. And staying high meant not thinking about things that made her sad.

A familiar fleeting pull swept through Amy's stomach. It shot up her body like a firecracker, passed her brain and went straight for her eyes. Amy stilled. Gulped. Then shook her head. Shook the feeling away. Where had *that* come from? There was no time for sadness. No time for thinking about anything that made her unhappy. No time for thinking about all the people she'd hurt or those people who had hurt her. She wanted to have fun. She wanted to laugh. She needed to talk to Willa. Now.

With a somewhat forced skip in her step she headed for the banquette that held Willa and her boyfriend, Rob, as well as their other friends, Scott, Kate, Chantal, Brodie and Jess. Amy counted them all off in her head, knowing she was the last one to arrive. She was often the last one to arrive these days. Work was becoming more manic as she took on more clients but that was the way she liked it. Busy.

Amy stilled. She counted her friends' heads again. There should be seven. But there were eight. Another head. An unfamiliar head. A male head with its back turned towards her. Amy wondered for a moment who the newcomer was. Their group was pretty tight. Newcomers weren't usually a thing, and if anyone was to introduce anyone it was usually her.

Amy's eyes skirted to Jess, who was looking at the newcomer with a strange, faraway look in her eye. *Aha!* That was it. Jess had invited a man. But that didn't make any sense, because Amy had spoken to her this morning before dashing out through the door and Jess hadn't said anything about a man.

Not that she had time to worry about Jess and her man or anything else. She'd won a massive contract. There were tales to tell and cocktails to be ordered.

Amy swung the Louis Vuitton bag she'd splurged on with her last bonus cheque onto the low seat the strange man happened to be sitting on and used her best PR voice.

'Ladies and gentlemen, hold your applause, but I must inform you that you are about to share copious amounts of alcohol with Bird Marketing's newest superstar.'

Everyone looked up and smiled at her encouragingly. Amy focussed on Willa, barely containing her need to say something outrageous and make her laugh. Willa had a strange smile on her face. A smile that wasn't quite a smile. And her eyes kept looking downward, then scooting back up. What was she *doing*?

'And, furthermore, I've managed to convince the idiots in charge that allowing me full control of their newest and most important client as well as their three million dollars was the best bloody idea they've ever had.' Amy laughed.

Scott stood and gave her a hug. Jess squealed in delight and called out congrats, and Brodie said loudly that her bosses must be nut-jobs.

Strangely, though, Willa didn't move. She smiled a tight smile. Frankly, Amy had expected more. A laugh, a joke, a call for drinks all round. But Willa sat still, that silly strange smile still planted on her face and her eyes now frantically moving up and down.

'Amy…' she started, finally getting up from her seat.

Her eyes were still scooting down and Amy finally realised where she was looking. At the stranger. Who Amy could now feel was looking at *her*. So Amy looked back. Then she looked at Willa. Who had stopped still. As had Amy. Her brain seized. Every cell in her body froze. No air was being released from her lungs and she was pretty sure her heart had actually stopped beating.

'Ames…'

Willa again. Amy willed herself to breathe. She felt the warmth of her best friend's hand on her arm and she was grateful for it. Because right at the moment she wasn't sure that she wouldn't faint. Her knees gave a little as her eyes met Willa's, holding them steady.

A conversation went on between the two friends without one word being spoken. A telepathic conversation that they had a knack for.

Is it?

Calm down.

No. Tell me it can't be.

Hold steady. It'll be okay.

I'm not prepared. What did I say? Did I make a fool of myself?

Just look at him.

So Amy did. She looked down at him. But right at that moment he stood. All six feet of him. Tall. Solid. Strong and dark. Amy forced herself to swallow and made her eyes trail up his chest, past his broad shoulders and to his face. A face she thought she'd forgotten. A face she'd never forget. It was him. He was here. In the flesh.

Luke.

Amy tried to speak but nothing came out. She tried again. She knew what she wanted to say. She'd practised what she wanted to say. Ever since she'd got back in contact with her old friend Willa months ago she'd been going over and over what she might say should she meet Luke, Willa's brother, her former boss and the man she'd had the fiercest crush of her life on. Who also happened to be one of only two people who knew her deepest, darkest secret. But all those words were gone. Somewhere. In the ether.

'Hello, Amy. It's been a long time.'

Yes, it has. Hello, Luke. Nice to see you. How are you? There were any number of things Amy could have said right at that moment. She dug her nails into Willa's flesh and jerked her friend towards her.

'I'm…gonna go get a drink.' Then she turned and fled, pulling her poor friend with her.

'Now, Amy, before you lose it…'

'*Before* I lose it? Before I *lose* it? Willa—I've already lost it! Why didn't you tell me Luke was coming? You should have warned me!'

'He literally just landed today and texted me. I told him to come along but honestly I didn't think he would.'

'Oh, God, what did I say? I can't even remember.'

As was the norm whenever Luke was around, Amy became a little ditzy. That logical, clever part of her brain evaporated when she saw him. Which was crazy. It had been—what? Seven years? No. Eight. Eight years since she'd seen him. Eight years since that night. The swooping roared through her stomach again.

Amy pulled her face into a smile.

'Okay—that's okay. It's fine. I'm fine. I was just shocked, you know…? I want to see him. I'm happy to see him. Let's get a drink—what are you drinking? Actually. drinks all round! We're celebrating. remember?'

Willa's eyes were soft, her expression so readable.

'Don't look at me like that, Willa. I'm fine.' Amy

said it firmly. With one of her signature smiles. Before turning to the bearded, tattooed bartender.

'Dave, darling. You look hot tonight! Sweet haircut. Sharp.' She smiled with all her teeth and winked. It was the smile she used when she wanted people to smile back.

She wanted everyone smiling tonight. She wanted everyone talking and happy. She needed her heartbeat to return to normal so she could turn around and face Luke. She wasn't even sure what she was getting so wound up for. Luke was an old friend—that was all. Sure, she'd had some silly little crush on him once. But that had been years ago. She'd only been eighteen then. A teenager.

She was a woman now. With a lot more confidence and plenty more experience. She'd changed. She'd moved on. And she was sure he had too. He probably barely remembered her. Or what had happened. That feeling again. Swooping through her. Every time she thought that feeling had finally disappeared a night like this would come. A night when it would return and lurk and keep tapping at her like an insistent salesman at a door.

'*Go away!*' she whispered to herself.

'Not exactly a warm welcome. I've only just got here.'

Amy felt him before she saw him. His warm, dark presence behind her. That slightly gruff and very deep voice in her ear. When she was eighteen it had made her melt and giggle. But today she wasn't melting. She wasn't giggling. She'd just landed a highly coveted three-million-dollar PR account, for God's sake. She was strong and powerful and in control. Strong, powerful women didn't melt.

But Amy grabbed the bar anyway—just in case.

'I wasn't talking to you.' Her voice came out all breathy and high. *Dammit.* Amy schooled it into something deeper. Her best PR voice. 'How have you been, Luke? It's been for ever!'

'Eight years.'

Luke didn't move. Amy had used to love that about him. How he was so still and solid. Big. Brave. Everything she wasn't.

At best she remembered herself as being flaky during the months she'd spent working at Weeping Reef as a receptionist for the tropical resort. At worst selfish, self-centred and a right little brat. No wonder Luke wasn't smiling. She'd always been his little sister's troublemaking friend. He'd never seen her as anything but that. And she'd always seen him as Willa's annoyingly controlling big brother. *Hot* big brother. As in smoking hot.

And right now, up close, Amy realised that hadn't changed. Actually, if anything, he was even hotter. He'd always been tall, but now he'd filled out more. His jaw was wider, his shoulders broader. His voice was even deeper. His hair was still thick and dark, but it was clipped a lot shorter than in the old days, when unruly curls had fallen carelessly over his forehead.

And gone were the board shorts and the resort polo shirts he'd used to wear. Luke stood tall in an expensive-looking suit. Complete with tie. Somehow, even though he looked a little restrained by all the neatness and correctness, it suited him. It definitely suited the grim look on his face.

Amy lifted her eyes to his. His eyes were still the same. Green. They were like those old mood rings they'd used to peddle in the gift shop. When he was happy they'd turn bright, like the Whitsunday ocean, and when he was angry or upset they'd come over a shade of stormy dark green. She remembered the stormy green. Luke had always seemed to be upset with her over one thing or another. But she'd only ever seen them violently green once. That one time...

Amy clung to her stomach, willing it not to swoop again. She didn't want that unwelcome feeling to reach her eyes as it threatened to do each time. She wouldn't cry. She'd *never* cry over that. Not again.

'Eight years. Wow. And still looking over our shoulders, ruining all our fun.' Amy smiled, hoping he'd take her words as she'd meant them—teasingly.

'And by the looks of it you two haven't changed much either. Still giggling over boys and drinking too many cocktails.'

Something resembling a smile lifted the corner of his mouth and he flicked his suit jacket back to push his hands into his pockets. He got it. He got *her*. He always did.

'You just wish we were giggling over *you*.' Amy smiled again. She couldn't help it.

She'd always liked to tease Luke. She'd always pushed and pushed till the grim look on his face cracked into a smile. It was a game she'd enjoyed

playing when she was eighteen and had had her whole
life in front of her. Now, at twenty-six, she should be
more cautious. She should have learned a few les-
sons. But it seemed with Luke she was still clueless.
Because flirting with him felt good. *Still*.

'I'm sure you are.'

He leaned in and Amy caught his scent. The same
fresh, oceany goodness that she remembered. His lips
brushed her cheek just lightly. As if he was afraid to
go near her.

Amy was grateful. It was important to keep her
distance. Especially with Luke. There was no doubt
she'd been looking forward to seeing him again. She'd
thought about it often since rekindling her friendship
with Willa. She'd asked Willa about him a few times.
Subtly. Without letting on to her friend how she felt.

Not that she was *sure* how she felt. Luke was someone from her past. Her very long ago past. And even
then he hadn't been anything to her…just a crush.
And she hadn't been anything to him. Just his sister's
silly little friend. An idiot who'd needed rescuing.

Amy clutched at her stomach and turned back to
the bar, where Dave was now racking up the drinks.
She smiled, she flirted, she paid all her attention to
Dave. So much so that she could see him blushing
underneath his beard. Her stomach settled. Her heart
returned to normal. She wouldn't think of that night.
She wasn't sure why she kept thinking of it—she'd
learned to block it out years ago.

Maybe it was because Luke was here. And he
smelled the same. She still remembered breathing

him in as he carried her out to the Jeep and took her to
the hospital. She remembered clinging to him shamelessly as he laid her in the back seat.

'Don't leave me.'

'I'm not. I'm right here. But I have to drive.'

'No!' The tears from her eyes had met her still wet
cheeks. 'Please. Just hold me.'

She'd been irrational. She'd known that at the time.
But she hadn't been able to help it. For those three
minutes the fact that his arms were around her had
been the only thing stopping her from collapsing,
and she'd been convinced she'd stop breathing if he
let her go.

He'd reached for her hair, stroked it back off her
forehead. Then with one finger he'd traced the cut in
her lip. She hadn't winced. His touch had soothed the
pain. She'd clung to his hand.

'No one is going to hurt you again, Amy. I promise you.'

'But…'

'Amy—look at me.'

That was when she'd seen his eyes so violently
green.

'I *promise* you.'

She'd believed him. She'd looked into his eyes and
into his soul and seen her protector. She'd let him go
then and sat silently until they'd reached the resort
hospital.

CHAPTER TWO

'I THINK YOU may have sufficiently embarrassed the barman, Lollipop.'

Amy's face broke out into an uncontrollable grin and she turned back to where the voice behind her was coming from.

'Don't call me that.'

'What's wrong, Lollipop?' He smiled. The slow, lazy smile that he specialised in. 'Lost your sense of humour?'

'No…' Amy grinned. 'But I *have* lost my tolerance for your teasing. And if you haven't noticed…' Amy put one hand on a hip and pushed it out '…I'm not as skinny as I used to be.'

Yeah, he'd noticed. Luke beat down the heat pumping through his veins. Amy wasn't the skinny teenager of eight years ago. She'd changed. Filled out. His eyes slipped to her chest. *Really* filled out. And although he'd always considered her a pretty girl, she'd always been just that—a girl. But she wasn't a girl any more. She was a woman. And, by the looks

of the body she was showing off in a tight white skirt
and tan silky blouse, she was *all* woman.

But she was still his little sister's friend. Her silly,
irresponsible friend. The girl who was too pretty for
her own good. The girl who made an art form out of
flirting. And that hadn't changed. The barman was
still flushing and throwing furtive glances Amy's
way.

'Some things have changed, but not everything.'

He nodded towards the barman and Amy turned
to see the direction of his gaze. The barman smiled
shyly before fumbling with a glass and allowing it to
drop with a loud smash to the ground.

He leaned in close to Amy's ear so no one else
could hear. 'Still making men do stupid things.'

As soon as the words had left his mouth he regretted them. He watched her stiffen. He felt her shrink
away from him and her cheeks burned an instant red.
He hadn't meant *that*. Not what she thought.

'Amy, I…'

She smiled. Wide. Fake. 'It's okay.' She gathered
drinks. She hoisted her purse under her arm, flicked
her hair and left. Making him feel like the most in-
sensitive man in the country.

He knew what had happened all those years ago
wasn't her fault. She'd been a kid. Sure, she'd been
silly, naïve—reckless, even. But who wasn't at that
age? She hadn't deserve what had happened to her
and he'd made sure that the loser who'd attacked her
understood how wrong he'd been.

Luke watched her walk back to the table filled

with people he hadn't seen in years. People who had once been closer to him than his family. People who'd made him feel normal. People who'd made him feel as if he belonged somewhere for the first time in his life. For the *only* time in his life. He'd never felt like that since.

The memory of that summer on Weeping Reef had got him through some tough times in his life. Had it only been a few months they'd all lived together on the island? It had seemed like longer. It had seemed that summer had lasted for years. It was the place where he'd remembered being young. Having fun. Being himself. But that was over. His reality now was work and responsibility and money and more work.

And he liked his life. He didn't want to go back. He'd grown up so much since then, learned so much. He was different now. Stronger.

But as he watched Amy walk away, clearly angry and upset, he didn't feel strong. He felt twenty-four again. Inept. Out of his depth and totally unable to decide what to do next. At twenty-four he would have ignored it. Ignored *her*. Ignored the way she felt and the fact that he'd put his foot into it. He would have sat with the others and said nothing. Carried on as if nothing had happened.

But he wasn't twenty-four any more. He was turning thirty-two in a month. And over the years he'd learned that the only way to solve a problem was to throw himself into it. Avoiding problems always made them bigger, more bad and harder to solve. Walking away was for sheep, and he wasn't a sheep. Not any more.

His feet flew across the floor and he had his arm on hers before she even sat down. 'Amy, I'm sorry. I didn't mean that the way it came out.'

Her eyes shot up to his. The same pretty brown eyes he remembered from all those years ago, but now a little more lined around the edges. From laughing. Or perhaps from crying. Probably both. If her life had been anything like his it would have been filled with both over the last eight years.

There were no tears in her eyes now, but there was something else. A fierce, angry determination he'd never seen before.

'It doesn't matter, Luke, that was a long time ago.'

She turned away, but he wasn't letting her go. She didn't fool him. There was no way she didn't still think about what had happened. He did. A lot.

During the last year in particular he had thought about it constantly. Since Koko. Since he had almost been the father of a daughter himself. He'd thought about all the things that could go wrong. All the trouble a girl could get into. He'd braced himself. He'd been as prepared as he could. He'd actually been looking forward to it after the initial shock had worn off.

'Amy.' He took the drinks from her hands and placed them on the table before moving a little closer to her. 'I'm sorry.' He held her eyes. 'I meant you're still an impossible flirt.'

'Is that what you think of me?' Her eyes hardened. 'I'm just a silly flirt who deserves everything she gets?'

She hissed the words and as he held her arm he could feel her shake just a little. Clearly it wasn't okay. Clearly she still thought about what had happened all those years ago. And clearly he'd put his foot in it big-time.

Her eyes darted from one of his to the other. Challenging. Hard. No fear, just distrust. That made his gut clamp hard. He didn't want her to feel that way about him. For some reason that was important. He didn't want her to feel she couldn't rely on him.

'No, Amy. That's not what I think. I like how you flirt with everyone you meet. You're friendly and sweet…if a little naïve. But I like that about you. I always did.'

He didn't move his hand from her arm or his eyes from hers. He couldn't let her go. Not until she realised that he had her. He wasn't going to hurt her. Something inside him burned to let her know that.

'I was just teasing you.'

She stayed silent but didn't move. The noise of the bar whooped around them but right then Luke couldn't concentrate on anything but her and his need to make her understand what he meant.

'What happened to your freckles, Lollipop?'

Her brow furrowed and her eyes lost that angry gaze. 'What?'

'Your freckles…across your nose.' He softly grazed the top of her nose with the tip of his finger. 'They've disappeared.'

A smile involuntarily moved his mouth. That summer they'd spent most of their time in the sun. Amy had worked on Reception but she had often gone out 'delivering a message' or 'taking a parcel'. He'd known what she was up to. She'd skipped out as much as possible to enjoy the sun and find his sister to get into mischief.

As the resort manager he should have hauled her into his office, gave her a warning—told her off, at least. But Amy had had a way about her. Cute, cheeky, sweet with just a whiff of sexy. He'd never been able to do anything more than give her slap on the wrist. And she known it. And she'd taken advantage of it. Batting her eyelashes and flashing her magnetic smile whenever she wanted something.

His eyes moved from her nose to her eyes. They weren't batting their lashes at him now. They were still. And hot. He saw something. Something that hadn't been there eight years ago. A sudden curious hunger that he knew he was transmitting right back to her.

No, no, *no*. This wasn't right. He stepped back a little, letting go of her arm. He couldn't feel *that*. Not with *Amy*. Not with little, scrawny, troublemaking Amy. His sister's best friend. His *little* sister's best friend.

But she wasn't that little any more. She didn't seem young at all. She looked… His eyes landed on her lips. Full and soft, they were covered in hot pink lipstick. She looked…*delicious*. His tongue darted out to wet his own bottom lip. Everything in his body stirred. She was right—she was no lollipop any more. The pretty little nymph had blossomed into a gorgeous woman, and she was looking at him now as if she was thinking exactly what he was. *Sin.*

'There are a lot of things about me that have changed, Luke.' Her voice had changed. It was deeper, with a hint of husk. 'And one of them is that now I know when to flirt harmlessly…' She moved closer, her breasts brushing his arm. He looked down and watched them—tanned and bouncing slightly as she moved. 'And when to flirt with intent.'

'And what are you doing right now?'

'Oh, I think you know *exactly* what I'm doing.'

His eyes moved up quickly and checked hers. 'Well, I hope you know what *you're* doing. You don't want to find yourself in more trouble than you can handle.'

She moved even closer and the stirring in his body started to roar. Quietly, slowly, but persistently. This wasn't little lollipop Amy any more. This was a woman well aware of her power.

'You think I can't handle you, Luke?'

Luke's mouth dried up. The idea of her handling him was doing violent things to his body. Things were springing to life. He had to calm this down.

'I think you might have enough to handle with all the booze being passed around this table.' He nodded towards the table full of glasses. Some shots of tequila had arrived and were being scattered amongst the others.

She looked away quickly, then back at him. Hard. Hot. He held steady.

'Not scared, are you, Luke?'

'Scared? Of what?'

She smiled. A magnetic bright white that glowed in the dark bar. She shrugged a little. 'You tell me.'

Luke's heart beat steady but hard. She'd pegged him. He *was* scared. Scared that he actually wanted to take little lollipop Amy home, get her naked and kiss her entire body. And that he'd enjoy it. And he'd want to do it again and again.

But he wasn't going to do that. Not with her. She was too close. She wasn't someone he wanted to hurt. And hurt her he would, if he let himself go there.

'The only thing I'm scared of is that this lot are going to get kicked out if they get any drunker.'

He looked behind him at the group of old friends. Laughing so hard they were falling off their stools. Passing shots of tequila around, talking louder. and getting more animated with every drink. *Fun*. That was what they were. Fun, easy and carefree. And Luke wanted a little bit of that. He'd just gone through the toughest year of his life and he was back here in Sydney for this. Fun. Not Amy. Not relationships. Tequila. Laughs. Old friends.

He swiped two shots off the table and handed one to Amy.

'We may as well join them, Lollipop.' He swept the liquid into his mouth and enjoyed the burn as it travelled down his throat. Get drunk. That was what he was going to do tonight. Then he'd be able to forget and relax and maybe live a little.

What he *wasn't* going to do was his little sister's best friend. He planned on staying right away from *that* little wasps' nest, because he sure wasn't ready to get stung again.

CHAPTER THREE

THE HOT TEQUILA warmed Amy's already hot blood. She watched Luke as he necked another shot. What the hell was she *doing*? Flirting was something she did. With everyone she met. She'd always done it. She'd realised from a young age that she often got what she wanted with a little bit of sugar rather than salt.

From a young age she'd also realised that her flirting could sometimes land her in trouble, so she'd taken great care to tone it down in the past eight years. She only flirted outrageously with people she knew well—like Dave the barman, who happened to be one of her little brother's mates. But she shouldn't have flirted so outrageously with Luke. Could she make it any more obvious how she felt about him?

Amy sidled in next to Willa on the red velvet banquette. More partygoers had arrived and the room was filling with hot bodies. Inside her chest the usual thrill of excitement thumped. But tonight there was something else in there. Caution. An unmissable beat.

Calm the hell down. But it was hard to tell her

heart to do that with Luke sitting right opposite her, with his big hard body and his come-to-bed eyes that had just locked with hers so hard she'd thought she'd never prise them loose.

'What the hell happened? That was a pretty heated conversation.'

Amy glanced at Luke as Willa spoke. A couple of vodka sodas and her friend's whispering hiss echoed like a train in the desert.

'Shh.' Amy moved a little closer so she could hiss herself into Willa's ear. 'Your brother hasn't changed at all. He still thinks you and I are two little girls who can't take care of ourselves.'

'What did he say?'

He'd said she was still making men do stupid things. As soon as he'd said it she been able to tell he regretted it. She knew he hadn't meant it as it had come out. She couldn't remember how many times he'd told her over and over that night that it wasn't her fault. That just because she'd been friendly it hadn't given that loser the right to expect anything from her or to do…what he did.

Amy pushed down the swooping, then glanced at Luke. His eyes met hers and her stomach settled. He hadn't meant that. He'd rushed straight over to her to tell her he hadn't meant that. But what if he was right? Maybe she *was* flirting a little too fiercely. Amy hitched at her shirt. Maybe she was exposing too much skin.

No. No! Stop! she scolded herself. What had happened hadn't been her fault. The way she dressed and the way she spoke to people had nothing to do with what had happened. It had been *his* fault. This shouldn't ever have been her problem, her hang-up.

Amy shook herself physically. When she'd come home from Weeping Reef her mother and father and even her little brother had wrapped her up in their little cocoon of a family and helped her recover. That was when she'd met Laurie. Sweet, nice Laurie. Who'd loved her. Who'd made her feel whole again.

She'd hadn't thought about what had happened in years. It had only been in the last six months, since her old friends from Weeping Reef had come back into her life and their stories had been rehashed, that she'd thought about it again. But she was strong. She was tough. She wasn't going to let the memories of one bad night make her into a victim.

'Ames? Was he awful?'

'No, not at all.' Amy shook her head and turned back to her friend. 'Sometimes I'm just too sensitive. And besides, I think I'm still in a little bit of shock that he's even here. You should have warned me!'

'I'm sorry about that, Ames. It happened so suddenly. And anyway, there's no need to be embarrassed. You had a crush on him years ago. He probably doesn't even remember anything about it… or…anything else. And he wouldn't even care. You know Luke—keep the peace, stay cool, never let anyone know what you think.'

'Yeah…'

That *had* been Luke eight years ago. She'd fallen over herself back then to get him to notice her. That night with that horrible guest had been all about trying to make Luke jealous. She'd been trying for months to get him to notice her but he hadn't. All Luke had wanted to do was work and haul her into his office to tell her off every time she bent a staple.

The old Luke would never have apologised. The old Luke would have said nothing. He'd have let her walk away. She knew his theory—*not my monkeys, not my circus.*

But tonight he hadn't let her walk away. He was different. He *looked* different. Older. Harder. Stronger. Sexier. Amy bit her bottom lip as she sneaked another glance at him. That same strong jaw—only now wider. That same thick dark hair—shorter, but still with a hint of wave. His skin wasn't as tanned, and he'd put on weight, but she could tell that underneath that suit he was all muscle.

He had taken off his jacket now and was laughing at something Brodie said as he rolled up his sleeves. His large forearms strained against the fabric and heat settled in Amy's core. Her skin tingled. Even after eight years she still found him attractive. She still wanted him more than any other man she'd ever wanted. Even Laurie.

A flush of heat passed across Amy's forehead and am ache rushed to the back of her neck. She'd never forgotten Laurie's tears at the airport when she'd left Melbourne. But she'd had to go. She hadn't been in love with him any more. She'd known she was breaking his heart by leaving, but she hadn't been able to keep on lying and saying everything was fine. She hadn't wanted to be with him any more. She'd been healed. She'd needed to move on.

But now, as she looked at Luke, she wondered if she really had.

The night wore on, as many of their nights together did. Full of laughter and stories that started with, 'Do you remember that one time…?'

Normally Amy would be at the centre. Her stories the loudest and most animated, with just a hint of exaggeration to make everyone laugh. But tonight Luke's presence made her retreat a little. She worried about what he thought. She couldn't help it. Even after all this time and eight birthdays she still wanted him to like her.

'So what else have you been up to, Amy? Besides work? Cause that's all you seem to do, according to these guys.'

Luke was looking much more relaxed after an hour of so of drinking and swapping insults with Scott and Brodie. He'd edged closer to her, so now his knee was just inches from hers.

Amy was feeling the effects of the tequila and the vodka. She'd relaxed and was enjoying taking a back seat for once. Instead of being the one who was always up and down getting drinks, or moving between conversations, she was sitting back and enjoying watching her friends have fun.

'Having fun. Keeping this lot entertained. You know what it's like—there's always a party to go to or someone wanting a piece of you.'

Amy smiled. She loved her life. She loved being busy, and having a big circle of friends was important to her. At first coming to Sydney had been hard. She'd been used to being part of a big group of family and friends in Melbourne and she'd found herself all alone. That was until she'd moved in with Jess and started to go out—and then, when she'd run into Willa by chance one night in a restaurant restroom, her social life had become manic.

Catching up with the guys from Weeping Reef was almost a full-time job—they'd all aged, and their relationships had definitely changed, but one thing hadn't. This group loved to party.

'I know what that's like. It isn't easy, being pulled in a dozen different directions. Do you miss home? How are your parents? And your brother—Antony? Does he still have all his animals?'

Amy's brow furrowed and she leaned back a little. 'You remember my brother?'

Luke had never met Antony. She hadn't remembered ever telling Luke about him, and even if she had it was impressive that he could remember after all that time.

'Sure. You told me about his obsession with saving animals. I remember you saying that every time he came home from school he had another injured animal in his backpack.'

Amy laughed. That was her little brother. When they were young their family home had always housed at least a dozen animals Antony had rescued and nursed back to health.

'He's a vet now—which was no surprise to anyone. At least that means the animals stay at the clinic and don't come home. Although I was talking to Mum the other night and she said Antony had lobbed up with a wallaby for her to feed while he went away for the weekend.'

Luke smiled and his eyes crinkled. Amy watched it. She watched the way his mouth broke out into that smile.

'So you still talk to your parents a lot?'

'Not as much as I'd like.' Amy stared into her half-full drink. 'I miss them. They're crazy and loud, and Mum is always trying to force me to try some new recipe that contains the latest "superfood", or get me to drink things like chlorophyll and whatever else she's read on the internet. But they're…you know… home.'

'Home.'

Amy met Luke's eyes and they were locked on her. She'd felt him watching her for most of the night. As if he wanted to keep her in his sights. He was probably afraid she was going to do something stupid again, as she'd had a habit of doing when she was eighteen.

'Where's home for *you* these days, Luke? Willa tells me you're some millionaire, swanning around on yachts with a different gorgeous woman on your arm every night. A hotel magnate, or something.'

Luke let out a whisper of a laugh. 'Willa makes it sound much more fun than it is. Home for me is wherever work is. It's been Singapore for the last two years. I started a new development there and I've been trying to get it off the ground. The Singaporean government are usually easy to deal with when it comes to western investment, but for some reason they dragged their tails with this one...' Luke smiled and looked away. 'But you don't want hear about that.'

He straightened his spine and rested his hand on his knee. Amy watched as his fingers spread. Long, thick fingers. The alcohol was clearly taking hold, because all she wanted to do was reach out and lace her fingers through his. Feel the warmth of his skin.

Really bad idea, Amy scolded herself. *Not Luke.*

Amy had met a few hot men in Sydney to relieve the pressure, but she'd found it difficult to meet someone she was interested in dating. She'd found it difficult ever since Laurie, really. The men she met seemed interested in her looks and where she lived, but she hadn't actually met anyone interested in *her.*

'Sure I do. My new account is with a hotel chain, so I'd love to hear about your work, actually. I have absolutely no idea about the industry, so I'll be hanging off your every word hoping you let some juicy PR secret out.'

Truth was, she liked to listen to him talk. He was one of those rare men who actually had something to say.

'Feel free to drop in to my office here in Sydney any time and talk to my PR. Tonight I don't want to talk shop, though. I just want to get drunk and relax.'

The booze *had* relaxed him, but for the first time Amy noticed the dark circles under his eyes. He ran a hand absently thought his hair. He looked tired and worn. Something he'd never looked eight years ago. Weeping Reef had been his first proper management job and back then he'd taken it very seriously. You didn't step out of line when Luke was in charge or you were out.

'Hard day at the office, dear?' Amy teased, and Luke glanced her way with a smile.

'Hard few years, more like it.'

'So does that mean your home is here now…for a while?'

Amy didn't want to sound anxious, but she was. Although she knew she could never be with Luke the way she wanted, the idea of him being close was strangely comforting.

'For a while.'

He smiled directly at her. That killer smile he'd used on the island when things had been going well.

'Good.'

'Why's that good?' His green eyes darkened.

Amy couldn't help it. She shifted forward till their knees touched. She just wanted him to *know*. She wasn't sure if it was the tequila or loneliness or nostalgia, but she wanted Luke to know that she was glad he was staying and that her foolish girlish heart still found him hotter than a car bonnet on a summer's day.

'It's good because it might be nice having you around. I've kind of missed having you tell me what to do, and criticising my work, and the way you used to say, "Not *again*, Lollipop."'

He laughed out loud when she lowered her voice to mimic the way he spoke.

'I did used to say that a lot, didn't I?'

'At least once a day. You were a horrible boss.'

'I was a very tolerant boss, if I remember, and *you* were a terrible receptionist.'

'I was the resort's greatest asset.'

'You certainly knew how to keep the guests entertained.'

Amy stilled.

'Don't go getting all offended again, Lolli. You know I didn't mean it like that. What I meant was that our rebooking rate was one hundred per cent because of you and the way you kept in touch with every guest—emailing them about special deals and sending them postcards saying we all missed them on the island. Those ideas were marketing genius. If you'd put that much effort into filing your paperwork maybe you wouldn't have had to spend so much time in my office.'

Amy laughed. 'Maybe I stuffed up the filing because I *wanted* to spend more time in your office.'

She winked and Luke's brow furrowed.

'What…?'

'You know…'

'Know what?'

'About my mad crush on you.'

'Yeah, right. I think you may have had a mad crush on just about *everyone* back then.'

'Maybe. But you were my maddest. And don't say you didn't know. I practically threw myself at you.

How about the way I used to wear my shirts unbuttoned almost to my belly button?'

'Yeah, you did. I was forever telling you to dress yourself properly.'

'And all those after-hours bar dances. They never happened when you weren't there.'

'Sure they did.'

'No. They didn't. I could tell you about a hundred times when I embarrassed myself, trying to get you to notice me—but you never did, did you?'

'Sure I did. I noticed. I noticed an extremely pretty girl who had a lot of growing up to do.'

'Well, I'm all grown-up now.'

'Yes, you are.'

They sat like that for minutes—too many minutes.

Then Chantal and Brodie called from the other end of the table. They were leaving. Amy pulled her eyes from Luke's and checked her phone. Midnight. She had to go into work tomorrow—she really should think about going home too. But something about Luke made her want to stay. She wanted to be close to him, to be near him. He made her feel…something she hadn't felt in a long time. Something comfortable and warm and exciting all at the same time.

'We're moving on, Ames—you coming?'

Willa stood to leave. She and Rob and the others would probably end up at Milly's—the nightclub around the corner where they often partied until daylight.

'Not tonight, Wills. I have to get up and work tomorrow. I think I might have to call it a night.'

'What?' Jess was very drunk. Her hair had come loose and she'd spent the last ten minutes hugging everyone in the bar goodbye. '*No!* Come on, McCarthy—we're going out!'

'No—no, I'm not.'

Those words were hard to say, and they tasted strange coming out of her mouth. But she had to say them. Despite wanting to kick the party on with Jess, and despite the irresistible pull towards Luke. She was a grown-up now. Her bosses really were expecting her to nail this account, and she really couldn't let them down. She had to leave.

'You can't go home alone, Ames…'

'I'm a big girl, Willa.'

'I know, but you really shouldn't travel by yourself.'

Amy rolled her eyes. She'd managed to get herself around Sydney every day and night for the last nine months, but Willa still worried about her. It was sweet, but unnecessary.

'She won't be travelling by herself. I'll take her home.'

Amy's head whipped round at the sound of Luke's deep voice.

'No, Luke. You don't have to do that…'

'Yes. I do. If you think I'm letting you find your own way home at midnight in the city then you're drunker than I thought.'

Amy wasn't drunk at all. Not by her usual standards, anyway. She was sober enough to realise that having Luke take her home was safer than going alone. But she was also sober enough to realise that she was drunk enough to maybe throw herself at him, given half the chance. And she didn't want to do that.

And then he stood and rose up before her like a Viking, all tall and strong and broad…

Where had *that* association come from? Maybe she was drunker than she'd thought. She let her eyes drop and they rested right on him. On the part of his body she was most curious about. Slowly she licked her lips. She'd fantasised so many times about sex with Luke. Would he be gentle and accommodating? Or would he throw her against the wall, make her shut up and have his dirty way with her? She couldn't decide which one she wanted first, but she suspected that she wanted to try them all.

Slowly Amy's gaze rose to meet his eyes. 'I don't need a chaperon any more, Luke, I've managed to take care of myself quite well over the past eight years.'

'Well, maybe I do.'

Amy stilled. What did *that* mean? Luke hadn't left her side all night, and she'd noticed him looking at her. She wasn't an idiot. She knew there was something there. An attraction. The old Luke would have ignored it, but the new Luke seemed a little different. A little more aware of his feelings and more prepared to deal with them. She wondered what he'd do with his feelings for her…

Ten seconds later she had her answer. 'Get your coat, Amy—we're going home. Together.'

It didn't take long to find a taxi. The night was hot,

and people were careening noisily down the laneways of the inner city suburb, but the taxis were out in full force, picking up the Friday night revellers as they moved from bar to club.

Amy slipped into the seat and Luke followed, sitting a little too close, pressing his big leg up against hers.

The ride to Amy's flat in Bondi was silent, but the air was filled with tension. Every movement, every sigh, every look put Amy on alert. The buildings sped past on the main roads, but as they got closer to the beachside suburb the taxi slowed down to navigate the twisty turns of the narrow streets and the plethora of speed bumps that littered the way.

Luke wasn't looking at her, but his leg was still pressed up against hers. She felt it, hard and definite. The rocking of the taxi was lulling her and letting the alcohol settle in her blood. She felt content. Safe. Safer than she had in months. Ever since she'd left Melbourne and Laurie.

But sitting in the taxi with Luke was nothing like sitting with Laurie. Not even in the beginning. She and Laurie had met through their parents, and he had been just what she'd needed at the time. He'd adored her. He'd thought she was the most beautiful, wonderful person ever to grace the earth and had expressed to her constantly how lucky he was.

He'd soothed her soul. He'd brought back her happiness. And she was grateful to him. But one day she'd realised she just wasn't in love with him any more. And she'd wanted out.

Laurie had bent over backwards, trying to get her to change her mind. And she'd tried to stay with him—she really had. She'd tried to convince herself that it was just a rough patch.

But one night she'd gone out with some workmates and kissed someone else and it had been then that she'd realised staying wasn't fair on either of them.

So she'd left—decided on a fresh start in Sydney.

Her parents had been upset. His parents had been angry. Laurie had called every day for the first three months. Amy had wanted to relent. She'd spent three months crying and talking and trying to explain why she'd needed to do what she had but they hadn't listened.

It had made being in Sydney even harder. She'd felt deserted. Judged. And all she'd been trying to do was be happy. But the people in her life who claimed to care about her the most had seemed to want the opposite of that. They'd wanted her to settle. Be happy with what she had because it made *them* happy.

The only thing that had got her through was Jess and Willa and her work. Her parents had come round eventually too, but she still had to stay busy and high—otherwise she'd be reminded of how she'd let everyone down, and then all she'd want to do was go back home and make it up to them. Go back and make everyone happy.

'You're quiet, Amy. You're never quiet. What's wrong?'

Luke's voice broke gently into the silence.

'Nothing. Just tired, I guess.' She *was* tired. Tired

of always trying not to think about the things that made her unhappy.

'I'm tired too. So much for me being a massive party animal tonight.'

He smiled and shoved his shoulder gently into hers. She shoved him back and he shoved her again. Their gentle shoves soon turned into pushing, and finally a little wrestling.

Luke grabbed at the back of her head. 'You always did think you were tough, Lollipop, but I know you're not.'

Amy pushed Luke's hand away. 'I'm tougher than you think, Boss.'

Luke smiled, 'You haven't called me that in a long time. I think I like it.'

The wrestling stopped. The air in the taxi turned a little thick. Amy stopped moving and stilled her hand where in rested, on his thigh. High on his thigh. *His* hand stilled on her head.

'You like it when I call you Boss?'

Amy's eyes skated to Luke's lips. They were slightly parted. She wanted to kiss him. She wanted to touch him. She wanted to do bad, bad things to him.

'I like having your hand there.' Luke's voice was deep, and he shifted his leg a little where her hand sat.

There was no mistaking what he wanted and how he felt. It sent a thrilling ripple through her to think that she could finally have what she'd wanted all those years ago. Time alone with Luke. Luke wanting her. It was everything she'd wanted as an eighteen-year-old and she could finally take it—if she wanted.

Carefully she shifted a little closer, her eyes still on his lips, her hand inching further up his thigh.

'Like this?'

A deep, low growl escaped from Luke's lips and Amy felt herself heat from the sound of it. *This was it.*

Quickly she pulled her hand away. 'You wish,' she said lightly, trying to clear the fog in her brain and the memory of his green eyes on her as she moved her hand up his leg.

Luke didn't answer. She couldn't tell if he was angry or embarrassed.

But then his hand moved and settled on her thigh. 'Good move, Lollipop,' he said quietly as the taxi finally came to a stop.

The heat of his hand on her thigh seared through her clothing. Why had she chosen that night to become responsible and sensible? She didn't *want* to be sensible. She wanted to be eighteen and reckless and to throw herself on Luke right here in the back seat of the taxi.

But she knew she couldn't. Because there was no way it would be a one-night thing with Luke and she couldn't offer him any more than that. She wasn't ready for another relationship. She didn't want to get involved in anyone's life. She still hadn't dealt with the fallout of her last failed relationship—she sure as hell wasn't about to throw herself into another mess.

She also knew that if Luke only wanted a one-night thing she'd be heartbroken. And, as she felt her body heat from her toes to her forehead at the mere touch of his hand on her leg, she knew in an instant that anything with Luke would get messy.

'Thanks for bringing me home, Luke. You didn't have to—but thanks anyway.'

'Any time, Lolli. I'm here for a few months now. I'll be around if you ever need me…for anything.'

Anything? Like hot sex?

'I should be all right. I've survived eight years without you so far.' Amy laughed, trying to keep it light. Trying to prevent him from seeing what she really wanted—for him to grab her, kiss her and insist on coming in.

But he didn't do that. He took his hand off her knee and opened the door to get out.

'No! No. Don't get out. I can walk to the front door.'

'I'm walking you to your front door, Amy.'

'No. You're not.'

She would punch him square in the face if she had to. She didn't want him walking her to the door, because she wasn't sure she wouldn't throw herself on him for a kiss goodnight, then force him to come upstairs and have his wicked way with her. No. A nice, chaste goodbye in the cab was the right thing to do.

But the kiss he landed on her cheek felt anything but chaste. It was soft at first, then he moved a little, closer to her lips and kissed her again, using his lips to soothe and caress her cheek. A kiss on the cheek—that was all it was—but Amy felt like melting right into him.

'Luke…' She wasn't sure what she wanted to say.

Don't. Stop. But those words wouldn't come out and the way she said his name sounded like a sigh.

'Amy.' He kissed her again, this time using his big hand to pull her cheek closer to him.

One touch. That was all she needed. To feel his skin one time. That would be enough.

Amy rested her hand back on his thigh and turned to face him. She kept her eyes on his—that way she'd know when he got too close and be able to pull away. But he didn't kiss her again. His mouth turned up a little at one side, but he kept his eyes on hers.

Amy's hand moved slowly but surely to his torso, and up further. She could feel the hardness of his stomach underneath her touch. She wanted skin. She needed to feel his warmth. So she tugged at his shirt till it was released from his waistband and enjoyed the relief coursing through her body as she hit his skin and continued moving upwards till she rested her hand on his chest. Hard and hot.

'That'll be twenty-four-fifty.'

The voice of the taxi driver broke the spell. Luke moved quickly, extracting the money from his wallet, practically throwing it at him, then flying out through the car door before Amy could protest. He was at her side and opening the door before she had time to breathe.

Stepping out into the night air should have felt better, should have cleared her head, but as the taxi sped away Luke stepped closer and she breathed in his scent again. Her head fogged. She turned into that silly besotted teenager all over again.

'Now how are you going to get home?' Her voice whispered it in the night.

'Maybe I won't go home.' His words were clear and gruff in her ear.

Amy moved closer as his arms encircled her waist. Maybe if she just felt his skin again she'd be done. She'd be able to move on.

'I like the feel of your skin.'

No. She wouldn't be done. His skin was hot and smooth, except for a sprinkling of hair on his stomach. She fingered it before moving her hands up and gripping his chest. She felt him tense and flex. This was more than flirting. This was dangerous territory. But with Luke it didn't feel dangerous. Exciting. Wrong. But not dangerous.

Luke breathed her in as he moved his hand over the silky blouse on Amy's back and gripped the back of her head gently. He needed her nearer. He moved her head closer to him. Dangerously close.

He needed to stop. But he wasn't going to. The alcohol, coupled with the relief of being home in Sydney and the surprise of seeing her again, had got under his skin. Everything was moving slowly. He could smell the prospect of sex in the air and he realised how much he wanted it. He needed it.

He curled his fingers through her hair. It was shorter now. Cut blunt to her shoulders. Nothing like the long, almost uncontrollable blonde hair she'd had back on the island. Back then her skin had been browner, her smile ready and willing. Here, she was different. Refined. Controlled. So unlike her.

He wanted to untie her, let her loose again. He wanted to see the carefree girl that he could still see in the flecks of gold that circled her brown eyes. But right now she wasn't carefree—she was serious. She was at her flirting best and he felt what those other men must have felt. The attention was intoxicating. The way she looked at him...as if he was the only man she'd ever looked at. The only man she'd ever felt this way about. Innocence and experience in one look.

'I like your lips,' he murmured to her.

They were still hot pink and full and slightly wet. He wanted to taste them. He wanted to taste *her*. Her hands massaged his chest. She wanted him too—he could feel that. And he wanted her.

He moved his other hand to her chest and touched lightly, circling her cleavage. Her eyes fluttered and she breathed more heavily. He watched every movement. He wanted to know how to turn her on. He let his hand cup her breast. He wanted to feel her underneath the silky shirt she had on. He wanted more of the soft warm skin he'd just been playing with. He wanted to touch all of her skin and kiss it, to bring out that wild girl he knew she had trapped inside. He wanted her to moan and squirm and scream and then he wanted to do it some more.

Amy's eyes met his. There was a heat in them he couldn't mistake. He knew what she wanted and there was no doubt she knew what he wanted. All he had to do was lean down, press his lips to her and drink her in.

This was Amy. Willa's little friend. The girl who got herself into more trouble than anyone he'd ever met. She never thought, so he should be doing the thinking for both of him. But his body wasn't listening. His body wanted her to move her hands down.

And as if she was telepathic, she did. Gently cupping him, then firmly wrapping her fingers around him through his pants.

He lost it. His mind stopped functioning. Logic and reasoning and everything he should possess left his body and all that was left was pure hot lust.

Swiftly, he took her lips. He pressed himself against her; let his hand fall to her chin so he could hold it steady. He wanted to keep her there till he'd finished what he was doing. His tongue moved against the seam of her lips and she let him in, shifting closer till those breasts were pushed right up against his arm. He shifted, letting her closer, and their mouths moved together. Slowly at first, but building up to such a frantic pace Luke was sure sweat was beginning to form on his forehead.

She was eager, pressing closer, and her hands were now on his back. It was just what he needed. Comfort and a warm body.

'Luke, you have no idea how long I've waited to do that,' she murmured, pausing only for a second and talking in a sleepy voice, her head tilted back so she could look at him before pushing herself closer and kissing him again—this time with force.

He wanted her. She smelled so good and tasted so sweet and her skin was soft beneath his fingers. But as soon as he heard those words he stopped. He couldn't do this. He *shouldn't* do this. She wasn't just a warm body. This was *Amy*. Little Amy. He couldn't let anything bad happen to her.

He'd let down enough women in his life. He wasn't going to do it again.

With a gentle push that spoke of finality he moved his head until she let go. Panting, she stared up at him, her eyes dark with lust, her lipstick almost kissed off and her perfect hair wild and falling softly over her left eye. Everything in his body went hard. She looked perfect. But he couldn't have her. That would be trouble, and the last thing he needed right now was more trouble.

'What's wrong?' she asked, moving her hands across his chest again.

It felt so good. Her hands were small but firm as they explored his muscles, making him feel bigger, stronger and better than he was. But he held her wrists and pulled them away.

'I'm not sure this is our smartest idea, Amy.'

She blinked as if coming out of a daze, then let out a breath. 'No. You're right. This is wrong.'

He didn't want to let her go but he had to. There were hundreds of thousands of eligible women in Sydney. He just needed to find one of them. Not Amy. Not her.

'This is a bad idea.'

'Very bad.'

She stepped back and wrapped her arms around herself. Right then she looked eighteen again. Innocent, unsure and wondering what she'd got herself into.

A memory of her sitting in that room flashed through his mind. Willa had called him. 'Amy's been attacked,' was all she'd said, and he'd flown to their villa.

Willa's eyes had been manic when he'd seen her and he remembered the way his stomach had sunk. He hadn't known what to expect, but when he'd opened the door to his bedroom he'd known he hadn't expected what he saw.

Amy had been sitting on her bed. Her wet hair plastered to her face with tears. Blood still fresh on her lip, her shirt torn and her bra exposed. She hadn't said anything. She'd just looked at him, then at Willa—clearly unhappy with him being there.

She'd been his responsibility. All the staff had. And for this to happen had his blood. But for some reason for it to have happened to sweet, carefree Amy had boiled him even more.

He'd kneeled before her. Asked her what had happened. She hadn't spoken. She'd just looked at him with tears rolling down her face. He'd held her eyes steady as Willa relayed the story.

It had been that slimy guest, Justin. He'd noticed them together. The jerk had been smooth. He'd been flirting with Amy all night, touching her. Luke had wanted to step in then, but he hadn't. He'd kept his opinions to himself. He'd known Amy was a bit reckless, but he hadn't thought she'd actually fall for the guy's lines.

He'd lost sight of them a little while later, when there'd been an emergency in the electricity room. They'd been gone when he'd come back. He should have checked on her. He should have made sure. But he hadn't. He'd gone back to his office to catch up on paperwork…

'I should go inside,' she said now.

'Yes, you should. And lock your door.'

'I will. Bye, Luke.'

'Bye, Amy.'

Amy gave him a strange look before walking up the path. He watched her punch in her security code. He waited till she'd climbed the stairs inside the glass door. He stood on the street till he saw a light go on at the second floor, where he assumed her apartment was. He waited for another twenty minutes on the street, watching another light go on, which he assumed was the bathroom—then all the lights went off.

And then, and only then, did he walk to the main road and flag down another taxi to take him home.

CHAPTER FOUR

THE FOOD AT THE waterfront hotel was good. The wine was chilled and the sun was beating down on their backs, but Amy's mood was still black.

'So what do you think it means?'

Willa was talking to her. She was saying something interesting and important, she was sure, but Amy couldn't remember a damn thing she'd said.

'I don't know, Will.'

'You're not even listening to me.'

'I am—I am.' Amy sat up straighter and looked her friend in the eye—or where her eye would have been behind the mirrored glasses she was wearing. 'You were saying about Rob and the flowers…'

'That was twenty minutes ago.'

Amy sucked in a deep breath. It was hot, and a headache was forming at the back of her head, and she knew exactly why.

She resisted the urge to check her phone. Again. Luke hadn't contacted her. It had a been a week. He knew where she lived—his sister was her best friend, for God's sake—he knew where to find her number but he hadn't. He hadn't called to check if she was okay after what had happened at her door and he hadn't called to catch up. Which he should have done.

'Right, Amy. Spill. I know you better than that. Something's up.'

Amy had told Willa that Luke had taken her home in a cab and left. She'd said he hadn't even got out. She didn't want to tell Willa the truth and that was churning her stomach as well. She told Willa everything. But the truth was she didn't even know how she felt yet, so she couldn't discuss it with Willa.

Luke was nothing. The kiss was nothing. So why did it feel like everything?

'I don't like it when you act strange, Ames. You're the only person who can make me get over myself and tell me the truth. And I need a hit of you. Where are you? Because you're not sitting here with me.'

Amy peered out past Willa's head to the water beyond. This wasn't like her. Amy didn't dwell. She got on with things—she moved on. Why the hell was she stuck on this? And on him. If he'd just call she was sure her brain would refocus and keep moving. She just needed to hear his voice.

'I'm sorry, Wills, it's this account at work. There's so much involved and so much to learn. I think my brain is a little frazzled by it all.'

'What you need is a night out.'

A night out. That was exactly what she needed. Cocktails. Cute boys and a killer dress. That would take her mind off Luke and her annoyingly persistent attraction to him and her ridiculous need to talk to him. She didn't need to talk to him—she'd not talked to him for eight years. A night out always fixed everything.

'You're right, Wills. A night out is exactly what I need—and I know exactly where to go. Our firm is representing Pete Middleton, who's just opened a hot new nightclub in the city. Envy, I think it's called. I'll get our names on the door for the VIP room. Call the girls.'

'Yay! Amy's back—I love it!' Willa clapped a little. 'But can our girls' night include a boy?'

'No. It's a girls' night. No boys allowed.'

'But I'm worried about Luke.'

Hearing his name froze something inside Amy. Willa wanted to invite the exact man she was avoiding? *No.* That wasn't the plan.

'Luke's a big boy, Willa—I'm sure he's fine.'

'He's been acting strange since he got back. Calling me a dozen times a day and asking me about Rob and if we're okay. He's never been that concerned before.'

'He was always over-protective.'

'Yeah, but he let me do my own thing. He always accepted my decisions. But he seems to be questioning everything at the moment. He wants to know Rob's background, and where he's from, and if he's making me happy. It's driving me crazy!'

That *was* a little strange. Luke had always been one to watch and keep an eye out for Willa, but he only ever stepped in if he needed to. And what made it even stranger was that he bloody wasn't calling *her*! Clearly he wasn't concerned about *her* welfare.

Heat crept all over Amy's body.

'Well, if he's so interfering, why do you want to invite him along? Wouldn't it be best to stay as far away from him as possible?'

Good advice. She should take it herself.

'I think he may be feeling a little lost and bored. I think he needs some distraction. Maybe if he does a few things he'll not be so concerned with me.'

'Maybe he needs a girlfriend.'

She was bitter. She knew that. But she couldn't help it. *He hadn't called!*

Willa's eyes softened and Amy knew what was coming. For some reason the two girls seemed to have a way of reading each other's thoughts, and right now Willa knew exactly what was going on.

'He didn't just leave in that cab the other night, did he, Amy?'

Amy remained silent. Anything she said could and would be used against her.

'Amy? What happened? Is there something going on between you two?'

Willa smiled, and Amy knew what she was thinking. Willa *wanted* something to happen between them. First, Willa knew the extent of Amy's crush on her brother all those years ago, and second, the idea of her best friend also being her sister-in-law would float Willa's boat.

Amy took a long sip of water. She was going to disappoint her friend. Not only was there nothing going on between her and Luke, she also knew there never could be.

It would be a nightmare if things went pear-shaped—which they would. It would risk her newly rekindled and much needed friendship with Willa, and Amy wasn't going to sacrifice that.

Amy knew that a random kiss with a stranger was all she could handle right now. Relationships were not on her to-do list. Not only was she still feeling guilty about the whole dumping Laurie and everyone hating her situation, she also wasn't sure if she'd be able to have a normal functioning relationship with anyone. Laurie had been Laurie. Kind, patient and accepting of her craziness—but would anyone else be so generous?

She wasn't sure, and nor did she want to find out.

'No, Wills. Don't get excited. The only person getting any action around here is you.'

'If you say so, Ames. If you say so.'

Amy could hear the smirk in her friend's voice but it was the truth—more or less. Disappointing though that was…

CHAPTER FIVE

Luke's name isn't on the door.

THE TEXT MESSAGE flashed on Amy's phone. *Damn*.
She'd thought Willa had gone off the idea of inviting
Luke. Clearly she hadn't, and now they were here and
she couldn't just turn him away. Although that was
exactly what she felt like doing. Particularly since the
jerk *still* hadn't called.

Amy avoided Luke's eyes when she met them at
the door. Instead, she spoke only to Willa.

'I thought you weren't bringing him.'

Amy knew she was being rude. Talking about
Luke while he was standing there. Tall, strong, and
with the fierce look on his face that had used to make
her melt. But she wouldn't melt this time. She was no
silly teenager any more. She was no one's slap and
tickle. *He should have called.*

'Trust me—I didn't want to come.'

Amy looked at his eyes then. What did *that* mean?
Did he regret the kiss? Did he not want to see her?
Well, two could play that game.

'No one's forcing you.'

'Fine. Good. I'll go. Call me when you need a lift home, Willa.'

'No!' Willa grabbed his arm as he made to turn. 'No, Luke. You're coming in and you're having a wonderful time.'

Luke didn't look happy but he stalked in—all darkness and clouds.

'Be nice!' Willa hissed to Amy as soon as he was out of earshot.

'I'm all rainbows and lollipops, Willa. It's your stupid brother who's got an attitude.'

'I know. He's had a bad day. But please try and be nice. For me.'

For Willa. Amy would do anything for Willa. And she wasn't exactly angry at Luke—just confused. What was wrong? Why was he being so damn rude?

The nightclub was clearly the current 'in' place to be in Sydney. Every B-grade celebrity had shown up, and Amy made her way around almost all of them. Her bosses would be even more in love with her when they found out about the publicity opportunities she was organising.

As the champagne flowed and the party bubbled along Amy managed to rack up event attendances, product endorsements, and even convinced a local TV presenter with massive boobs to bring her success-ful travel show to the hotel chain she was managing.

The night was going well, and Amy was getting what she needed—a temporary high. Except every time she glimpsed Luke her high left her. He wasn't looking at her, or talking to her, and every minute of neglect from him was making her blood burn.

'Amy McCarthy, your tits look amazing in that top!'

Matthew Davey. The biggest sleaze on the Sydney party circuit. He hit on everything that moved and had been pestering Amy for a date since she'd moved there.

'Matthew. You're…here.'

Normally Amy would turn on the charm. Matthew may be the biggest knob in the entire universe, but he had a super-successful health food supplement business and was currently in the market for a new PR agency. But there was something about Matthew that Amy didn't like. A certain way he'd look at her or accidentally touch her that made her skin crawl.

'Yes, I'm here. Have you been waiting for me?'

Amy didn't smile. 'Sure. Have you got a drink?'

His glass was full but she was more than happy to go away and find him another one. And then maybe 'accidentally' get lost on the way back.

'Yeah, I'm good, babe. Did you get my text the other day?'

She had.

The grassy knoll. One p.m. Saturday. Be there.

Amy had ignored it. Sitting amongst Sydney's most unbearable hipsters and putting up with Matthew on a hot, sticky afternoon sounded like her version of hell.

'Yeah, I couldn't make it—work, you know. It's hectic!' She raised her glass and sipped, looking away to see whose eye she could meet.

Where the hell was Willa? She'd get her out of this in the flick of an eyelash.

'You work too hard, babe. Listen—there's something I want to discuss with you. I've made my decision on who I'm going to go with for my account.'

'Mmm?' *Please not me, please not me.* Amy sipped her champagne again.

Matthew stepped closer. His aftershave wafted around her. It was a nice scent, but for some reason on him it just smelled cheap and nasty.

Matthew lifted a hand and gripped the upper part of Amy's arm. He was squeezing too tightly and it hurt. A searing heat ran through her. She schooled her breathing, turned her head to look at his hand, raised one eyebrow and looked him square in the face.

'Matthew, I don't know who you're going with for your account, and frankly I don't care. But if you don't take your hand off me you're going to wake up tomorrow with the blackest pair of balls known to man.'

'Oooh!' Matthew smiled, not removing his hand and moving in closer. 'Kinky. I like that.'

'What's going on here?' Luke's gruff voice broke into the space.

'What?' Matthew let go and snarled at Luke. 'Who are *you*?'

'Never mind who I am. I think it's time you left.'

'Why?' Matthew drew himself up. He was tall—

almost as tall as Luke—but nowhere near as thick-set. 'Go away, mate.'

Luke stepped deliberately in front of Amy, blocking her view and meeting Matthew's eyes. 'I said, *leave*.'

'Okay, okay, okay…' Amy shoved herself in front of Luke. 'I think that's enough, Luke—everything's fine here.'

'You stay out of this, Amy.'

Luke's brutal, patronising words made Amy's body buzz. She understood what he was doing. She knew he was trying to help her. But she'd been helping herself for these past eight years. The last time he saw her she might have been a pathetic teenager who made stupid mistakes and got herself into bad situations but that had been a long time ago. She'd learned to be more cautious. She'd learned to trust her instincts. She'd learned to stick up for herself and she didn't need him busting in, trying to be the hero.

'I *won't* stay out of this, Luke. I'm handling it.'

'It's all right, Amy, I've got this.'

He glanced at her and she saw the flash of green in his eyes. He was angry. But Matthew hadn't done anything really wrong. He was obnoxious and annoying, but she'd already let him know his attentions weren't welcome.

'No, *I've* got this.' Amy turned to Matthew. 'Go away, Matthew.'

Matthew's eyes opened wide, as did his mouth. But he didn't say anything. He just threw Luke another dramatic look and left.

'You're lucky I was here.'

Amy turned back to Luke, her own face as shocked as Matthew's. 'Lucky? Why am I *lucky*? I had the situation under control.'

'You're not known for having situations under control, Amy.'

'*Excuse* me?'

'I was just trying to help.'

'No, you were trying to interfere. You stepped in without asking and just assumed I'm some idiot who can't control my own life.'

'That's not what I did, Amy. You were having trouble with that loser, so I stepped in before anything got any worse...'

'Oh, I *see*. You assume that I'm as stupid and naïve as I was eight years ago. That's it, isn't it? You don't see me as anything else but a silly eighteen-year-old and you never will. The same way you see Willa. Just a stupid little girl who made a bad choice and married the wrong man all because *you* weren't there to save her. That's why you're driving her crazy now. That's why you won't leave her alone. You're suffocating her, Luke, and she doesn't like it.'

Luke stared back at her, his eyes still flashing green. 'My sister is *my* responsibility. And, yes, I see Willa as someone I have to look after—but not because she's stupid and can't take care of herself. Because I let her down. I knew she shouldn't have married that man. I knew she was too young and he was too old for her. But I said nothing back then. Just like when—'

His eyes searched hers.

Was he talking about the night she'd been attacked? Amy flushed. She hadn't seen Luke again after that night. She'd shed a lot of tears over what had happened, but so many more over what Luke must have thought of her. And now she knew. He thought she was silly and naïve and couldn't take care of herself. The thought made her heart feel heavy—she didn't want him to think like that about her.

'There were times I let things happen that I shouldn't have, and that was wrong. So I'm sorry if you think that my coming over here and stepping in is interfering, Amy. I'm sorry if you think I shouldn't be the kind of man who steps in and takes action to stop the people I care about from getting hurt. But I *am* that man. I may not have been eight years ago—hell, I wasn't that man a year ago—but I am going to be that man now. I don't want to lose any more people in my life just because I sit around and wait for bad things to happen.'

Emotion rolled off him like a morning fog. His fists were clenched and he stood too close. His eyes glowed and Amy realised there was more going on with Luke than he was letting on.

He might think she was silly and always getting into trouble—he might not want her or even like her—but she knew when someone needed a friend, and from the look on Luke's face, she knew he needed one right now.

'Luke…' He'd turned to go, but Amy caught his arm. 'Luke, wait. Stop.'

He stopped and turned. 'What?'

Amy realised now why he was all up in Willa's grill. Because he needed to talk…about something that was bothering him. His speech about not being there for people when they needed him had been passionate and emotional, and that was so unlike him. Hard, cool and distant. That had been Luke eight years ago. Something had changed.

Eight years ago Luke had been there for her when she'd needed him. He'd been a friend in the most difficult time she'd ever experienced. And tonight Amy was going to return the favour.

'Do you still have that crazy sweet tooth of yours?'

Amy smiled and Luke's brow furrowed into two dents between his eyes.

'What?'

'Come with me, Boss. I'm going to take you to heaven.'

CHAPTER SIX

LUKE KNEW HE WAS probably sporting his orgasm face right now, but he couldn't help it. He was literally in heaven. Amy had taken him to a late-night bakery called Heaven and inside he'd found cakes, slices, ice cream, macaroons and every other sweet thing his boyhood dreams had been made of.

He avoided this type of food because he knew how much he loved it and would always eat too much of it, but tonight it was just what he needed.

He'd had a bad day. The Singaporean government had brought up more issues. His manager in Singapore had been able to take care of it, but it had irritated him. He'd come to Sydney for some much needed rest, but so far he'd done nothing but stress. About the Singapore project, about Willa, and now about Amy.

He'd been thinking about her since that night. He'd tried to stop but he couldn't. She was still that same girl he'd known all those years ago but something had changed. He couldn't put his finger on it. She'd always been confident, but it was different now. Not a reckless wild confidence in her looks and the way she could turn men on. Now her confidence seemed more internal. As if she'd actually learned to like herself instead of always wanting to feel that attention from others.

Sure, she was still a flirt, but she seemed more in control of it now and was somehow able to turn that confidence in herself into a generosity that had him captivated. Like tonight. Instead of staying angry, as she should have when he'd stepped in and interfered, she'd seen that he was upset and left the party to make him feel better.

Luke shifted a little closer to her. Somehow, in some crazy way, that made him feel even more protective of her. He wanted to protect that good, kind heart of hers and not let anyone hurt it.

'Good?'

Amy was smiling. Tonight she looked even better than she had before. With a slick of red on her lips that matched the fire-engine-red strapless top she had on, she looked polished and perfect. Professional with an incredibly sexy edge. He could see why she was perfect in PR. She was the ideal combination of warmth and smarts. If she hadn't already been kicking goals and clearly happy in her job he would have tried to poach her for himself.

'*So* good. You're going to make me fat, Amy.'

She laughed, and he was reminded of old Amy. That bright laugh had used to echo across the office constantly. She didn't laugh as much now, he noticed.

'You'd never get fat, Luke, you're way too disciplined for that.'

She was right about that. He made sure every hotel he built housed a well-equipped gym. Keeping his body under control was something he *could* do—and with his sweet tooth, it was necessary.

'How did you remember about my sweet tooth?'

She laughed again, and he found himself moving even closer to her on the curved bench they were perched on. He licked another piece of cake off his spoon.

'You always worked. You were always in your office, or scooting off on a golf cart to check on some problem. The only time you emerged and actually sat with us was on the days someone had a birthday and we got cake. Sometimes we made birthdays up just to lure you out.'

'No? You didn't!'

Amy laughed again. 'We did once. Remember we wanted new uniforms and you didn't have time to go through them and choose? We went and got your favourite cake—chocolate rocky road—and had all the uniforms out and ready for you.'

He didn't remember that. But he *did* remember not having enough time. He'd worked hard over the years on that, and now made sure he was across everything.

'You always were a ratbag, Lollipop.'

'And you always were hard to deal with.'

Amy lifted her spoon to her mouth and Luke watched as she poked out her tongue to lick it clean. Long strokes, getting every last piece of cake. His body hardened. He'd tried to stay away from her. He hadn't called or contacted her because he knew his attraction to her was wrong. And now he was re-minded of why he should have stayed away tonight.

She dipped her spoon in for another piece. Her tongue came out before the spoon hit her lips and she closed her eyes as she sucked it. Luke put his cake down, his appetite gone. For food anyway.

'I'm not hard to deal with at all.'

Amy crossed her legs and her bare knee was now pointed at him. He wanted to touch her, just rest his hand there and feel that skin again.

'I'm a pussycat,' he said, trying to keep his voice level.

She laughed again and he smiled, right down deep inside. He liked it when she was happy. She deserved to be happy.

Amy placed her plate on the table but kept the spoon and absently licked it. He watched her tongue go in and out, wishing like hell that she was paying that type of attention to a part of his body that was now become uncomfortably large.

She leaned forward a little and her cleavage filled the red top. Swallowing, he lifted his eyes to hers. They were dark and warm, like the caramel fudge he'd just been eating.

'You're no pussycat…you're a big, unfriendly old lion. Even tonight you weren't happy to be here.'

'I've had a bad day. A bad week. I'm sorry.'

She sucked in a breath and her breasts moved up and down. Flicking her hair back, she leaned an elbow on her knee and rested her chin on it. Her dark eyes were big and she blinked at him. He licked his lips. Hot—it was so hot in here.

'And how about not calling me all week? Are you sorry for that?'

'Do you want me to be?'

'Luke, you don't kiss someone like that and then not call them.'

'I thought we'd agreed getting involved was a bad idea?'

'Did I say I wanted to get involved?'

'Well, what *do* you want, then?'

She moved closer, her face now level with is. Her scent met his nose and all his thoughts left his head. It was a week ago again, and this time he couldn't blame the booze. He wanted her.

'You. In my bed.'

'Be careful what you wish for.'

His blood pumped. He wanted this to happen. She wanted this to happen but knew it shouldn't. He *knew* that. But as her hand touched his leg he couldn't remember why.

'The thing is, Luke, I haven't had sex in a long time. A *very* long time. I find it hard to meet men I feel comfortable enough to want to get naked with. I know you think I'm a flirt and that I've probably got men tied up all over town…'

Luke had visions of her on top of him, his wrists tied and her doing whatever the hell she wanted. He put down his spoon.

'But I haven't. And the truth is I find you incredibly sexy. And I want you. And I know this is a terrible idea, but—to be honest—I think you'd really be helping me out.'

For the first time Luke realised Amy wasn't flirting with him. Her words were sincere. There was no fancy flattery. She was matter-of-fact, and he found himself liking it. She knew what she wanted. Sex. With him. And he realised that it was exactly what he wanted too.

She had the spoon in her mouth again, so he took it, slipping it from her lips. 'I can help you out, Amy, but you need to get rid of this damn spoon.'

In seconds, he'd replaced the spoon with his lips and she drew herself closer, licking his tongue the way she had been the spoon seconds ago. She tasted like cake and he kissed her deeper, his arms circling her small frame, dragging her to him. She responded with a little moan which only made his body harder.

'We should leave,' she murmured, and he took no time in getting her the hell out of there.

Amy's flat was only two blocks away but it seemed too far. Every time she got more than two centimetres away from him he grabbed her, pulled her close and started kissing her neck. She responded by turning and lifting her arms around his neck before kissing him back.

He wanted more of her—needed her horizontal. She seemed to want the same, because she was pulling on him, pulling him down closer, her hands everywhere—on his back, behind his head, through his hair. She gasped as she kissed him, barely coming up for air, and her desperation turned him on.

'If we keep kissing here we'll never get to your flat,' he whispered into her hair as she pulled him close again.

'I know, but I can't stop.' She pulled him again and he stumbled a little, accidentally pushing her so she stumbled too, but he caught her before she fell.

He laughed. 'Someone's going to get hurt.'

Grabbing at her from behind, he forced her to walk. But he didn't get far before the lure of the skin on the back of her neck called to him again.

This time she practically growled as she turned and jumped on him. Surprised, he stepped backwards, but found himself tripping on something. Before he could stop himself he was falling backwards into a bush in someone's garden, her right on top of him.

They clashed heads and landed in the leaves and Amy let out a little yelp.

'Are you okay?' he asked, holding her arms steady.

Strange noises came from her. At first he thought she was crying, and he struggled to get them upright, but she wasn't crying. She was laughing. It started as a giggle and ended in a contagious laugh with which Luke couldn't help but join in.

The bush rustled as they lay there, uncomfortable and sore, but unable to free themselves as they laughed heavily at nothing. She clung to him and he clung to her until their laughter subsided.

'You're just what I need, Amy.'

Her laughs evaporated and she looked at him. Her dark eyes were almost black in the night.

'Ouch,' she said, and moved to get up.

Not the reaction he was expecting, but possibly the best one she could give. This wasn't a relationship. This was just two friends helping each other out. He was glad she realised that, because they'd have more than a few scratches if they weren't on the same page.

'Help me up!' she whispered as the lights in the house were flicked on.

'Who's there? Is someone out there?'

They stilled, but the bush couldn't hold them, and then Amy shifted a little so that Luke had to adjust his position to hold her up.

'Who is it? I'm calling the police.'

With a struggle and a push Luke managed to get them both upright, and then he grabbed Amy's hand and pulled her hard. They ran off down the footpath, with abuse being hurled at them from behind.

CHAPTER SEVEN

AMY'S LUNGS BURNED. They'd run so fast, and she'd already been out of breath from all the kissing she'd been doing.

Kissing Luke was even better than she'd imagined it would be. He was confident and sure, and he'd held her so close and so hard she'd felt his desperation for her. It made her feel wanted and special. But she had to remind herself what this was about. *Sex*.

She'd decided to forget about Luke a few hours ago. But when he'd exposed himself to her with that speech about Willa being his responsibility and him wanting to be the kind of man who fixed things she hadn't been able to resist.

She wanted him all over again. Badly. And the truth was she hadn't felt that way about someone in a long time.

'Code?'

He was asking for her security code to get them into the building. He still had hold of her hand and it felt so good there.

'Zero, three, one, zero.'

He turned to face her. 'You shouldn't tell anyone your security code, Amy.'

Amy blinked. He was right. She *shouldn't* tell anyone her code. She would never normally tell anyone her code. But she'd blurted it out to him without any prompting. What was *wrong* with her?

'Don't worry, I'll have it changed by the morning. I don't want you breaking into my house while I'm not here and going through my underwear.'

His stern face disappeared and was replaced with a slow, sexy smile. He moved closer, slipping one hand down the front of her skirt to brush his fingers against the lace of her underwear. She sucked in a breath—a deep one. His fingers were confident and she wanted him to go further, explore deeper.

'How about I just do that out here?'

Deep and sexy, his voice made her legs shake.

'Open the damn door, Luke.'

He did—but not before he kissed her again, deeply, and with a force she'd never felt from Laurie. In comparison Laurie's kisses were soft, almost reverent. But there was nothing reverent about the way Luke was kissing her and moving his hand to get underneath the lace of her underwear.

Amy led the way up the stairs, pausing once to turn and kiss him again. She was finding it hard to go more than three seconds without feeling his lips on hers, and thankfully he responded the way she wanted him to. He stopped and kissed her back, his hands tangling in her hair as he pulled her face closer to him.

'Up, up…' he panted, and she moved backwards up the stairs before reaching the top and fumbling in her bag for the swipe card that would let her into her flat.

Before the door was even shut Luke had her up against the wall in her hallway. His hands worked on the zipper of her skirt as her hands fumbled with his buttons.

He was strong, and he held her as if she weighed nothing more than the packet of condoms she had in her bedroom—still unopened. Condoms she needed right now.

'My bedroom is down that way…' She struggled to get the words out as he kissed her lips, her eyes and her neck. That spot right between her collarbones. She'd never been kissed there, and she wasn't sure why it felt so damn good but it did.

The buttons undone, she finally got a look at the older, bigger, stronger and *tattooed* Luke. Across one side of his chest and down his shoulder were the black markings of a large tattoo. She couldn't make out what it was, and nor did she have time to look.

Luke was swiftly removing her top, pulling it up over her head, and he had her bra on the floor in seconds. His mouth moved down to her chest as he held her backside up against the wall. She ached to feel his tongue on her nipple. She wanted him to suck and lick and bite. She needed him right now, with a force she couldn't explain. This wasn't tender loving sex, like Laurie had offered, this was wild animal sex. And it was just what she needed.

'No time for bedrooms,' he said as he finally let her feet fall to the ground.

He moved down her body, his hands touching before his tongue licked. Her neck, her breasts, her nipples, her stomach… And finally he was pulling down her skirt and kissing the lace of her underwear. It was the only barrier between them now and she wanted it off. She tugged at it, trying to get it off.

The heat of his breath hit her bare skin as he helped her and she moaned loudly when he finally let his mouth kiss her swollen lips. She held his head steady as his tongue forced its way in. He licked with long strokes, and then with fast short ones. He moved his head a little to the side and kissed her, long and hard and deep, and Amy felt everything in her core shake.

She wanted to climb up onto his shoulders to get herself closer, but with a swift movement he already had her leg up. She pushed closer and he kissed deeper, delving with his tongue and sucking on her clit. Amy pressed closer. Laurie had never done it like this. *Never.*

She felt what Luke was feeling. He wanted her. Every bit of her. And he wasn't stopping until she was satisfied. But the orgasm wouldn't come. She clamped her stomach tight. She shifted away. She didn't want him to get sore, kneeling before her.

'Relax,' he murmured into her, which made a warm trickle flow up her spine. 'Relax, Amy. Let go. Enjoy it.'

His words murmured through her and she did what he said. She relaxed her muscles, she thought of nothing else but him and what he was doing, and within seconds the hot flash of a shaking orgasm tore through her. She bucked. She shook. It tingled up her body and then it was over.

Luke looked up at her, panting a little, his lips moist and his eyes greener than she'd ever seen them.

'Now we can move,' he said, a slow smile forming on his lips.

But she wasn't going anywhere. She pushed on his shoulders till he was on his back on the floor and then she tore at his belt. She had his pants down in seconds and hovered above him.

'Condom,' she said.

'Condom...' he repeated. But he didn't move.

Clearly he wasn't prepared—but she was. Quickly she sped into her room and fumbled through her drawer, trying to locate the pack she'd put there, intending to put it to use but not having done so yet. She slipped one from the packet and was back on top of him, ripping it open, in seconds.

But she was trembling too much to put it on. The orgasm was still freshly running through her body. So he took it from her hands and sheathed himself.

As soon as his hands hit the base she started. Slowly, purposefully sliding herself over him. A thrill ran over her as she lifted herself and then slid back down again. He was big, and she felt him throbbing inside her, but his face turned her on more than anything.

His mouth was almost a snarl and his eyes were focussed on her. Not her breasts, or her body, or what they were doing but connected right to her eyes—and she felt as if she could read his thoughts. His animalistic thoughts of just being in the moment and enjoying what she was doing to him.

His hands gripped her thighs and he moved her forwards, then backwards, faster and faster. She felt his gaze. It made her feel wilder, more free. She lifted her arms to her hair and let her mouth make the noises it wanted. She moaned, she sighed, she called his name.

He pushed her back and forth more frantically until he quietly growled, 'I'm going to come.'

She looked at him then—right into his eyes. 'I want you to come.'

And he did. Pulsating and pushing into her until another orgasm burst through her and shook her body. Abandoned, she shifted and moved until every last spark was spent, and then all she could do was fall on to his chest. Exhausted and dazed and much more satisfied than she'd felt in months.

CHAPTER EIGHT

THE SUN PIERCED Amy's eyeballs and she cursed loudly. She always remembered to pull the blinds before she went to sleep. *Always*. Because every morning the sun hit that spot that would fry her eyeballs and then sit there…just long enough to make sure she was awake and not able to go back to sleep.

She moved slowly, expecting her hangover to hit violently as soon as her head lifted from the pillow, but surprisingly her head felt okay. Was she hungover? No, of course not. She hadn't drunk that much last night. But she *was* hot.

She pulled the covers off, but just as they flicked to the other side she felt something she wasn't expecting. Warm flesh. Amy's head spun and everything returned in a rush. The nightclub…Heaven…falling in the bushes…the frantic backwards walk up the stairs and then the hallway…oh, the hallway.

Amy couldn't stop the smile that was spreading across her face. Because it hadn't been just the hallway. They'd made it as far as the lounge before they'd had to start kissing again, and then they hadn't even made the bed before he was on top of her and looking into her eyes again. Hard, direct and hot.

They'd laughed, and Amy had gone to get water, but by the time she'd returned he's been curled up in her bed. Naked and gorgeous. Which he still was now.

Amy wasn't sure whether it was the fact that it was Luke, but she'd never had sex like that before. Frantic and fast, desperate to taste, touch and be as close as possible to each other. He'd seemed to want her so badly, and it had made her want *him* even more badly. And as they'd kissed and touched and explored it had seemed nothing was off-limits. As if he was willing to do anything she wanted. And, God help her, last night she'd been willing to do anything to please him.

It was new. And dangerously addictive. But Amy had willpower. Loads of it. And she knew what this was. A reaction to a past life. Scratching an old itch. A way to pass the time while Luke was in town. It wasn't real and that was good. She didn't want real. She didn't want a relationship. Because relationships never lasted and someone always got hurt and she wasn't ready to do that again.

Luke moved. He rolled over, then opened one eye. He looked at her, and she smiled before giving him a little wave.

He opened his other eye and lifted his hand to wave back. 'Hi.'

'Hi.'

He lifted himself up with a yawn and a grunt and stretched. His thick torso shook as his fists rose up high over his head.

Amy bit her lip. *Willpower.*

'How are you feeling this morning?' he asked, his voice deep and sleepy.

Horny. 'Good. You?'

He met her eyes and paused before replying, 'Hungry, actually.'

'I have bread and… Actually, that's about it. Sorry.'

She and Jess didn't shop for groceries. They ate out. Toast and Vegemite was about all they had available in-house. And wine. There was always wine. But she guessed he didn't feel like wine.

'Bread?' He screwed up his face. 'That isn't going to cut it.'

'What do you want, then? This isn't a café I'm running, you know.' She mirrored his movements and propped herself up on one hand.

He smiled then—a lazy, slow smile—before bringing his big hand up to touch her thigh under the sheet. Amy shivered. Instantly her body overheated. Too many sheets covering her. She wanted to be completely naked. Exposed. And doing whatever he wanted. Hell, if he wanted to eat croissants off her stomach she'd let him.

Wait. No. Willpower.

'How about a bit of this?'

He grabbed a handful of her backside and roughly pulled her closer. Amy's nipples sprang to attention. Every hair on her body stood and her core started to throb. Slowly at first but then, as his hands moved and explored her skin, before coming round to rest right on her swollen folds, the throbbing beat overtime. She tried not to move. One move and his fingers would be inside her.

Willpower.

This visceral reaction was new. With Laurie it had taken foreplay and talking and a whole lot of negotiation. It had never been immediate like this. Laurie had never made her hairs stand on end. He'd loved her. Gently. Slowly. Respectfully. Laurie would have never grabbed her ass and pulled her so close she could feel him hard against her. She hadn't wanted him to.

But with Luke it seemed that clearly she did. Or her body did. It felt as if it was sparkling—as if it was alive for the first time in a long time—and she liked it. She didn't feel numb, for once, and she had Luke to thank for it. But that was all this was. Just an awakening. With a hot man she'd once had a thing for. Who she didn't have a thing for any more.

'A bit of what?' Amy teased, knowing what he wanted and wanting it too, but wanting to hear him beg. 'Don't you think you've had enough of that?'

'Not nearly enough.'

He snuggled in close and kissed her right behind the ear. Amy's back arched. A hot tingling streamed from the spot he was kissing right down to her toes.

'We should eat,' she protested, pulling away from him and meeting his eyes. They were almost blue. A sea-blue that reflected the ocean way offshore.

'I'm planning on it,' he growled, and kissed her long and hard on the lips.

Then, before she had time to breathe, he grabbed her by the waist and flipped her onto her back. She made all sorts of fake protesting noises but he cleverly ignored them. She squirmed a little, so he held her hips steady and sat up on his knees.

Amy admired the view. His chin was covered in a growth of twenty-four-hour stubble, his hair—although short—was standing in all directions. He looked a little beastly and a lot hungry. For *her*.

Amy had never felt so hot in her life. Normally she'd cover up, or make an excuse to calm things down so they wouldn't get out of control. So she could keep a handle on what was going on. But this was Luke. She'd known him for years. He knew her deepest darkest secret.

Her stomach swooped and he must have seen something flash in her eyes.

'Stop thinking. Just relax. Let me make you happy.'

He smiled and the swoop turned into something else. A more violent wave of sexual energy and excitement. The squirming to get away turned into a squirming to open her legs. Wider and wider, so his head could make its way down to where she was hot and swollen and oh, so wet…

'Delicious…' he murmured, using a finger to stroke her up and down before he pushed his way in.

Amy let out a guttural noise as Luke let his tongue explore, stroke and lick her. She shuddered happily. She tasted so good, and he loved being there in her warmth, feeling her buck against him. Her noises were becoming more frantic. She was close and he needed to slow it down. He wanted this orgasm to last a long time. He wanted her to really enjoy it and feel *everything*. But she tasted so damn good and was so responsive he couldn't let her go.

He tugged at her hips, bringing her down to his face.

He wanted to tell her to relax but he couldn't speak. Last night had been frantic and crazy, and when he'd woken this morning he'd wondered if it were all a dream. Then he'd seen her. Her blonde hair messed up, her eyes black from make-up and the sun belting in behind her, bathing her in some weird angelic light. Naked except for the sheet she'd held carelessly to cover her breasts. Then she'd waved, and a naughty look had crossed her face, and he'd been immediately hard all over again.

She was fun—he'd expected that. She loved sex. He hadn't expected that. He'd known she was flirty but he'd noticed a caution in her. Whenever a man spoke to her she wouldn't let him get too close. She often touched women when she talked, waved her hands about and lightly touched their arms when she laughed, but with men he'd noticed she was further away. Her voice was light, her laugh loud, but her body language was clear. *Don't get too close.*

Which was why, when they'd left Heaven, he'd been so surprised at her response. She'd leapt on him. She'd pushed herself into him, her lips hungry for the taste of him and her hands constantly moving over his skin. She'd made him feel bigger and stronger and so desired he'd lost his balance near that bush.

She'd ended up on top of him and he'd wanted to

wrap her in his arms and carry her home like some caveman. As if she were his. But she *wasn't* his. Not really. But right now she was—and right now it was his responsibility to give her the best damn orgasm of her life. And he was going to do it. She just needed to relax.

CHAPTER NINE

HE SHIFTED TO kiss her thighs gently, using the time to catch his breath and allow her to relax. She moaned and moved her hips. Her lips were swollen and open to him, and all he wanted to do was feast on her again, but he had to be patient. He wanted her to remember him.

He knew their time together wouldn't last long. It never did, and this in particular should never have started in the first place. But it had, so now he was determined that she'd remember him as the best damn sex of her life.

Swiftly he took her in his mouth again. He licked, then found the hard nub and sucked it gently while his tongue worked everywhere else. When she gripped the sheets tight and started to pant he knew she was close. Her hips rose up to his face…she pushed herself closer to him. *Wait. Wait. Not yet.*

Still he laved her, enjoying the feel of her on his lips and the way she was now gripping his hair, trying to get him closer, moving faster. *Now.* She was going to burst.

Luke gave her one last long suck before using two fingers to find that spot inside her that would make her scream. And she did scream. Loud. It was music to his ears and everything on him stood bigger and stronger and harder.

When her hips stopped bucking he sat up to look at her. She wasn't smiling but she looked beautiful. She used a hand to rub her face and over her hair. Blonde strands fell across her eyes and she looked so much like the old Amy of Weeping Reef. Young, carefree and in love with life Amy. And *he'd* done that. He'd made her feel that way—just for a moment.

Rising up above her, he didn't wait for her to be ready. He had to have her. *Now.* He slid in with force, grabbing her hips and forcing her back and forth. But she didn't deny him. She moved and rocked and moaned and called his name and the pressure built as she started to get control of her body. She matched him. She liked the way he moved—he could tell. She was hungry for him, greedy for him, and it just made him want her even more.

She sat up with him still inside her, her legs encircling him, her arms on his chest as his muscles moved. She watched them, watched what they were doing, and he lost it. Watching her watch made something inside his brain burst and he came without a second's hesitation.

For a moment everything went black, and Luke took the time to enjoy what had undoubtedly been the best sex of his life.

CHAPTER TEN

For Amy, the next two weeks were spent in a bubble. Working hard on her new account was easier when she knew that at the end of every day she'd get rewarded. With Luke. And his insatiable appetite…for *her*. Her body, her pleasure. He seemed to like it all.

He didn't call her during the day, but whenever she felt overwhelmed or bored, or felt like talking to him, he took her calls. He answered her texts. He paid her attention—he made her feel she was someone worth listening to and it was intoxicating. *He* was intoxicating. And the sex…

Amy shivered in her seat as she stared out through the plate glass window on the eighteenth floor of her work building. They were constantly hungry for each other. Every time was like the first time. He looked at her as if she was the most beautiful thing he'd ever seen, and she couldn't believe how much he fascinated her. She'd touched every muscle, every inch of skin on his body. She'd traced his tattoos with her finger, asking what each one meant.

She usually didn't get much of an answer, though,

because touching always turned to kissing, and kissing always turned to something more. It was wild and passionate and everything she'd never had with Laurie.

When she'd had a crush on Luke all those years ago she'd seen him as someone older, elusive and hard to pin down. Now it was different. She wasn't attracted to his cool, calm exterior any more. She was attracted to his warmth. To the way he made her feel. Alive. Buzzing.

She knew she shouldn't get too into this—he'd told her that he was only home for a little while, and reminded her plenty of times that relationships didn't work out for him because he was always travelling, but she couldn't help it. This wasn't just a fling— this was something else. They couldn't be that into each other and then let it fade away because he had to leave.

This relationship, although it was only two weeks old, felt more real than any relationship Amy had even had. She could be herself. She could expose herself and no matter what—he still wanted her. Was hungry for her. Not because he wanted to heal her or help her but just because he wanted her.

The phone in Amy's office made her head spin back to the computer and what she was working on. *Work*. She had to get back to it. She was meeting with the new clients later and they wanted to see her progress on the social media plan. Which she was nailing.

'Hey, Ames—what's up?'

Willa. Amy's heart beat a little faster. She'd been

neglecting her friend lately. Between work and Luke, she didn't have much time for their usual after-work drinks or lazy lunch dates. She needed to make it up to her.

'Heaps, darling. Working on this social media plan—it's hectic.'

'Clearly. I haven't seen you in so long I forget what you look like.'

Willa's tone was a little accusatory. Amy winced.

'I know, babe, and I'm sorry. I need to see you, but I've just been busy…you know.'

'Yeah, with work…'

'Yeah.'

'Definitely not with my brother.'

Amy stilled. That beating heart stopped. She hadn't said a word to Willa about her and Luke. She hadn't had the chance, for one—and also, if it didn't work out, she didn't want Willa to be upset. But to be honest the real reason was that this thing with Luke was new. And fragile. And so good. And she didn't want anything to touch it. She didn't want to be talked out of it. Because it was crazy, and she knew that, but she just didn't want to face it. Not yet.

'What do you mean?'

'I mean you have been spending a lot of time with Luke—haven't you?'

How the hell did she know that? Had Luke said something? Something about that idea made Amy's head and heart swell. He must like her if he was talking to his sister about them being together. What had he said?

'I… What…?'

'Jess told me.'

Jess. Of course. They'd tried to be discreet, but Jess had seen him at the flat. Leaving. Arriving. Jess had tried to ask Amy about it but she'd shut her down. She usually discussed everything with Jess—but she didn't want to discuss this with her either.

She also suspected that Jess had a bit of a crush on Luke, and although she hated to admit it she was slightly panicked by that thought. Jess was hot and fun and edgy and out there, and a part of Amy wondered if maybe Luke would prefer that, given the chance. It was a crazy thought—but Luke made her a little crazy.

'He's just popped in a few times…to talk about things. Has he been better with you?'

Turn the conversation around. That was the best solution.

'I know you're trying to turn this around to me, Ames, but we're talking about *you*. And Luke. And when he's turning up late and leaving in the morning he's not there to "talk about things", is he?'

Amy could tell Willa was a bit peeved. But she wasn't sure why. Was it because she hadn't told her what was going on or—worse—was it because she didn't approve? She'd known this would happen. Other people's opinions *always* affected things. That was why she hadn't wanted this to get out yet. She'd wanted to get to know him on her own. Enjoy him on her own. But it was out now and she'd have to deal with it.

'Don't be mad, Wills.'

'I'm not mad. Just confused. Why haven't you told me? Why does Jess know and I don't?'

That was it. Willa was worried about their friendship. Which was crazy as Willa was the best friend Amy had ever had and ever would. They'd been through so much during that summer on Weeping Reef, and since they'd become friends again it had been as if the past eight years' absence hadn't happened.

'Jess doesn't know, Wills. She's just been in the flat and seen some things and is assuming a lot. But you're right. We need to talk. But I can't today—I have a super-important meeting. How about drinks tomorrow night at Saints? I'll tell you everything then.'

Willa paused. Amy could hear her breathing. And thinking.

'Okay. But don't bail on me—or I'll hunt you down, okay?'

'Okay, I won't. See you then, my lovely.'

Amy hung up with a full heart. She had so much right now. A friend who loved and cared about her. A fabulous job. A great lifestyle. But for some reason it all paled when she thought of those times spent with Luke. He made her feel more alive and bright than anything else.

She'd never been this excited about a man and she'd never let a man's interest in her affect her other relationships or her emotions. How had Luke got under her skin so quickly? Laurie's love had been easy and secure, and she'd always known where she stood, but with Luke it was different. Every day she wondered if it was her last with him, or if it was even going anywhere.

And now people were beginning to talk. Maybe she needed to find out. As much as she wanted it to keep going on the way it was, perhaps it was time to find out if this thing they'd started was anything—or nothing. If anything, having this talk now might save her a broken heart—because she was pretty damn sure that even though she hated the idea of it she was falling like a stone in the ocean for Luke.

Luke checked his watch. She was late. He was getting used to that. She was always late. He hated it when people were late, but when it came to Amy—like everything else about her—he liked it. It added to her charm. Which was utterly stupid.

He tried to think of something he didn't like about her, but he couldn't. And that was what was annoying him. Too often lately he'd been thinking about her. He'd always made a point of not contacting the women he was sleeping with. He didn't want them to think he wanted more.

But when *she* called him or texted him he couldn't help but respond. He liked hearing her voice. He liked listening to her problems. He liked the sound of her voice. It turned him on. It calmed him down. It made him feel better. Which was why he was nervous. Letting someone else affect the way he felt was dangerous. It made him lose sight of what was going on.

He spotted her coming down the street. Her skirt

was tight and her heels were high. He loved it when she looked all professional and smart—it turned him on. But then when she was at home and in bed naked, with her hair everywhere, it turned him on as well.

Damn, *everything* about her turned him on. He needed to find something about her he didn't like. Just something small he could focus on. Because he'd realised this morning when she hadn't texted him and he'd missed it that he was feeling a little too much for little Miss Lollipop. *Big mistake.*

'How did your meeting go?'

He'd barely got the words out before she landed on him. Her arms around his neck, her soft lips on his. He liked that about her. She always wanted him. Always wanted to touch him. Always showed him how she felt. It was a nice change from most of the women he met, who preferred games over real emotion. But he was supposed to be finding things he didn't like—not things he did.

He held her arms and pushed her back. 'Did you win them over?'

She smiled. He liked that too. She had a beautiful smile. Sunny…bright. Nice straight white teeth and a dimple in either cheek.

'Of course I did. They love me. Why wouldn't they? I'm amazing.'

He liked that too. Her cheeky confidence. She never made excuses. She knew who she was and what she was and that turned him on.

This wasn't going well.

'That's true. You *are* amazing.'

She smiled and he realised he liked her eyes as well. Caramel-brown, they were looking at him softly now and his body hardened. How the hell could her damn eyes turn him on?

'But I have a surprise for you.'

She raised an eyebrow. Yep. Turned on.

'I like surprises…'

She held his hand and rose up on her toes to kiss his cheek. This was a disaster. But he was about to give her a surprise he was sure she *wouldn't* like. Then he might see another side of her. Bitchy. Moody. Inflexible.

He pulled her to the side of the road. 'I'm taking you for a ride.'

She turned to where he was looking. His fully customised 1975 Harley Fat Boy sat arrogantly on the road. A motorbike. This would test her. Riding a bike with him would mess up her hair. She was wearing heels. Her skirt was too tight. She would complain. Most women did.

Amy let go of his hand. She stepped off the kerb, her eyes trailing over the length of the bike. She reached out a hand tentatively and stroked the custom-painted tank. Luke had built the bike himself. He'd taken pains to remove everything nice on the original bike. Everything on it now was raw, pared back, and as un-pretty as he'd been able to make it. This wasn't a show bike. It roared. It cut through the traffic like a beast. It was a hog and a pig and he loved it. But he was sure she wouldn't.

'Wow.'

His heart sank. Was that a sarcastic 'wow'? He had wanted to pick her up on the bike today so he'd see that bad side of her, but now that she'd said it he realised he was a little disappointed.

'You don't like it?'

She turned to him. 'It's magnificent. It's so...*you*. Are you going to let me ride on it with you?'

Luke's heart stopped. She *liked* it. She wanted to ride it with him.

He should have known. That reckless, carefree Amy was still in there. All locked up behind her power suits and bravado—but she was still there. Still looking for new adventures.

His blood bubbled. She wanted to ride and he wanted to show her. He wanted her to feel the way he did on a bike. When his mind clicked off and the wind and the speed made his heart race and he felt fearless and immortal. She'd love that.

But this was supposed to frighten her. She was supposed to complain. This was supposed to be the thing he didn't like about her. She'd surprised him once again. And it turned him on.

If it wasn't for all the people walking along the street right now he'd rip that tight skirt right off her, lay her on his bike and show her how much he liked her right here.

The beast she'd awakened in him growled and he beat it down with a whip. His attraction to her was getting dangerous and it had already been two weeks. It was time for him to move on, get distracted, feel suffocated. But he hadn't yet. And that was irritating him. Maybe it was just because he wasn't working all day long. Usually he had that to focus on.

'The helmet will mess your hair up—just warning you.'

She stepped closer, her hands on his chest, and looked up at him. 'I'm not scared of getting my hair messed up.'

'What *are* you scared of, then?'

Her eyes flicked from one of his to another. She was thinking about her answer.

'I'm scared of lots of things, but not when I'm with you.'

Her answer was quiet and her voice had changed. He felt it, stabbing right in his heart. Another thing he liked. She liked him. But that was exactly the thing he *shouldn't* like.

'We'll see about that. I've heard it's pretty scary on the back of my bike.'

She smiled and reached around to the back of her skirt. There was a long zipper there that she zipped right up. She took the helmet from his hands and put it over her head. She fumbled with the clasp, so Luke reached out and did it up for her. He didn't want her to hurt herself if she fell off. Which she wouldn't. He was an excellent rider.

He took her handbag and stuffed it in his saddlebag. He really pushed it down but she didn't complain. She just raised an eyebrow as he hauled himself on to the bike. She didn't even ask any questions. She just slipped off her shoes, shoved them into the bag as well and climbed on the back.

Luke pumped the peg. Her breasts were firm against his back. He pumped again and the engine roared into life. He let the clutch go and the bike jerked, throwing her forward a little until she was pressed right up against him. He couldn't see, but he was sure that skirt of hers was high up around her thighs. She tightened her grip on him with her legs and slipped her arms around his waist. His fists tightened on the grips.

He needed to ride. He had to stop thinking about her and the way she felt against his back. So trusting and so close. He just wanted to ride back to his place and get her naked—but he wasn't going to. He'd just find more things to like about her. The way she looked with nothing on, the way her skin felt—silky and smooth—and the noises she made. The soft moans and the loud screams. He liked it all.

He needed to lose himself in the wind and the speed and pretend that everything was all right and he had everything under control. So he rode. And she pressed herself closer, hugging him harder on the corners and yelling in his ear at the traffic lights. And he liked her even more. She was having fun, and she got it.

When they hit the open road her grip relaxed and she stayed quiet, and he enjoyed the feel of her pressed up hard against him as if they were one body, riding free. No destination in mind, just enjoying the ride.

Amy felt more free on the back of Luke's bike than she had in longer than she could remember. With the rush of wind flying past her ears there was no chance to talk. And there was no reason to either. They didn't need to talk. She sat close to him on the bike, every part of her pressed against him and buzzing with the road underneath. It felt intimate and comfortable.

Every bump or turn in the road just brought her closer to him and she snuggled in tight. But not too tight. Her grip was firm, but he was able to move and guide her if he needed to. They were in unison, in perfect sync, and Amy realised that this was what she'd never had with Laurie.

She had never been Laurie's equal. He'd loved her too much and had put her on a pedestal so high that she'd never have been able to love him that much. But here with Luke she felt as if they both knew what was going on and they both wanted the same thing. Today. With each other. On this bike. In the sun.

She wasn't sure how long they'd been riding. The sun was still up, but falling, and Luke had slowed down to manoeuvre through the gates of the national park. There was a track, but the trees were close. It twisted and turned but strangely Amy felt safe. She never felt as if she'd hit one of those trees. He knew what he was doing and she completely trusted him as a rider.

The bike stopped and Amy still buzzed. She climbed off a little shakily, and Luke caught her and laughed.

'Might take you a few minutes to get your land legs. Sit down and take your helmet off. I want to show you something.'

Amy sat, a smile planted firmly on her face. She had no idea where she was but she didn't care. Adventure. Fun. Mystery. Excitement. That was what was missing from her life. She'd been playing it safe for so long she'd forgotten what this was like. This was the sort of thing she'd done all the time on Weeping Reef—she'd always been looking for something to make her heart beat faster.

She guessed her need for excitement was due to the safe and fairly subdued way she'd grown up, in a house full of loving and gentle health nuts and the safe but so confining all-girls school she'd gone to. It was no wonder she'd broken out and gone crazy on Weeping Reef. It had been the first time she'd met people who were like her. People who wanted to have fun and see the world and have adventures.

And they'd all had some fun. Until that night. When everything had changed. When fun had seemed to die.

Amy watched Luke as he rested his helmet on the seat and pulled a knapsack out of the leather bag tied to the side of the bike. Luke was one of only two people who knew what had happened that night. Amy had never told her parents or Laurie. Her mother had suspected that something had happened on the island, and one night she'd come close to guessing, but she hadn't, and Amy had been relieved.

She didn't want to reveal how naïve and stupid she'd been and she didn't want to talk about it. All she wanted to do was forget. She knew now it wasn't her fault. But somewhere deep inside she had one regret.

That she'd left. That she'd packed up and run away and hadn't confronted the man who'd affected her so much. That she hadn't told him what she thought of him and what a coward he was. Somehow, in some way, it made her feel that he'd won and she'd lost.

'Ready?'

Luke smiled and Amy's mood brightened instantly. He grabbed her hand and hauled her up easily from the rock she was sitting on. The day was warm, but not hot, and they were alone in the bushland. Sticks and dry leaves crunched underfoot and the only other sound was the calling of birds and cicadas as they pushed their way through the low-lying branches.

A hum was the first indication that the landscape was changing, and it was only seconds later that Amy had to stop and look.

'Luke, it's beautiful…' she said absently.

Falling from a cut of rock high above them was a large waterfall. It wasn't blue, but nor was it green, and it didn't rush down heavily but fell gently, with occasional rushing swoops into a pool below that was surrounded by rocks. The water created an atmosphere of cool air that Amy felt whisper over her shoulders.

'My dad used to bring me here when I was young. We'd ride all day and camp here at night. Back then you could light fires, so we'd cook up some sausages and talk about nothing.'

'Do you two come here any more?'

'No. We haven't been back since Mum died.'

Amy remembered Willa talking about her mother a

few times. She'd died when Willa was in high school. It had been hard for her. Luke had been away at university and she'd been alone with her dad, who had been grieving.

She'd told Amy how alone she'd felt. Amy had always imagined that they had become so close because Willa had been dying for some female company. When they'd first met Willa had been so shy and reserved. It had been fun to try and bring her out of her shell and make her see the world differently.

Amy was sure she'd done most of her outrageous things just to show off to Willa. And of course to Luke. Perhaps that was why Luke hadn't liked her back then. Perhaps he'd thought his sister should have been cocooned for longer instead of being thrown out into the big bad world and encouraged to live the way Amy wanted to.

Back then Amy had been looking for fun without thinking of the consequences. Now all she did was think of consequences. She wondered if there was some way to find a balance. A way to have fun, like she was having with Luke, but still be good at her job and feel safe. She felt safe right now. Holding his hand, enjoying the sun. She felt safer with him—a man she'd really only known properly for two weeks—than she had with any man she'd met since Laurie.

And the difference was that she wanted Luke so badly she ached. He seemed like the perfect combination of sexual freedom and safety. Except he wasn't. Because he'd told her so many times that he didn't do relationships, and she still wasn't sure that going out with her best friend's brother was her smartest idea, so how was *that* safe? But right now she didn't want to think about that. She just wanted to enjoy what was left of the afternoon with Luke.

Amy's body shimmered in the water. It hadn't taken much convincing for her to get naked and dive in. She was brave and bold and game for anything. She surprised Luke every time. She was thirsty for adventure, but never reckless about it. And sexually she wanted to do whatever it took to please him—just as he wanted to do whatever it took to please her.

He was sure he just had—on the riverbank. Now it was her turn. She turned back to him, a sexy half-smile on her face as she cut through the water with long, confident strokes, only coming up for air when she was near the waterfall. She dipped her hands in it, then gasped when she tried to put her head under and it pushed her down into the water.

He was at her side in seconds, pulling her up from where she'd sunk. She coughed and spluttered and pushed the hair out of her eyes. He pulled her close. He wanted her where he could see her. Where he could keep her safe.

Her breasts pushed up against his chest and her legs wrapped around him. She totally trusted him. She didn't for a second think he'd break her heart, and that made him feel a little too hot. She smiled slowly and he kissed her, long and hard. He let his tongue stroke against hers and moved against the smooth skin of her legs.

This afternoon had been perfect, and he didn't want it to end, but it had to. And so did this thing with Amy. Not because he'd found anything wrong with her, but because he *couldn't* find anything wrong with her. There was only ever one reason a man couldn't find fault with a girl, and that was… Well, it was better not to think about that.

Suddenly Amy's eyes went dark and the smile disappeared from her face as she shifted to allow his length inside her. He knew he was so close it was dangerous. Amy moaned as he moved to fill her and her fingernails scraped over his back. The pain from the scratches felt good, and pressure built from feeling her move against him.

He needed traction, so he moved them back towards the rocks underneath the waterfall. Grabbing her by the waist, he lifted her up and off him and onto the rocks. She lay back, waiting like a beautiful mermaid. He wanted her. Had to have her. He wanted her body and to hear her laugh and to keep her safe. And as he climbed up on top of her, to slide in long and smooth and slow, he knew he was falling.

This couldn't go on.

She groaned in appreciation.

This had to end.

She lifted herself up and wrapped her arms around his neck. He pushed himself in deeper. Her moans got louder, her panting wilder. and he couldn't stop. He watched her face, her eyes—the way she threw her head back to expose the bones at the base of her neck and her hard nipples. He kissed them. He kissed her neck and behind her ear. He found her mouth and kissed away her screams as he allowed himself to go, allowed himself to love her—just once.

And when he came to and saw her breathing heavily, her skin glistening, not smiling, exhausted from their lovemaking, he knew it had to end.

CHAPTER ELEVEN

THE MESSAGE ON Luke's phone beeped angrily at him.

Huynh has revoked the approval. Everything has to be submitted again.

Kel Huynh had been the thorn in his ass since this whole project began. She was tough and strict and had made him jump through every hoop she could find during the whole process of building his hotel.

It was his most ambitious project to date. He'd never built a hotel this large or complicated before. There was a retail precinct, bars, restaurants, and he'd managed to lease out a large portion of the hotel to one of the richest companies in South East Asia to open their state-of-the-art casino. But Kel Huynh had fought him every inch of the way.

She was against the casino, but without it the project wasn't feasible. They'd managed to get the casino in, but now she was stopping them getting a twenty-four-hour licence—which would totally ruin the whole project.

His man in Singapore was one of his most trusted employees. He'd managed and transformed Luke's very first hotel and Luke knew he'd be able to handle this on his own. But it irritated him that there was another hitch. Maybe it could be sorted without him... but maybe a trip back to Singapore was just what he needed. Distance. Time. Perspective.

This afternoon at the waterfall with Amy had been awesome. For the first time in a long time he'd thought of nothing else but now. But that didn't sound too smart to him.

He'd always been a planner. He'd always planned for the future, tried to foresee problems before they happened so he could deal with them. So he could be prepared. So much in life was unpredictable—planning was his way of trying to stay in control. But with Amy he didn't even think about planning. Each day was a new adventure. And despite what he knew he should do it felt great to be living in the moment. Too great. Dangerously great.

'What is it?'

Amy was pulling on her helmet. She'd forgone the skirt this time and was planning to ride behind him in nothing but her underwear and his shirt tied around her waist. With her wet hair drying messily and her shirt unbuttoned to reveal a slice of her gorgeous breasts, she looked hotter than he'd ever seen her.

'There's a problem with the Singapore hotel. A big one.'

'What's wrong?'

'It's the twenty-four-hour opening. They've denied our licence. It's a big problem.'

'But haven't you got someone to handle all that for you?'

'It's a big problem, Amy—the whole project could fall.'

A slight exaggeration, but he needed to buy some time. She put her hands on her hips and let her head fall to the side. Hot. Sexy. He wanted her again.

'I might have to go back to Singapore.'

'What?' She stood up straighter. 'When?'

'Soon. Tomorrow.'

He knew they could handle it without him. But he also knew no one else could do it better than him. Kel Huynh was clever and she was quick. He really should be there in the room when his people met with her.

'I've never been to Singapore.'

Luke stilled. Amy's expression had changed. She stood awkwardly, her hands clasped in front of her.

'I've always wanted to.'

'It's… I wouldn't say it's the most exciting city.'

Bars, restaurants, a nightlife like no other, constant warm weather—the place was exactly up Amy's alley.

But if she was there he wouldn't be able to think. Or work. This crazy feeling of falling for her would never go away and he needed it to. This was *Amy*. Little Amy. His sister's best friend. Reckless, careless Amy, who would get hurt when he let her down. He couldn't fall for Amy.

'I don't know—I've heard good things. And it would be really helpful to see a hotel of your size in action. To help with my account, I mean…' Her caramel eyes looked at him, then looked at the ground. 'Unless, I mean… Unless you don't want me tagging along. I shouldn't—'

'No, it's not that. I… It's just. I'll be working and I won't have a lot of time to…spend with you.'

'No. Of course…I know.' She looked up again. 'But I'm a big girl—I could look after myself.'

The silence went on too long.

Luke didn't know what to say without sounding like the world's biggest ass

'Okay, yeah. Sure. You can come…if you want.'

She shrugged and her cheeks reddened. 'Only if you want me to.'

'Of course…'

Luke moved to put his arm around her waist. He went to kiss her forehead but she thought he was going to kiss her lips and moved, but not fast enough, and he ended up kissing her eyelid instead. *Smooth*.

'Of course I want you to.'

'Okay…then…'

The ride back to Amy's apartment was quiet. She didn't yell in his ear at the traffic lights and she didn't press herself up against him. When she got off she thanked him and retrieved her bag and skirt with an awkward blush.

Luke's palms itched. He didn't want it to be like this. Even though he knew they couldn't go on, he didn't want it to be like *this*. But it was. And it was probably going to be like this for a week, because now she was coming to Singapore with him.

'I'll have someone book a flight for you and let you know the details.'

He kissed her on the cheek. She didn't look at him.

'Okay, sure. No problem. I'll wait to hear from you then.'

'Good.'

'Great.'

'Okay, then. Bye.'

'Bye.'

When Luke's motorcycle had roared into life and sped down the street Amy lifted her expensive handbag above her head and threw it onto the ground with a force she hadn't realised she had. Then she swore so badly she was sure it would have made a trucker blush. Then she picked up her bag and her pride and stalked into her house to find as much wine as she could and shout at herself for being such a fool.

The sweat dripped slowly between Amy's shoulder-blades and down her back. The taxi was clean, but there was no air con. She was hot and tired and re-gretting everything.

She knew she looked a wreck. Frizzy hair, make-up sweated off and massive bags under her eyes.

The eight-hour flight from Sydney to Singapore had been awkward and embarrassing. First class was always a nice way to travel, but Amy hadn't been able to enjoy it. Luke had spent the entire trip next to her on his computer, sending emails and filling out forms.

Amy had tried to talk to him but he'd shut her

down with one-word answers and she'd spent the entire trip feeling as if she was disturbing him.

Everything had been going so well. They'd been enjoying each other. She'd been happy and he'd seemed happy. It hadn't been until she'd asked to come to Singapore with him that everything had changed. But why shouldn't she have come? They'd spent almost every day together in the past two weeks, and he'd seemed to be as into her as she was him.

But obviously she'd got it wrong. *Again.* She'd trusted someone she shouldn't have *again.*

The taxi stopped in front of a tall space-age style building. Luke was still silent as he stepped out of the taxi and ordered the bags to be brought in. As soon as the doors rolled open he was met by five staff members and Amy found herself walking behind him. Forgotten. Neglected. This wasn't the Luke of the last two weeks. Who *was* this man? This seemed more like Weeping Reef Luke. Absent and obsessed with work.

Check-in took no time. Luke was handed a key, and he finally took Amy's arm as he led her to the elevator.

'What do you think?' he asked when they stepped into the cool mirrored lift.

She shook her hair out, confused. 'About…?'

'The hotel. Do you like it?'

Did she like the hotel? *That* was what he wanted to talk about after an eight-hour silent flight?

'Sure. It's amazing.'

It was. From the garden in the foyer to the busy,

efficient service of the staff. But she hadn't expected anything less of any hotel Luke owned.

'Good.'

More silence. The lift stopped on the very top floor. Of course. The doors opened to reveal a private penthouse. Of course. Amy should have felt better about it than she did. They were here in one of the most exciting cities in the world in possibly the most beautiful hotel room she'd ever seen and she wasn't happy. She was furious.

'I have some work to do. I'll have to go into the office. There's food and drinks in the fridge—help yourself and call the concierge if you need anything at all.'

That was it. That was the very limit.

'What I *need*, Luke, is for you to stop acting like the King of Jerks and talk to me.'

He looked at her blankly and her anger spread.

'Or is this how it's going to be? You avoiding me and neglecting me and treating me like some mistress? Because that's not good enough, Luke. I'm not your mistress. I'm not here for a sordid little affair. I want to be with you and spend time with you and that's exactly what's going to happen!'

Amy didn't expect what happened next. She didn't expect him to come at her with force and grab her around the waist and kiss her with a passion she hadn't felt before—even from him.

'Luke?' She tried to speak between kisses.

'I thought you were regretting your decision to

come here,' he said, coming up for air before putting her face in his hands and kissing her again.

'I thought *you* were.'

'No. Not at all. I *want* you here. I want you with me. I couldn't stand you not talking to me on the plane.'

Amy clawed at his shirt. She needed him naked. His desperation for her was turning her on.

'You were the one not talking to me.'

'No, that was *you*.'

He tugged at her top until it came off over her head and she desperately unbuttoned his shirt. He pulled it free and she moved to his belt as he pulled her pants off easily. She stepped out of them and gasped when his hand drifted down her stomach and into her underwear, his fingers gently coaxing her to come to life. It didn't take much. She was already hot and wet for him as she fumbled with the remainder of his clothes.

'Why are you so difficult?' she demanded as his fingers expertly drove inside her.

She clung to his shoulders, then let her teeth clamp on his lips as they kissed. His moan echoed in her ear and spun her brain out of control. His skin was hot and he was naked now. She could feel him hard and ready against her belly. She couldn't wait for a bed. She wanted him now. Eight hours on the plane—not touching him, not talking to him, not having him close to her—and she was mad with anger and desire and want. Apparently he felt the same way.

'Not difficult. Maybe a little challenging. But you

seem like the type of woman who likes a challenge,' he answered, lifting her up with one arm and pulling her underwear down with the other.

She hoisted her legs around his waist before sliding her hand down his taut torso and letting her fingers grip his silky shaft. She knew what it felt like, what it tasted like, and she wanted it inside her right now.

'There's challenging, and then there's downright rude. You didn't talk to me for *eight hours*, Luke. You made me feel rejected and unwanted.'

She squeezed and his arms held her tighter, his eyes meeting hers. Hot. Direct.

'I'm sorry. Sometimes when I don't know what to say I say nothing.' He kissed her shoulders, then lifted her up a little to kiss her breasts.

Amy used both her hands to cup his face—she needed him to hear what she had to say. 'You can say anything to me, Luke. *Anything*. Even if you think I don't want to hear it. The worst thing you can do is leave me in the dark. Then I jump to conclusions and I get scared—and I hate being scared.'

He stilled and she felt his big arms pull her in closer. His forehead was close to hers…their lips were almost touching.

'Don't be scared, Amy. I have you.'

Amy couldn't hold back any more. The tight knot in her heart was taking up all the space and her heart was beating hard and heavy. She kissed him desperately, wanting him to know exactly how she felt right then.

'I know you do,' she murmured as his kisses became deeper and even more frantic.

'Say you want me, Amy.' His demand was growled in her ear.

'No, you say it first.' She was throbbing for him. She wanted his length where his fingers had moved and were now eagerly exploring.

He leaned down, let his tongue slide on her earlobe and growled in a deep, gritty voice, 'I want you.'

Every thought left Amy's head.

'Now,' she demanded. 'Now!'

Luke lifted her at the waist and let her slide onto him. He was big and hard and he filled her, and she wanted more. She moved up and down and around until the heat inside her body coiled in her core. This was what she'd missed. Him being close. Him needing her and wanting her and depending on her.

She massaged his big shoulders and whispered in his ear, using the dirtiest words she knew. That seemed to fuel him even more and he drove himself into her almost angrily, definitely greedily, and Amy took his anger and his greed and paid it back just as violently.

Luke brought out something in her she'd never felt before—a desire to please and be pleased. A need to protect and take care of someone. As selfishly as she enjoyed sex with him, the desire to give herself selflessly to him was almost impossible to control. She was doing things with Luke she'd never done with Laurie. She'd never whispered dirty words to him.

She'd never wanted Laurie so much she couldn't wait even to lie down.

Luke was different. He made her feel as if nothing was taboo. As if sex was a normal—no, a vital part of their relationship and was the way they communicated sometimes. Sex was like breathing and eating and talking. It kept them close and together and sane and made her feel that they needed each other the way they needed food.

Luke was moving slowly now and she knew what was happening. It was his calm before the storm. His way of preparing himself before using all his strength. And she knew this was her time to let go and feel him rubbing so close, making her clit come alive, making her orgasm bubble to the surface. She rode him and he rode her right back.

'I'm coming,' he growled, and she responded with more dirty words. More reasons for him to use all the strength he had to take her to the place only he could.

This time the orgasm lasted longer, and the aftershocks kept her clinging to him for minutes. She couldn't let go. Their bodies were almost fused together. It took a while for their breathing to calm and for a laugh to escape from both of them.

'*That* was an orgasm,' he said, his voice deep and sleepy.

Slowly, carefully, he let her off and she found the chaise longue that sat nearby and collapsed onto it. He collapsed next to her and kissed her mouth before shifting to one side and running the backs of his knuckles up and down her arm.

'Don't ever do that again,' she said, still breathless and panting.

'What?'

'Leave it that long before making love to me. I'm pretty sure I lost some brain cells then.'

He laughed, and the sound warmed her from the inside out. She loved it that she could make him laugh.

'Me too. It was pretty intense.'

'It was—because you ignored me for so long.'

'No, you ignored *me*. I was trying everything I could to feel your leg under that blanket.'

Amy furrowed her brow. 'That's what you were doing? I thought you were pushing my leg away.'

'No, you ratbag.' He turned to face her and his arms came around her as her body sank into comfortable relief. 'I was trying it on. Trust me, if you feel my hands anywhere near you I'm trying it on. Never pushing you away.'

'Then you should *say* that and not let me jump to conclusions.'

'You should ask and not let me think you don't want to talk.'

Touché.

They lay like that for a long time, drifting in and out of sleep. Exhausted from lovemaking and being wound up and from the flight.

After a while, they got hungry, and Luke insisted on ordering food from Din Tai Fung. He wanted her to have the dumplings, insisting they were the best. And they were. And they ate and talked and laughed and watched as the sun set over Singapore's skyline.

As they sat together, their legs entwined, full of dumplings and content from hot sex, Amy's shoulders relaxed. Luke was asking her about why she'd left Melbourne and what she'd left behind.

'His name was Laurie…' she explained. She hadn't talked about him to Luke yet. She hadn't wanted him to know. She was worried he'd judge her as everyone else had. 'His parents were good friends with my parents, which was why my leaving became so messy.'

'Messy how?'

Amy remembered the sadness and the anger and the guilt she'd felt. It hadn't happened overnight with Laurie—it had taken a while. It had started with little things. Things that had annoyed her about him. Mostly the way he had become so dependent on her. She'd started to feel suffocated and as if she couldn't make a move without it affecting him. She'd thought that sex with Laurie had been great at the time. It wasn't until now, when she'd had sex with Luke, that she realised how safe and staid it had been.

Amy snuggled in closer. 'Our break-up wasn't just about the two of us. Our families got involved…everyone had an opinion. It was actually my brother who helped me make my mind up. He said that if I wanted to leave he would be there for me. That he was on my side and it was better for everyone if I listened to myself and what I wanted. He said they'd get over it eventually.'

'And have they?'

'My mother was angry about it for a long time, but she loves me. I know that, and I know she wants me to be happy. So she doesn't even talk about it now—except to occasionally mention that she runs into Laurie from time to time.'

'And how did he take it? Laurie?'

'Badly. He begged me to come back. Cried. Wrote me letters. Posted sad quotes on social media. I almost caved so many times, but Antony told me to stay strong. He said that life is yours to live—not anybody else's. He said I wouldn't ever be happy if I didn't do what my heart wanted and that eventually my unhappiness would start to affect everyone else. He told me that it was just the change—the prospect of everything being turned upside down—that was making everyone so upset, not the fact that I wanted to leave.'

'And did it make you happy? Leaving?' Luke asked quietly.

Amy felt his hands start to stroke her hair and she felt almost like a cat, curled up and comfortable and not wanting to move an inch.

Yes. She was happy right now. She'd been so happy since she'd met Luke again. For the first time in a long time she didn't feel the need to go anywhere, see anyone or do anything. She didn't need anything to make her feel high, to make her forget. She just wanted to be here with him. Still.

'I will be,' she said quietly. 'What about you? I don't know anything about your significant relationships.'

Luke breathed in heavily and stopped stroking her head. She didn't move an inch. She wanted him to keep going. After a few seconds he did and she breathed out, curling up even closer to him.

'There was one of significance. Well, our *relationship* wasn't significant. We didn't know each other long. I was in Malaysia for business and we met at a business dinner. She was English—divorced. She'd been living in Malaysia for six years. She needed company. I needed…well…I needed company too. It lasted three weeks. I liked her a lot but there was no real connection there. We were just friends.'

'Why was it significant, then?'

'She got pregnant.'

Amy froze. *Luke had a child?* How had she not known this?

'She lost the baby, though. At fourteen weeks. I wasn't there when it happened.'

Amy sat up and looked at him. His eyes were red and he looked tired. He ran a hand through his hair, messing it up. It made him look younger. Unsure of himself.

'It was a pretty bad time,' was all he said.

Amy didn't know what to say but she knew what to do. She kissed him. Lightly, gently. And he kissed her back. 'I'm sorry, Luke.'

Luke's smile was small, but it was there. He pulled her back to where she'd been lying and started stroking her hair again.

'It happens all the time, apparently,' he murmured, in a tone that plainly said even if it did, it still wasn't fair.

'Do you still talk to her?'

'Koko? No. Not any more. It happened over a year ago. She's married again now—or so I heard.'

Amy suspected he hadn't 'heard' at all. She suspected he kept a close eye on Koko. Because that was what Luke did.

'It's hard to lose someone. Especially a child.'

'No one should have to lose a child,' Luke said quietly, his hands steady in her hair.

'It must have brought back memories for you.'

His hand stopped. 'Memories?'

'About your mother…'

His silence made her fear she'd said the wrong thing.

She stayed still. 'I'm sorry, Luke, I didn't mean to…'

'No, no, it's okay. I just…I haven't talked about… Mum…in a long time.'

'You don't have to if you don't want to.'

'No.' He began stroking her again but adjusted his legs and she moved, giving him more room. 'It's okay. It was a long time ago. I was an adult when it happened. Willa felt it more than me.'

'Nineteen must have been a hard age to lose your mother. Isn't that when you were away at college?'

'Yeah, I was at university and getting involved in hotel management. I'd been working in hotels throughout school. Mum got sick while I was away. I wasn't there when…when it happened. Afterwards, Dad suggested I stay away. He said it would take my mind off things.'

'That's an odd thing for him to suggest, don't you

think? Wouldn't it have been better if you'd stayed with your family?'

'I should have been there for them before. I suppose Dad thought I may as well make something of myself, seeing as I'd already missed my last opportunity to see Mum. It didn't really affect me the way it did Willa. I didn't miss her like she did.'

Amy turned again to look at him and he looked down at her. The sadness in his eyes didn't match his words. He'd missed her. And by the look on his face he still did.

'You didn't do anything wrong, Luke. You were young and you were living the life you needed to live. Your mother would have been proud of you.'

'You don't know that.' His words were abrupt. He shifted.

'You don't still feel guilty about anything that happened do you?'

This time he shifted again—hard. He lifted his arm and checked his watch. 'This has been nice, Amy...too nice. I really do have to work while I'm here.'

The change of subject took her by surprise. Amy moved so he could free his legs. 'Now?'

'Now. Sorry. I really do.'

He stopped to kiss her. Long and hard and sincere. It soothed her a little. But only a little. She wrapped her arms around herself as he jumped off the chaise longue and padded into the shower. It didn't take him long and he emerged fresh and clean as if it were the morning. But it wasn't—it was almost six o'clock in the evening.

'There's a rooftop bar in the hotel. Get dressed and go up there. I should only be a couple of hours and I'll meet you, okay?'

He pushed his tie up to his throat and kissed her cheek and in seconds he was gone. Just like that. As if the past few hours hadn't happened.

He left Amy feeling a little cold and very confused.

The lights that had seemed so pretty—almost magical a few hours ago—were now burning holes in her retinas. He still wasn't back.

Amy flung back the remains of the fruity cocktail she was drinking. She'd lost count at four. He was silent and absent and neglecting her again. He hadn't been like this in Sydney. In Sydney he'd been attentive and sweet and...*present*. They'd been in Singapore no more than a few hours and already he was gone—neglecting her again as he had on the plane. She'd made it clear that she hated silence. He knew she'd start to get scared if he didn't let her know what was going on in his head.

Amy checked her phone again. No messages. No Snapchats. Nothing. He'd said he would meet her in a couple of hours. It was now almost ten o'clock.

Amy held her hand up to gain the attention of the waiter. She needed another drink. She shifted and smoothed down the cool jersey fabric of her dress. He had no idea how good she looked right now. Because if he did he'd be here—buying her drinks and paying her attention. Not neglecting her. Making her feel as he had on the plane—as if she was invisible and unimportant.

The waiter appeared with another cocktail and she stared into it. What was she doing here? Getting angry...jumping to conclusions.

This had started as an innocent fling with someone from her past. She hadn't wanted to hope that it could go anywhere, but now... After spending so much time with him, and after their conversation earlier, she knew that hope had burrowed itself deep into her heart. She wanted him and she wanted this, and if she didn't sort out what was going on she knew she'd end up with a broken heart. And after the whole disastrous Laurie business she wasn't sure she could handle that.

She knew Luke had changed. The cold, distant boy had grown into a warm and passionate man. But there was still some of the lonely workaholic buried there. Someone who was used to being on his own and who got uncomfortable if he felt someone was getting too close. That was why he'd fled earlier.

Or maybe he was avoiding her because he didn't want this to turn into anything. He hadn't wanted her to come over here in the first place. Perhaps he wasn't scared of relationships but of a relationship with *her*. He knew who she was. Who she'd been. He knew her deepest, darkest secrets. Perhaps he couldn't take this or her seriously because deep down he still believed her to be the silly party girl she'd been eight years ago.

Amy swallowed to moisten her dry throat. Her past had finally caught up with her. She'd spent the last eight years running and hiding but now it had caught up. She was all exposed, out in the open, and she felt eighteen again. Young. Naïve. Scared and not knowing what to do next.

Amy stood and grabbed at her shawl and clutch. She wasn't eighteen again. She *wasn't*. She was twenty-six. Things had changed—she'd changed. She'd grown up, even though she didn't feel she had sometimes. She knew what she wanted. She wanted Luke and she didn't want to do anything stupid again. Like trying to make him jealous.

If her past had taught her anything it was that she should tell people how she felt and not try and manipulate them with jealousy and mixed messages and silence. Bad things happened when you did that. It was time to be direct with Luke. If he was avoiding her because he didn't want to be with her she needed to know. Before she got in any deeper. Before she started to think crazy things like he actually felt something for her.

She escaped the darkness of the bar and travelled down quickly in the elevator. Her heels clacked across the paved footpath.

She checked her phone. GPS said his office was just four blocks away. Four blocks for her to figure out what she was going to say. Four blocks until she told him that she needed to know what was going on. Four blocks and she was going to tell him how she felt. And he needed to tell her too.

There was a time to be working but this wasn't it. She knew he was using his work as a sort of emotional shield. This was classic old Luke. For all his appearance of changing and maturing, becoming a man who'd dealt with his past, he was still haunted by it. Was working too hard to avoid dealing with things. Like he had at Weeping Reef.

Luke had all but admitted earlier that he'd felt shut out when his mother died. His father had spent all his time worrying about Willa, which had left no one to worry about Luke. A man who'd hidden his emotions and feelings about his mother's death by burying himself in studying and then working himself into the ground ever since.

That was why he hadn't participated in the staff's lives back on Weeping Reef. That was why he'd partied with them all but had always left when they'd got drunk and started talking about their feelings. That was why he'd done nothing when he'd seen her and Justin together that night. Denial. Emotional avoidance.

She should have seen it long ago. Her marketing training had given her the ability to peg everyone's consumer behaviour. She should have seen that Luke wasn't buying into love or even close emotional relationships because he couldn't deal with them. Willa, his father, his staff and his friends...and now her.

It wasn't fair. He'd made her feel as if he actually *felt* something for her, but he wasn't going to take it anywhere. She could see that now. He would just keep pushing her away because he didn't want to get close to her. She'd revealed herself to him over the last two weeks. He'd known her emotionally, mentally and physically in more ways than any other man ever had—even Laurie.

And now he was pushing her away. As if all of that didn't matter. As if she couldn't be trusted with his feelings. She'd trusted him with her deepest, darkest secret and he didn't trust her. How. Dared. He?

CHAPTER TWELVE

THERE WAS NO WAY Amy could have told anyone how she'd covered those few blocks to Luke's office. She wasn't sure how she'd made it there herself. But she was mad. Mad at Luke for putting her off and not having enough respect to let her in on what he was thinking. Mad at her family and Laurie for making her feel so bad about wanting more—about wanting to leave them to make the life that *she* wanted, not the one they wanted. And mad at the man who had attacked her.

He was the one who made doubts creep into her mind when they shouldn't. He was the loser who'd taken her to the beach that night when she was full of booze and tried to have sex with her when she wasn't ready.

He'd called her a tease. A slut. He'd told her she deserved it when he'd pushed her down onto the sand and pulled his jeans down. He'd hissed angrily in her ear as he'd pushed her head closer to his penis. And she'd been too young to be angry. All she'd been was terrified.

She'd pushed and shoved and kicked and screamed and yelled until finally she'd got away. And after that she'd felt nothing but guilt and shame. As if she'd done something wrong. But she hadn't. Walking to the beach with him that night and kissing him had never been an invitation. They were human beings, not animals, and when she'd said no he should have respected it.

But he hadn't. He hadn't respected what she'd wanted. Neither had Laurie and now neither did Luke.

Amy was shaking by the time she found Luke's building and pushed open the door. It was late, but there were still people around. She found the name of his company on the list and pushed the 'up' button for the lift.

Luke was *not* going to disrespect her. He was going to listen whether he liked it or not. He was going to hear what she wanted and he was going to give it to her—or at least give her a reason why he couldn't.

The lift was empty when she stepped in and pushed the button.

He had work to do—she understood that. Her own career was hectic, and she knew how easy it was to neglect your relationships when you needed to work. But that shouldn't happen. Everyone needed a life outside of work. Otherwise work was pointless. Life was no fun without friends and family and people to share it with.

Maybe Luke didn't realise that yet. Tonight he was going to learn that lesson.

The foyer of Luke's office was deserted. The lights

in the area behind the reception desk were off. Amy headed towards the light down the hall, her heels muffled on the carpet.

She heard his voice before she saw him.

'We've been over this a dozen times. Our staff numbers have *not* escalated. The figure we gave you at the start of the year is the same. We've hired additional contractors for the build, that's all.'

A pause.

'As I discussed with your planning manager, we've got that organised. We're just waiting on supplies.'

Another pause.

'Ms Huynh, I respect your policies, but this has gone on for three months. I'm losing money and this project is in danger of falling over. I understand that… I respect that, but… Yes. I understand. I will take care of it and have it to you within the hour. Goodbye.'

When Luke looked up he jumped in his chair.

'Amy! What are you doing here? I didn't hear you.'

Luke's hair was askew, as if he'd run his hands through it a million times. His eyes were lined with red streaks and his tie was off. He looked tired. Overwhelmed. The words that Amy had been practising evaporated. Luke was stressed—she could see that. She knew how that felt. When there were a dozen things to achieve and you felt as if you were the only one who could do them. As if the weight of the world was on your shoulders. She understood his need to get his work done.

It wasn't fair of him to exclude her, but when she

saw him smile she knew she wasn't ready to give up on him. Without speaking Amy walked to his side and turned his chair to face her.

'What are you doing here? I'm sorry this is taking so long, Amy. You look gorgeous… What time is it?' He glanced at his watch. 'Damn. I'm sorry, babe.' He put his hands on her hips and met her eyes. 'I'm *sorry*.'

When Amy looked into Luke's eyes she realised that work was his life because it *had* to be. He'd been on his own for ever. The only thing he knew was to get the job done on his own. Maybe working had served him well when things in his personal life had got rough. But that was in the past, and the past was over.

'What are you doing here, Luke?'

'I just have to get this finished. It won't take too much longer. I'm sorry, Amy. I'm not great company at the moment.'

'Don't you have people to do this for you? It's ten o'clock.'

'I *have* to get this finished.'

'I understand that, Luke. But that's not why you're here so late and not with me, is it?'

His brow furrowed.

'You're here because you don't want to deal with me. With *us*. You're using work as a way of not dealing with what's happening between us.'

'Amy…'

'No. Stop avoiding me. Don't do that again. Look

what happened the last time we stopped talking to each other.'

'Amy, it's just not simple…'

'No, it's *not* simple. Life gets complicated and sometimes you have to take a risk. *I'm* willing to take that risk, Luke, but are you?'

His eyes searched hers and his hands didn't leave her hips. Then he breathed in deeply. 'It's late, Amy, and I'm tired. I'm sorry that I didn't come and meet you. I lost track of time, that's all. I'm not avoiding you, or using work to not deal with anything. I just need to get this done.'

For some reason his speech made Amy sad. She'd wanted him to say yes, that he was willing to take the risk. She'd wanted him to say more. She wasn't sure what, but…*more*.

'I can see you thinking, Lolli. And worrying. Don't.' He pulled her in closer and her arms fell around his shoulders. 'Everything's fine. *We're* fine. I've got you. I just need to get this done.'

Amy wanted to shout and demand that he tell her he wanted her. She wanted him to explain why he was here and not with her. She wanted to know what the hell was going on. But he'd said 'we're fine', as if there actually was a 'we', so instead she just rubbed the back of her hand on the stubble that had formed on his cheek.

His face seemed so familiar to her now. So comfortable in such a short space of time. She knew every line and eyelash. She wanted answers, but she knew he wasn't going to give her any. Not tonight anyway.

He was distracted and stressed and instead of demanding the answers she desperately needed now all Amy wanted to do was help. She wanted to massage him, run her hands over the tight, worn muscles on his body—make him feel better.

'I tell you what—how about I help you with this? Then we can go back to the hotel and you can *show* me that everything's fine.'

His face broke out into a wide smile. 'I wish… But you can't help, Lolli. I've got to do this on my own.'

Amy's hand flew off his cheek and gripped his shirt—hard. His eyes opening wide in surprise.

'Do you have *any* idea who I am?' she asked, going for a sinister look on her face.

Luke raised an eyebrow in a fantastically sexy move that made Amy's body heat in the way only he could make it do.

'I am Bird Marketing's number one PR executive. I've negotiated deals and organised campaigns that have made millions of dollars. My skills are legendary and I'm here, practically sitting on your lap…' Luke shifted his legs and she moved in closer—so close her breasts were almost touching his chin. A violent shiver rolled up Amy's spine at the heat of him so close. 'I demand you take advantage of me.'

Heat shone in Luke's eyes as they shifted to her lips. His hands grabbed her hips violently and shoved her closer to him till the heat of his chest burned through her dress and right into her now throbbing core.

'I don't answer to demands.'

His teeth bit down on his bottom lip as he moved his head closer to her breast. She saw what he was planning, and her nipples ached to feel his mouth on them, but she pushed him back.

'Then we should negotiate.'

'I don't negotiate.'

She peered down at him, her eyebrow raised the same way as his, and she saw the same reaction in him as she'd felt. His hands skated up her back and pulled her in tighter, but again she pulled back.

He reconsidered. 'What would your opening offer be?'

She pretended to think as she held him back. She strained against him as his mouth sought her breasts. 'How about this? You spend at least an hour kissing my entire body and I'll help you with whatever's going on here. Then we go back to the hotel and I'll spend an hour kissing *your* entire body.'

He considered her for a second, before his mouth reached for her breasts. She had to push against him violently so he could not make contact. His face flushed and she knew what he wanted. She'd seen that look in his eyes so many times.

Amy reached down to lift the edge of her dress up over her knee, then shifted herself so she was sitting in his lap. She wanted to find a way to make him feel better…she wanted to help. First by relaxing his mind and then by seeing what she could do to make his job a little easier. Now she was perched on Luke's long legs her breasts were tantalisingly close to his mouth. She knew he was frantic by now—she could feel him hard beneath her. *This* was the help he needed right now. Physical release.

'Deal,' he said gruffly, and his lips met her neck with a violent, deep kiss.

Amy let out a satisfying moan as his hands pulled her in close. She couldn't hold him back any more. His mouth kissed up her neck to her mouth and his kiss was hard and demanding. She pulled away, breathless—her entire body pulsating with white-hot desire for him.

'You haven't really grasped the concept of negotiation, have you?'

He kissed her neck again, then slipped his thumb under the strap of her dress to lift her it off her shoulder. When it dropped her breast spilled free, and he hesitated for only a second before cupping it in his big hand and slipping her nipple into his mouth. Her head fell back. She moved her hips to feel him hard and strong against her.

'I've achieved the outcome I wanted,' he said, only lifting his mouth off for a second to answer her.

'You're easily pleased. But unfortunately for you, I'm not. My expectations for this deal are high, Mr Moore.'

'They will be exceeded, Miss McCarthy.'

She wanted to say, *We'll see*, but she didn't get a chance to. He lifted her up off the seat and had her back on the desk before she could speak. With one sweeping move her flimsy dress was over her head and all that lay between them was a very small item of underwear.

Amy fumbled at his belt buckle but he removed that for her too. His manic desire for her turned her on. The look in his eyes turned her on. The way they'd come to an agreement turned her on. She was gone. She knew that now. There was no turning back and no caution. She was his and he needed to know that.

Tonight there was no time for talking, but tomorrow—there would have to be. Because Amy could feel herself slipping into a feeling she knew she'd not be able to get herself out of.

'Off—it needs to be off.' She tugged at her underwear and he helped her remove it before climbing on top of her, his knees perched on the desk.

First he used his hands to stroke the length of her body. Not missing anything. Touching everywhere. He left a wake of trembling flesh, and Amy did what she'd learned to do with Luke—let go. There was no use trying to stay in control when she was with him and no use worrying.

She closed her eyes for a moment to enjoy his touch, then opened them. She wanted to see him watching her. She wanted to *know* him. When they were together like this there was no thinking or negotiating. They just *did*.

Using each other's sounds as a guide, they slid their way around each other's bodies, kissing and teasing and tasting until one or the other had had enough. This time it was Amy. She grabbed at his hips and moved them where she needed them to be. To where she was hot and swollen. She couldn't take another second without feeling him there.

She gasped when he entered her. No matter how many times she felt him inside her, it always surprised her. It wasn't just his size, it was the way he moved—as if he was hitting every spot she had, as if he knew exactly what she wanted. He thrust hard and she tried not to make a noise. She couldn't remember if she'd seen anyone else in the office, but with him moving like that she wasn't sure if she cared.

'Thank you for coming, Amy,' he whispered, letting his chest fall onto her.

'You're—' She gasped again as he raised himself up to thrust once more. 'Welcome!'

It came out as a moan and Luke smiled, knowing she was ready. The thrusting became deeper. Amy lifted her hips to meet him, her feet wrapped hard around his buttocks. She still wasn't sure if there was anyone else in the office but right now she didn't care. She had to cry out.

He gripped the back of her neck and lifted her up off the desk. His thrusts became purposeful and his face took on the angry, dirty look she knew so well. He was almost there, and Amy wanted to come with him.

Quickly she took his hand and let it slip between them. He knew what to do. His thumb circled her clitoris. First slowly, then more frantically and violently. Her orgasm grew. He felt her shake. He moved with her until her final scream pronounced her done, and as she shook he let himself tip over the edge as well, a deep, satisfied moan leaving his lips as she took everything he had to offer, cupped his chin with both hands and watched his mind clear of all his worries and be consumed by one thing. Her. Them. *Now.*

When Luke finally came to Amy was sitting on the desk in front of him, naked, with her hands still cupped around his chin. Her eyes glowed…gold rings around the brown. Her cheeks and chest were flushed and her once perfect hair was wild and forming a halo around her face. She was beautiful—and that was the problem.

Little Lollipop was no longer his sister's naughty friend—she was *his* naughty friend. A gorgeous, sexy woman who managed to make him forget himself whenever he was with her. Something he shouldn't do. He'd tried so hard in the last few years to be strong—for everyone. To take his business to the highest level, to keep the people he loved safe. But no matter how hard he tried bad things happened.

As he watched her lips form a satisfied smile he wondered what bad things would happen with *this* relationship…

'Feeling better?'

The words purred off her lips. Her face was so familiar to him now. He loved the way her lips smiled on just one side first, before forming a full smile. He smiled back—he couldn't help it—before kissing the tiny freckle that sat on her collarbone. He'd explored every inch of her body—dozens of times—but she'd surprised him tonight.

He knew he'd been neglecting her. He knew that he should have left the office earlier. But he'd wanted to make sure everything was taken care of. And in the back of his mind he knew she was right. He was avoiding her. Not because he didn't want to be with her but because he'd realised this afternoon how it would feel if he didn't have her.

Her silence and distance had been torture. When she'd finally spoken to him he hadn't been able to help rushing at her and making love to her. He'd been so relieved. And now, afterwards, when they were sitting together watching the lights he felt so comfortable. *Too* comfortable.

This whole thing had been a mistake. A delicious, exciting, magnificent mistake, but a mistake nonetheless.

'I'm feeling much better.'

His teeth connected with her shoulder. He wondered if she was cold. Picking up his shirt from the chair behind him, he wrapped it round her shoulders. She took it, letting her arms slip into the too big sleeves.

'Well, then, now we need to tick off the other part of our deal.'

Help. She wanted to help. But she couldn't help. There was too much to do and not enough time to do it. There was no way she'd be able to help.

'There's no need for that. How about this?' Luke wrapped his arms around her and held her close, hoping his warmth would soothe her. 'How about I get this taken care of and you go back to the hotel and order us some food? I'm starving after that, and if I know you I bet you are too.'

She pushed at his chest. Hard. Surprisingly hard. 'We had a deal.'

He knew that look in her eye. She was getting mad. He needed to calm her.

'I know that, but I need to take care of this…'

'No.' She crossed her arms. 'That wasn't the deal.'

'Amy—'

'Sit.'

She used a foot to push him and the back of his legs hit the chair. He landed on his ass with a thump.

'It's time you listened to me. We had a *deal.*'

Amy uncrossed her arms and stood over him, one arm either side of the chair. Her hair fell forward and her eyes narrowed. She was angry. And dead sexy. He resisted the urge to pull her onto his lap and kiss her. *Just.*

'And the deal was that we relax you, then fix whatever problem you have. Together. You and me. Not you on your own, taking on the responsibilities of the world. Not you on your own, thinking no one else can do this. I've come a long way since Weeping Reef, Luke. I've had to grow up. To manage people and figure things out. And I've figured *you* out.'

She turned her chair so the window was at her back. The lights of Singapore sparkled behind her and his shirt billowed out in front. It wasn't the lights he was looking at. It was her. Angry and determined and making him listen like no other woman ever had.

'You think the only way to stop bad things happening is by taking on all the responsibility. But life happens either way. You can't take on the responsibility for everyone. People make their own choices and they deal with the consequences. Your job is not to save them but to be there for them when they fall. Because they will. Everyone does at some point. I know. I fell once and you caught me.'

But he *hadn't* caught her, had he? He'd let that bad thing happen to her. And he'd let his sister marry the wrong man. And he hadn't been there for Koko. He knew Amy was just trying to help, to make him feel better. And he liked her for that. Other women would have walked away when he neglected them, but not Amy. She'd tracked him down, sat him down and made him accountable. That was what he needed. Someone who saw his darkness and liked him anyway.

With a gentle kiss he let her know that he appreciated her and her lecture and that slow little smile of hers crept over her face.

'Good. Let's get started. What's the name of that witch making your life hell?'

'Kel Huynh.'

'I'll start with her.'

Amy *had* changed from her Weeping Reef days. There was still a lot of fun and cheeky jokes, but there was no wandering off and getting distracted, no trying to get out of what she was supposed to be doing. She was all business.

She pulled out all the paperwork he needed. She read through his to-do list and suggested ways to delegate. He didn't agree with all her suggestions—

after all, she couldn't know the ins and outs of this project and who would be able to handle it and who wouldn't—but she had a way of convincing him to try it her way.

Her salesmanship was magnificent. She complimented, joked, dropped little-known facts, used distraction—all the tricks in the book. But mostly she flirted, and *that* was when he couldn't resist. Amy in full flirt was like nothing he'd ever seen. She knew just how to tilt her head and play with her hair and smile and bat her eyelashes. She knew just what to say—innocent with a slightly shocking twist—as if she knew exactly what she was talking about. Which she did.

Amy was an expert. She knew how to get what she wanted—she always had. But he didn't mind her using her charms on him. He liked her charms. Especially when her charms were dressed in just his shirt. Watching her breasts peep out from where she'd loosely buttoned the shirt made all thoughts fly from his head. He'd do whatever she wanted and she knew it. He had to fight to stay in control. He had to fight to stop himself from grabbing her and kissing her every five seconds.

'All done, I think.'

She smiled as she punched the last of his data into the spreadsheet. He watched her from where he stood, next to where she was sitting. He watched her fingers fly over the keyboard. She didn't look at them—just kept her eyes on the screen.

Amy had always been a quick learner. When

they'd changed the computer system on Weeping Reef a month after she'd started she'd been the first in the office to master it. He remembered the time she'd spent at the others' desks, showing them what to do. At the time he'd been frustrated. She'd been neglecting her own work. She hadn't got things done. But now he realised how lucky he'd been to have her. He hadn't had the time to show the staff the new system. She'd been doing him a favour by taking their questions and explaining things to them.

He hadn't appreciated her back then. In his head she'd always just been his sister's silly friend who talked too much and didn't get her work done on time. He wished he'd seen her then as he did now. He wished he'd noticed how generous and caring she was instead of focussing on himself and what needed to be done. Maybe she would never have had to go through with what she had if he'd taken more notice of her. Taken the time to get to know her. Listened to her.

Luke moved closer and slipped his hand across her shoulder. She stopped to put a hand over his and smile at him. But he didn't smile back. He couldn't when all he could think about was that she deserved more. So much more than he could give.

'You're amazing—you know that?'

She smiled and dimples embedded themselves in her cheeks. 'About time you realised that.'

It was. About time.

When they'd finally packed up and gone back to the hotel she decided he needed to watch her slowly undress before she climbed on top of him and made each and every one of his thoughts disappear from his head. And he found himself wondering again why the hell he hadn't realised how amazing she was eight years ago.

CHAPTER THIRTEEN

WHEN AMY SAID she had a surprise for him the next morning he was hoping it involved more nakedness, but she was dressed and standing in his office—he'd managed to convince her to let him go there for a few hours.

'Time to go,' she said firmly, her eyes connecting with his.

He knew there was no use arguing. And with her help yesterday some of the pressure had actually been relieved. He'd delegated some of the less pressing tasks and managed to get everything together and now it would be on the desk of the demanding Ms Huynh.

There was nothing left to do but wait. And enjoy the delights of Singapore. With Amy.

'Back to the hotel?' he asked hopefully, getting up to put his arms around her waist and kissing her hard on the lips.

She twisted her arms around his neck and pressed herself closer. Her breasts pushed against his chest and he hardened instantly. No one had ever turned

him on more that Amy, although a niggling fear had
bored itself into his brain like a spider and taken up
residence there. Pressing on his nerves whenever he
started to think things he shouldn't. Like this might
last. Like this was something important. Like he
never wanted to let her go.

'No...' she murmured between kisses.

He liked it that she couldn't get enough of him either. He enjoyed the way she became breathless and
a little vague every time they kissed. As if kissing
him made her forget everything the way kissing her
did him.

'No. Not back to the hotel. Somewhere better.'

She smiled that slow smile of hers and his heart
clamped. She was an amazing flirt. He had to remember that and not take all this too seriously. It had only
been a few weeks that she'd been back in his life—it
was moving quickly. Too quickly. He needed to slow
this down. Stay in control. Keep his eye and his damn
heart steady so everything stayed where it should be.

'Nowhere could be better than the hotel with you.'

Luke let his hands slide up her back under the
white shirt she was wearing. Her skin was soft and
smooth and he wanted to kiss it. Kiss her everywhere.
Sex would help him forget what he was worrying
about and it would mean she couldn't ask any more
questions he didn't want to answer.

'Trust me—you're going to love it.'

'Surprises weren't part of our deal.'

'No, they weren't, but this is not negotiable. You've

flown me all the way here and I want to see some of Singapore.'

'We're not going on one of those awful double-decker buses, are we?'

'Don't worry—you'll enjoy it.'

'As long as you're there I will.'

Her eyes met his for too long. He had to remember not to say things like that. That type of thing sounded a little too 'relationshippy', and he didn't want her to think that that was what this was. Not that Amy wasn't someone he could see himself having a relationship with—if there was anyone he'd want to spend every day with it would be her—but he was better at taking care of people from a distance.

'That sounded as if you're starting to like having me around, Luke Moore.' She smiled breezily. 'Tell me the truth: is it my devastatingly awesome PR and management skills that turn you on so much?'

No. It was the way she teased him and never let him take himself too seriously. And the way she worried about him when he worked too hard. And the way she knew exactly what he needed. And the way her body seemed to fit so perfectly with his. There were a million reasons he liked having her around and only one reason why he couldn't. He'd already let her down once. He'd let something bad happen to her and that had changed her. He couldn't be responsible for someone like Amy.

'That must be it.'

'Or maybe you're starting to realise what a catch I am?'

'You *are* a catch, Amy. You're gorgeous and smart and funny and I've never seen anyone work a spreadsheet quite like you. You'll make some lucky man very happy one day.'

Her expression froze for just a second. But then she smiled and the hesitation in her eyes was gone. Perhaps he'd just imagined it.

'We should go,' she said brightly.

For a moment he thought about the man who would eventually marry Amy and a wave of hot jealousy rolled over his body. Amy needed someone reliable. Someone she could depend on. Someone who didn't make her angry like he did. Someone who wouldn't let her down as he once had.

She chatted breezily as they went downstairs to get a taxi. She mentioned that Willa had called earlier that day and had wanted to tell her some news but had been called away. His sister had a habit of making spontaneous decisions—like the one she'd made when she got married. That had ended in disaster. He wondered what scheme she was coming up with now. Of *course* she'd call Amy about her crazy plans. The two were thick as thieves. Even thicker now than they had been at the resort all those years ago. Which was another reason a relationship with Amy wasn't a good idea. It would become awkward…it was all too close.

Luke glanced at Amy in the cab. It was a typically hot Singaporean day. Amy's hair wasn't as blow-dried and straight over here as it was back home in Australia. The humidity gave it a kink and it looked a little like the way she'd used to wear it back on the reef.

Only then her hair had been longer, and usually dripping in jewellery and leather straps and gemstones. And back then she'd usually worn a lot less.

She'd become rather conservative over the eight years when he hadn't seen her. In Sydney she mostly wore suits, but over the last couple of days the old Amy had begun to emerge. Today she had on a top that exposed her belly and some very short shorts. And instead of a bra he could see a bikini top tied around her neck. He liked it. He liked the bohemian she hid beneath her corporate slick. He knew who she really was. Troublemaker Amy, with a definite thirst for adventure and fun.

So opposite to him. He had responsibilities, and he needed to be the reliable, dependable man he'd been working hard to be—and yet he couldn't help admiring the way Amy didn't let her own responsibilities stop her from living life. Not that he'd ever be able to live like that.

He slipped his fingers through hers and held on tight. She smiled and shifted a little closer and he liked her there. Close and warm and completely his… at least until life and work inevitably got in the way. But he didn't want to think about that. Not today. The sun was out and there was a beautiful woman wanting to make him happy. Today the only thing he wanted to think about was Amy.

Amy had slipped the cab driver a piece of paper with the address of where they were going on it, so he still had no idea where they were headed, but when they passed the huge sign signalling the entrance to Sentosa Beach he started to wonder.

'The beach? You want to go to the *beach*? There are possibly five hundred better beaches in Australia than this, you know.'

'Not the beach.' She smiled and squeezed his hand.

'Then where…?'

The taxi sped past the manmade beach and the amusement park that was so popular with families and tourists and continued on.

'The *wharf*?'

'Yep. The wharf. I've chartered a boat. And I've wiped your schedule. Today I have you all to myself, with no mobile connection. We have champagne and food and paddleboards and that's it.'

It sounded like the perfect day to Luke—but no mobile connection…? 'What if Kel Huynh needs me?'

'She'll have to wait.'

Amy sidled even closer and rested her head on his shoulder. They couldn't go on for much longer like this. It was impossible. But a day out on a yacht with Amy for company sounded so good that for now he just wanted to enjoy it.

Amy smiled at Rocky, the captain of the yacht she'd chartered with a little help from the concierge at the hotel. He'd given them the safety speech and was now firing up the engine. Luke had volunteered to uncork the champagne, so Amy had come to the front of the boat to enjoy the views that were whizzing past her as they headed for one of the small islands that lay around Singapore.

The sun was warm, but not too hot. Unlike in Australia, there were no flies here—the humidity was horrendous for her hair, but somehow that just made it feel more like a holiday.

Amy stood with her back to the window of the cabin. She breathed in deeply and the salt air filled her lungs. She was happy, and it was a strange kind of happiness. Something she'd never felt before. A kind of dozy, lazy happiness in which she was completely conscious of all the problems in her life but it was as if there was some strange drug running through her veins, making those problems seem so much more insignificant than they had just a few short weeks ago.

'Here we go.'

Luke passed her a champagne glass. He'd opted for a beer, and Amy loved that about him. He was honest and real. He clearly didn't like champagne, but rather than drink it and say nothing, as Laurie would have done, he'd got himself a beer and done what he wanted.

Amy slipped a hand in his and moved close to him. He put his arm around her and for a moment everything was perfect. She wasn't sure if it would last, or if this would all end in tears, but right now it didn't matter.

The boat tipped and water sprayed up to cool them down as it sped out to sea. A few other boats were speeding past and the people on them waved as they caught their rip.

Luke leaned down to talk in her ear over the roar of the engine. 'I have to admit, Lolli…'

Amy smiled, the sound of his voice making her want to get naked right there. No one had ever done that to her. Luke had awakened some kind of sexual sprite in her and she was loving it. She loved trusting someone with her body. That had been taken away from her years ago, but with Luke's help it was back.

She slipped a hand up in between his shirt and his skin. He pulled her closer. He felt it as much as she did. She knew he couldn't get enough of her. He seemed to want to rip her clothes off every time they were alone…and sometimes when they weren't. His desire for her made her feel powerful and strong—something she hadn't felt in a long time.

Luke was healing her in a way Laurie never had. He made her angry and sad and happy and so turned on she couldn't bear it. Luke was bringing her back to life when Laurie had allowed her to sleep. He was giving her the strength to enjoy the life she'd left home for. He was making her finally think that making the move from Melbourne had been a good one.

But something niggled at her still. The way he always put his work first. The way he could neglect her. It screamed of the old Luke. Closed and cold. And earlier he'd said she'd make someone a lucky man one day. But not him. That thought irritated her. What did he mean? Did that mean he thought they were going nowhere?

Amy's thoughts rattled in her head, getting mixed up and confused, and she shook her head. She couldn't think like that. She couldn't start reading into things and thinking about things that way. He'd probably meant nothing. She just wanted to feel happy—like she was now. She wanted to trust her feelings for once. She wanted to trust *him*. She wanted this to be real and she wanted it to last. It had to last because… because this was different. It wasn't safe. It wasn't predictable and it wasn't one-sided.

She could see that Luke cared for her in the way he looked at her when he thought she didn't notice, and the way he touched her, and the way he was constantly trying to protect her. And she cared about him too. A lot. She…she *loved* him.

Amy tried to shake herself back into the moment. As she looked across at Luke he grinned at her. He had mirrored sunglasses on, so when she looked at him all she saw was her own reflection. A pair of trusting brown eyes staring at him. Even she could see the pathetic puppy dog love in them.

She smiled and took a deep breath. It was okay. He had her. He'd had her back at Weeping Reef. When the absolute worst had happened it had been Luke who'd had her and he had her now. Yesterday, when they'd had that fight and she'd thought she'd lost him, he'd assured her that he had her and it had made her feel safe and out of control all at once—and she'd liked it. The feeling was addictive and she wasn't ready to let it go yet.

'I have to admit this was a pretty good idea,' he said, leaning down again.

'I only have good ideas.'

'That's true. You're with me, aren't you?'

Her grin was wide. 'Perhaps that was *not* one of my best ideas. But I'm a glass half-full kinda girl— I can make the best of any situation. I'm sure I can work with you,' she teased.

He took the bait. She could always rely on him to. He *got* her.

'You can work with me, can you? Tell me, Lolli, what would you change about me if you could?'

His smile was wide and it showed off the tan he was starting to acquire since coming home to Australia and not working as much, spending more time outdoors. Sunshine and fun agreed with him.

She considered her answer. What would she change? Nothing. Except for his overbearing need to take care of everyone and be so responsible all the time. But she even liked that about him. As annoying as it was, you knew when Luke Moore cared about you because he didn't let you out of his sight.

'I'd change that belt. Black belt and brown shoes? *So* not working.'

He chuckled and looked down at his outfit. He was wearing his usual work attire today, *sans* the jacket, but she'd thought of that and packed him a pair of board shorts down in the cabin. She'd bring them out when they anchored. Seeing his gorgeous body in a pair of low slung boardies was going to be one of the highlights of the day.

'Besides my apparently appalling taste in fashion, of course.'

'Besides that?' She considered him, then raised her

hand to lift his sunnies. She wanted to see his eyes. He pushed them to the top of his head and she studied him. From the wrinkles at the sides of his eyes to his stubble-covered jaw. 'Nothing.'

He breathed deeply and something changed between them. Something crackled to life that hadn't been there before.

'And that's what I'd change about you too. Nothing.'

'We must be perfect.'

'We must be.'

Their conversation was simple. And Amy liked it. It made her feel that maybe she was right. Maybe she *should* love him. Maybe this was actually real.

His eyes locked with hers and he brought his arms down to encircle her waist, keeping her tight against him and still. Slowly, carefully, he bent his head and kissed her. Amy felt the bones in her body disappear. She leaned into him. This wasn't one of his usual manic, sexually charged kisses. Although it was still damn sexy. This was slower, deeper. He was taking his time and creating a soothing, slow rhythm with his tongue.

She responded, holding him tightly around his neck and communicating with him the way he was with her. She knew it now. He loved her back. No one could kiss someone like that and not love them.

They stood for too many minutes, kissing and being totally unaware of what was going on around them. Amy wasn't sure how long they kissed, but when they stopped she was out of breath and so was he. He looked as if he was about to say something, but at that moment Rocky appeared and they realised the boat had stopped.

Rocky coughed awkwardly. 'I just need to get in here and release the anchor rope.'

They moved aside and shared a grin as Rocky anchored before disappearing back down to the cabin.

'I think that means it's time for swimming. You wait there.'

Amy's heart was so full she was scared it would burst. After that kiss there could be nothing else for him to say but that he loved her. She wanted to hear it. She wanted to feel the words wash over her. She realised it had been for eight long years she'd wanted him to feel this way about her, and today it was going to happen.

Grabbing the board shorts, she headed back up, her heart pounding. When she saw him smiling at her, her hands shook. She wanted to hear him say it, so why was she so anxious now?

'Here you go—I packed these. I didn't think you'd have boardies on underneath that suit. You can get changed—or do you want to go down to the cabin? There are a few boats about—maybe you want to go down?'

She was rambling. Her words were coming out too quickly. She tried to think of more. What was she *doing*? It was as if she didn't want him to get a word in. As if she didn't want him to say the words she was longing to hear. What was *wrong* with her? Of course she did. She wanted him to feel that way about her. She wanted to know. What the hell was she so scared of?

His brow furrowed. 'You okay, Amy?'

She nodded. 'Of course—perfect. I think I just need more champagne. I'll go get some. Unless you want to get changed first? Or we could go together? There's plenty of room down there. You'd have your privacy. I mean, if you need it.'

His arms were around her in a second. 'Amy. You've seen me naked plenty of times. I don't think it matters if you see me get changed.'

'Yeah—yes. Of course.' Her laugh was forced. Nervous. What the hell was going on with her? 'So we should…go…together.'

'We should.'

He laughed, taking the board shorts from her and holding her hand before leading her to the back of the boat and the cabin below.

Rocky passed them in the doorway on his way out. 'So I'll leave you two for a couple of hours and come back?'

They watched as he boarded a paddleboard and headed towards the shore. Amy watched him go and the fluttering in her belly started to grow. *Come back now!* she felt like screaming. For the first time since she'd seen Luke on that chair at Saints she was frightened to be alone with him. What the hell for?

'All alone…what should we do now?'

There was no mistaking the look in his eye. She knew what he wanted. She wanted it too. As she watched him peel off his shirt she wanted it so badly.

But after they were done he would probably say what he was going to say, and she wasn't sure she was ready for that. Not yet. First they should do some paddleboarding. Yes—that was what they should do.

'You get changed and I'll get the paddleboards ready.' She fled before he could argue.

When he emerged, gorgeously tanned, his muscled torso was begging to be touched. But she didn't touch him. She handed him a paddle.

'You're really keen for this paddleboarding thing, then?' he teased, taking the paddle and playfully smacking her behind with it.

Amy turned away. She needed to think. She had to figure out what the hell she was scared of right now—and watching him there, half naked and teasing her, wasn't helping.

Amy pulled off her clothes and pushed a paddleboard out into the ocean, before diving in and emerging to haul herself up on it. Within minutes she'd mastered the oar and was paddling fast—away from the boat, away from Luke, and away from the conversation she wanted to have but which scared the hell out of her.

A half-hour later Amy's arms were burning. Her thighs were sore and she could feel the burn of the sun on her shoulders.

'You're doing it wrong.'

Luke appeared like a shark in the water and tilted her board. Amy faltered but kept her balance. He laughed and she growled.

'You've gotta be a little more stealthy than that to

fool me, Moore.' She poked at him with the oar and he disappeared under the blue-green water—only to appear on the other side.

'What are you doing out here all alone? I thought you wanted to entertain me?'

He shook the board again but she stood steady, still swiping at him from her position up high.

'I never said I was here to entertain you.'

'Then what *are* we here for?'

Amy steadied herself and glared at Luke, whose hands were wrapped ominously around her board, and sat down, one leg either side of the board.

'I wanted to sightsee.'

'The only sight you need to see is me.'

Amy let out a little gasp and an embarrassingly girly squeal as Luke pushed on the board.

'Permission to climb aboard, Captain?'

'No! Permission not granted. Stop! We'll both fall!'

The board rocked dangerously but Luke kept coming, sliding his stomach onto the board before swinging a leg over. He grabbed her shoulders and held her steady as she tried to keep still.

'No, we won't. I've got you, Amy.'

'No, you haven't!' She grabbed at him, desperately trying to stay upright.

'Stop moving, Amy. I've *got* you. Hold still.'

His deep voice reverberated through her head and she listened to him. He had her. All she had to do was be still. Amy breathed in deep and looked at his face, his smiling lips and his eyes. He had her. She just needed to stop.

'There. What did I tell you? You need to learn to trust me, Lollipop.'

He grinned, and she grinned back. Trust. That was what they had. That was what she'd never had. Not since that night at Weeping Reef. Not really. That jerk had taken away all her trust, and even though Laurie had helped she knew she still kept a thick wall up.

She hid it well. Behind the non-stop working and the late-night parties and the quick jokes and the perfect outfits. But Luke had managed to get behind her wall. She was here, with limp, frizzy hair, in a vulnerable position, and he had her. Why had she been avoiding him? He *had* her. He'd had her eight years ago and he had her now.

Luke was facing her, one leg either side of the board, and she shifted so she was a little closer. Then she placed her hands on the board in front of her and carefully, while trying to maintain her balance, pushed herself towards him. His eyes darkened. His grin disappeared. He made a deep noise in the back of his throat before leaning forward and meeting her lips.

Their kiss was fast and furious and gained desperation as time wore on. He shifted closer and she did the same, all the while clamping her thighs around the board.

'That's better,' he muttered. 'Nice and close— that's where I want you.'

'That's where I want *you*.'

He smiled beneath the kiss. 'Yeah, right—until you

have another party to go to. I know you, Amy. You're a wild animal. Can never be tied down or tamed.'

She smiled back. 'Maybe not, but there's something to be said for staying wild.'

'There is?'

He spoke between kisses and Amy's body heated. She wanted him. Right here, on this board, in the ocean, with an audience of at least fifteen boats full of people around them. This was what he did to her. He made her feel as if no one and nothing else existed. Just him and her.

'Of course there is. Domesticated animals get fat and lazy and scared, and they depend on their owners for everything. That's not a life. Wild and free—that's a life.'

Luke leaned back, stopping the kiss. Amy missed it. She wanted to taste more of him. She leaned forward again but he hesitated.

'There's something to be said about domestication too, you know,' he said.

'Is there? I can't think of anything.'

His brow furrowed. 'That animal knows where his next meal is coming from. He knows he has a safe home to come to at the end of the night. He has a family who take care of him.'

'Maybe. But where's the fun in *that*?'

Amy was keeping it light and cute. She wanted him to kiss her again. But whatever she was saying wasn't working. He didn't lean forward again.

'So what you're saying is…you want a cat?'

'No.' He smiled. 'No. I don't want a cat. I want a tiger.'

Then he leaned forward and kissed her so hard and so fast that any chance of balance completely left her and they toppled together into the ocean.

Water went up Amy's nose and she emerged spluttering and laughing, her eyes stinging from the salt. But she wasn't alone long, because Luke had his arms around her and was kissing her again.

'I forgot—tigers can't swim!'

Amy laughed and pushed on his chest. '*This* tiger can.'

And she left him smiling as she cut long, smooth strokes through the water. Her time on Weeping Reef hadn't been completely wasted. One thing she could definitely do well now was swim. She'd spent every morning on the island in the resort pool, and even after all this time she was so fast Luke didn't catch her until they were back at the boat.

As they climbed Amy playfully pushed him back in, and when she laughed and offered him a hand he pulled her back into the water. She knew she looked like a drenched rat. She had no make-up left and her hair was plastered over her face. But she didn't care. He didn't care. And she knew. She was in love with Luke and he was in love with her and she was finally ready to hear it.

'You go on up top,' Luke insisted when they finally managed to get on board. 'I'll get us some food and drinks. You dry off.'

She smiled, wanting to kiss him and wanting to

punch him as well. Of *course* she wanted him to say he loved her. Her apprehension had nothing to do with him and everything to do with her. She'd been a good girlfriend to Laurie for years. She'd been faithful and loyal and just as loving to him as he had been to her. But then she'd changed. What she wanted had changed. That didn't mean she was bad and didn't deserve love.

Luke had made her feel that she did. With Laurie, sex had been slow and respectful. With Luke anything went. Luke had been the one to save her from the attack on the island. He'd helped her then and soothed her, made her feel that what had happened hadn't been her fault, and he was doing the same thing now. She loved him for that. And she deserved the love he was offering in return.

Lying back on the deck, with the ocean below, Amy started to relax. This had always been meant to happen. She'd been meant to have this break from Luke. In order to grow up. In order to gain some perspective. And they were meant to meet now. It was right. It was time. And she was ready.

Luke didn't take long with the food and drinks and their former comfortableness returned as they teased each other and fed each other and laughed and played on the deck of the boat. When they'd finished Luke rubbed sunscreen into her already red shoulders and back, and she did the same for him.

She lay on his lap, her face turned towards the sun, and they just sat—full and content and not needing to talk for a long time.

'This has been just what I needed, Amy. How do you *do* that?'

'What?'

'Know exactly what I need?'

'I'm your soul mate—that's how.'

The words fell out before she could stop them. Her heart lay heavy and her breathing stopped.

Luke was silent, and a tingling caution crept over Amy.

'Do you believe in soul mates, Luke?'

For a long time he didn't answer. Her nervousness returned. She couldn't help but notice his hesitation.

'I don't know about that, Amy. You meet people, they teach you things—and then they leave. That's normally how it works.'

'Not everyone leaves.' Fear edged her nervousness. What was he saying?

'Everyone leaves.' His voice was quiet.

'Even you?' She wasn't looking at him. She was talking into the breeze. She couldn't face him.

'Even me.'

The world stopped turning. Amy's heart stopped beating. A primal instinct she hadn't known she had roared within her. Slowly turning, she faced him, sitting up.

'Luke…' She tried to smile. 'You don't mean that.'

His hands were behind him, he looked relaxed and casual, but he took off his sunglasses and met her eyes. 'I'm not a keeper, Amy. We both know that.'

'What does that mean?'

Amy's heart beat faster. This wasn't what he was

supposed to say. *I love you. I need you. I can't live without you.* Not this.

'You know what it means. You know what I'm like.'

'No. Tell me. What *are* you like?'

'Married to my work. Absent. Unreliable.'

Amy's brow furrowed and breathing became difficult. What was he trying to say?

'You're a hard worker. So am I. That doesn't mean you can't have a relationship.'

'No, it doesn't. But the person I have a relationship with would have to be very understanding. And forgiving. Nothing like *you*.'

He laughed, and her fear and nervousness gave way to something else. Anger.

'Nothing like me? Oh? Why? Because I'm a wild animal? A thoughtless, silly party girl? Because I can't be serious? Because what you want is someone more *domesticated*?'

'No…'

'Or is it because I can't hold down a relationship? Because I change my mind? Because I put myself first? I told you about Laurie the other night because I thought you'd understand—not because I thought you'd hold it against me.'

'That's not what I meant, Amy. I just meant that you need someone who can take care of you. Who knows how to handle you. Who can protect you.'

Amy stood up over him. 'I don't need a keeper. I need a partner. Which is what I thought you wanted to be for me. I guess I was wrong.'

Why had she said that about soul mates? This wasn't how the conversation was supposed to go. He was supposed to be saying he loved her, but he wasn't doing it. He was making her heart hurt. Why had she said that…? But then again, what if she hadn't?

Luke stood too now, and towered over her. But she wasn't afraid. She deserved love. Luke had taught her that. She wanted him and they were supposed to be together—she knew that now. She'd found herself in these past few weeks. She'd realised that what she wanted wasn't wrong. He'd helped her find that out and he wasn't getting out of it that easily. She knew he loved her—she'd felt it. So why was he saying this?

'You need someone to take care of you.'

'No, I don't. I need you.'

Luke stared at her. He didn't move. She could see his mind ticking but he still didn't speak. And then he just turned and left her standing alone in the bow of the boat. Angry, confused and hurt.

What the hell had just happened?

No. He wasn't doing this. He wasn't going to shut her out. Not after the last three weeks. Not after this perfect day. And not after she'd finally realised what she was looking for. *Him.*

'Don't walk away, Luke. We need to talk about this. About us. About what's happening here.'

Luke didn't answer. He just kept walking until he got to the cabin and pulled another beer out of the fridge.

'Luke…'

'I shouldn't be here. You know Kel Huynh is getting back to me today and yet you drag me out here.'

Luke picked up his phone and moved it in the air.

'Luke, forget work. We need to talk about *this*.'

'Forget work? Do you know who I *am*, Amy? Do you know what I *do*? You say you work hard, but you don't have a business to run. You don't have a family to take care of. What about Willa? You said she called—maybe something's wrong? I haven't spoken to my father since I came back to Sydney, and this project will fall over if I don't sort all this out. Don't you understand? I don't have time to be out here on a boat, rubbing suntan lotion into your back and talking about our feelings. I have *work* to do. You know— like a responsible adult. I'm not an overgrown party animal, Amy. I'm not wild and free like you. I'm domesticated and I *like* being domesticated. People rely on me. They need me. And while you're around I'm letting everyone else down.'

His speech ended in silence. Luke didn't even know what he'd said in the end. He'd just been talking, moving his lips. Distracting her. Distracting himself.

He'd felt something earlier. In that kiss he hadn't been able to break away from. A dangerous connection that had felt so right and so bloody wrong at the same time. He couldn't do this. He needed to get back to work. He couldn't look at her face for one more minute because he'd let her down again. Maybe not today, maybe not tomorrow, but eventually. And he couldn't face that.

He checked his phone. No reception. No connection. All he had to look at was her disappointment and hurt. Just as he had that night, all those years ago. A man had taken from her what hadn't been his to take.

He'd found that man that night, and he'd made him sorry he'd ever come to Weeping Reef. Then he'd packed the bastard up and sent him away. Banned him for life from that resort and any other resort Luke had ever worked at. Now he was the one who needed to be exiled.

Without another word he went to the boat's radio and contacted Rocky, and within ten minutes they were heading back to the city. Back to real life and not this fantasy world where anything could happen. Where Amy could actually be his. She thought it would work out because she was young and hopeful and optimistic, but he knew what would happen. He'd never be able to give her what she truly deserved from a relationship—not long-term.

When the boat docked Amy was off and onto dry land in seconds. She didn't say goodbye. She hadn't said anything since his outburst and he didn't blame her. But this was the right thing to do. They couldn't fool themselves and think this might be something it never would be. Better she knew that now rather than five years down the track, when they were married and had a couple of kids.

He watched her go, her legs moving fast and her arms folded tightly across her chest. He didn't stop her. Why would he? What would he say that he hadn't said already? The best thing now was to let her go and hope that one day she would find someone she could rely on. Someone who could prevent bad things happening from her.

His phone beeped manically. Twenty-five messages. He needed to get back to work. He needed to focus. He had to get back to reality and not think about the wild animal that was now running as far away from him as she could.

Amy felt a kick on the back of her seat for the eleventh time. They hadn't even taken off. She should be in first class right now. Enjoying a relaxing glass of champagne and sharing a blanket with Luke. But she couldn't sit next to him. She couldn't even look at him.

As soon as she'd got back to the hotel she'd gone to Reception and got another room. She'd expected him to call or message her but he hadn't. Not once. Not even to check that she was all right. He didn't care. He never had. That thought made her feel the same way it had the last two hundred times she'd thought it. Sick.

The thumping behind her began again. Then came the crying and the calling out. 'Mummy!'

Amy stuck in her earplugs and closed her eyes. She tried to stop the tears in her eyes from falling but she couldn't, so she put on an eye mask and cried for eight hours straight.

When she landed back in Sydney she told herself to stop.

'Enough.'

Her phone beeped insistently as soon as she'd picked up her luggage. Ten missed calls. Two from work and eight from Willa. She dialled her friend's number immediately. She hadn't called Willa back about her news. She didn't want to speak to anyone but it was time now.

'Amy! You're back! Yay! Yay!'

Willa was smiling. Amy could feel it through the phone.

'I'm back.' Amy tried to smile too. *Enough,* she told herself again.

'I've been trying to get hold of you for two days. What's been happening—how's Luke?'

Amy hadn't told Willa about her relationship with Luke. She'd told her friend she was going with him to Singapore to research his hotel business for her own work. She was sure Willa hadn't bought it, but—as the good friend she was—she'd pretended to.

'Fine. I think. What's happening with you—why have you been so desperate to get hold of me?'

'Oh, Amy. I have news and I needed you to know first! But I couldn't get hold of you—and I had to organise the party—it's this Saturday. We wanted to get everyone together while they're still in town!'

'Slow down, Wills. What party? What are you talking about?'

Willa laughed a joyful, happy laugh that made Amy's heart ache just a little bit.

'We're engaged, Amy! Rob and I are getting married!'

Of course they were. Perfect. Just what she wanted to hear after a disastrous break-up with the man she loved—the man she'd always loved. Possibly the only man she'd ever love.

Amy smiled as wide as she could. 'Willa, that's amazing news—congratulations!'

She really was happy for her friend. Willa had been through so much, and for her to find love again was wonderful. Amy thought perhaps she was being a little greedy, finding two men to love and marry within eight years…but that was irrelevant. She was over the moon that her friend was happy. But the news still made her chest ache and her stomach heavy.

Willa didn't seem to notice. Nor did she notice Amy's apprehension when she told her about the party on Saturday night. Luke would be there. She'd have to face him. See him and still be in love with him, knowing all the time that he didn't love her. That he'd put his responsibilities and his work before her. That he didn't consider her relationship potential because she was too 'wild'.

It was stupid and irrational, and a ridiculous reason not to love someone, but she couldn't help feeling hurt all the same. Because she wanted him to love her. So much. And she missed him already. The feel of his skin, the scent of his neck and the taste of his kisses. She needed him right now. With his big arms around her. Holding her up. Saving her as he always did.

But he wasn't there and he never would be. And on Saturday night she'd have to smile and act happy and pretend everything was okay. This was going to be the performance of her life.

CHAPTER FOURTEEN

AMY HAD BARELY had time to think about anything since she'd arrived back in Sydney on Monday. Her work had become manic and Willa had been calling her non-stop.

Amy was glad of it. The only time she cried now was when she was in the shower, and that didn't count because the tears might have been water and no one would know except for her puffy eyes the next day. Which she excused away with claims of jet lag and tiredness after a big weekend.

And yesterday she'd managed to go a whole hour without thinking of Luke. She'd been trying on dresses with Willa, and seeing her friend so in love had made her thoughts veer to him, but once her friend had started talking about how happy she was, and they'd begun trying on shoes and jewellery, talking about the new home Willa and Rob were going to build, Willa's excitement had taken over and Amy had felt genuinely happy. No pretending.

It had been a nice feeling, and she wanted to feel

that way again, but now the party was starting and she was hot. A storm was brewing over the humid city.

The party was being held at a harbourside restaurant. Willa had recently sold the harbourside mansion she'd shared with her ex-husband and was now living in an apartment that was way too small for the hundred or so people now mingling in the restaurant.

Cracks of lightning lit the starless sky and Amy counted the seconds before the boom of thunder. Ten seconds. Which meant the storm was ten kilometres away. Depending on which way the wind was blowing, they could expect rain in less than an hour. Torrential rain, by the look of the dark clouds that had rolled in and which now blanketed everything in a surreal darkness.

It was sticky and hot and uncomfortable, and the air was filled with a weird sort of apprehension. Which made her feel as if she wasn't the only one in the city tonight feeling sad.

She hadn't spotted Luke yet, and even though she told herself she didn't want to she knew she was dying to see his face again and watch him—see if he was happy, or miserable like her. He hadn't called. He hadn't made any contact. That was ripping at her inside, but she had to smile and get on with things. She couldn't change how he felt. All she could do was power through this tough time and hopefully come out not too scarred at the end.

Yeah, right, she scolded herself. The scars were going to be thick and deep with this one. She knew that already.

'Hey, Amy, thanks for helping this week. Willa's been a bit crazy. She settled down once you came home, though.'

It was Rob, Willa's soon-to-be husband. Amy liked Rob. He was calm and strong and he loved Willa fiercely. She wanted that for her friend. Everyone deserved to be loved like that. And it didn't hurt that he was handsome as all get-out.

'I've been happy to do it. I needed the distraction.'

'Distraction from what?'

Willa appeared, her hair pulled back in an elegant chignon and dressed in a gorgeous cream designer dress that made her pale skin glow.

'Ah…work…mostly.'

'Liar.'

That was the thing about best friends—you had to keep the good ones for life: they knew too much.

'I'm not lying. I've been busy since I got back— seems they can't operate without me…'

'Liar,' Willa repeated. 'Rob, could you go get me a drink?' She smiled sweetly at her fiancé.

'Of course—female code for, *Go away. We're about to have a deep and meaningful and you're not invited.*'

'That's why I love you, darling—you're so smart.'

Willa smiled and kissed her fiancé. Amy turned away.

'Now, Miss I'm-Going-to-Singapore-for-Research, are you going to tell me what the hell is going on between you and my brother or am I going to have to beat it out of you?'

She knew. Of course she knew. It was obvious. Willa had known about Amy's crush on her brother all those years ago and Willa had seen their connection in the bar that first night. Willa also knew that Amy could sell snow to the Eskimos, but she couldn't lie to her best friend.

'Nothing. Absolutely nothing. He's moved on.'

'Has he? Is that why he hasn't stopped growling at me since you two got back? Is that why he's spending the night out on the balcony, arguing with anyone who walks past about how Australia was robbed in the cricket?'

'Willa, I don't want to do this here. Not tonight. It's your night. Your engagement party. We'll talk about it another time.'

'No, we won't. We'll talk about it now. My best friend and my brother are unhappy and angry and I need to know why. I *deserve* to know why.'

Amy took a deep breath. She did deserve to know. She told Willa everything else and she should have told her about this. Maybe she wouldn't have cried so much. Maybe she wouldn't have fallen for him the way she had. Maybe her friend would have advised caution and told her to hold back. And maybe that was why she hadn't told her in the first place.

'It's just a disaster, Wills.'

The tears welled again in Amy's eyes but she wasn't going to cry. Her eye make-up was on point tonight and she wasn't going to ruin it.

She took another deep breath. 'We had a…a thing. It

was good. It was great. At least I thought it was. Then we went to Singapore and everything turned bad.'

Amy explained that she didn't think Luke had even wanted her there in the first place. How he'd told her about the guilt he felt about his mother and about Willa's divorce. She told Willa how they'd talked about Laurie and how she felt she'd let him down.

Amy fought back tears again when she explained how Luke had made her feel that night. Loved. Accepted. Normal. Then how he'd shut down and left her alone. She told her about their night in the office and their day on the yacht and how she'd thought that everything was good and they felt the same way about each other.

Then she told Willa about the argument, and how Luke had said that she was a wild animal and he didn't want a wild animal. And about how he'd looked her in the eye and told her he had responsibilities and that she had no idea what that meant. After spending weeks paying her attention and making her feel like the most important person in the world, it had taken one day and one argument for her to feel like nothing to him.

The tears did fall then, because she realised what she was so sad about. He'd never let her down before. He'd been there for her in her darkest time—he'd always had her. But that day on the yacht she'd felt that everything they'd had was a lie, and that was what cut her the most.

Willa listened without interrupting and without

moving. Then she breathed in through her nose and let it out, and took both Amy's hands in hers.

'Amy, I'm going to tell you something and I want you to know it's for your own good. Do you trust me?'

Amy nodded even while her heart pounded. She knew her friend. She knew that she was about to tell her some home truths and Amy wasn't sure she wanted to hear them. She knew it was over with Luke, but to have someone else say it would be terrifying. She wasn't sure she was ready for that.

'I've known you a long time, Amy, and I know what you're going to say and do before you even do it. I know that you sometimes act before you think. You speak without hearing. And I say this with love in my heart, Ames, but sometimes you're so busy trying to stay busy that you miss the most important things. You're a beautiful person, with a generous heart. You're quick to love and you're the most supportive and loyal friend anyone could ever have…but you never give anyone any *time*.

'Luke is the type of man who needs time. You can't rush him. He doesn't do well with snap decisions. And if he feels rushed, or pressured, or backed into a corner, he'll lash out. He says he's not a wild animal, but he is. Inside he *is*. He's spent most of his life being pressured into responsibility and doing the right thing. Then he meets you. And you do whatever the hell you want whenever the hell you want and *he* wants that. He wishes he could do that. And that's what frightens him about you.'

The tears were falling thick and fast now. Amy

gripped Willa's hands tightly. 'He doesn't love me, Wills. I love him. But he doesn't love me.'

Amy's words were soft. She could barely get them out. She knew she was being pathetic, but she'd kept it all in for so long now. It hurt. *She* hurt. She needed to let it out.

Willa took action. She pulled at Amy's hands until they found themselves in the ladies' room. Inside were two of Rob's aunts, reapplying their lipstick, and Willa swiftly asked them to leave. They looked peeved, but they did as they were told. Amy wasn't sure how she did it, but Willa managed to lock the door, and when she turned back she only said one word.

'Cry.'

But Amy couldn't. The tears had stopped. Her friend was here, she'd let it out, and she had nothing left.

'I'm okay…really.'

'You're not. You're a mess and it's my stupid brother's fault. Here.'

Willa opened her small bag and Amy peered inside. It was filled with make-up and tissues and Band-Aids and aspirins and everything else a girl could possibly need.

'Fix yourself up. Calm down. I'll be back in ten minutes. And then we're going to have a drink and celebrate my engagement and you're going to have fun and forget about my brother and the dastardly things he said and did. Got it?'

Willa was reserved and shy, but at times she could

be the strongest woman Amy had ever met. She nodded at her friend and they hugged the way only two girls in a bathroom could before Willa left her alone to fix herself up and prepare herself for a night of not thinking about stupid boys and their hurtful words.

Luke was angry. The man in front of him had had the hide to say New Zealand's batsmen were superior to the Aussies. Which was outrageous. Everyone knew that the current Australian line-up was the best they'd had in years.

'You've got no idea, mate.'

'Ha-ha—it's just a game, though, isn't it?'

Just a game? Who *was* this loser? 'If you think it's "just a game" maybe you shouldn't even be watching it.'

He stepped forward. This moron deserved a punch.

'Settle down, mate.'

'What did you say to me?'

Now he really *was* going to punch him.

'Okay, so everyone's happy here, are they?'

Willa had arrived.

'I think I need a drink.'

The moron left. Lucky. Because he'd been thirty seconds away from a piece of Luke Moore.

'Okay, Luke, I think that might be enough.'

'I've only had two beers, Willa, I'm not drunk.'

His sister raised her eyebrow. 'Not enough alcohol, but enough unprovoked aggression. You're going to drive all my guests away and then there'll only be you and me left here to party.'

'He was an idiot. Why do you always make friends with idiots?'

'I don't know, big brother. But I *do* know I'm related to the biggest idiot of all.'

'What?'

Surely Willa didn't want to pick a fight now? Not *now*. Not when he felt like this.

He hadn't seen or heard from Amy since they'd got back. She hadn't contacted him. She hadn't made any attempt to call him. She'd just walked out of his life as if the last three weeks meant nothing. Which was what he'd wanted her to do, so why the hell did it bother him so much and why the hell couldn't he stop thinking about her?

Everything reminded him of her. Smells, sounds, sights. It didn't matter what it was, he could come up with a story about how it was connected to Amy. He missed her so much. And it hurt. And he knew he couldn't have her because she didn't deserve someone like him. Someone who would let her down.

He turned to face the dark sky that was streaked with lightning. He waited for the boom of thunder. Five seconds. Five kilometres away.

'Luke. What's going on? You've been so angry and distant since you got back from Singapore. What happened?'

His whole life had been turned upside down—that was all. He'd let everything he wanted walk away—that was all.

'Nothing. I'm just worried about the Singapore deal.'

'Why? You said they approved it—what's to worry about?'

Nothing. She was right. Kel Huynh had finally approved everything. It was going ahead as planned, on budget and on time. That wasn't what was bothering him but he didn't want to tell Willa that. She didn't need to worry about him or anything else.

'You don't understand, Willa.'

He felt the punch on his arm and turned in surprise to see Willa staring at him, her eyes flashing.

'I *understand*, brother. I understand that you are an A-grade idiot. You let the woman you love slip away—and why? Because of some ridiculous guilt you have about our mother or me or something else you didn't do. There was nothing you could do about any of that. You couldn't save Mum. Dad couldn't save her. No one could. Then you took it upon yourself to become my keeper, which I didn't need you to do. I was fine. I had Dad. I had friends. I was fine. I *am* fine.'

'*Real* fine, Willa. You married an absolute loser and I did nothing about it. Don't worry, I've checked Rob out and I've let him know that this time around he'll have to answer to *me* if anything goes wrong.'

'I don't need you to do that! I'm not eighteen any more. I'm a grown woman. I can look after myself. I just need you to be my brother. To be there when I need you. The way you were there for Amy when she needed you.'

Willa's words felt like a punch to the guts. He hadn't been there. He'd let her down. Then and now.

That was why Amy had walked away. That was why she hadn't come back.

'As usual, Willa, you have no idea what you're talking about. Why do you think that thing happened to Amy that night? I saw them together. I *saw* that sleaze talking to her. I knew he only wanted one thing. And what did I do? *Nothing.* I walked away. I let it happen because that's what I do. I walked away from you, I walked away from Amy, and I walked away from Koko. And when I was lucky enough to get a chance to have Amy back in my life you know what I did? I walked away from that too.'

'Why, Luke? *Why* did you walk away?'

Luke stilled. Why *had* he walked away?

'Because he didn't love me.'

Amy's voice was like an elixir. His head moved towards the sound and he drank it in, and when he spotted her he drank her in too. She looked beautiful tonight. He'd spent the evening on the balcony, avoiding the chance of seeing her, knowing what it would do if he did see her. Knowing it would kill him to see her and not be able to have her.

'Amy.' It was all he could say.

'That's why he walked away, Willa. Because he realised that I loved him and he didn't love me back.'

It took a second for Amy's words to sink in. *What* had she just said?

'Isn't that right, Luke? You were okay with everything that happened between us until it came time to love me. You couldn't bring yourself to do that. Not silly, wild Amy. Someone you can't tame.'

'I don't want to tame you, Amy.'

'Then what *do* you want? Because I've spent the last five days trying to figure that out.'

He wanted her—that was what he wanted. But he was scared.

'You're just caught up, Amy. What we have—it isn't reality. It's fantasy. You know what would happen if we were together?'

'What? We'd fall in love and live happily ever after?'

'You'd be reminded every day of how I let you down.'

'How exactly *did* you let me down, Luke?'

'I let it happen. I let that bad thing happen to you. Then I hurt you in Singapore. I left you alone and then I hurt you.'

'You did hurt me. But you didn't let me down on Weeping Reef. That would have happened no matter what. If you had come over and tried to stop it I would have just been more determined. You know what I was like. And I was only with that loser to make you jealous. If you had reacted I probably would have done something even more unsafe.'

A beating started in Luke's heart. A steady thump that meant he was coming back to life.

'I should have stopped him. I should have beaten that loser before he had a chance to do that to you, not after. I should have kicked him off the island when he first arrived, not after he'd hurt you.'

Amy was silent and another crack of lightning lit the sky. One…two…three… Only three kilometres away.

'So Willa was right. You punched him?'

'Of course I punched him. I tracked him down and made sure he was sorry for what he did. And then I kicked him off the island. I watched him go. But I didn't stop it from happening.'

The lightning lit Amy's face as she came toward him. 'Thank you, Luke,' she said quietly. 'That was my only regret, you know—that I didn't say something to him. At the time, I thought he'd got away with it. I thought he'd stayed when I left and that made me feel like a victim. I didn't want to feel like that but I did—for so long.'

Luke watched her eyes. She was sad…he could see that. And *he'd* done that to her. He didn't want to make her sad. All he wanted to do was make her happy.

His chest filled with something that wasn't air. He wanted her close, holding on to him. Needing him. Not tamed, but still.

'Amy, I'm sorry.' He stepped closer to her, wanting to touch her. Wanting to reach out and pull her into his arms. 'I'm sorry I couldn't stop that. I'm sorry you got hurt. I'm sorry for the things I said on the yacht. I'm *sorry*.'

When she lifted her face the lightning caught it again. The boom of thunder came only a second after.

'I'm sorry I never told you that you were my hero that night. You saved me. You made me feel safe when I didn't think I ever would again. And now you're back. And you're saving me all over again.'

Lightning. Thunder. Then another crack and the

rain sheeted down. But Amy didn't move. She stood still and solid. His wild animal, looking up at him with her wild eyes. Soothed. Safe. All because of him.

'No, Lollipop—you've got it wrong. You're the one who's saved me.'

He reached for her then—he couldn't wait any longer. Willa had disappeared and everyone else had rushed inside as the rain started to fall. It was just the two of them and he needed to hold her close. He wanted to protect her from the rain and from anyone hurting her ever again. She was *his*. She was the most amazing, wonderful woman he'd ever known and he'd be damned if he was going to let her go. Not now that he had her back.

Slowly, but with confidence, he lifted a palm to her chin. 'Looks like I'm the damsel in distress and you're the knight in shining armour.' He smiled, and to his relief she smiled back. That slow smile he loved to watch creep over her face.

The lightning and the thunder cracked and boomed and the rain fell around them and over them. And all he wanted to do was kiss her. To feel her pressed against him. To feel her lips against his so that he knew where she was and she knew how he felt. He loved her and she loved him and they had each other and that was all they'd ever need.

'I guess we'll just have to save each other,' she said, and he knew it was time.

He leaned down and tasted the rain on her lips before she let him in. They kissed long and hard and deep, with the kind of desperation you only felt when you thought you'd lost something for ever only to find it again.

'I think we've wasted enough time, Amy.' He kissed her neck and her cheeks and then her mouth again as he murmured his words into her ears. 'I adore you. I love you. I need you.'

She broke away from the kiss for long enough to look into his eyes. 'Then this is the deal, Mr Moore. First you take me home and we make crazy love like the wild animals that we are.'

She smiled that gorgeous smile he couldn't get enough of.

'Then you marry me, forget about going back to Singapore, and we live happily ever after.'

His chest filled and his mouth smiled bigger and wider than it ever had. He'd never been more sure of anything in his life. He loved her. That was it. They'd met for a reason back on Weeping Reef, and that was so they could get to this point in time.

For the first time ever Luke believed in soul mates—because he'd found his.

'Deal.'

Then they sealed the deal with a long, deep, passionate kiss.

* * * * *

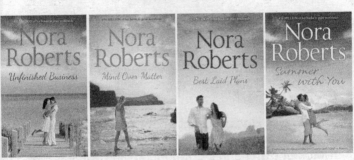

MILLS & BOON®

It's Got to be Perfect

IT'S GOT
TO BE
Perfect

UNCORRECTED
PROOF COPY

HALEY HILL

* cover in development

When Ellie Rigby throws her three-carat engagement ring into the gutter, she is certain of only one thing. She has yet to know true love!

Fed up with disastrous internet dates and conflicting advice from her friends, Ellie decides to take matters into her own hands. Starting a dating agency, Ellie becomes an expert in love. Well, that is until a match with one of her clients, charming, infuriating Nick, has her questioning everything she's ever thought about love...

Order yours today at
www.millsandboon.co.uk

MILLS & BOON®

The Thirty List

* cover in development

At thirty, Rachel has slid down every ladder she has ever climbed. Jobless, broke and ditched by her husband, she has to move in with grumpy Patrick and his four-year-old son.

Patrick is also getting divorced, so to cheer themselves up the two decide to draw up bucket lists. Soon they are learning to tango, abseiling, trying stand-up comedy and more. But, as she gets closer to Patrick, Rachel wonders if their relationship is too good to be true…

Order yours today at
www.millsandboon.co.uk/Thethirtylist